UNCONDITIONAL

Sawyer laid her hand on Holling's arm, communicating her feelings without words. Fear and trust mingled together, letting him know that even though by now she was scared, whatever he decided to do, she would support him.

Move, Holling said to himself. Move while they still could. He put his index finger to her lips, indicating silence and caution, than began to crawl on his hands and knees. Sawyer followed, biting her lip to keep from crying out against the jagged rocks that dug into the soft flesh of her palms and worked their way through the knees of her jeans.

"Holling!" Sawyer mouthed to him.

"Keep moving," he said, his voice a ragged whisper. She nodded tightly and picked up her pace.

He pushed Sawyer in front of him. Twenty feet to the path. Maybe fifteen. Maybe, if they could get there before being seen, before they set the dog loose, maybe they might still have a chance . . . So many maybes.

Fifteen feet. Thirteen . . . a little farther now. Just a little more. Ten feet. Holling grabbed her roughly and spun her around to face him. "Sawyer, listen to me . . . listen good and do exactly as I say. When I say go, you make a straight line for the path. Keep going. Don't look back, darlin'. Don't look back. . . ."

Unconditional

GERI GUILLAUME

BET Publications, LLC
http://www.bet.com
http://www.arabesquebooks.com

Acknowledgments

This novel is dedicated to my children—RáVen and William—for their unfailing belief that good guys should always win.

I'd also like to thank my supervisor, mentor, and friend Mary Crowe, who knows what "fair" is.

And for my mother, Mary Ann Williams, who breathes love and life into her family with every breath she takes.

Chapter 1

Three o'clock in the morning. The one thing Shiri Deneen wanted to hear even less than the rumbling snore of her husband, Jack, was the sound of a ringing telephone. Groaning, she clamped her pillow down over her ears, taking care not to press down too hard on her recently braided hair. The silk pillowcase could only protect her so much from the eyebrow-tugging strain of her honey-blond microbraids.

"Shiri," Jack mumbled, jostling her with his elbow. "Phone."

"You get it this time," she said, through a jaw-popping yawn.

"Nuh-uh. You get it."

"I got it the last time, J.D," she complained.

"No, you didn't. I did. Remember? It was the defensive coordinator reminding me that they've moved the practice from eight-thirty to seven."

"That was before Mama called reminding me about the family meeting tomorrow. Remember?" Shiri spoke loudly, competing with the jangling of the phone.

Jack grunted in acknowledgment. He sat up, punched his pillow into a more comfortable position, and then lay down again. "You know, I think you're right, baby. The phone's probably on your side of the bed anyway. So, why don't you go on and answer it?"

Shiri raised her head, looking for the cordless handset sitting on her nightstand. It wasn't there, though she could still hear it ringing. She rubbed her eyes, clearing away the sleepy film covering them. *Extended-wear contacts, my left eye!* She made a mental note to go back to her old prescription. She squinted at the clock.

"It's three o'clock in the morning!" she exclaimed and gave an irritated punch in the middle of her husband's bare chest.

"What was that for!" He gingerly rubbed the spot.

"Nobody but one of your football buddies would be calling us this late. Probably calling you to come to some stupid after-game party."

Jack cracked open one eye, leering at her. "You know Big Dog. Once he gets his party on, he wants everybody in on it."

"After two years of marriage, haven't those jock heads figured out by now that your catting-around days are over?"

She paused as the phone fell silent. Still irritated at the interruption of her beauty sleep, Shiri grumbled. "They need to leave you alone, Jack. You don't play for the Steeldogs anymore."

"But I'm still part of the team, Shiri," he said.

"There's such a thing as too much closeness. Assistant coach from nine to five on nongame days. There's a reason you quit playing, Jack," she reminded him.

Jack's position as assistant coach kept him close to the gridiron action without the grueling punishment to his body playing both offense and defense that arena league football team had required of him.

"Gotta stay true to my boys, baby. You know what they say, once a dog, always a dog."

"Well, *this* dog is gonna turn into a grouchy bitch if that was Big Dog on the phone, Jack," she warned him.

"Come here, Shiri." Jack held his arms out to her, inviting her back into the position they'd fallen asleep in. Shiri laid her head against his chest, snuggling close as he stroked her back and shoulder.

"I just don't want you to wear yourself down," she said in a more subdued tone.

"It's not the plays on the field sapping my strength," he teased her. He kissed the top of her head. When Shiri lifted her face to him, he kissed her again on the forehead. She made a soft sound of contentment, curling her body around his. Jack's hand shifted, cupping her rear and pressing her closer against him.

"Personal foul, Coach," Shiri said in a breathy whisper.

"Tell it to the ref," Jack retorted. He shifted, rolling from his side until he was lying on top of her.

When the phone started to ring again, Jack muttered a curse of irritation, then rolled off of his wife.

"Whoever it is must be crazy," she said. "Or desperate." She searched around for the phone as it continued to ring. "I'd heard that . . . what was that heifer's name . . . Damitra . . . was asking Big Dog about you."

"Who?" Jack said innocently, raising his eyebrows.

"Don't be cute. You know who I'm talking about."

"Can't help it being cute, Shiri. It's in my genes."

"As long as you're only unzipping those jeans for me," she cautioned.

"I love it when your jealous side shows," he said. "We have the best make-up lovin' after your eyes go green."

"I'm feeling very jealous now," she said, wagging her finely arched eyebrows at him.

"Let the damn thing ring," he said huskily. In a moment, the answering machine would pick up.

Jack drew Shiri back into his arms. His hand drifted

under the hem of her camisole, resting possessively against her breast. For a moment, she resisted his advances as every jealous bone in her body rearranged itself into her rigid spine.

"Come on, Shiri," he coaxed. "Don't be that way." Now that he was awake, all of him was fully awakened, including his desire. Especially his desire. Jack was grateful that he still had such strong feelings for his wife. When he'd been diagnosed with multiple sclerosis two years ago, that was his biggest fear—that he would not be able to physically satisfy her. That fear had almost cost him their relationship. It had made him turn away from her, rather than risk disappointing her. Not so now. He couldn't turn away from her now if he tried.

"What if it's Mama calling me to let me know that Bren's gone into labor?" Shiri objected.

Jack almost made a face. When wasn't somebody in Shiri's family going into labor? Or getting married? Or divorced? Or put in jail? She had such a large family, whenever one of them called, anything was likely to have happened. "Then they'll call again on the cell phone. C'mon, Shiri. Let it go. I promise, they'll call back later."

"*Ummm,*" she moaned, moving against him. "Call back later."

Her need for sleep was quickly replaced by another need, as insistent as the chiming phone while Jack's hand absently caressed her skin. Shiri turned her face to him as Jack leaned up on his elbow.

"You sure you don't want me to get that?" His tone was low, teasing, as his hand dipped lower and found its way to the waistband of her pajama bottoms.

"Get what?" Shiri said with a throaty chuckle. "I don't hear anything."

"Me neither," he agreed, helping to ease the floral cotton

pajama bottoms down over her hips. She shifted her feet, working them down around her ankles.

Jack settled over her again. His hands roamed along the familiar planes that never failed to excite him or amaze him even after two years of marriage. Shiri responded instantly, parting her knees to allow him greater access. That was all the encouragement he needed. But even as he came to her, he knew that though her body was with him, her mind was distracted. It was that damned telephone.

Sighing in frustration, Jack leaned over his side of the bed and dug the cordless phone out from under the stack of decorative pillows he'd tossed aside when they climbed into bed.

"Yeah?" His tone was curt, considerably less than gracious when he answered the phone. "Hello?"

Shiri sat up on one elbow. "Who is it?" she mouthed to him.

"Don't know. They're not saying anything." He put the phone to his ear once more, frowned when he thought he heard the soft sound of crying. A woman. Through sobs and an occasional hiccup, he thought he heard her ask to speak to his wife. One of Shiri's relatives.

"It's for you," he said, handing the phone over to her.

Tucking strands of honey-colored braids behind her ear, Shiri raised the phone.

"Hello?"

"Shiri?"

"Who is this?" Shiri frowned, not immediately recognizing the speaker on the other end of the line.

"Shiri, it's me. It's Sawyer."

"Sawyer?" She cupped her hand over the mouthpiece and relayed to her husband, "It's my cousin Sawyer."

Jack blew out a frustrated breath and let his head fall back limply against the pillow. Sawyer Garth. Yet another cousin on Shiri's paternal side. Grandpa George's brother's grand-daughter . . . or something like that. It was just easier to think of her as a cousin. How many cousins did Shiri have? Two years of marriage and he was still discovering them.

"What does she want *this* time?" Jack said ungraciously.

He'd only met her cousin Sawyer a few times—once at his and Shiri's wedding and again during a book signing for Sawyer's first published novel. He had started reading it but he'd never finished it. The mixture of historical fiction, Western-style action, erotica, and fantasy time travel was too out there for his tastes.

He had to wonder what kind of mind could dream up stories like that. Since that first book, she'd cranked out four more. Each more fantastic and bizarre than the previous one. From what little he knew of Sawyer, the book was a reflection of her eclectic personality. She lived in a world of her imagination, her own creation. Jack called it the Bizzaro World. You never quite knew what you were getting with Sawyer. She was wild and unpredictable. Independent. Private. Some-times to the extreme of being reclusive. Other times, she was the proverbial party girl, even giving someone like Big Dog a run for his money. She didn't drink or do drugs, that he knew of. That was probably why she could outlast even the most hard-core partier. No one could top Sawyer when it came to having a good time. That was her problem. That was when she got into the most trouble, trying to snatch the at-tention from everyone else.

But that was only when she wasn't in trouble. When she was in trouble, then she had to draw the whole family into her woes. He suspected that she'd called Shiri tonight be-cause she needed someone to help her out of another tight spot.

Even though he'd only met her a couple of times, her in-fluence on the Johnson family was keenly felt. She was con-stantly involved with some kind of drama or the other. And to hear her tell her side of the story, none of it was ever her fault. Always someone's else. Jack had to wonder about a woman who never took responsibility for her own actions. He had to wonder about a woman who craved chaos. He and Shiri had just had a conversation about Sawyer last week when she'd called to tell Shiri that she was going to take a cross-country tour on her motorcycle with a bunch of other women she barely knew.

When he'd mentioned the fact that Sawyer might be heading for another mental spiral, Shiri had done what she always did for her cousins. Jumped to their defense.

"Sawyer's not crazy. She's just *different*. So what if she's a bit of an oddball?" Shiri had protested.

"You mean a head case," he'd corrected. "The girl's in serious need of some therapy."

"How can you say that about Sawyer? She's never been anything but nice to you."

"That's because Grandma Lela was always in the room, holding on to her reins, making her behave. Otherwise, she would have been all over the map."

"Some men find that spontaneity attractive. That guy she's with now . . . Ryan . . . he seems to like it."

"He's got a vested interest in liking it," Jack scoffed. "He's her publicist. The crazier she acts, the more publicity for her books. As long as he's making money off of her, you'd better believe that he's gonna like it. If he doesn't like it, he'll put up with it and put on one hell of a performance to keep getting what he's getting from her."

Jack attributed Sawyer's eccentricity to too much money left by her deceased mother as part of her trust fund and too much intelligence, her being the only daughter of a man with a suspected IQ of genius level. Though Sawyer seldom attended family functions, Shiri and Sawyer had somehow forged a special bond. Shiri the ultraresponsible one, and Sawyer the poster child for Peter Pan's Neverland. She was a grown woman who refused to grow up. She was so young. Twenty-three or twenty-four. But she was still old enough to know better.

As much as he applauded his wife's connection and devotion to her family, sometimes their closeness was damned inconvenient. Right now, he was hungering for a little closeness with Shiri of his own. But judging from Sawyer Garth's tone on the phone and the expression on his wife's face, wasn't nothing happening in the husband-wife department tonight.

"I don't know what she wants," Shiri whispered back, covering the phone with her hand.

"Shiri, can you meet me? I have to talk to you," Sawyer pleaded into the phone.

"Now? Sawyer, it's three o'clock in the morning!" Shiri protested. But even as she spoke, she was starting to climb out of the bed.

"Oh . . . sorry . . . I didn't realize that it was so late. It's just . . . uh . . . I need someone to talk to and I . . . that is . . . you're the first person I thought of. You always said that if I needed anything I could call you."

"And I meant that. Sawyer, hang on a minute, okay?" She glanced apologetically over at Jack before swinging her feet off the edge of the bed and moving into the bathroom to talk without disturbing him. She folded the seat down on the commode and propped her feet up on the huge, two-person, whirlpool, spa-type bathtub. Rummaging through the basket on the side of the tub, she dug out cotton balls and fingernail polish remover. *As long as I'm up,* she thought with resignation. *Might as well make good use of the time.*

Keeping her tone hushed to avoid the echo in the large bathroom, Shiri cradled the phone between her shoulder and ear as she said, "Okay, now tell me. What's going on with you, Sawyer?"

"It's blue, Shiri."

"Excuse me?" Shiri was only half paying attention as she held up two selections of nail polish in front of her. One was cotton-candy pink. The other was maraschino-cherry red.

"The stick. It's blue."

"The stick. What stick? I'm sorry, I'm not following you." Shiri painted one fingernail pink and the other red. She blew on her hands to quickly set the colors.

"The stick!" Sawyer said again, louder this time, as if talking louder would make her meaning that much clearer to her cousin. "The damned thing turned blue on me."

"Stick turned blue," Shiri echoed. She paused as understanding finally dawned on her, then said, "The stick . . . you mean it's blue. . . . Oh, ooohhhh! You mean it's blue? Does that mean what I think it means?"

"Yeah, Shiri. It's blue. That means I'm pregnant."

"Sawyer, are you sure?"

"About as sure as I can be. I took the home test three times. Three different times. I tried the one with the plus and the minus signs, the one with the single and double lines, and the one that turns blue."

"And . . . it's blue," Shiri finished for her.

The sizzling curse from Sawyer's lips was confirmation enough.

Shiri winced. It was the same curse of frustration Jack gave when she decided to take the phone call. "I take it that this wasn't something you've been expecting. No pun intended."

"I'm going to assume that calling you so early in the morning has dulled your usually sharp mind. Of course I wasn't trying to get pregnant!" Sawyer screeched into the phone. Shiri held it away from her ear until the screaming on the other end stemmed into ragged breathing. "Would I be calling you at three o'clock in the morning if I was trying to get pregnant!"

"Don't get snotty with me, Sawyer Garth. You called me, remember? I'm only trying to help you out."

"I'm sorry. I'm sorry. It's just . . . I'm so scared, Shiri. I wasn't expecting this. Why is this happening to me!"

"Well, what did you think was going to happen?" Shiri snapped back. She thought back to the last time she saw her cousin. She'd received an invitation to her first book signing but could hardly get close to her. Could hardly speak to her. Sawyer's agent, slash, publicist, slash live-in hovered around her, his hands all over her—as if to show everyone the true nature of their relationship.

"I don't need a lecture, Shiri. I was being careful. Very careful."

"You were using protection, weren't you? *Please* tell me that you were," Shiri begged.

"I was. I swear I was. But something happened. It must have broken or leaked or something."

"Was it Ryan?"

"Of course it was Ryan. Why would you ask me something like that?"

"I don't know. It just came off the top of my head."

"I know I like to have some fun, just as much as the next girl. But I don't sleep around, Shiri. I'm not a slut."

"I didn't say you were," Shiri said, to soothe her cousin's wounded feelings.

"Ryan's my first . . . my only, Shiri." Her tone was wistful.

"Have you told him yet?"

"No, I haven't. Not yet. I kept hoping that if I took the test enough times I would get a different result."

"What about your dad?"

"You must be on something." Sawyer's tone was incredulous. "Of course I haven't told him yet. I can't tell him. It would kill him. But first he would kill us. First Ryan, and then me."

"Simeon wouldn't do that to you, Sawyer. He loves you."

"He loves me. Hates my lifestyle. Hates the drama and

disorder I bring into his perfect world. Can you imagine what a grandchild would do to him? First, it would force him to admit that he was even old enough to have a grandchild."

"Then why do you keeping aggravating him, Sawyer?" Shiri demanded. "Why do you keep doing the things you know are going to drive him crazy? Those spooky goth friends you hang out with . . . those whacked-out books that you write . . . running off and disappearing for days without telling anyone . . . I swear, Sawyer, sometimes I think you're *trying* to hurt yourself."

Sawyer's voice grew deathly quiet as she said, "Trust me, Shiri, if I really wanted to do some damage to myself, you know that I could. It would be so easy. I know folks who can make things happen. Get my hands on some pills. A swallow here. Half the folks I know carry shanks. A slash of the wrists there. Doesn't have to be anything devious. I could just throw my hands up when I'm on my bike."

Shiri had images of Sawyer on her motorcycle, driving so fast, too fast to stop. "But you don't want to, do you!" Shiri didn't try to hold back the alarm in her voice. This was the part of Sawyer that very few ever saw. This was the part of her that made Jack so nervous to be around her.

"Shiri!" It was Jack calling out to her. He must have heard her cry out. "Is everything all right?"

She clamped her hand down over the phone and reassured her husband, "Everything's fine, J.D. Go back to sleep." She then said stridently into the phone, "Sawyer, you'd better tell me now, you're not thinking of doing anything stupid, are you?"

"Of course I'm not. Don't be silly." The laugh Sawyer gave back didn't completely convince her cousin. "I'm too afraid to try anything that would leave permanent scars. All my scars are emotional ones."

"I don't know about you, Sawyer. Sometimes I wonder about some of the stunts you pull. I don't see how you've survived them. Remember that time you went drag-stripping and nearly wound up smeared all over the road?"

Sawyer quickly shifted blame. "That wasn't my fault. The engine blew a seal."

"Grandma Lela almost blew her own gasket. You know she had the entire church set up a prayer vigil for you? You're on four different prayer request lists."

"So *she's* the reason I've got my own private guardian angel sitting on my shoulder," Sawyer teased. "And my ever-loving family to watch out for me to keep me safe."

"We can't be all of the time," Shiri insisted.

"I just wish my father was there even *some* of the time," Sawyer lamented.

"Where is your father?"

"Somewhere off in Liberia. Trying to make peace in the world. . . . Funny, huh?" Her tone was bitterly sarcastic. "When there's so much turmoil right here in his very own home. You think if I called him and told him that I was pregnant he would come home? Even for just a little while?"

"Is that why you do some of the crazy things you do? To get his attention? No wonder he's annoyed with you."

"Annoyed doesn't even begin to describe how he feels about me!" Sawyer snapped. "I think he blames me for Mama dying. Have you ever thought about that?"

"Girl, what have you been smoking? Simeon loves you. He's given you so much."

"Oh, that's right. I forgot how you and the rest of the family have put him on such a pedestal. He's so perfect. Everyone knows and loves Simeon Garth. The great mediator. To hear him tell it, everyone one from the pope to peanut vendors are all seeking his advice. I'm lucky if I get a postcard on my birthday. Not even signed by him. Forged by his administrative assistant."

"Well, if it's attention you want, walking around with your belly as swollen as a basketball is not the way to do it."

"That's not funny."

"Do you hear me laughing, girl?" Shiri said earnestly.

"Even though I'd love to see the expression on his face when I bring yet another problem into his house, I'm not going to tell him until I have to."

"Before, I was taking pity on you. Now you're just sounding like a brat."

"I don't know why I even called you, Shiri."

Shiri could tell that Sawyer was going to hang up on her. That's what she always did when she didn't like the direction of the conversation. For someone who thrived on drama, she sure did turn tail and run when things didn't go her way.

"Don't you hang up on me," Shiri threatened. "You called me because you know that no matter what, I'm going to be there for you."

"You're family. You're just saying that."

"You know that's not true. I've always been there for you. Who was the one who told you that you had a lick of talent and that you should write a book?"

"You did," Sawyer said reluctantly.

"And who was the one who came up with the bail money to get you out of lockup when you and your goth friends started that fight at that hole in the wall . . . What was that place called again?"

"The Hole in the Wall," Sawyer admitted.

"Uh-huh. And who was the one who found you, brought you back, when you ran off because your father didn't buy you that pony for your birthday?"

"That would have been you, and Essence, and Brenda," Sawyer said. "Jeez, you had to dig for that one. I was only nine years old then."

"Hey, what do you expect? It's freakin' dawn-thirty. I should be snuggled up to my husband, starting off his day with some TLC. But I'm not. I'm here for you, girl. I told you,

I'm your cousin. Your friend. And I love you. Unconditionally. No questions asked."

"I love you, too, Shiri," Sawyer said, her throat closing up. "I'm so lucky to have a cousin like you. Thanks for listening to my crazy ranting . . . again."

"You're not crazy, Sawyer. You're just, uh . . . *different*."

"I know what that means." Sawyer laughed. "That's just a nice way of saying nutty as the proverbial fruitcake. You don't think I know what you guys say about me when I'm not around? I can almost hear your hubby. 'Your cousin's got issues, Shiri. She needs a couple of six-packs of Prozac.' " Sawyer perfectly imitated her husband's inflections. She was a natural mimic, making Shiri want to laugh despite her concern.

Instead, she cleared her throat and tried to sound sincere. "The only thing we say about you is that we wish you hung around us more . . . dazzle us with that eccentric personality. You know it's not just me. We all love you, Sawyer. We all support you. So, are you going to tell the rest of the family about your little bundle or not?"

"I don't know." Weariness and confusion seeped through the phone.

"What do you mean you don't know?"

"I don't know means I don't know. I don't know what to do, yet, Shiri. I'm still reeling from the realization that there's a tiny person growing inside me. Leeching off of me. Sucking me dry. Ruining my life . . . as screwed up as it already is."

"Most people wouldn't see babies as leeches, Sawyer. Some might even consider them a blessing . . . especially those who have been trying for a long time to conceive. You do realize that you have options, don't you?"

"I know."

"Don't think just because you're confused and scared that you have to make a decision, one way or the other. You don't have to choose any one of them just yet. How far along do you think you are?"

"Three, maybe four weeks. My periods were never regular, so I'm not exactly sure."

"Why didn't your doctor put you on the pill?"

"She did. They made me sick. Even the low-dosage hormone ones."

"And that contraceptive patch?"

"They gave me a rash. Trust me, I thought I was doing what I could to protect myself."

"Everything except abstinence," Shiri muttered.

"I heard that. I dare you to tell me that you were a virgin when you married Jack."

"Hey, we're not talking about me. We're talking about you. Have you made an appointment to see your gynecologist?"

"I told you, I haven't made up my mind what I wanted to do."

"That shouldn't stop you from seeing a doctor, Sawyer. If you say the condom broke, then you should to be tested for STDs."

"Ryan's been my only partner, Shiri," Sawyer said, a slight edge in her voice. She wasn't used to people doubting her. Her sanity, maybe. But not her word.

"Maybe for you. But can you be so sure about him?"

"Shiri, Ryan and I really care for each other. We're committed to each other. He told me that as soon as my book was published, we'd get married. He just didn't want to burden me with all of that wedding-planning stuff while I was writing."

"Yeah, right," Shiri said in derision. "You're published now. Five books to your name. And the latest one is shooting up the charts. What's stopping him from slipping the ring on your finger now? He's already slipped you another unexpected surprise."

"Shiri! That's a tacky thing to say," Sawyer exclaimed.

"It's the truth. He can stick that ring around his penis but he can't put one on your finger? So the condom broke. Accidents happen. You didn't plan for the baby, but you can plan for the wedding. You've got plenty of time. In the meantime, you need to see a doctor. I'm just trying to cover all of the bases, girl. I'm not questioning whether or not you love each other. You've only been together for a couple of years. But who knows who he was with before you or how careful he's been? You need to get to a doctor. Don't play around with your health, Sawyer. Or the health of that baby."

Shiri could hear the reluctance in her cousin's voice. "Okay, okay. I'll call and make an appointment."

"When?" Shiri demanded. "I know you, Sawyer Garth. You can find excuses when you really don't want to do something."

"In the morning," Sawyer said, in a mingling of irritation and admiration for her cousin's straightforward speech and take-charge attitude.

"Do you want me to go with you?"

"You'd do that for me, Shiri?"

"Of course I would! You're my family. I'm there for you. No matter what you decide."

"You won't tell anybody about this, will you? You've got to swear that you won't say anything." Sawyer was starting to sound panicky again.

Shiri lowered her voice and glanced at the bathroom door. She'd tried to keep quiet, but how much had Jack heard? "It's not for me to tell, Sawyer."

"I mean it. You can't say anything. Not even to Brenda and Essence. I know how tight you three are. And now that Brenda's pregnant with those twins, everybody's gone baby gaga."

"If you don't want me to say anything, I won't. That's your decision and yours alone."

"I'm not looking forward to having that conversation. My father's going to be so disappointed. But why should that be any different? I'm already a disappointment to him. His one and only child had to be a girl. I didn't even have the good grace to be a boy, to carry on his name."

"You need to drop that emotional baggage you're lugging around, girl. Simeon loves you, Sawyer. He might be hurt at first, but he'll get over it. Who knows? He might even surprise you. Maybe you're gonna make him a granddaddy. Maybe that'll be enough to get his attention. Some positive attention for a change."

"Oh, *puh-lease*. What do you think your folks would've done if you came to them and told them that you'd gotten yourself knocked up?"

"Not much they could do since I'd probably make sure I'd make the phone call from the farthest city away from Birmingham when I'd told them. I hear Anchorage, Alaska, is very nice this time of year."

"Is that supposed to be a joke?"

"Sorry. It was in poor taste. But I was just trying to help you see the brighter side. Our family may go off the deep end sometimes, but we're always there for each other. No matter what."

"I just get tired of being a disappointment to everybody."

"Then stop," Shiri said simply.

"I can't help it. I'm trying to be true to myself. But every time I try to live my life to please myself, I wind up needing somebody to get me out of the mess I've made. I don't want to go to my father one more time asking him to forgive me. Not this time. Not when I thought I was doing right."

"If you need me there when you talk to Uncle Simeon, I'll be there for you, too."

"Thanks, Shiri. But it's not Daddy I was thinking about now."

"Who?"

"Aunt Rosie."

"Aunt Rosie? What has she got to do with this?"

"I'm her favorite, you know," Sawyer said.

Shiri burst into laughter, then hushed herself, peeking through the door to see if she'd disturbed Jack again.

"I hate to be the one to break it to you, Sawyer, but we're *all* her favorites," Shiri confided.

"Well, that's what she told me when I told her that I'd be joining her in Seattle for that bikers' rally."

Rolling her eyes, Shiri said, "Well, as much as I love our great-aunt Rosie, she's just gonna have to get over the disappointment of you not being able to join her for one of those crazy, cross-country motorcycle gang rallies."

"We're not a gang," Sawyer corrected. "We're not even an official biking club. We don't have colors. None of that worrying about offending anybody when we ride through their territory. We're just a group of women who enjoy each other's company."

"Well, whatever you are, you're gonna have to sit this out, Sawyer."

"Why?"

"What do you mean why? You can't go tooling around the country in your condition."

"You sound so old-fashioned. Just like Grandma Lela."

"If talking sense means sounding old-fashioned, then lock me up in a retirement home and pass the tapioca pudding. I know you're not still thinking of riding out there to join Aunt Rosie, are you?"

"The ride was a charity event, Shiri. An all-woman ride raising money for breast cancer awareness. It wasn't just a few biker chicks looking for a good time. I was really looking forward to taking that trip with Aunt Rosie. The down payment for that bike was a graduation gift from her."

"Why couldn't she have given you jewelry like she did

the rest of us?" Shiri grumbled. "It's bad enough that you're endangering yourself riding around on that two-wheeled death trap, but now you're talking about the life of your unborn child. You can't be that selfish."

"I'm not sure I even want the thing!" Sawyer snapped.

"Sawyer!"

"It's the truth, Shiri. I can't deny that. I'm twenty-three years old. I've still got a lot of living to do."

"You sound like you've got one foot in the grave already. Having a child isn't going to be the death of you."

Shiri could almost feel the cold silence coming through the phone. She cursed, then slapped the palm of her hand against her forehead. "Oh, Sawyer, I'm so sorry. I didn't mean to . . . that is . . ."

"Don't worry about it, Shiri. You can't miss a mother you've never known." Sawyer's tone turned hard again.

"She loved you so much. Was so excited about the very idea of giving birth to you. Those pictures of her and your father . . . the videotapes she left behind as her special messages of love for you . . ."

"Daddy said that my name was the last word on her lips. Died right in the labor and delivery room. You think that's something I'm looking forward to facing? No way in hell. Call me selfish if you want to."

"Nobody's calling you selfish. A little nutty, maybe, if you think you're still going on that ride."

"I have to go, Shiri."

"No, you don't."

"Yes, I do."

"No . . . you . . . don't," Shiri said emphatically.

"You can't stop me."

"You think I can't? Watch me. I know you're stubborn and you think you're going to get your way like you always do, but not this time. If I start dialing right now, tonight, telling everybody what you're planning to do, I'll have legions of Johnsons over at your condo so fast, you'll get whiplash watching your head spin around."

"You swore to me that you wouldn't say anything!"

"Some things are worth breaking a promise for. Saving your life and your baby's is one of those things."

"I'm not going to do anything crazy, Shiri."

"You're damned right you're not. I'm not going to let you. So you can get all thoughts of joining Aunt Rosie in Seattle out of your head. You hear me, Sawyer Garth?"

There was silence on the other end of the line so Shiri repeated herself, a slight edge in her voice.

"Hello? Sawyer?"

"Yeah, I hear you, Shiri. I hear you."

Chapter 2

Sawyer's gloved hand pressed a button on her handlebars, sounding the horn as she crossed the state line from Wyoming into Montana, but she didn't really hear it. Even with the tinted, smoke-colored face shield of her helmet snapped down to block the western sun's glare, the wind still managed to find its way into her helmet—an odd but familiar humming in her ears. She'd honked the horn, just like she'd heard in a song at the last place she'd stopped for gas. It was a country-and-western song by a popular girl group blaring from the outside PA system. Something about horns and babies crying and small towns. It seemed appropriate. Sawyer had seen a lot of small towns these past few days.

She clutched with her left hand and flipped her right wrist a couple of times in quick succession, throttling back a bit as the paved highway started into an upward S-curve. Leaning slightly into the turn, she effortlessly worked the throttle to give her an easy surge forward. Nice. Safe. Easy. Just as she'd promised herself she'd take it. Just as she'd promised Shiri she'd take it as she roared away, leaving her concerned cousin standing in the parking lot of the doctor's office four days ago.

Four days. That's how long she'd been on the road, leaving Birmingham without bothering to stop by her town house for as much as a toothbrush. She had to get out of there. Leave it all behind. Her home, her work, her man. Though, from his reaction when she'd told him that she was pregnant, Sawyer didn't care to consider him her man anymore. She wasn't sure what she was expecting, but it certainly wasn't *that*.

"You're pregnant?" Ryan had echoed when she made the announcement. "Well, I'll be a son of a—"

He pulled his hands out of hers, the hands she'd taken when she led him to the bed, sat him down, and told him that she had something serious to discuss with him.

"I know you weren't expecting this," she went on in a rush. She talked fast to keep herself from thinking too long and too hard. If she talked fast, maybe she could convince herself that she really wanted this baby. If she talked fast, maybe Ryan would take it as enthusiasm and would be caught up in the emotion, too.

She needed him to be there for her. As much as her cousin Shiri supported her and encouraged her, she needed to know that the man who had planted this seed within her would stand by her, nurture her until she developed the maternal feelings necessary to raise the child. She was no fool. She knew that in many of her relatives' eyes, she was little more than a child herself. But together, they could get through this. With their support, more education, some child-rearing classes, and plenty of patience, they could all grow together.

"I wasn't expecting it, either. But now that it's happened, we can go on as we were. We'll just have a third one to consider now . . ." Her voice trailed off her when the look he turned on her wasn't shock or disbelief or excitement. Her carefully prepared speech was falling on deaf, unwilling ears. The look her gave her instead was pure denial.

He shot up from the bed as if burned. The same bed he'd led her to time and time again, the same bed that creaked and rattled with the enthusiasm of his lovemaking, made a painful, hollow ringing noise as he rose to put some distance from her.

"What do you mean 'we,' Sawyer?"

"Who do you think I mean? You and me. The mother and father of this surprise package you delivered," she said, putting her hands on her stomach.

Ryan shook his head violently from side to side. "Can't be my baby, Sawyer."

"Of course it's your baby, Ryan."

"Nope," he flatly denied. "Couldn't be. I had the old plumbing stopped up five years ago. Vasectomy. No babies poppin' out of that chute, honey. Impossible. If you've been steppin' out on me, I'm sorry for ya. But I'm not taking the hit for this one."

Almost twenty years her senior, Ryan had entered the relationship with her willingly, enthusiastically. He'd found a true jewel in Sawyer. She was bright and funny, as passionate about her books as she was in bed. Well, maybe not so great in bed lately. But he just attributed that to the fact that she was working too hard. He could deal with that. As long as she was working, he was working. As long as she was churning out best-sellers, his publicity firm was doing well riding on her wave of popularity. As an extra bonus, she made excellent eye candy when he took her to publicity functions. Five feet four, but with generous curves, she always turned heads when she entered a room. Always.

With potentially the hottest black woman writer to hit the stands since Toni Morrison, his publicity agency had hitched itself to her rising star. He was her business partner, her friend, her mentor, *and* her lover. But he would not be father to her child. He couldn't be. Children meant that he had to meet more than contractual obligations. He wouldn't do it. He just wouldn't do it, even if it meant losing Sawyer to another agency. With enough eager writing talent out there, he was as sure that he could find someone else to take her place as he was of the fact that he was not the father of her child.

Sawyer had listened to him give a thousand reasons why he couldn't be the father. She only had one to prove that he was. Ryan had been her first. Her only. Even though she wasn't exactly thrilled that she was about to become a parent, she didn't expect him to reject the idea with such cold, calculating insistence. And to accuse of her of cheating on him! He couldn't have hurt her more if he'd punched her.

"This is your baby, Ryan," she'd shrieked at him. "It *has* to be!"

"I told you, it isn't. I'm cut, baby. Nothing is coming out of these pipes but sweet, sweet music."

"I don't understand," Sawyer said. "If you had a vasectomy, Ryan, why did you bother with the condoms?" she demanded. She hated those things as much as he did. They were a necessary evil. No matter how much they claimed to allow maximum sensation for both partners, they always just felt like rubber to her.

"For this very same reason. I don't know what you'd bring home with you . . . bring into our bed."

"I do *not* sleep around, you callous son of a—" Sawyer stopped herself, reined in her anger. "Check the numbers. A vasectomy isn't one hundred percent effective. This is your baby. And if I have to get a court order to haul your ass to a clinic to submit to a paternity test, I will."

"Are you threatening me? Have you forgotten who you're talking to? I'm the one who pushed to get your crappy books out there. I'm the one who got you the book signings and the public appearances. Without me, you'd still be trying to sell your self-published books out of your daddy's car. Don't you try to push that bastard off on me, Sawyer. I'm not buying it. If you even think about it, I'll make sure that nobody will buy the next pile of trash you put out, either. I'll stay up, all night long, call in every favor I can to make sure that you won't make one signing engagement."

"You can't do that! We have a contract!"

"Contracts are like rules, Sawyer. Made to be broken."

Contracts and hearts, Sawyer thought bitterly. The fact that he'd threatened her livelihood didn't bother her. She was not lacking for the things money could by. Her mother's trust fund made sure of that. She'd become a writer not for the money, but for the pleasure of having something creative, something people wanted to buy, come from her fingertips. Not to mention the attention that she'd received. She loved public appearances, basked in the glow of book signings where the people she met raved on and on about her books. Meeting them filled the hole in her soul left vacant by her absentee parents.

Now that Ryan had pulled away from her, leaving her feeling empty again, Sawyer came to one conclusion. She would *not* bring a child into this world growing up as she did. She would not have a child of hers lying awake at night, crying herself to sleep, wondering why her father didn't want her.

So, she'd gone to the doctor with Shiri, secure in the decision that there was only one option to her. She didn't want the child. Ryan didn't want it. What else could she do?

"Are you sure about this?" Shiri had asked, her voice trembling as she handed Sawyer the paperwork that explained to Sawyer the risks associated with terminating a pregnancy.

"Yes," Sawyer said, meeting Shiri's gaze with unwavering resolution. Shiri's soft brown eyes were filled with worry. In startling contrast, Sawyer's green eyes were hard, seeming cool and unbothered by her decision. Her body. Her choice. It was as simple as that.

Her hand was steady, swift, supplying all the information the forms requested with her neat, block script. Last menstrual period. Blood type. Known allergies to medication. Effects of anesthesia. Outpatient care requirements. Down the list, over to the next page, finally to the signature line. Only then did she pause. Her hand hovered over the line, suddenly, unexpectedly trembling as if afflicted with palsy.

Sawyer looked up; her gaze swept over the waiting room. The cheeriness of the décor only frightened her more with its mauve and pale green sprigs of flowers, reproductions of prints depicting smiling cherubs, and cross-stitched homilies touting the joys of parenthood. She couldn't stand it. The room seemed to close in around her. It was almost full to capacity. Pregnant women in the last trimester, their bellies swollen and distended as they shifted uncomfortably in the waiting room chairs with not quite enough padding for them, some of them older, some of them barely into their teens, young mothers with babies in strollers or babies crawling around the waiting room floor, couples nervously holding hands, others hiding behind magazines, like *Parenting* or *Working Mother*.

Sawyer felt for all of them. She rejoiced for the ones who'd finally conceived after months (or maybe years) of trying. She lamented for the ones who were still trying and mentally saluted the ones who'd made the same difficult decision that she had made.

The frosted glass separating the waiting area from the doctor's staff slid open. A young woman with bright auburn hair and cotton-candy-pink scrubs partially stood from behind the desk and sang out, "Ms. Garth?"

It was her turn. Time to go back in. She'd already been in earlier to take a confirmation blood test. It had come back with the same result as that damned blue stick. If she had any last doubts, an ultrasound would confirm it when she went in to perform what her doctor's euphemistically called an "office D and C." Time to perform the irrevocable. Sawyer reached out and clasped Shiri's hand.

Shiri squeezed back, trying not to notice how cold and clammy her cousin's hand had turned.

"I'll be right here waiting for you," Shiri whispered to her.

"Like hell you will," Sawyer said fiercely, leaping out of her chair. The clipboard with the unsigned consent papers clattered to the floor. "Let's get out of here."

"Are you sure?" Shiri tried not to sound hopeful. She wanted to be supportive, strong for her cousin. At the same time, she was secretly glad that Sawyer had changed her mind. One more addition to the family. One more cousin.

"Get me out of here before I change my mind again," Sawyer said in a harsh whisper before she fled the room. Down the hall and to the elevator. She stabbed at the button. The button light came on, but the elevator couldn't get to the fifth floor fast enough for her. Turning in an about-face, Sawyer decided to take the stairs instead. Her sneaker-clad feet flew down all five flights. By the time she reached the ground floor, she was gasping for air, dry-heaving, trying to squeeze out the contents of a near empty stomach. One hand clutched her stomach as she pushed through the doors and stumbled to the side of the building. She ignored the smattering of protesters picketing in front of the building, holding up signs and passing out "Support Life" literature to all those entering. She'd taken the flyer, but crumpled it up and tossed it into the trash as she'd gone to her doctor. She'd ignored them when she went in and gave them the same disregard when she game out—as sick to her stomach as she was in her heart.

She vaguely remembered Shiri suddenly appearing at her side, grasping her shoulders, and keeping her from sinking completely to the ground.

"You m-must think I'm an id-id-idiot," Sawyer stammered. "Panicking like that."

"Don't be silly," Shiri said stoutly. "You're not an idiot."

"I couldn't do it . . . I just couldn't. I kept thinking, what if my mother had signed papers on me? I wouldn't be here today. She gave her life for me and this is how I repay her? What kind of sorry daughter is that?"

"If she was here now, I know she'd be so proud of you, Sawyer."

Sawyer turned haunted eyes to Shiri. "And you were going to let me go through with it."

"It's what you said you wanted," Shiri protested.

"Next time I tell you I want to do something that crazy, you knock me flat on my behind and sit on me until the lunacy passes. Got that?"

"You've got a deal." Shiri sealed the promise with a kiss on her cousin's forehead. "So what now? What are you going to do?"

Sawyer shook her head. "I don't know. I guess I need to start spreading the news before I start spreading."

She pressed both hands against her stomach. With the fetus no bigger than a popcorn shrimp, she knew that it was some time before she would start to show.

"Don't you even try it," Shiri said with mild disgust. Sawyer was petite. Probably had clothes specially made for her. Clothes manufacturers didn't make sizes in the negative numbers. "You know you'll be one of those women who'll stay cute and sexy all the way through the pregnancy. I'm jealous of you already."

"Eight months and counting," Sawyer said. "I've got a lot to do between now and then."

"Go shopping for maternity clothes, register for baby

shower gifts, start picking out names." Shiri ticked off on her fingers.

"All in good time," Sawyer said. "First things first. Let's go." She started for the parking lot.

She unclipped her motorcycle helmet from the seat. As she fastened the buckle under her chin, she reasoned that everything was going to work out. Everything was moving along to some grand plan. She wasn't meant to have that abortion. Somehow, deep down, she knew that she couldn't go through with it. Why else would she insist on driving herself to the clinic instead of accepting the ride that Shiri had offered? Even though the paperwork stated that she'd be okay to drive after the anesthesia had worn off, Sawyer had never ridden her motorcycle under the influence of anything. Not even a glass of wine or light beer. That was her aunt Rosie's doing. When she'd gone with Sawyer to pick out the bike, she made her promise that she'd never ride with her senses impaired. She'd stressed that fact again when she went with her to take her motorcycle driving test. Once she turned the ignition key and revved up the motor, she must always be clearheaded and in full control of her faculties. With so many careless, unwatchful drivers out there, road hogs, and just plain mean people, her senses might be the only thing she had to rely on to save her life.

So, when she climbed aboard her black and silver Suzuki Savage, pressed the ignition button to start the motor, and announced to Shiri that she was heading straight for Seattle, Washington, Sawyer knew that she was completely in her right mind.

Despite Shiri's explosion that she had flipped her wig, Sawyer had simply smiled and promised to call her as soon as she joined up with their aunt Rosie in Seattle. That was four days ago. Four days on the road. Four days of thinking about what she had done—or rather not done—and not regretting a moment of her decision.

"Sorry I ever thought I could deny you the pleasure of being a grandma angel, Mama." She'd lifted her eyes to the sky and apologized more than once. She still wasn't sure what kind of mother she'd make. But her mother had given her nine months' worth of memories in letters and recorded messages. Could she do no less?

It was two weeks before she was supposed to meet up with Aunt Rosie for the May Flowers' biker rally. May Flowers was the name Aunt Rosie's biking friends had given themselves for their annual May-June road trip. Two weeks on the open road—her last wild fling before she settled into her new life as "the mommy."

Sawyer Garth leaned forward and addressed her stomach before peeling out of the parking lot. "Time to make some memories for you, baby."

Chapter 3

Jon-Tyler Holling remembered the extra order of pecan pie for his father, but only after he'd already climbed into his Chevy Suburban and started up the engine.

His shoulders slumped as he blew out a frustrated sigh. With his hand still on the keys dangling from the ignition, he debated going back inside Marjean's Café. It was the beginning of the supper crowd, and the owner and head cook, Marjean, had her hands full.

Since the department of transportation had added that spur from the interstate through White Wolf, official population of 306, at every meal the one and only restaurant that served home-style cooking here was filled to capacity.

The same could be said for the only gas station in town, the corner grocery store, and the laundry. And the liquor store? On a Saturday night, Holling knew you could practically forget getting in and out of there in less than ten minutes. The only structure where anyone could usually find elbow room on any given day was the Methodist church that stood quietly, patiently, on the north end of town waiting for its share of activity.

Maybe I should just forget about the pie, Holling considered. Maybe he should settle for a stack of those prepackaged apple pies served by that fast-food burger joint up the road. Or he could swing by that drive-in restaurant and bring his pops home a couple of flavored slushy ice drinks. Even as he sat and debated, three full van loads of workers from the Montana Department of Transportation pulled up to the parking spaces on either side of him, temporarily blocking him in as they piled out. If their arrival didn't top Marjean's capacity limit, Holling didn't know what would. He could hear snatches of their conversation.

"Santiago, you make sure you roll up those windows, son. I don't like the look of those storm clouds rollin' in."

One of them stopped, stretched out overworked muscles, and stared up at the sky.

"A little water on the inside might be an improvement, Wyatt. When's the last time you cleaned out this van? Whew, boy! Smells like something crawled up in here and died."

"That's your mama you're smellin' back there. She made me clean out the van the last time she lay on her back for me."

The rest of their conversation was cut off as they trudged through the front entrance, trading insults and arguing about whose turn it was to pick up the meal tab.

Overhearing that conversation was enough to make up Holling's mind. He didn't want to be out in the weather. As bad as his pops's sweet tooth must be plaguing him, Holling knew that if he didn't come home with that pecan pie, he would just have to turn around again and drive through the pouring rain to get it.

Muttering a curse, he slammed the SUV door behind him as he climbed out. Holling figured that if he had any real sense, he would just pop over to the E-Z Mart and pick up the ingredients to make his own pie. He'd done it before. But that was about four years ago. And after tasting the sticky sweet mess, his father had expressly forbidden his ever trying a stunt like that again.

To save them all from going into a sugar-induced coma, from now on they would agree to leave all the cooking to Chale Cimarron. But their live-in housekeeper wasn't there, gone to Houston to celebrate his granddaughter's *quinceañera*. It was a special time for his fifteen-year-old granddaughter— as important a milestone as a debutante party, with preparations as elaborate as a wedding. They couldn't refuse Chale the vacation time. He had to be there.

That didn't stop Holling and his father, Nathaniel, from exchanging concerned glances when he'd announced that he'd be gone for a couple of weeks. The guests that stayed at their ranch bed-and-breakfast always raved about Chale's cooking. Every comment card left behind mentioned him. Not that he and his father couldn't cook for themselves if they had to. They just preferred not to. It was easier on their stomachs that way. Kinder to the guests. Since it was the summer hiatus before the real tourists starting reserving time at his ranch, they didn't have to worry too much about scaring off any more patrons, or the skeleton crew remaining to handle odd jobs, with their rudimentary cooking skills.

In preparation for his vacation, Chale had cooked and frozen enough entrees for him and his pops to last a couple of weeks with dire warnings for them to stay out of his kitchen.

"You touch a single pan and I'll know it," he'd threatened. "All you've got to do is put the food in the oven and heat. *Mas fácil*. So easy even an old dumb cowboy like you can understand. *Diez minutes*." He held up ten fingers. "No cooking. *Comprendes?*"

"Yeah, yeah. We understand," Nathaniel Holling had grumbled.

But Chale had extended his stay, going on three weeks, and now pickings in the proverbial Holling cupboard were getting slim. Holling blamed the lack of goodies on his father. They would have lasted a while longer, and he wouldn't have had to make these frequent trips to Marjean's, if his pops hadn't wolfed down all the desserts within the first week of Chale's vacation.

The double-layer chocolate cake with homemade whipped frosting, the tin of oatmeal cookies with plump golden raisins, the bowl of fruit salad sprinkled liberally with coconut, even the six-inch-long bars of lemon zest—so tart they made even your teeth pucker—were gone. All gone.

When Nate was reduced to eating frosted shredded wheat for his attack of the sweet tooth, he decided that enough was enough. It was time to go after the real thing. Since he blamed his son for their lack of desserts, it was up to Jon-Tyler to go after some more.

"I don't see how it's all my fault," Holling had protested as his father tossed him the keys to the Suburban.

"Chale's not here. You can't cook. And you won't get a woman in here of your own who can."

"Get your own woman." Holling tossed the keys back. "And while you're at it, go get your own dessert. I'm just as happy snacking on an apple."

"What do you think I am, a horse? I like my sugar refined. Just like my women. I'm almost sixty years old, boy. Your prospects of findin' a woman who'll put up with us looks better than mine." Nate flung the keys back.

Holling snatched them in midair. "Prospects? What prospects? What are you talking about, old man?"

"There's that Malveaux girl for starters. If you'd gotten with that Malveaux girl like I told you to—"

Holling had to snort in amusement at that. "What do you mean gotten with her?"

"You know exactly what I'm talking about. That girl had her eyes on you, Holling. I've seen the way she was looking at you when we were having supper at Marjean's."

"Pops, she wasn't lookin' at me. She was lookin' at the triple burger that Marjean had served me. You don't want me hookin' up with her, Pops. She'd eat us out of house and home within a month."

Nathaniel stroked the bristly gray and white hairs of his neatly trimmed beard. He held the door open for Jon-Tyler, rushing him along. "Yeah, come to think of it, she was kinda on the hefty side."

"You're just bein' polite, Pops. The girl had the combined weight of the entire Billings Outlaw football team."

"But you have to admit, the girl can cook. If you went on ahead and married her, our food bill for the month might triple, but at least we'd all be eatin' good."

"And put Chale out of a job? I wouldn't be so cruel. Call me a sentimental fool, but I don't think it's a good trade-off. I'd rather make a hundred trips back and forth to Marjean's Café than deal with a woman who was more interested in what is on my plate than what's in my heart. So what if Annalise Malveaux can cook?" He shrugged in feigned indifference. "I need to cut down on the calories anyway."

"Now, that's just plain crazy talk. You don't need to cut down on calories. You need to cut down on your complainin'. How come every time I suggest a woman for you, you turn me down, boy?"

"How come you're always suggesting women that suit your needs more than they suit mine? You only wanted me to get with Annalise Malveaux because she knows how to cook almost as good as Chale can."

"And there's something wrong with that?"

"That's your stomach talking, not your heart."

"Okay, so Annalise wasn't the one for you. What about that Branson girl?"

"The one with the lazy eye?" Holling said, squinting his eye at his pops to imitate her off-kilter stare.

"Yeah, that's the one. What was wrong with her?"

"I can think of about twenty things wrong with her . . . make that twenty-fifty. That's about how far she can see with that cockeye."

"Now, you can't say anything about that Willis gal. She had it all." Nate held out his gnarled hands, waving them in the air to give an exaggerate silhouette of Kyla Willis.

"You mean, had 'em all. Yeah, Kyla's sweet. On everybody in White Wolf, that is. If I wanted to take her out, I'd have to take a number."

"You're so picky, Holling. One of these days, boy . . . one of these days . . ."

"I know, I know." Holling had heard it all before. "Pow!" He swung his fist to give the air an uppercut. "Right in the kisser!"

"That's right," Nate said, bobbing his head. "It'll hit you just like that. Knock you right off your feet. You mark my words," he predicted. "You're gonna find a woman who'll take that picky list of yours and rip it to shreds. And when you do, heaven help you. What happens when you won't be able to find a flaw in that gal? Then what're you gonna do?"

"Pigs are gonna fly before that happens, Pops."

"Then you get this road hog to flyin' and bring me back one of Marjean's pecan pies. I'll call ahead, make sure she's got one fresh out of the oven. And while you're at it, pick up dinner. I don't feel like cookin' tonight."

"You haven't felt like cookin' since we hired Chale," Holling retorted. That was about fifteen years ago. Holling had been ten years old then. When Chale had whipped up a batch of peanut butter cookies from scratch, Holling's favorite, even sprinkled powdered sugar over the top, he'd told his father that they had to hire him. They just had to. None of the other candidates would do.

He was glad someone around there felt like cooking, Holling thought as he reentered the café. It was what Marjean did best. That much was obvious by the almost-standing-room-only dinner crowd.

Every chair and bench in the small waiting area was filled as Barbara Jean, Marjean's nineteen-year-old daughter, ushered patrons in groups of twos and threes to any available booth and table. Barbara Jean was the spitting image of her mother, right down to the frosted feathered hair, electric-blue eye shadow, and penciled-in eyebrows.

Holling lifted his hand, trying to get Barbara Jean's attention. He was a regular and a resident. Hoping to trade in on that familiarity, he figured that had to be worth something.

"Be with ya in a minute, Mr. Holling," she called out to him.

Holling nodded to show that he'd heard her, then eased back to try to find a spot along the wall to wait. The first few minutes weren't so bad. Some folks that he knew came in not long after he did—Felicity and Sam Felder. Married as they'd been for almost forty years, Holling thought with mild amusement that they looked more like brother and sister than man and wife. Tall. Rail thin. Both had graying, frizzled hair, watery blue eyes, and lips pressed together in a constant state of disapproval. He wore a cap bearing the logo of a local feed store. She wore a bandana of the same color. Denim shirts. Both wore boot-cut Wranglers. If it weren't for the visible ring from always carrying Sam's can of Copenhagen dipping tobacco in his back pocket, Holling was sure that from the rear he wouldn't be able to tell them apart.

Holling tried to imagine what it must be like, living nearly half your life with someone, putting up with someone, who wasn't your blood kin. It was inconceivable.

"Surprised to see you here, Holling," Felicity said, smiling at him. She was only teasing. She'd seen him there just yesterday. He and Pops had stopped into White Wolf to pick up a few fencing supplies and decided to swing by for lunch.

"I'll bet you'll be glad when Chale gets back," Sam added.

"Your guests will be gladder. How many do you have out there now?" Felicity asked.

Holling shook his head. "None. The last one left the day before Chale took off for Texas. We timed the summer hiatus just right. Most of our hands are on vacation. Just a small crew who didn't have travel plans is hanging around, helping Pops out with odd jobs until things pick up. By the time he gets back, we should be startin' to see more traffic."

"Speakin' of which, what do you think of all this road construction?" Sam counted the heads of the MDT workers dotting the restaurant.

"We all voted for it," Holling reminded them.

"I don't know. It's hard on us now. Folks could barely find us as it was and now the roads are all torn up," Felicity complained. "I didn't know it would take this long to build a simple highway."

"I don't think we'll take too bad of a hit," Holling predicted. "I finally got our Web site up. So even if they can't find us off the interstate, they'll be able to find us in cyberspace and book the rooms."

"Most of your guests come to you on horseback anyway, following the old trails," Felicity said. "As bad as things are torn up around our place, you'd need a helicopter to airlift someone in. I'm just afraid that with one good rain, all that mud and runoff from the construction will overrun us."

When Barbara Jean finally swept by him, her expression harried, Holling grasped her lightly by her elbow.

"Remember me?" he said, trying to keep his tone light. But anyone who knew Jon-Tyler Holling knew that when he tightened his jaw, narrowed his eyes, and gave that slight tilt of his head, he wasn't pleased and probably wouldn't take much more of whatever it was that had displeased him. At just under six feet, with 220 pounds and a greased-lightning right cross, Holling didn't get displeased too often.

"I'm so sorry to keep you waitin', Mr. Holling. What can I do for you?"

"I'd ordered a pie from your mama. A pecan pie. I just want to pick it up and then I'll get out of your hair, Barbara Jean." He raised his hands, releasing her arm.

When her eyes grew as large, brown, and round as that pie, Holling had a feeling that he'd be stopping by that E-Z Mart and baking for his pops tonight, despite the ban on his cooking.

"Oh . . . that pecan pie. I'm sure sorry, Mr. Holling. When you took off and left it, Mama thought that maybe you changed your mind. We've already cut it up . . . and . . . well, that feller over there got him a piece of it . . . and then that lady over there and her four kids each got a slice . . . and . . . well, sorry, Mr. Holling. I hate to say it, but ain't much left now but crumbs."

"I was only gone three minutes. Five at the most!"

"Mama tried to call you back when you left the counter, but I guess you didn't hear her. It got like a zoo in here as soon as you walked out."

"Yeah, I can see," he said, moving aside as still more customers squeezed into the waiting room area.

"I woulda sent Waydell out to your place with it but he was out in Cut Bank visiting his mama. She finally had that operation. You know, the one to get that extra toe removed. Mama says it's about time. It was a shame she had to wait so long to—"

Holling held up his hand to cut her off. Barbara Jean was better than the town newspaper when it came to passing on information.

"Anyway, he called us and told us that he can't get back. Rain's coming down hard, heading this way. He could barely see, even with the wipers on that old truck, so we told him to pull over until it clears. I'm really sorry. If you care to wait, we can whip you up a new one. Might take a while though."

"Naw, that's all right, Barbara Jean. I'll just tell Pops he'll have to have his supper without anything sweet to eat. Guess that makes up for all the times he sent me to bed without my supper." He'd meant it as a joke, but the look of remorse on Barbara Jean's face told him that maybe he should leave all the cooking and the joke-telling to Chale.

"Oh, now I really feel bad. I know how much Mr. Nate likes his sweets. Just give me a few minutes, Mr. Holling. I'll run to the back and see what we can get for you."

"Don't trouble yourself, Barbara Jean. It's all right. Take care of your other customers first. I'll come back later."

"No, sir. I won't hear of it. You paid for a dessert and you're one of our best customers. We'll make it right and the next one is on the house for your trouble. Wait right here, all right?"

"All right," he agreed reluctantly. Holling resumed his position, leaning against the wall, trying to make himself small and out of the way of the steady flow in and out of the restaurant. With his arms folded across his chest, one booted foot resting against the peeling faux walnut paneling, Holling erected his own wall of personal space around him that seemed to withstand the press of bodies. No one wanted to jostle the man of stone. Hard, chiseled face, body sculpted by years of hard work. Irresolute. Immovable.

He hadn't been waiting long before the storm foretold by the MDT workers and Barbara Jean rolled in. The winds picked up first. Each time the door opened, the old tension spring couldn't keep the wind from smashing it against the outer wall. The door creaked in protest as it whipped against the wall. Holling expected at any time for it to be ripped off the hinges at the rate the wind was blowing.

White Wolf was nestled in a small pass at the base of the

Bridger Mountains. The walls of the mountains acted as a chute, forcing air through and over the town. Couple that with a hard rain and runoff from the mountain, and he could count on being here for a while, too. He should have left a long time ago. Now that he was here, he'd have to stay until it blew over, along with anyone else not living within walking distance.

A few patrons had just parked on the outskirts of the full parking lot when the sky turned to pitch and the first drops of pelting rain struck. They sprinted for Marjean's. Through the huge glass panes lining the front of the café, Holling watched the approach of yet another motorist trying to beat the weather.

A biker nosed its way past most of the parked cars. Up, then down the parking lot, looking for a space close by the front door.

Holling clucked his tongue, a soft sound of sympathy. *Good luck,* Holling thought. The postage-stamp-sized parking lot was jammed solid. Parking on the street was also full. When the doors opened, the last of the stragglers coming in with laughter and loud declarations of the meanness of the weather, Holling heard the gravelly purr of the motorcycle motor revving up.

The biker hunkered low over the handlebars, coasted between two vehicles, turned up the handicapped-access ramp, and made its own parking spot on the sidewalk under the overhanging eaves of the café. Just in time. A clap of thunder rattled the windows and set off almost every car alarm in the parking lot. The electronic wails of the security devices mingled with frequent crashes of thunder. Streaks of lightning cracked the sky, competing with the flashing headlights of cars whose alarms continued to sound off no matter how many times owners used their key remotes to disengage them.

By the time the biker shut off the engine and swung a leg

over the seat to dismount, pea-sized hail bounced off the eaves and scattered along the ground without touching the gleaming black and silver bike. Instead, the frozen chunks of ice peppered the other unprotected vehicles. In themselves, the pellets could do minimal damage. A cracked windshield here, or a chip in the paint there. It wasn't the fact that it had begun to hail that bothered Holling. It was what often came behind a hailstorm that made him uneasy. Tornados. Somewhere out there, a funnel cloud was likely. And here he was, stuck at Marjean's, waiting on a damned pecan pie.

He fished his cell phone out of the clip at his belt and stabbed at the speed-dial number with his thumb. The phone rang several times without answer.

"C'mon, Pops, pick up," he muttered. He hung up, then dialed the number to the bunkhouse. It picked up on the first ring.

"Holling's Way," was the response. Standard greeting for anyone who dialed the ranch.

"Red Bone." Holling recognized the gravelly tone of one of the hands. Lowell Redmond had signed on three years ago. Diagnosed with throat cancer, he'd undergone surgery to remove part of his larynx.

"Mr. Holling."

"Is my pops around there?"

"Yeah, we're all here. Me and Corey and Cale, Matías, and Mr. Nate. Weather's turnin' nasty."

"Yeah, that's why I'm checkin' in."

"Where are you?"

"Stuck here at Marjean's." Holling's disgust was obvious by his tone.

Red Bone gave a snort of laughter. "Mr. Nate said you wouldn't come back without that pie."

"If I'd known I had to go through this to get it, I woulda let him come out and get his own damned pie. What's he doin' anyway?"

"We got ourselves a real good poker game goin' here, Mr. Holling. Don't you worry yourself about us. You sit tight and ride out that storm."

"I don't think I'm going anywhere. Not anytime soon."

"Like I said, don't worry about us. The horses are all put up. Doors latched tight. Patio furniture is stored. We're watching the weather on Corey's TV. If we get the word or hear the siren, we're all down in the cellar quicker'n spit."

"I'm not worried that you'll get out of the weather. I'm worried about your poker playin'. If Pops is in the game, you make sure he wears sleeves that fit tight at the cuff."

"You don't got to worry about that none, either. We're playin' strip poker. Right now, he's down to his T-shirt and boxers."

Holling burst into laughter, then snapped the phone shut.

The storm must've dropped the air temperature ten, maybe fifteen degrees outside. As the biker yanked on the door, the air swirling through the entrance had a bite to it, making those still seated in the waiting area edge away from the entrance or huddle closer together to avoid the wind and rain that was driven in.

The biker turned around, pulling on the handle to get the door to close. But the wind was much stronger and threatened to send the door slamming against the wall again. Holling was closest to the door. He reached for the handle and allowed the biker to pass by him.

"Let me get that for ya, son," he offered.

Small wonder, Holling mused, that the biker seemed to be having so much trouble closing that door. Nobody but a tourist would underestimate the force of the wind during a Montana storm. This one seemed especially ill equipped to handle the sheer ferocity of it. Even with the heavy protective biker gear—leather bomber-style jacket, insulated gloves, blue jeans, chaps, and thick-soled boots—he couldn't have weighed more than a hundred pounds. Noting how slight he was, Holling marveled that he managed to get the bike onto the sidewalk. That took some fancy maneuvering, even on a calmer day. Holling guessed his height to be about five feet three or four. The top of his head with the helmet on just reached the middle of Holling's chest.

He had to give the kid credit. He had just enough sense to get in out of the weather. The way he'd ridden that bike up on the sidewalk, Holling had first figured him to be a hotshot, overly confident in his ability to handle the machine. It was that overconfidence that could get a biker smeared all over the road. He should know. He'd taken a spill or two in his riding days.

A broken collarbone and a couple of permanent pins in his femur were enough to convince him that youth, enthusiasm, cockiness, and speed weren't always a good mix. He'd bought that Harley-Davidson when he was seventeen. By the time he was eighteen, the bike was put up for sale. That was seven years ago and he hadn't looked back or regretted his decision since. The twinge in his leg when the weather turned just like this was reminder enough of why he didn't ride motorcycles anymore. He got his kicks from real live horsepower now, helping his father gentle the horses that could be rented to explore the numerous nature trails throughout the state.

"Good thing you got out of the rain there, son," Holling remarked as another crack of thunder set off a fresh round of car alarms. "Riding around in this weather ain't no joke."

When the rider pulled off his helmet, the joke, Holling thought with a fair amount of surprise, was on him. Surprise and embarrassment.

"You don't see me laughing," the biker responded, raising a finely arched eyebrow over the most striking green eyes Holling had ever seen. Not a he under all that gear, Holling mentally corrected, but a very definite she.

Chapter 4

Tucking her helmet under her arm, Sawyer raised her gloved hand to her mouth and tugged on the fingertips with her teeth to loosen the gloves. She removed one glove, then the other. Ignoring the curious looks from the people in the waiting area, she tucked the gloves into her jacket pocket. It was several degrees warmer in the café, so she also unzipped her jacket.

She seemed impervious, unmindful of the open stares she received. The hush that fell over the waiting area as she came in was measurable. She was used to the open stares by now after four days of traveling across several states—from sprawling metropolitan cities to out-of-the-way podunk towns like one.

What was the name on the roadside sign? Sawyer tried to recall. White Wolf, that was it. She was stalled out here in White Wolf, Montana. She wasn't even sure it would rate an ink dot on the map with a population count that didn't even break a thousand.

Probably included the cattle, too, Sawyer thought with mild amusement. She expected the stares. And if she stayed too long, she expected that because she was a biker they didn't recognize and was unaffiliated with any club, there would be questions—if not from local law enforcement warning her not to cause any trouble, then from suspicious, small-minded individuals that she'd made nervous.

She was a woman alone, riding on what was typically a man's mode of transportation. What exactly what she? Biker gang member or just plain butch? Either way, some just didn't like outsiders and would rather see her ride on.

Not now, Sawyer thought stubbornly. She was hungry and tired. Her bottom was beginning to ache. She resisted the urge to reach back there and rub the troubled spot. The last time she'd stopped in a town like this and went reaching behind her, she'd been in a bank, waiting in line, trying to withdraw money since the automatic teller machine was being serviced. Someone thought she was reaching for a weapon. And before she could protest, three local "heroes" had her pinned to the floor and were yelling for the cops.

It had taken her two hours to convince the local authorities that she wasn't casing the place. She was just riding through. Having a rap sheet didn't help her situation. If there had been more on that sheet than malicious mischief, she was sure that she'd still be there now trying to talk her way out of lockup.

Yeah, she had to be really careful when she stopped in these small towns. Small towns, small minds, Sawyer was beginning to think. She'd been on the road for three hours without a significant stop. Though she'd wanted to push on to the nearest roadside motel, she couldn't chance the weather. She'd promised Shiri that she would be careful. There was no need to push herself past the point of exhaustion. She wasn't scheduled to meet Aunt Rosie in Seattle for two weeks. That gave her plenty of time to take the scenic route, to explore the paths less taken, to store up as many memories for the baby as she could manage.

It was because of the baby that Sawyer pulled into the first place that appeared safe for her to stop. Plenty of vehicles parked out front. The more people around, the greater chance for her to fade into the background. All she wanted to do was get something to eat, collect her strength, and wait for the storm to blow over. If she laid low, there wouldn't be any chance for trouble. Now that she was here, she had to do something quick to allay the collective fears of the folks gathered inside the restaurant.

"It turned nasty out there quicker than I thought," she said aloud to no one in particular and gave her most pleasant smile. She "enhanced" her Southern accent, figuring that it would go over well in a town filled with folks who talked "just as funny."

No one really smiled back. That is, none of the women smiled back at her. A few of the men did, though she really couldn't call the smiles friendly. More like presumptive. She'd seen that look before, too. Sawyer knew from experience that those kinds of smiles had something to do with the leather chaps that she wore. Once they figured out that it was a woman underneath all that gear, the idea of a woman in leather was something of a turn-on, even though she really didn't mean it to be. They were worn for function more than fashion. They cut the wind, keeping her legs warm and from stiffening up after holding them in the same position for the long stretches when she rode.

At the intentional snub, Sawyer gave a small sigh, ready to wrap herself up tightly in the air of anonymity and self-reliance that had seen her through most of this road trip.

"Yeah, it happens that way around here sometimes." The one who'd helped her with the door spoke up from behind her. "Clear blue sky one minute, and the next thing you know, all hell breaks loose."

Sawyer half turned to address him. "It must make things

really interesting around here," she said sarcastically. *About as interesting as watching cattle graze,* Sawyer thought.

She turned her back on him and stepped up to the WAIT TO BE SEATED sign. From the looks of folks gathered at the lunch counter, filling all the tables throughout the restaurant, and standing around the waiting area, she wasn't the only one with sense enough to get in out of the rain. Sawyer sighed again, swiping away strands of thick black hair from her cheeks and running her fingers through it to fluff it up. She'd recently had it done in a short, razor-cut shag in anticipation of the long ride. Made it easier to wear her helmet than when she'd worn her hair in the shoulder-length, flat-ironed style.

Looks like it's going to be a long wait, she lamented. Sawyer took off her jacket to make herself more comfortable. She then peered around the restaurant, trying to catch sight of someone who could seat her. She saw one woman behind the counter, setting down orders, picking up empty plates, and pocketing tips as fast as her wide-hipped, ample-armed, orthopedic-shoed body could make her move.

On the far side of the restaurant, another young girl with hair and makeup that was stuck in a 1970s time warp moved from booth to table to pickup window with charm, enthusiasm, and a whole lot of smiling. The smiles grew bigger as the tips left on the table grew bigger as well.

That girl certainly knew how to work this crowd, Sawyer thought admiringly. Flirting with men and boys, respectful to their women, cuddly with the kids, she must have snatched up fifty dollars in tips in the past five minutes alone.

As hungry and as tired as Sawyer was, it would be worth fifty bucks if the girl would turn some of that attention her way and get her a table.

"So, how's the service around here?" she addressed the man from the door, still standing behind her and slightly to her right. "How long is the wait?"

"Not long," he said. He lifted his hand and gave the young

girl a wave. Sawyer didn't see how she could have seen him. Her back had been partially turned as she addressed another customer. Yet, she turned and looked directly at him as if he'd shouted her name from across the room. He then pointed down at Sawyer.

The girl said something to the customer she was handling, then came back to the hostess station.

"Welcome to Marjean's," she said to Sawyer. "How many in your party, ma'am?"

"Party of one," Sawyer said.

"Smoking or nonsmoking?"

"Nonsmoking, please," Sawyer said, though she didn't see how it would make a difference. The café wasn't that large. A thin blue haze of smoke hovered at eye level. Only some of the smoke could be attributed to the grill.

"Yes, ma'am. It'll be a little bit of a wait. Fifteen minutes or so."

"Try to make it closer to the fifteen than the or so, would you?" Sawyer suggested. She pulled out her wallet and slipped the girl a five-dollar bill.

"I'll do my best, ma'am, but it's crazy around here this time of evening. Your name, please?"

"Sawyer," she supplied.

"Yes, ma'am. I'll call you as soon as something's available." She then looked around Sawyer to the man standing behind her. Not so far behind, Sawyer noted. He'd inched up closer since she'd come in but stood just far enough away so as not to crowd in on her personal space.

"I haven't forgotten about you, Mr. Holling. I'm heading back right now to get you that dessert I promised. I think Mama said something about a key lime pie that's almost set well enough to serve."

"Actually, Barbara Jean, if it's not too much trouble, I think I'll wait on that pecan pie."

The girl's face scrunched as if she didn't quite hear him correctly. "Sir?"

"I'll wait on it. About half an hour to get it made, right?"

"Or so," she qualified.

"I'll be here, then."

"Are you sure, Mr. Holling?"

"Yep."

"All righty, then. I'll go back and tell Mama to whip you up another pie."

"Sure do appreciate it, Barbara Jean."

Barbara Jean looked down at her list again and called out the next names to be seated. The couple that was called had been one of the lucky ones. They'd gotten to Marjean's soon enough before the dinner crowd to grab a waiting bench. As soon as they moved to follow the hostess, two of the MDT workers that had gone in before him started toward the bench, but Holling moved to stand in front of the empty seat and gave the appearance of a man who wasn't about to budge, despite being outnumbered by the road crew.

"Been ridin' long, ma'am?" he called out to get Sawyer's attention. She half turned and nodded.

When he tilted his head, indicating the empty seat, she raised that eyebrow at him again. She wasn't sure if she should accept the offer. The last time she accepted his help, he'd called her "son." Her feminine pride was pricked. Did she look that bad? Her vanity almost won out over his valor.

When she didn't move toward the bench, the man insisted this time as he gestured with his hand. That ever-active hand. First, it got that hostess's attention and now it had hers. She had been riding a while and was actually looking forward to standing up on her feet for a while to give her body a stretch. But she was also tired. Maybe it was the higher altitude, the stress of driving with extra care that worked against her.

But there was a change she noticed in her body due to the

baby. Her energy level wasn't quite what it used to be. She found herself getting tired quicker than she used to. Before the baby came along, she used to be able to stay up all day and night, especially when a writing deadline was fast approaching. Not anymore. Sometimes sleepiness would overtake her—even in the middle of the afternoon. It wasn't anything for her to lie down for a brief catnap and wind up sleeping away half the afternoon. And since she didn't believe in taking drugs or artificial stimulants to keep her energy level up, Sawyer decided to listen to her body and let instinct guide her on how to care for herself. Instinct was howling in her ear now, as fierce as the wind outside, to take the offered seat.

"Thanks for the assist with the door, mister," she said, sitting next to him as he slid over. "I thought that wind was going to send that door flying off . . . and me with it."

"Don't mention it. Doesn't do well for the town's reputation if we let our tourists go flyin' halfway 'cross the state. Though sometimes folks here in White Wolf say that's the only way Wyoming can get a decent tourist . . . snapping up the ones that've left us."

"What makes you think I'm a tourist?" Sawyer asked, both amused and annoyed that he would make the assumption. His first assumption about her gender hadn't been very close to the mark.

"Y'all don't sound like you're from around here," he said, deliberately imitating her soft drawl.

"No, sir, I'm not," she confirmed, turning the tables on him by deepening her voice and injecting just a hint of a nasal twang into her own response. This was a real cowboy—from the top of his wide-brimmed, black felt hat to the tips of his boots. She wasn't so much surprised to find a real black cowboy. Sawyer knew they existed, had researched their history in preparing for her novels. The fact that she'd actually found one here in Montana did surprise her. What was he doing here? He stood out here, just as much as she did.

Despite the crowded room, the rest of the café's patrons had all given him his space. He had a presence that commanded. It wasn't only his physical presence. He wasn't very tall, not even six feet, maybe five feet eleven. But he was powerfully built, with wide shoulders. When he'd come up behind her to close that door, he'd practically eclipsed her. His arm had reached out quickly. Large hands had pulled the door closed with hardly any effort at all.

At the same instance, somehow Sawyer sensed that he belonged here. He was somewhat rough around the edges. When he'd thought she was a boy and had spoken to her of the dangers of the weather, her initial reaction was to be insulted. She didn't need some jerkwater-town cowboy telling her how to handle her ride. She knew when to come in out of the rain.

Sawyer didn't like the condescending way he'd spoken to her, either. But the longer she sat next to him, the more she was starting to realize that he hadn't spoken to her like a parent speaks to an errant child. There was a backhanded kind of compliment in the way he showed approval of her decision to get in out of the weather.

"Maybe I'm not just passing through," she said, trying to get him to admit that he was wrong about her. "Maybe I'm coming back to stay with family."

"You don't have any family around here," he said, with as much confidence as if he'd mapped out her family tree and traced her lineage back for generations.

"Then where would you say I'm from?"

"If I had to guess, I'd say somewhere farther south. Mississippi, maybe?"

"No." She shook her head, glad that his track record with her was still iffy.

"Georgia," he guessed again.

"Getting warmer."

"Alabama." He nailed it.

"Very good." Sawyer clapped her hands. "I'm impressed."

"Don't be. I was about runnin' out of Southern-sounding states to throw at you."

"You're not a tourist," she guessed.

"No, ma'am. Born and raised right here in White Wolf."

"Let me guess, you plan to die here, too?" She'd come up against that mentality before. Short of the land being uninhabitable or a developer buyout, she'd come across families in her travels who'd lived on their properties for generations and couldn't be budged.

He paused, giving her an odd look. "Kinda morbid to think about my own death . . . but yeah, when my time comes, I think I will. Not a bad place to have as your final resting place. But, knock on wood, that won't be for some time yet. I've got too much kick in me to be thinkin' about lyin' down."

When he rapped his knuckles on the back of the wooden bench where they sat, and used the movement as an opportunity to stretch his left arm along the back of the bench, his arm brushed against her shoulders as she sat next to him.

Sawyer used the excuse of leaning forward to set her helmet on the floor beneath the bench to move away. When she raised herself again, she made sure that she'd scooted her bottom close enough to the edge of the bench to keep from leaning against his arm. She didn't mind him being friendly, but not that friendly. She didn't know him well enough. If that Barbara Jean girl came back to seat her, she wouldn't have to get to know him at all.

"Got my plot all picked out right down to the shape of the headstone and the message I want engraved on it," he continued.

"And you call me morbid?" she said, pointing to herself.

"Don't you wanna know what it'll read?" he asked.

"Not really," Sawyer said flatly.

He leaned closer and whispered, "Sure you do."

Sawyer mentally bit her tongue to keep her response to herself. What was it about these small-town, small-minded types?

"All right," she said in a tone that clearly said she was humoring him. "Tell me. What do you want carved on your headstone?"

He held his right hand out in front of him, as if encouraging her to see his vision.

"I want it to read 'Here Lies Jon-Tyler Holling.' "

Sawyer waited expectantly for something more, if not something profound, something homey-sounding. When nothing else was forthcoming, she nodded her head slowly and said, "That's . . . uh . . . pretty deep."

"Six feet deep," he said, his expression solemn. But something in his eyes told Sawyer that he was teasing her. His dark eyes crinkled at the corners. "So, what would you have carved on your headstone?"

Sawyer blinked in surprise. The question caught her off guard. The last conversation she'd had been about death was with her cousin Shiri five days ago. She'd convinced her that she hadn't been contemplating her own death. And now this stranger was asking her to consider it.

She lowered her head, trying to picture her spot, already laid out in the family plot. Neatly manicured lawn. Wreath of white roses and lilies. A simple, black onyx headstone. Sawyer turned to face him again.

"Trek," she said finally.

In her mind's eye, she was imagining the open road, how many miles were still laid out before her to go before she made it to Seattle. She was also thinking about her new role as a mother. She wasn't equipped, wasn't ready. How was she ever going to manage? It wasn't as if babies came with manuals. Not like motorcycles. If anything went wrong on her bike, she knew what to do. All she had to do was pop out the user's manual, turn to the page, grab the correct tool, and off she was again. If she couldn't fix the problem, she knew half a dozen motorcycle mechanics who could. Not so with babies.

"Trek?" he repeated. "You mean, like that science-fiction television show with the half dozen spin-offs?"

"No-ooo." She drew the word out. "More like a continuous lifelong journey. That's what I want others to remember about me."

"Trek," he said again.

"Yes."

"No name?" he encouraged. "You don't want your name written on your headstone?"

"My name?"

"Sure. So folks will know what to call you when they visit your grave site."

"Folks like who?" she asked, folding her arms across her chest. "Anyone likely to visit my grave site will already know who I am."

He laughed at her response, running his hand over his mouth and chin to wipe away the grin. He then leaned forward, resting his elbows on his knees, and clasped his hands. "You know, you're not making it easy for a person to get to know you, Trek," he said bluntly.

It took Sawyer a moment to realize that they weren't just making casual conversation. It was one of the strangest come-ons she'd experienced lately. Over the past four days, she'd been subjected to many come-ons. Cheap, cheesy, overly used one-liners. Most of them stale and uninspired, focusing more on her physical attractiveness. If she had ten dollars for every lecher who was more interested in focusing on the size of her breasts than what was in her heart, she could probably afford to send her child to the best schools in the country without having to dip into her trust fund.

But once this man said his piece, he turned the focus to her. He made it obvious that he wanted to know about her. He could see for himself what she looked like. That is, he didn't have to make any crude comments about her body to get her attention. He was asking her those questions to understand what was inside her head.

"Maybe in small, small letters I'd have my name engraved underneath—Sawyer Garth." She pinched her fingers together to show how small.

"Sawyer Garth," he repeated.

"Yes," she said. "That would be me."

"Come to think of it, there used to be some Garths around here," he said, now openly teasing her about being a tourist. "Lived just on the other side of White Wolf. Not anymore, though."

"Oh, really?" She went along with his joke. "Tell me, whatever happened to them?"

"The wind blew them all the way back to Alabama." He held his hand out to her. "Pleasure to meet you, Sawyer Garth."

Chapter 5

She had small hands, Holling noted, as he shook hands with the leather-wearing biker woman. Her hands were soft, with neatly trimmed, natural nails. No rings on her fingers, not even decorative ones. Not even a wedding ring. That was the first thing he looked for when she'd taken off her gloves. Small hands, but not fragile. Her handshake grip was firm and full of confidence.

Not like some women who let their hands hang in yours like limp noodles, Holling mused.

Holling hated that. Made him think that if he made the slightest move to shake, he'd squish their hands to a mushy pulp. He didn't get that sense with this woman. She was very strong. When she'd ridden that bike up on the sidewalk, fighting wind, rain, and negotiating the tight spaces between the parked cars, she'd handled the bike skillfully, with plenty of finesse and style. That biker woman knew what she was doing.

Sawyer, he mentally corrected. Her name was Sawyer Garth. Unusual name, but it suited her. Fit her as nicely as those skintight jeans she was wearing. He sucked in a deep breath. Lordy! Made him want to get off the wall, move closer to her to get a better look.

"Sawyer, party of one. Your table's ready, ma'am."

When Barbara Jean called her name, Sawyer scooped up her helmet, stood up, and said brightly again, "That would be me."

"Mr. Holling?" Barbara Jean then called out to him. "Your pie will be ready in just a while. Sorry to keep you waiting, sir."

"That's all right, Barbara Jean. I didn't mind the wait," he said, looking pointedly at Sawyer as he spoke.

Barbara Jean flashed him a knowing smile. "You're sweet to say so, Mr. Holling. But I know you must be itchin' to get on your way before this storm gets any worse."

"How much worse can it get?" Sawyer looked apprehensively back at the door.

Holling could almost read her mind. She was worried about her motorcycle and was probably wondering whether it would be prudent at this point to skip the meal and try to find somewhere to store the bike, somewhere less exposed. That's the way he would have felt if it had been his hog parked out there like that.

When he had been riding, he was known to take better care of that bike than he took care of himself. Polishing the chrome, tuning the motor, searching catalogs and salvage yards for parts to dress her up—almost every spare dollar he made went into making sure the bike was in top-notch condition. Every biker knew that if you took care of the bike, the bike would take care of you—keeping you rolling. Besides, at seventeen, he couldn't get enough of the attention he got when he roared through town. The custom paint job alone was enough to turn heads.

"Shouldn't the storm have passed over us by now? It was moving pretty fast," Sawyer said hopefully.

"We're under a tornado watch until nine o'clock tonight,"

Barbara Jean said, indicating one of the televisions mounted overhead near the far side of the lunch counter. Scrolling across the bottom of the screen were the counties under the watch.

"An hour ago, we were only supposed to be under the watch until about six. That's why it's still so packed in here, ma'am. Nobody wants to go out in this mess. And I don't blame 'em." She handed Sawyer a menu, then motioned for her to follow.

The man who'd finished his dinner and freed up the table for Sawyer brushed past them on his way to the exit. As soon as he'd opened the door, and Sawyer saw how bad the weather had gotten, she shook her head in dismay and started for the door as well.

Holling wasn't sure what made him do it. Before he could stop himself, he reached out and grabbed her arm, just above her elbow.

"Sawyer," he said, his voice full of caution. "Where do you think you're going?"

"I'm not leaving my bike out in that," she said, tugging her arm out of his grasp. She jerked her thumb in the direction of her bike. "That's my only ride home."

"You go back out there again and you'll be headed home tucked in the seat of a funnel cloud."

"Isn't there a covered parking lot around here . . . somewhere?"

"Nuh-uh," he said. "You won't find anything like that around here."

"Then how about a barn?" she snapped back. "There ought to be plenty of those."

"Enough to shake a stick at," he said, ignoring the sarcasm and the implication of her question. "But I can't let you go out there looking for one."

Sawyer opened her mouth to protest, then decided against that. Part of her wanted to argue for the sake of her pride.

Who was *he* to tell her what she could and couldn't do? He didn't know her well enough to have that kind of power over her. It only took a split second for her to realize that his restriction wasn't about power, but concern for her safety. Was it presumptive of him to automatically assume responsibility for her safety? Perhaps. Was she touched by the sentiment? Most definitely. She hadn't felt this fierce protectiveness since leaving her family back in Birmingham. The weight of that realization settled over her, deflated some of the fight from her.

Sawyer swore, then muttered, "I hope my insurance policy covers acts of God."

"I'm sure your motorcycle will be all right, ma'am," Barbara Jean tried to assure her. "If there's a tornado headed this way, we'll get the warning siren in plenty of time. The last tornado we had through here only took a few shingles off the rooftops, smashed a few windows, and knocked over a few light poles. Nothing we couldn't get cleaned up in a few days."

"You don't know what a comfort that is to me," Sawyer said, then immediately felt sorry for her tone when Barbara Jean offered, "If worse comes to worst, you could always pull your bike up in here. It won't make Mama too happy but it'll give the customers something to talk about for days."

"And the health inspector," Holling retorted.

Sawyer looked back at the door again, almost as if she was considering the idea, but Holling blocked her path. He had no intention of letting her out that door. Not any time soon. To make sure that she stayed put, he followed Sawyer all the way back to her booth. When she slid into the orange vinyl seats, he sat across from her, folding his arms resolutely on the wall-matching wood laminate tabletop.

"I'll give you a few minutes to decide what you want, ma'am," Barbara Jean said, pulling out cutlery wrapped in a white paper napkin and setting it on the table in front of Sawyer.

"You gonna get a bite to eat while you're here, Mr. Holling?" she asked him, setting another silverware set in front of him. "I don't see the takeout you ordered before."

"Fried chicken, mashed potatoes with home-style gravy on the side, green peas, a basket of biscuits, and an extra-large iced tea," he said, without even looking at the menu. Sawyer lowered her eyes to keep from staring. She didn't eat that much in a week. Ryan was a vegan. He wouldn't be caught dead eating meat or meat by-products if he could help it.

"Yes, sir. I'll be right back with your order."

As soon as Barbara Jean moved away, Sawyer put her own arms on the table and leaned forward. "You don't have to babysit me, Holling," she said irritably. "What do you think I'm going to do, slip out the back way?"

"What are you talking about?" he asked innocently. "You think I'm here to keep tabs on you?"

"The thought had occurred to me," she replied.

"No, ma'am," he said with conviction. "I've got better things to do with my time."

"There's that empty spot right on the wall by the door." She pointed near the entrance.

"Why would I pass up my opportunity to grab an empty seat? Look around here. The place is packed. Don't think my being here has anything to do with you. I'm just killin' time while I'm waiting for my pie."

He took off his black Stetson, placed it on the tabletop, and rubbed his hand over his head. Leaning back, he made it clear that he planned to be there for a while—especially since, Sawyer recalled, he hadn't ordered his food to go.

Now that he'd taken off his hat, she pretended to study the menu while taking in the details of Holling's face. She in-spected him with clinical detachment, a writer's way of noting details without making a judgment of what she'd found. She'd gotten into that habit, people studying, to help her round out the details of characters within her novels.

It wasn't a handsome face. Not by most conventional standards. She wouldn't have picked this array of features for any of her novel heroes. Then again, one reviewer had once said that her characters were all *too* beautiful, and wondered how anyone in her stories ever accomplished any of the fantastic feats she had them perform without marring or scarring.

Holling's face was more compelling than handsome, making her want to look a little longer to take in all of its intricacies. Lean. Hard. A dark face etched with deep lines. High cheekbones that were kissed by the sun. His bronze skin was taut, making it difficult for her to judge his true age. Somewhere between twenty and thirty. She wondered whether he had a little Native American in his ancestry. It wouldn't be uncommon for this part of the country. His eyes were almond shaped with the color of deep chocolate. Like M&Ms. She made the comparison, then wondered if the sudden thought of the sweet treat had anything to do with the pangs of hunger worrying her stomach. His nose was broad, flared, and looked to Sawyer as if it might have been broken. There was a scar just above the bridge of his nose. She wondered how he'd gotten it. A fight maybe? Somebody pounded it in retaliation of him sticking his nose in their business one too many times? That thought almost made her laugh out loud, until she realized that she was losing her emotional detachment.

Back to business, Sawyer, she admonished herself, continuing her examination to assess his mouth. Full lips were slow to smile. When he did, it took years from his face, giving him an almost mischievous look, like a little boy with a secret. A small chip on the bottom of his front tooth added to that naughty charm.

She didn't realize how long she'd been staring until she

raised her eyes and found him staring back with just as much curiosity. Curiosity and something else. Confidence. He knew that she was looking and it didn't bother him. Whatever flaws she'd found in her examination, real or imagined, he didn't seem to care. He was comfortable with himself and who he was. Sawyer sensed that instantly about him. It showed in the easy way he carried himself.

So different from Ryan; she couldn't help making the comparison. Ryan just didn't walk into a room, he strutted. All eyes had to be on him. He made sure of it. It didn't seem to be that way with this Holling. If anyone was staring at him, it wasn't anything that he did. It was because of who he was.

"Your pie?" she said, drawing them back to their conversation.

"Yes, ma'am. Pecan pie. Freshly made with Marjean's secret family recipe. So good, it'll make your stomach leap into your mouth to get a better taste. *Umh-umh-umh*."

The way he said it, leaning across the table closer to her as if to share a secret, even touching the tip of his tongue to the corner of his mouth, all seemed perfectly innocent to Sawyer. Just casual conversation. The effect it had on her was anything but casual. Sawyer's active mind flashed with a visual. She saw herself kissing Holling, tasting for herself the sticky sweetness of Marjean's pie. She imagined herself running her tongue over his firm, full lips, delving inside to explore hidden corners of sweetness. She could almost feel the warm roughness of his tongue swirling and sliding against hers, dipping in and out slowly, deliciously.

Sawyer bit down on her lip, muting the involuntary whimper of a sudden pang of desire. Her grandma Lela would call it lust. Pure, unadulterated lust. "That must be one helluva pie to make you want to risk being caught in a tornado, Mr. Holling."

She raised the menu, holding it up in front of her face to completely block him from her view. He didn't see her form her lip into an exaggerated O and exhale. No. Jon-Tyler Holling wasn't handsome. He was breathtaking.

"It *is* good," he said. "She doesn't skimp on the pecans. You know how you get some pies, there's more Karo syrup filling than nuts? Not Marjean's."

She lowered the menu and said with nostalgia, "My grandmother makes her pies like that. Deep-dish pies a body can really dig into. You stick your fork into one of hers and it covers the fork prongs from tip to top."

"So you know what I'm talking about."

"Yeah . . . but I don't know if I'd step into a gale-force wind to get one."

"You're safe here, Sawyer," Holling said, covering her hand briefly with his.

Maybe he'd meant it to be a gesture of reassurance. Sawyer wondered what it was about her that brought out the protector in him. Did she look fragile? Did she look like she needed his help? She'd gotten this far without him. As soon as the storm passed over, she'd keep on going.

Her expression clearly told him what he could do with his assurances. She didn't want his protection. She wanted her motorcycle. Holling quickly withdrew his hand.

"Marjean's is pretty solidly built. If I had to be anywhere, I guess here's as good a place as any."

Sawyer turned to peer out of the window. Barbara Jean had given her a booth in a row that ran along the outer edge of the café wall. Gusting winds drove the rain against the smoked glass so hard, water sloshed and slid down the pane in steady sheets. The *plink-plink-kerplink* of hail bouncing off the window made Sawyer nervous. A tree branch ripped from one of the decorative trees lining the sidewalk and slammed against the window, scraping along the side at least a foot before being caught up and swirling away. Sawyer gasped and shifted subconsciously away from the window, almost to the edge of the booth.

"Where are you headed?" Holling asked her.

"What?" she asked distractedly, not really listening to him, but staring out the window to see if she could find a break in the clouds. None. Even through the tinted gray glass, the sky was thick with blackish green swirling crowds.

"I said, where are you headed, Sawyer? You're on your . . . What did you call it . . . your trek?"

She shrugged in answer. As kind as he'd been to her so far, he was still a stranger. And she was a woman traveling alone. In any circumstances, whether she liked him or not, she shouldn't be revealing her traveling plans to him. A woman these days couldn't be too careful.

"Just touring the country," she said.

"Oh, I see," Holling replied, smiling at her. What a strange woman she was. He knew her grandma cooked killer pecan pies, but she wouldn't tell him her next stop on the road.

"I'm supposed to meet up with some friends," she continued.

"Are you on vacation?"

It was mid-May. He wondered what Sawyer did for a living that allowed her to take off for days at a time. He couldn't imagine her working at an office—all stiff and proper, wearing the corporate uniform. She seemed too unconventional for that. Unless she was her own boss. Now, that he could imagine. Whatever Sawyer did, she would have to call the shots. A woman who could ride a motorcycle was a woman who wanted to be in control. It was probably driving her crazy now, having to sit here, forced to stay put because of the whims of the weather.

"I'm taking a sabbatical," Sawyer replied.

Sabbatical? Yeah, right. That was just a fancy word for running away. She had to be running away from something . . . or someone. She had a cell phone clipped to the belt of her jeans. Yet, she hadn't used it. She'd been stuck here for at least an hour and she hadn't checked in with anyone. No one had called her, either. Not her grandma. Not her man.

If it wasn't people trouble that she was having, what was going on in her life that made her want to take off? Holling didn't get the sense that it was legal trouble hounding her. The last man to leave the café was a Montana state patrol officer, still dressed in his uniform. He'd nodded to her on the way out and Sawyer hadn't reacted. In fact, she'd barely given him a second glance when he walked by. A woman in trouble with the law wouldn't have stood so boldly out in the open.

Maybe it was because she was more concerned about the welfare of her bike than she was being recognized and being picked up. Somehow that didn't ring true to Holling. She wasn't nervous when he walked by her, because she had no reason to be. She wasn't on the run from the law. So, what was the reason behind the sabbatical? He opened his mouth to ask the next question, but she interrupted him smoothly.

"What about you, Holling? What do you do?"

She propped her elbow on the table and placed her chin on her fist, staring at him with open curiosity.

"Green," he said in response, just as easily switching the topic to the one he was more interested in.

She shook her head, uncomprehending.

"Your eyes," he clarified. "Is that your natural color or are you wearing contacts?"

"They're my natural color," she admitted.

"And your hair?"

"What about my hair?" she said, self-consciously running her fingers through the shag cut.

"I like it," he announced. "It's . . . sassy. It's your natural color, too?"

"You have a thing for nature?" she said, goading.

"I have a thing for uncomplicated," he corrected. Then he

leaned back, spread his arms open. "What do you think I do?"

"You mean besides throw your weight around, giving everybody orders?"

"Bingo!" He slammed his palm down on the tabletop, making Sawyer jump and the silverware rattle. "Give the little lady a prize. I am what you think I am," he said. "That is, what you see is what you get from the folks here in White Wolf. Those of us who don't work in the service industry, for the state, or the beef-processing plant are in the cattle business."

"Where do you fall?"

"Got my feet in a couple of camps. I maintain some property for the state of Montana, keeping it as a land preserve. About four hundred acres or so. Nature trails wind all through it. Our home is a stop where some of the trails converge. Me and my father manage a bed-and-breakfast, catering to tourists just like you, Sawyer."

"Oh, so you took one look at me and thought 'profit,'" she accused him.

"No, ma'am. Didn't have money on my mind at all when I looked at you. We also have a family side business supplying a good, prime grade of beef to the healthy, carnivorous appetites of the good people east of the Mississippi. Chances are if you've had a hamburger or a thick, juicy sirloin, you were probably eating one of mine."

"Sounds like a lot of bull to me," Sawyer retorted.

He winked at her and said, "That doesn't offend you, does it, darlin'? You're not a vegetarian, are you?"

"No, I'm not a vegetarian. But I'm trying to eat healthier these days."

"You don't have to give up beef to do that. You'd be surprised. With today's technology, we're developing heartier strains, more disease-resistant, leaner cuts of meat. Eat all you want."

"Uh-huh," she said, crossing her arms across her chest. "If it's all so wonderfully good for you, why'd you order fried chicken?"

" 'Cause variety's the spice of life," he retorted. "And too much of a good thing isn't always good for you."

Sawyer looked over Holling's shoulder and nodded as Barbara Jean came bearing a tray with his order. As the girl set the food in front of him, Sawyer felt a tightening in her stomach—an odd combination of hunger and nausea. The sight of the food, the thick, golden brown crust of the fried chicken, the mounds of real potatoes, flecks of the brown peelings whipped in, and plump green peas made her bite her lip to keep from drooling over the table. At the same time, the smell of the food made her stomach churn. It was as if it was the baby's way of expressing her displeasure at the heavy meal.

"Did you decide what you want?" Barbara Jean asked.

"Something that isn't swimming in grease and gravy." Sawyer moaned. She stood up, swayed, and then grasped the edge of the table to steady herself. "Your restroom?"

Barbara Jean pointed as Sawyer clamped her hand over her mouth and bolted in that direction.

Chapter 6

Sawyer didn't know what it was exactly that sent her racing to the bathroom. It couldn't have been just the sight and smell of the food. She was in a restaurant, for heaven's sake. As soon as she'd pulled off her helmet, her nose was assaulted by a variety of foods—most of them fried.

It wasn't just the fatigue making her ill, either. She'd been tired before and hadn't been affected like this. However, she had pushed herself well past her limit today. She'd done it racing against time and Mother Nature, trying to beat the weather before it got really bad.

She wasn't sure if she could blame her sudden attack of nausea entirely on the baby. She wasn't far enough along to start suffering from morning sickness, was she?

Whatever it was that hit her, it hit her hard. Brought her to the knees right before the porcelain commode. She was barely able to grasp a paper toilet set protector and slap it against the seat before her stomach wrenched. Anything and everything that had been in her stomach since yesterday found its way into the commode. And when there was nothing left, her guts continued to spasm, dry-heaving until she was physically exhausted and her head began to throb.

"Hello . . . hello in there. Are you all right, ma'am?" A light tap on her stall and she heard a voice of concern. Sawyer lifted her head off of the commode seat and turned it enough to see a pair of comfortable walking shoes and brightly colored neon socks from underneath the stall door. It was Barbara Jean.

Sawyer sucked in air, trying to regain her composure.

"I'm . . . uh . . . all right," she said, trying to sound normal. Hardly convincing with the way she was sitting on the floor and the sound of her retching barely finished bouncing and echoing off the walls.

She yanked on the roll of tissue and dabbed her mouth. Sluggishly, she pulled herself to her feet and opened the stall door. Just outside, Barbara Jean stood, nervously chewing on her fingernail.

"Are you all right, ma'am? Can I get you anything?"

"Some water?" Sawyer suggested shakily. "And maybe some crackers. Saltines, if you have them." She remembered her cousin Brenda going through a box of them in one sitting.

"Yes, ma'am." Barbara Jean backed away, looking unsure. "I'll get it for you and bring it to you in here."

"Just put it out on the table," Sawyer said. "I'll be out in a minute."

"Maybe you should stay here for a while," Barbara Jean suggested.

"I'll be all right," Sawyer insisted. She could almost read the girl's mind when she noted the doubtful look on Barbara's Jean's face. Sawyer figured that she was as worried about her as she was about her customers. What would they think seeing someone suddenly violently ill right after being served?

"Don't worry, Barbara Jean. I'm not contagious," Sawyer said dryly.

"Oh!" The girl breathed a noticeable sigh of relief. "The way you went runnin' out of there, I thought maybe it was something you ate that made you sick . . . but then, I haven't brought you anything to eat. *Duh!*" Barbara Jean slapped her forehead with the palm of her hand.

"I've got just a little morn . . . uh . . . that is, motion sickness. I've been on the road for a while and I haven't stopped to eat. As soon as I get something to settle my stomach, I'll be just fine."

"You had me worried for a minute when I heard you pukin' your guts out. Mr. Holling's worried, too. He's standing right outside, you know."

"He's waiting outside the bathroom door?" Sawyer asked incredulously.

"Yes, ma'am, he sure is. He's the one who sent me in after you. I think he woulda come in himself, but I told him that some of our lady customers might not appreciate him poking around in the women's restroom. Bad for business when we've got men staking out the women's bathroom."

"You tell him I said that he doesn't have to babysit me. I'm not going to sneak out the back way."

"Huh?"

"Never mind. It's a joke between me and Mr. Holling. If you could just set some crackers out on the table for me, I'll just freshen up a bit and then I'll be right out, okay?"

"Take your time, ma'am," Barbara Jean insisted. "All the time you need."

Sawyer steadied herself, then moved over to the bathroom sink. She started to run water in the basin. Cupping water in her hands, Sawyer closed her eyes and splashed it against her face several times.

Blindly, she reached for the paper towel holder.

"Here you go, honey." A woman's voice, high-pitched and elderly.

Sawyer cracked her eyes open, trying to squint through

the water streaming down her face. A woman with fluffy white, tightly curled hair, in a cream-colored pantsuit, placed a towel in Sawyer's hand and then stepped back and stood next to her, smiling sympathetically.

"Here, let me help you with that." The elderly woman pulled down several more paper towels and reached to dab at Sawyer's face.

Surprised, Sawyer leaned her head back and tried to avoid the woman's assistance. She hadn't heard her come in. Maybe she'd been in one of the stalls and had heard her being ill. Having Barbara Jean hovering over her was bad enough. She didn't want to get a perfect stranger involved. She turned back to the mirror, using the paper towels to swab the water she'd splashed onto the counter.

"Thanks. I can handle it from here." Sawyer looked up into the mirror, meeting the woman's gaze, and gave her a wan smile. It was meant to be gracious but dismissive. Maybe it was too subtle for the woman. She didn't budge.

"Let me help you, honey. You look peaked, if you don't mind me saying. And if I sound like a fussy old lady, you'll have to forgive me. The older I get, the faster I'm likely to speak my mind."

She placed one hand on Sawyer's shoulder as she started to dab around her forehead again.

"When your days are numbered," she said gently, "you don't want to waste time being mealymouthed. If you have something to say, go on and spit it out . . . that's what I always say. But I say to myself, Luce, mind your own business. But I just can't do that. If something needs saying, then I'm the one to say it. If something needs doing, I'm the one to do it. It's just who I am."

Sawyer's smile became less forced, more grateful. This woman's attitude reminded her of her grandma Lela. She wasn't one to mince words either.

"A woman in your condition shouldn't be skipping meals, you know."

"Excuse me? What did you say?" Sawyer blinked in surprise.

"You are expecting, aren't you?" Luce insisted.

Sawyer wasn't sure how to respond to that. She was grateful for the woman's assistance. Yet, did that give her the right to ask such a personal, invasive question?

Shiri had always joked that you don't ever ask a woman if she's pregnant. Not until you actually witness the child dropping out before your very eyes. That's the only way you can be sure that you haven't offended someone who might not be pregnant. She'd said it to be funny. But this woman's invasiveness didn't amuse Sawyer. Not at all.

"I've had four children, three girls and a boy. They've given me nine lovely grandchildren and one great-grandchild on the way," Luce went on say. "Whoever made up the term morning sickness obviously wasn't pregnant. Whatever it is you want to call it, I recognize it when I see it. You've got lovely glowing skin, honey. That is, up until the time you started throwing up, and now you're just as pale as I am." She laughed softly at herself as she leaned close to Sawyer—so close that they were almost cheek to cheek as they regarded one another in the mirror. Her light blue eyes met with Sawyer's green ones in the mirror.

"The sight and smell of food finally did you in, didn't it? How far along are you, honey?"

"Not too far along. About four weeks," Sawyer confessed. As surprised and annoyed as she was at the woman, she was also strangely comforted by her. She'd put her at ease, made her confess things to her that she wouldn't do under normal circumstances. Then again, nothing about this road trip so far was turning out to be normal. Luce continued to dab her forehead as she tended to Sawyer.

"I thought so. You're not even showing yet. You've still got your petite figure. No wonder Holling's taken with you. He isn't the father, is he?"

"What!" Sawyer exclaimed. Enough was enough! It was none of her business. "No, of course not. We've only just met today."

"Where is the baby's father? He's not traveling with you?"

"No," Sawyer said sharply. "And probably won't ever be." She took the paper towel out of the woman's hand and tossed it into the trash with open vindictiveness. The gesture was symbolic. She was simplifying her life, getting rid of emotional baggage, cleansing her soul of the trash that had weighed her down.

"Shame. A woman doesn't need to be alone at a time like this. You need someone to take care of you."

"Look . . . Luce, is it?"

The woman nodded, acknowledging her name.

"I can take care of myself," Sawyer said testily.

"Yes, honey, I'm sure you can. But a woman shouldn't have to. Trust me. I know what I'm talking about."

"Because you've had four kids of your own? And I suppose that makes you an expert." Sawyer didn't mean to sound unkind. The words were pulled out of her mouth of their own volition.

"Oh, I'm sorry. I'm afraid I have offended you, haven't I? I didn't mean to be rude," Luce soothed.

"You didn't offend me." Sawyer crossed her fingers against the stretch of the truth. She made an excuse. "I'm just tired and hungry."

"Well, I'll say just this one thing more and then I'll mind my own business and let you get back to your table. You've got to keep your strength up. That means plenty of rest. And don't you go skipping any meals again, either."

Sawyer smiled. She half expected the woman to wag her finger at her. Her grandma Lela would have. What was it about that maternal finger wagging that could put a grown woman to shame?

"I won't, Luce. I had no intention of doing that again now that I know what can happen."

"And as for you taking care of yourself . . ." She touched Sawyer lightly on the cheek with a warm, smooth hand. "If you have someone who wants the job, let them have it."

"I'll keep that in mind," Sawyer replied. "If you'll excuse me, I guess I shouldn't keep my water and crackers waiting. Thanks again for . . . uh . . . well, taking care of me."

"It was my pleasure, honey." She backed away from Sawyer, then headed for the exit.

After she'd gone, Sawyer breathed a sigh of relief. She tugged her clothing back into order and walked slowly to the bathroom door. She wanted to be sure that her stomach was settled, and that there would be no more mad dashes back to the stall before she went out into public again.

As soon as she pulled on the handle and opened the door just a crack, she saw Holling leaning patiently against the far wall. His hands were tucked into his front jean pockets, one foot propped up against the wall. The door widened and his head shot up.

"Sawyer! Are you all right?"

Sawyer tried to make light of her predicament. "You didn't have to stake out the ladies' bathroom, Holling. I told you that I wasn't going to sneak out the back."

He winked at her. "Call it an ego thing. No man likes to think that being in a woman's company turns her stomach."

"I'm fine," she insisted. "I told Barbara Jean that I'd just been on the road too long. Too tired. Too hungry. It just all caught up with me."

"I was worried about you. You were in there a long time."

"Don't worry. Between Barbara Jean and Luce, I was very well taken care of."

"C'mon," he said, taking her arm and guiding her back to

their booth. This time, Sawyer didn't pull away. Luce's advice echoed in her mind.

If you have someone who wants the job, let them.

Barbara Jean was on her job, too. There was an entire box of saltine crackers waiting on the table for her by the time she got back. A pitcher filled with water and ice cubes dripped with condensation onto the tabletop. Gone, Sawyer noticed, was Holling's huge plate of food. In its place were three plastic to-go boxes. He didn't say a word about them as he sat down across from her. And she didn't ask.

Sawyer unwrapped one of the cracker packages and munched in relative silence. One cracker, then another. Her impulse was to wolf them down, she was so hungry. But she forced herself to eat slowly, to give her stomach time to settle. When she reached for the water pitcher and tried to pick up the nearly full container, her hand trembled just a bit so that the ice rattled and water sloshed onto the table.

Without asking, Holling clasped his large hand over hers, wrapping his fingers around the pitcher grip, and helped her to pour her drink into the glass. When he set the pitcher down again, Sawyer couldn't help but notice that he wasn't in a hurry to pull his hand back.

"Thanks," Sawyer murmured, withdrawing her hand. She raised her glass to her lips, taking a small sip. Again, she resisted the urge to gulp. The crackers had made her thirsty. Most of all, keeping her eyes lowered to her glass gave her an excuse not to meet Holling's gaze. His stare was too direct, too openly interested in her. She didn't want to make the investment of getting to know him. Something told her that she already knew more than she should know about him. She knew enough so that he wasn't just another face in the crowd. She knew enough about him to keep him in her thoughts long after she'd climbed onto her bike and ridden away. Jon-Tyler Holling would not be so easy to dismiss.

"Is that all you're planning to have?" he asked, as if he was counting the number of crackers she'd eaten.

She shook her head. "But it's what I hear you're supposed to eat whenever you have an upset stomach."

"When I was little, my pops used to give me warm soda. Coke or Pepsi or Dr Pepper. Anything with lots of sugar and caffeine. To this day, I can't think about a soft drink without thinking that I need to be lyin' in bed somewhere takin' it easy."

Sawyer gave a dry chuckle. "With as much as you eat, Mr. Holling, I don't believe you were ever little." She pushed the crackers aside and folded her hands on top of the table.

"Speakin' of my pops," Holling murmured. He looked down at his belt clip, peering at the flashing display of his phone. He checked the caller ID. Sawyer heard the barely audible strains of his cell phone ringing. Something sweet. Classical. Beethoven's "Für Elise," if she wasn't mistaken. Yet another dimension to him she had not expected. This part of the country, all she expected to hear was country music.

He shut the phone off without answering it. "Feel like you can handle something more substantial now?" he asked. "Some real stick-to-your-ribs cookin'?"

She nodded her head. "I think so. "

Holling raised his hand and called Barbara Jean over.

However, the girl never got the chance to respond to his request. She never got the chance to impress Sawyer with their fine café cuisine. Sawyer wasn't sure if she'd even heard him. There was no way the young girl could have. She stopped, dropped everything in her hand at the earsplitting wail of the tornado Klaxon blaring from one of the utility-pole-mounted speakers.

Chapter 7

"Time to go!" Holling said tightly, reaching across the table to take Sawyer's hand. But he was in a hurry and wound up clamping down on her wrist instead. He was thankful that she didn't resist or question him. The fact that she simply slid across the vinyl seat to trail behind him was a testimony to his ability to foster her trust.

She didn't strike him as the kind of person that trusted easily. It was a feeling he had about her the first time he ever laid eyes on her—once, he admitted to himself with embarrassment, he figured out that Sawyer was a woman. When she'd first come through that door, her body language, the way she stood, the stiffness of her spine warned anyone away from her.

When he'd touched her, tried to stop her from going back outside to take care of her bike, she'd jerked away from him. Not that he blamed her. She didn't know him from Adam. She couldn't know his true intentions and didn't want to risk second-guessing them. If she'd been carrying a weapon, she could easily have pulled it on him, claimed that she was only trying to protect herself, and fully expected not to be arrested for doing so.

Though she hadn't completely lost some of her edginess or let down her mental guard against letting him get too close, she didn't question him when he abruptly left the table. Maybe she didn't need to. She knew what that warning siren meant. She didn't need him to tell her that. Still, when she could have gone her own way, trusting in her own instincts to protect herself, she'd followed him without a word.

Maybe it was the urgency in his expression, the curtness of his tone that made up her mind. This was no time for questions or even talking more than necessary. It was time to move. Move now! Holling knew by experience that after the warning Klaxon sounded, the time before the funnel cloud was on top of him could be a matter of minutes. Mere minutes. Sometimes less than that.

He cleared the booth and nearly collided with another couple seated in the booth next to them.

"Watch it!" the man muttered, trying to shield his wife from the surge of customers all running for cover.

Not running fast enough, Holling thought with impatience. Not if they intended to outrun the brutal force of a Montana storm. The man was herding his wife from behind, his hands planted on her shoulders as he shoved her ahead of him. She lost her footing, her high-heeled shoe slipping on food that had spilled onto the floor in the confusion. Down she went, giving a cry of dismay, as her husband knelt down to help her.

Holling stopped short and managed to maintain his own footing as Sawyer plowed into him from behind. He was distracted for a moment as he felt the softness of her breasts press into his back. The smell of her perfume, light and floral, managed to cut through the aroma of fried food and the muskier smell of human bodies suddenly jammed into a narrow corridor. As Sawyer's upper thigh made contact with the back of his leg, Holling felt a jolt as real and as stunning as if he'd been standing barefoot in a pool of water with a small electric appliance running in his hands. For the briefest of moments, he wondered what she would feel like without the layers of leather and denim separating them.

"Sorry," Sawyer murmured, trying to back off. There wasn't much room for them to maneuver.

"Time to get those brake lights looked at," he joked as he darted around the fallen couple. "Is she all right?" Holling asked the man ahead of him.

The man nodded, putting his arm around his wife's waist to help her up.

"That's it, everybody, just keep calm. Keep it moving. This way!"

Marjean, the owner of the café, stood on top of the lunch counter, shouting and pointing to direct the flow of her customers to her storm shelter.

"Where are we going?" Sawyer finally asked Holling.

"Marjean's got a storage room beneath the café. We should be all right in there until this blows over. Trust me. I've spent a time or two down there waiting for the skies to clear. She's got air-conditioning, a color television, and enough snacks to put the spread at a Super Bowl party to shame."

"Storage room? Is that where we're all being herded to? All of us aren't going to be able to fit in a storage room," Sawyer objected. "There must be twenty or thirty customers in here."

"It'll be cramped, but it'll be all right. You might even call it cozy."

Sawyer tugged against him. "I am *not* going down there," she said emphatically.

Holling turned to stare at her. "What did you say?"

"You heard me. I said I'm not going into any storage room."

This time, she did pull away from him. If he'd had any trouble reading her lips, the expression on her face said more than enough. She wasn't going.

Holling took a deep breath, blew it out through his nose. Maybe that cozy crack did get her hackles up. If he was out of line he would apologize later. But if she was resisting him to prove a feminist point, now was not the time. Precious seconds were ticking by. It could mean their lives if they delayed much longer.

"What's the matter with you, Sawyer? This is serious business. You don't mess around in weather like this."

"I know how serious this is!" she snapped. "If I'd listened to my instinct before now, I wouldn't be in this mess." She folded her arms across her chest, shaking her head in regret. "I never should have stopped here in White Wolf. Something told me that I should have just kept on riding clear on to the next state."

"You can sit and reflect on your travel plans *after* we've gotten to shelter, woman." He pointed at the door and the darkened entry where at least a third of Marjean's customers had started to descend.

Holling mentally calculated the number of people trying to get in with the space available. The last time he'd been down there, he'd taken refuge on a padded folding chair, tucked between two shelves lined with canned goods and soft drinks. There he'd watched the opening day of a baseball game in relative comfort.

"Are you gonna get yourself down those stairs or am I gonna have to carry you?" he threatened, taking a step toward her.

"Don't even think about it!" she warned, stabbing her index finger at him. "Who do you think you are! You don't know me well enough to—"

"I'm the man who's tryin' to keep your behind from being splattered clear into the next state," he retorted. Holling reached for her again, but Sawyer wasn't having any of that. She backed away from him, and would probably have back-pedaled all the way outside if she hadn't run into a wall. She glared at him, practically daring him to try to move her. Holling stepped up to her, answering the challenge.

Marjean cupped her hands and shouted to be heard over the tornado warning Klaxon and the rising wind. "Hey, you two! You two can make goo-goo eyes at each other later. I'm shutting that storage door in thirty seconds, that's with or without you!"

"Do you hear that?" Holling said, his head swiveling in Marjean's direction, then back to Sawyer again.

"Holling, don't make me go down there!" Sawyer pleaded. "I can't. I won't!"

"Now you're just being stubborn," he said. "And stupid. If you're thinkin' I'm gonna try somethin' down there, you can get that out of your head. If it'll make you feel any better about being down there with me . . . with the rest of us . . . I'll sit on my hands until this whole thing blows over."

She closed her eyes, lowered her head so that he had to stoop to hear her. "You don't understand. It's not you, it's me. I'm afraid of tight spaces. Terrified of them."

"You're—" He didn't complete the sentence.

"Claustrophobic," she finished for him. "Once, when I was a little girl, I was playing hide-and-seek with my cousins. I hid in an old fridge in the garage that my dad was supposed to haul off to the junkyard. I was only six. The door closed and . . . and I couldn't get out. I screamed and yelled and kicked and clawed. But nobody could hear me. I don't know how long I was in there. Seemed like hours. . . ."

Sawyer's chest started to heave, almost as if she couldn't breathe just thinking about it. "I couldn't breathe . . . so hot . . . and dark . . . I know I almost died. If it hadn't been for my cousins finding me . . . Anyway, I can't stand closed-in spaces. If I have to go into that storage room, if you make me go, I'll be a screaming, raving maniac before Marjean closes that door. You think Marjean would want me to panic her customers that way?"

"Sawyer, you don't have a choice," he said, grasping her shoulders. "It's not safe up here. If this town gets hit with a twister, every flying piece of debris, anything not nailed down, maybe even your bike, is gonna come flyin' through that window. Have you ever seen that movie *Biker Boyz?* Remember that scene when the bike goes crashin' through the window? It'll be that and ten times worse up here if you stay."

Marjean eased her bulk from the lunch counter.

"You two coming or not?" she demanded.

"Yes!" Holling said sharply, pulling Sawyer toward the door.

"No!" Sawyer countered. Bringing her arms up, she threw them apart and broke his grip on her shoulders.

"Well, I'm going down. When you two figure it out, you bang on the door real loud. If I hear ya, I might let you in."

Holling swore, a sizzling curse that made Sawyer's cheeks burn. Not that she hadn't heard the word before, or even used it herself when she was particularly frustrated. The fact that she'd driven him to do it made her feel awful. Just awful. But not as awful as she'd feel if he'd closed her up in that storage room.

"Go on, Marjean," Holling told Marjean, dismissing her. "Get yourself inside."

"You sure, Holling?" She raised her penciled-in eyebrows.

"Yeah. Go on. We'll be all right."

"You're stone crazy!" she snorted. "Just knock the silly thing over the head, sling her over your shoulder, and be done with it. She probably doesn't weigh more than a hundred pounds soaking wet."

"Don't you even try it," Sawyer said, backing away from him. "You go on, if you have to. I'm staying right here."

"I'm not leaving you up here by yourself, Sawyer. What kinda man you think I am?"

"Seeing that I just met you an hour or so ago, I really can't say what kind of a man you are," Sawyer shot back.

If Holling felt the sting of her words, he didn't show it.

"Well, darlin', you're about to find out just what kinda man I am," he said as he watched Marjean waddle past them, down the hall to the back of the café. When the heavy, reinforced steel storage room door closed behind her with a thud, effectively leaving them on their own, Holling turned back to Sawyer. His expression was resigned.

"Now what?" she asked him.

"Now we duck and cover," he said simply. Glancing around, he didn't see much in the café that could provide adequate cover for them. The tables would be tossed around like matchsticks. The booths were bolted to the floor, but they were too close to the windows. He considered the kitchen, but didn't want to be trapped inside if the natural gas line that Marjean used for grill cooking ruptured.

"What about over there?" Sawyer suggested, noting the long, L-shaped lunch counter.

He nodded, then directed her to the corner where the two halves of the counter joined.

"Down," he said tersely.

Sawyer sat down with her back against the counter's wall. She drew up her knees, hugging her legs close to her chest.

Holling took a few minutes to clear away the counters directly facing their hiding place. He swept aside empty coffee mugs, stacks of plates and saucers. Shoving aside bell-shaped dessert displays and wire racks containing a variety of bagged chips and cookies, Holling didn't have much hope that these normal, everyday items wouldn't become projectiles if the wind did manage to tear through the building. But it made him feel better to be doing something—anything—to give him a fighting chance now that he had made the decision to stay.

Then he hunkered down next to her, trying to make himself as comfortable as he could in the confining space.

"You really are crazy, you know that?" she said, partially in awe, partially in derision.

"You'll get no argument from me," he agreed.

"Why are you doing this for me? You don't know me. You don't know anything about me."

"To tell you the truth, Sawyer, I'm not sure why I'm here. Any sane person would have just said 'so long,' turned around, and followed Marjean down those stairs."

"You should have gone," Sawyer insisted. She raised her eyes, sending up her prayers that the storm would pass them over.

"I told you, I couldn't leave you here."

"Not that I want to wish ill on anyone, but I'm glad you're here," she said, trying to smile through her fear.

"So," he said, with forced brightness, "what do we talk about while we're waiting for the building to come down on our heads?"

"Marjean must trust you a lot to leave you up here with her cash register."

"She knows as well as I do that dead men don't steal," he retorted.

Sawyer bit her lip with worry. "How bad do you think it's going to get, Holling?"

"If the warning siren has gone off . . ." He shook his head and shrugged.

He was irritated that she couldn't choke back her fear long enough to save her own life. If she'd just followed Marjean and the rest of them down to the storage room, it all would have been over soon. An hour, maybe? What was one uncomfortable hour out of the rest of her life? It didn't make any sense to him.

More than he was angry at her, he was angry with himself. Angry that he could not convince her to go with the others. As he sat there and reflected on their confrontation, he knew that his inability to convince her was only a blow to his ego, his male pride. He'd tried to inflict his will on her, even to save her own life, and she'd pushed back with a strength of will all her own. He wasn't used to people bucking up against him. Not him. Not Jon-Tyler Holling.

If Sawyer had been a man behaving irrationally, Holling might have just clubbed the idiot on the jaw and carried him down the stairs for his own good. The thought had occurred to him. And, later, if she decided to bring assault charges against him, he could take small comfort in knowing that he'd probably saved her life. Yet, he hadn't because she wasn't. She wasn't a man. She was a woman. So he'd kept his hands to himself. And in doing so, he'd probably signed both their death certificates. What kind of woman, he thought, would make him risk so much?

"I don't know," he said, in answer to both her spoken question and to the unvoiced one in his head. "Like Barbara Jean said," he continued, "the last twister to blow through here last spring was only a category one. More of a nuisance than a threat. Still, when the warning came, we didn't take any chances. We all ran for cover . . . and I ain't ashamed to admit it."

"There's still time," she said. "You can still go."

"No." He shook his head in denial. "I can't. Not if you're not."

Sawyer lowered her head, rested her chin on her knees. "You must be bucking for sainthood, Holling, trying to hang around here saving me."

"Every man needs a cause," he returned. "Makes him feel

like he's worth something. More of a man. At least, that's what my pops always taught me."

"And what was your cause before I showed up in White Wolf?"

"Save the whales," he replied sarcastically.

"Whales?"

"Yep."

"In Montana?" she countered.

"Yep," he repeated.

"Wouldn't that make you the patron saint of lost causes?"

"I think that would be General Robert E. Lee. You being a Southern girl, you ought to know that, Sawyer Garth."

Sawyer laughed despite herself, easing the tight lines around her mouth and the furrow between her eyebrows.

"So, you can laugh," he teased her.

"Yes, I can laugh," she said, smiling back reluctantly.

"I was beginning to wonder. You look so serious." He raised his hand, smoothed it over his face, and pulled the corners of his mouth down like a mime changing expressions.

"How many people you know can smile through what I've been through so far this evening?"

"Not many," he admitted.

"I'll tell you what, Holling, if we get through this—"

"*When* we get through this," he stressed.

"When," she conceded. "When we get through this, I will grin for you from ear to ear."

"That I'd like to see," he said in hushed tones. Holling reached out and touched the corner of her mouth with his thumb.

Sawyer narrowed her eyes at him and pulled her head away. She was vulnerable and she knew it. Trapped here, in this town, in this café, cowering down out of sight with a man who most likely was used to getting his way with women— what was she thinking?

"I'm not grinning yet, Holling," she retorted.

"No, I guess not. Nothing funny about—" He broke off suddenly, looking around him as the lights flickered for a moment, then went out completely to plunge the café into total darkness.

Chapter 8

Sawyer swallowed hard. Swallowed her pride and her fear. As she scooted closer to Holling, she didn't even protest when he put his arm around her shoulder, drawing her closer to his chest.

"It's all right," he soothed. "Don't worry. It's going to be all right."

She wasn't sure if he was trying to convince her or himself. She took that comfort for what it was worth. Without any lights, it seemed to Sawyer that every noise that she could ignore or discount when the lights were on crowded in on her. Every creak, every crash, every moan of the wind got to her. She felt like a child afraid of the dark and the monsters—real or imagined—that haunted her. She cringed, burying her face in his chest.

"I don't like this," she murmured. "I don't like this at all. Shouldn't there be an emergency generator? Backup lights or something?"

"Oh, it's not so bad," Holling said, hugging her close to him. "Like I said before . . . kinda cozy."

Cradling the back of her head, he continued to murmur to

her. What exactly he said, Sawyer was sure she wouldn't be
able to repeat. It wasn't so much what he said, but how he
said it—full of calm, steadfast assurances. If he'd told her
that they'd be safe from a thousand flaming radioactive me-
teors crashing down on them, somehow she'd believe him.
She listened to the sound of his voice and let it drown out
everything else, including the sound of the wind, the rain
splashing against the windows, even the continuous thud of
hail against the café roof. All of it seemed to fade into noth-
ingness. Near silence.

Sawyer felt the tension easing from her back and shoulders. The louder the silence grew, the more relaxed she became. Was it really over? Had the storm passed over them?

The sudden silence had the opposite affect on Holling.
Sawyer felt him tense. Every muscle in his body seemed to
stiffen so that she felt as if she were holding on to a wall of
stone.

"What is it, Holling?" Sawyer asked, lifting her head.

"Hold on, Sawyer," he said. If possible, he drew her closer
to him. "This is it."

"What do you mean hold on!" she repeated, raising her
voice. "What's it? Isn't it over? The storm has passed us by,
hasn't it?"

He just shook his head, his dark eyes somber.

Sawyer popped up and peered over the edge of the
counter. From her hiding spot, she could see out of the wide,
floor-to-ceiling window along the front of the café.

"Oh . . ." Her breath came out in a small moan. "Oh my
God!"

Holling scooted around, too, and watched for a few precious seconds of stunned silence as the black clouds coa-
lesced above them in a swirling turmoil. It was close. Too
close.

"Last chance, Sawyer," he said, clasping his hand over

her forearm. "If we're going to that storeroom, we gotta go now!"

She relented. Her eyes were wide and worried. "Let's go."

He stood up, pulling her with him. "Everything will be all right, Sawyer. We'll just ride it on out, and if you start to freak out on us down there, we'll just give Marjean and the others a good laugh at our expense."

He unfurled himself from their spot, started for the narrow hall leading to Marjean's storage room. It was too late. Mere seconds too late. In what seemed to Sawyer the span of a heartbeat, the funnel cloud was on them. She looked over her shoulder and choked out a soundless scream. Horrified, she watched as evidence of the funnel cloud's destructive force played out in front of her. It was unreal, like watching a kid's Saturday morning cartoon—the Tasmanian Devil— whirling down White Wolf's main street. Nothing remotely amusing about this devil. Wild. Vicious. Unstoppable. As the twister took a path down White Wolf's main corridor, structures flew apart as if made of tissue paper. Cars and trucks were lifted from the parked positions on the street and were tossed around like kites.

Holling banged on the storage door, tugged on it without much success. Either Marjean couldn't hear him or she didn't want to.

"Holling, look out!" Sawyer screamed aloud as a park bench sailed through the air, smashed through the café window, and embedded itself into what had been Barbara Jean's hostess station. The wood veneer podium shattered into splinters under the impact, panels flying in all directions. A shower of glass spilled onto the floor, skidding from one end of the café to the other in a mixture of rain and golf-ball-sized chunks of hail.

She turned her face around, using the back of Holling's shoulder as a shield. With the entire face of the café literally gone, Sawyer felt the air around her drawn out in a rush, with an odd *whooshing* sound, as if it wanted to join with the greedy, consuming tornado. Sawyer wasn't sure if Holling could hear her. She didn't waste time on words. Dragging Holling with her back, she dove for their hiding place, putting her arms over her head. She felt something warm and solid cover her. Holling. His weight pressed down on her, literally covering her from head to foot with his bulk.

Sawyer was sobbing in terror. Her entire body trembled. She knew it and wasn't ashamed. She was crying and cursing at the same time. Cursing her fear and her obstinacy. Why didn't she listen to Holling? Why couldn't she have swallowed back her fear? Sawyer didn't believe the terror of the storage room could match what she was feeling now. Maybe she hadn't believed that it would ever come to this.

Her thoughts were filled with recriminations. Why did she have to stop in this godforsaken town? Why didn't she just keep on riding? Why didn't she go down to the storage room with the others? Why didn't she listen to Holling's advice and take refuge? Because she hadn't, she put not only herself in danger but him as well. What did he ever do to deserve this? He'd been nothing but kind to her. From the very first moment, he'd gone out of his way to help her. And what had it gotten him?

Please, God, she prayed silently. *Please let it be over soon. Please!*

One way or another, she wanted it to end now. Not that she wanted to die. Now, more than ever, she wanted to live. Mostly, she prayed that once it was over, this man would be able to forgive her. If anything happened to him because of her stubbornness and her fear, she didn't know what she would do.

Sawyer sent up her thoughts. *Please don't let anything happen to him. It's all my fault. If anything, take it out on me.*

She heard a whispering near her ear. With his cheek

sealed against hers, Sawyer heard Holling murmuring a soft prayer to himself.

"The Lord is my Shepherd; I shall not want . . ."

By the time he'd uttered "I will fear no evil," Sawyer was praying in unison with him. It didn't take long for her to remember the words, though it had been a while since she'd said them on her own.

Holling stretched out his arm, managed to join hands with hers. His rough, callused palm closed over hers. Their fingers intertwined an intensity Sawyer thought would forever bind them.

". . . for Thou art with me."

Their whispered voices seemed loud to her. Loud enough to blot out the roar of raw nature crashing down on them.

Sawyer didn't remember the exact moment the bottom fell out of the sky. All of her senses were overloaded—skewing her perception of reality. The ominous creak of support timbers stressed beyond their limits, the acrid smell of scorching electrical equipment as ceiling light fixtures were ripped from their sockets, the sonorous rumble of wood beams crashing to the floor—all of it blended in Sawyer's mind in a haze of pulverized Sheetrock that thickened the very air that she breathed.

She sucked in a deep breath, choking and gasping. A continuous, sibilant hissing alerted her to the escaping natural gas that irritated her nose and throat. The sloshing of spilled water from the ruptured water line drew her attention to the mini river that wound its way through fallen obstacles in Marjean's Café. Uprooted booth seats, toppled tables, and broken crockery defined the water's course as it eventually puddled near the demolished entryway.

Sawyer lay on her side, taking stock of her surroundings. It took her a few minutes to realize that she was alive. Alive! She'd made it. The storm had passed over her and left her relatively unscathed.

"Thank you!" She raised her face to what used to be the ceiling. Instead, she found herself looking out to what was becoming a calm Montana evening sky. Black clouds lightened to purple, strangely rimmed in gold, touched by the last rays of the setting sun. It was beautiful. The magnificence of the sky made her throat close, took her breath away. Seconds after she realized that she was okay, she realized that she was alone. Completely alone.

"Holling?" she called out, trying to sit up. Disoriented, she looked around. Where was she? It was hard to tell. What might have passed for Marjean's Café was so very different now. Just a pile of wet rubble, bricks, twisted metal, and shattered glass. Somehow, she'd wound up outside the main wreckage, several yards away from where she and Holling had taken refuge.

"Holling, where are you?" Sawyer staggered to her feet, then immediately doubled over in pain. When she looked down to investigate the spot, she gasped at the large red stain smearing her shirt just above her right hip. Sawyer pulled up her shirt and found a gash, four inches wide, ripped into her skin.

"Oh God," she moaned. Closing her eyes, she forced herself not to be sick. "Get a grip on yourself, Sawyer, girl." No time to panic. The cut was bad, but not life-threatening yet. "Look at it this way, at least the cut didn't slash you all the way through to your intestines."

If she'd seen any of her innards poking through the gash, then she'd panic. For now, she'd just have to cope. She pulled her shirt down. For now, it would have to serve as a bandage to stanch the flow of blood.

She grabbed a pole from the rubble, a piece of white PVC pipe snapped off in a five-foot-long section, and used it to lean on to take the pressure from her injured side.

"Answer me, Holling!" she called out. When her way was blocked by a fallen section of the wall, she used the pole partially as leverage to move it out of the way. She ground her teeth against the pain in her side and leaned her full weight into the pipe.

When the wall didn't budge, Sawyer cursed in frustration and smashed the pole against the stubborn wall. If he was still in there, she had to get to him. How much longer could he survive under all of that? It didn't occur to her that maybe he was thrown clear, too. She refused to believe that she'd survived and he hadn't. He was in there. She knew it. Somehow, she felt him. He had to be in there and she was going to get him out.

"Come on, Holling! I can't do this by myself!" she yelled out. "Where are you?"

"Here, honey. Let me help you."

Sawyer spun around, nearly falling over in astonishment, when Luce laid her gnarled, liver-spotted hand on her shoulder.

"Luce!" she gasped. "What . . . Where . . . How'd you get here? Where'd you come from?"

"When I heard the siren, I took cover like everybody else."

"In the storage room with Marjean in the others? Are they all right?" Sawyer looked around her, searching for any sign of the restaurant owner and her patrons.

"Oh, I imagine they're all right, honey," Luce said in an offhand manner. "The storage room is actually an old war bunker from the forties. It's buried deep and sealed up just tight. They're all just fine. I imagine they'll venture out in a bit."

"Holling," Sawyer choked out. "He's in this mess somewhere. He wouldn't go down there with them when I refused to go. I have to find him."

Sawyer was crying again. Tears left streaks down her dust-covered face.

"Don't you cry now, honey. If he's here, we'll find him."

Sawyer reached for her pole again, but Luce pulled it out of her grasp. "What do you think you're doing? Put that down. You're too busted up to be moving anything heavy."

"I'm all right. Don't worry about me."

"Somebody has to," Luce retorted. She reached out and laid a hand against Sawyer's side. "You don't have a lick of sense. Remember, if you're in pain, the baby's feeling it, too."

Sawyer winced and sucked in a deep breath.

"If you don't sit down and rest, the bleeding won't stop."

"But what about Holling?"

"Help is on the way," Luce assured her. She turned her face to the main road, tilting her head as if listening. "Hear that? Sirens." She then smiled. "Looks like the cavalry's coming over the hill. Might take them a while if the rest of White Wolf looks like this, however."

"I can't leave him in there like that. He . . . he saved my life. Even when I was too stupid to do it for myself. I've got to find him, Luce. With or without your help."

"You are a stubborn one, aren't you?"

"Some folks call it hyperdedication." Sawyer gave a rueful laugh. She came by her stubbornness naturally. Every last one of the Johnson women, whether married into the family or born into it, had a stubborn streak.

"You keep your eyes peeled, honey. I'll move the heavy stuff out of the way."

"You?" Sawyer looked in disbelief at Luce. Even though she was taller than Sawyer, she was so thin and frail. It looked as though a summer breeze could topple her over. How she managed to survive the tornado, Sawyer couldn't even begin to fathom.

"Just like you, I'm a lot tougher than I look," Luce assured her. "Now tell me, what was the last thing you remember?"

"Diving for cover underneath the lunch counter," Sawyer said promptly. "After that, everything's a blur. The next thing

I know, I'm out here. And he's somewhere in there . . . I hope. Or maybe I don't hope. Maybe if he was thrown clear, he's alive and well somewhere. Maybe if he's still in there . . ."

Sawyer felt the walls of fear and doubt closing in on her.

"Only one way to find out," Luce said. "Under the lunch counter, you say?"

Sawyer nodded. "Yes."

"Unless I've completely lost my bearings, that would be somewhere . . . uh . . . over there. Yes, I think I see something."

Luce started forward, taking extra care not to touch any exposed wiring or jagged metal protruding from the demolished café. Sawyer followed behind her as best she could, holding her throbbing side.

Without warning, Luce held up her hand. "Do you hear that?" she whispered.

Sawyer shook her head. Water dripping, and an occasional crash as the building continued to settle to the ground.

"I think it's . . . yes, it is. It's music."

Sawyer strained her ears and eventually picked up the tiny, electronic strains of Beethoven's "Für Elise."

"It's a cell phone," Sawyer said in surprise. "Holling's cell phone!"

"Over there," Luce said excitedly, pointing with the tip of the pole. "It's coming from over there."

She reached out for Sawyer's hand and guided her around a fallen section of the wall to a crumbled section of the lunch counter. She moved aside a piece of plywood wall paneling and revealed one of Holling's boots. Only one. The rest of him was covered with debris.

Sawyer clamped her hand over her mouth. What if there was no *rest of him?* What if that boot was the only thing they could find of him? What if he'd been ripped apart by the twister and this was the only grisly remainder of him?

She knelt down to grasp his ankle. She ran her hand up

the boot, and gave a sigh of relief when she grasped the leg of his denim jeans. Sawyer squeezed and felt the warmth of his leg. Boots and jeans and a body still in them. A body still warm.

Luce knelt down and started to push aside the debris covering him. "Give me a hand, honey," she urged Sawyer.

It took a few minutes to excavate Holling. Some of the pieces were easier to move than others. And with each passing moment, Sawyer felt herself getting weaker. Maybe it was the loss of blood. Maybe it was fatigue and the fact that the only things she had in her stomach were a few sips of water and a couple of crackers.

After they'd pushed aside the remainder of the debris, revealing Holling's dust-encrusted face, Sawyer felt a tightness in her stomach that rose all the way up to her throat. She could barely speak. His lean face was drawn tight, as if even unconscious he was in pain.

"Is he . . ." Sawyer couldn't bring herself to ask.

"He's still breathing," Luce said. She took Sawyer's hand and placed it against his chest. "See? You can still feel his heart beating. Strong and true."

Sawyer edged around, cradling his head in her lap. She smoothed over his face, gently calling his name.

"He's going to be just fine," Luce said.

"How can you be so sure?" Sawyer demanded. Luce was so steady, so confident in her ability to make it happen just by speaking the words.

"Help is here," she repeated. Sawyer remembered the emergency sirens.

"Talk to him, honey," Luce encouraged. "Let him know that he's not alone."

Sawyer nodded, and leaned close to him, her mouth just inches from his ear.

"Holling," she whispered as she stroked his face. "I'm

here, Holling. I'm here now. Everything's going to be all right. Can you hear me? Everything's going to be all right."

When Holling moaned, his eyelids briefly fluttering open, Sawyer gave a small cry of delight. "Holling! Oh, thank goodness! You scared me to death."

She leaned down and pressed her face close to his. "I can't believe it. It's a miracle." She looked up, her eyes shining at Luce.

"I told you everything was going to be all right, honey. You just have to have faith." She glanced at Holling. "Looks like he's taken quite a blow to the head. I can't see how bad it is, though. Why don't you see if you can find one of those napkins or a rag or something to wet it down for me? Let's see about getting him cleaned up a bit."

Sawyer hesitated. Now that she'd found him, she didn't want to leave his side.

"Go on, honey," Luce urged. "I'll watch over him."

"I'll be right back, Holling," Sawyer promised. But she wasn't sure if he'd heard her. His eyes were closed again. Yet, his breathing deepened, returned more to a natural rhythm. With an encouraged smile to Luce, she pulled herself to her feet and started to rummage nearby.

"Found one!" Sawyer called out triumphantly, spotting a blue-and-white-checked napkin snagged on a piece of concrete. Sawyer made her way to what used to be the kitchen and dipped the napkin into the flow of water spouting from the broken pipe. She squeezed out the excess, then carried it back to Holling.

Sawyer knelt down beside him, giving a questioning glance to Luce.

"He's doing fine," the woman assured her. She scooted out of the way and let Sawyer minister to him. Gently, Sawyer began to dab at his face and forehead, wiping away the blood and dust. He stirred again, reaching up for her hand.

"Shhh," she soothed him, squeezing his hand before pulling it out of the way to his side. "Lie still, Holling. I'm not very good at this nursing thing. It's not as if nurturing comes second nature to me. So you'd better lie still before I wind up making you feel worse than you probably already do."

"Giving me a peek into your bedside manner, Sawyer?" he teased, then grimaced when a wave a pain hit him so hard that his hand involuntarily clenched, forcing her to lean closer to him to relieve the strain.

"You hang in there, Holling," she whispered fervently. "Cavalry's coming. Can you hear that?"

The faint strains of emergency sirens still echoed in the distance. As the wailing grew in intensity, Sawyer figured two, maybe three vehicles were tearing up the main road leading into White Wolf. Sawyer hoped that one of those vehicles was an ambulance. The cut on Holling's head, once she'd cleared around the crusted dirt and blood, looked bad.

"Maybe you should go stand outside what's left of this place, Luce, and let them know that we're here. Flag somebody down to get Holling some help."

Sawyer glanced back over her shoulder when the woman didn't respond.

"Luce . . . Luce?" Frowning, Sawyer murmured in irritation, "*Now* where did she go?"

Chapter 9

Holling wasn't sure where he was. When he'd first opened his eyes, he shut them immediately. It hurt too much to try to see. When he'd tried to lift his head, it throbbed with the intensity of a migraine. Only much worse. There was medication for migraines. He didn't think there was a pill on this planet that could take away the piercing, white-hot pain shooting through his temples. It blotted out everything so that he couldn't think.

The last thing he remembered was diving under the counter with Sawyer. After that, not much else. Roaring in his ears. Blinding pain in his head. And after that? Nothing. No, that wasn't quite right either. One moment there was turmoil, confusion, and the unfailing certainty that these were going to be his final few moments on earth. The next moment, a sense of complete and utter calm. Too much calm. Enough for him to mistake it for nothing. A void. An absence. No fear. No pain. No confusion. All of it taken from him in an instant.

In that brief instant when he sensed nothing at all, he wondered if he was dead. And if he was, why wasn't it like anything he'd expected? Where was the tunnel of bright light? Where were his loved ones who'd passed on before him? Why weren't they there to greet him and lead him to the other side? Where was his judge? If he was dead, shouldn't he have had to give an account of himself? And if he'd been judged and found lacking, where was his punisher? It didn't make any sense. The more he tried to straighten it out, to reconcile what was happening to him, the more confused he became.

Until he heard the voice—calling to him, calming him. He felt tender hands on him, caressing him, caring for him. Knowing that he was being tended to took away his concerns, and to some degree, his pain. He knew that he was alive. He was safe.

Holling opened his eyes and focused on Sawyer's face hovering over him. He remembered speaking to her and seeing the relief in her big green eyes. He tried to reach up to touch her cheek, to let her know that it was all going to be all right, but she was more intent on reassuring him. She was trying to be strong for him. Holling was content to let her carry that burden for a while. He felt tired, sleepy. He just wanted to rest. To spend the rest of his life lying on his back, being cradled in those caring arms.

"Holling!" Sawyer called out to him sharply. "Don't go back to sleep. Not yet."

Her tone jolted him back to wakefulness. His eyelids flew open. Squinting, he tried to focus again.

"You might have a concussion," she said rapidly. "You've got a nasty cut on the head. If you go back to sleep now, you might not wake up. Do you hear me?"

"Loud and clear," he said, his tone dry. He reached up and rubbed his head.

"Sorry." Her voice dropped to a near whisper. "I didn't mean to yell in your ear."

"Don't worry about it. It's . . . uh . . . good to hear your voice, Sawyer. For a minute, I had my doubts that I'd ever hear anything again."

"We made it through, didn't we, Holling?" Her tone was hushed.

"Yeah, Trek," he said. "It looks like we did."

"You know that I couldn't have done it without you, don't you? I guess that means that I owe you my life."

"I'll take my payment in small, unmarked bills, if you please," he said, trying to lighten her mood.

"I'm serious and you're making fun of me!"

"You told me in the café that you didn't know what kind of man I was. Now you know. I'm the kind of man who likes making fun of people who take themselves too seriously, Sawyer."

"I'll bet that made you a real riot in school."

"That was me. Mr. Popular. How 'bout you, Sawyer? What were you like in school?"

She laughed self-consciously. "Why do you want to know?"

"What else have we got to talk about? Looks like we're gonna be here for a while until they find us. You might as well fess up."

"If you must know, I was the geeky kid with her head always stuck in a book. Big buckteeth. Braces. Coke-bottle-thick glasses. My senior class voted me most likely to donate my brain to science."

He chuckled. "And just look at you now. You ought to go back to your school reunion and put all of those losers who made fun of you to shame," he said gently, reaching up to finger the strands of hair that fell across her cheek as she leaned over him. "You sure are a sight for sore eyes now."

"Oh, I'll bet you say that to all the motorcycle mamas who come through here."

"No, ma'am. You're the first one."

"I guess all the others had more sense than to stop

through White Wolf during a tornado threat. I'm the only nut who wanted to try it."

"I'm one man who's glad you did stop. If we hadn't met, I'd probably be a mangled lump of flesh, forgotten under a pile of rubble somewhere, waiting for the emergency response team to dig me out with their cadaver-sniffing dogs."

"Don't thank me. Thank your cell phone. If Luce hadn't heard it ringing—"

"My cell phone?" Holling said, his expression puzzled.

"Uh-huh. If it weren't for your phone, we wouldn't have found you."

"Who's we?"

"Me and Luce."

Holling looked around. It was just the two of them there now.

"I guess she took off right before you woke up. But she was the one who heard your phone ringing and that's what led us to you."

Holling reached for the leather case attached to his belt. "My phone?" he repeated. He worked open the flap and withdrew a small silver phone. Flipping open the cover, he began to punch buttons with his thumb.

"Checking to see who would be calling you in the middle of a natural disaster?"

"The last person to call me was my pops. I . . . uh . . . thought I'd turned the ringer off." He flashed her a weak smile. "Funny thing is, as soon as you went to the restroom, he called me a couple of times, wondering when I was coming back. I thought I'd turned down the ringer so that we could talk uninterrupted."

She pointed an accusatory finger at him. "See? It was your own folly that brought that storm down on us. Because you shut your father out, disrespected him, it brought Mother Nature's wrath down on us."

"Folly?" he teased, raising an eyebrow at her. "No wonder

you were teased mercilessly when you were a kid, using words like 'folly' and 'wrath.' If I'd known you back then, I would have teased you myself."

"And I would have thrown one of my countless tomes at your head."

He reached up and fingered the lump forming on the back of his head. "I wish I had known you then. Maybe with a few books thrown at me, I'd have a tougher head than now."

"How does it feel?" Sawyer asked, clucking her tongue in sympathy.

"Like someone dropped a building on it. How 'bout you? Are you all right?"

"I'm fine. Don't worry about me." She rocked back on her heels.

Holling took a moment to take in her appearance, noted the bloodstain on her shirt.

"Sawyer! Good grief, woman! What are you doing hovering over me? How bad is that?"

"Don't panic, Holling. It's just a cut. Not bad. It's not even bleeding anymore."

"When was your last tetanus shot?"

She shrugged. "About two years ago, I think."

"Let me guess, you cut yourself opening up one of your countless tomes."

"You don't get tetanus from paper cuts. Now, a staph infection is another matter."

"What happened to you?"

"I was walking barefoot on the beach in Florida and stepped on a rusty beer can."

"I'll bet that killed your romantic walk on the beach," Holling said. He was fishing for information—information he knew that she wouldn't volunteer on her own. Did she have a man or didn't she? It frustrated him that they'd been through so much and still he knew so little about her.

"Nothing romantic about it," she said hesitantly. "I was at

a family reunion. My cousins Shiri, Essence, and Brenda wound up getting me to the hospital."

Three names. Three women. Holling chose to believe that if there had been a special man in Sawyer's life, he would have been the one to take care of her. That is, if he was a man worth anything.

"Oh . . ." he said, on a long, exhaled breath. "So, you're telling me that if we, that is, you and me, should take a stroll along the beach someday, I wouldn't be steppin' over anybody's boots to get there."

"They have beaches in Montana?" she asked in mock surprise.

"You can find anything you want here, if you look hard enough. So?"

"So what?" she pretended as if she didn't understand what he wanted.

"You're avoiding the question, Sawyer. I'm askin' you, who's my competition? Are you gonna tell me?"

"No." She shook her head back and forth.

"Why not?"

"Call it sidestepping if you want to. All I'm doing is making sure that I don't ever get cut like that again."

She had said it in a way that let Holling know that she wasn't talking about beaches and beer cans anymore. Someone had hurt her. Hurt her deeply. How long ago, he couldn't tell. Whenever it was, the wound was still raw and causing her a great deal of pain.

If he was going to move forward with her, he would have to tread carefully. It wasn't a matter of deciding *if* he would go. He already knew that he would. He'd subconsciously made that decision the moment she'd taken off that helmet. Or maybe the decision had been made for him. Call it destiny. Call it fate. Call it plain old dumb luck. If he hadn't gone back in after that damned pecan pie, he would never have met her. If he'd been a pessimist, always looking on the dark side, he could also have thought that if it weren't for her he probably wouldn't have been caught out in that storm. There was a reason for everything—including her reason for being in White Wolf, at this point in time, at this point in his life.

"Sawyer—" he began, and was interrupted by an excited shout.

"Over here!"

"We found two more!"

A beam of light pierced the night air. The high-powered light from an extra-large flashlight swept back and forth, illuminating their sheltered spot in its cool white glow.

"Here!" Sawyer called out unnecessarily and tried to stand up to draw their attention.

"Just stay put, ma'am! We're sending someone over there to help you."

"Do you hear that, Holling?" she said excitedly, and on impulse leaned over and hugged him.

Holling had an impulse of his own. He hadn't planned it, but he'd be lying if he'd said that he hadn't thought about it—a persistent thought always in the back of his mind. Up until now he'd been able to resist the impulse. Not denying it. Simply choosing his moment on when to act on it. The time was right, right now. As Sawyer leaned over him, Holling raised himself up on his elbow, hooked his hand behind her head, and pulled her toward him.

"Holling, don't!" Sawyer objected, offering resistance as she placed her hand against his chest. She started to pull away from him. Holling could feel her strain against his hand. Her entire body stiffened in rejection, even as he felt the pulse under his fingertips increase at her neck.

Holling released her.

"Sorry," he muttered. "I guess I got ahead of myself."

"No, I'm sorry," she said, fumbling. "I can't . . . I mean, I shouldn't." She was too raw. Much too vulnerable. If she kissed him now, she would never be able to emotionally detach herself from him again. And she had to. She had to let go. She couldn't let these extreme circumstances forge a relationship that might not ever have occurred naturally, on its own. Holling wasn't her type. He was too damned independent. He wasn't needy enough for her. And she needed to be needed by someone. It would never work.

He cut her off. "You don't have to apologize. I just thought for a minute that maybe you wanted . . ."

"Wanted what? Wanted you to kiss me?" Sawyer laughed out loud. It sounded cruel, insensitive, and she knew it. But it had to be this way. Whatever he thought she was able to give him, emotionally, she had to squash that idea. "What in the world put that idea in your head? Don't get me wrong, Holling. I'm glad that you're alive and that you're not hurt. That's all it was. Anything else you thought you saw was your own imagination. I don't want you to kiss me, Holling. I don't want you to touch me. All I want to do is make sure that you're all right so that I can get the hell out of this town."

"Well, you certainly made that point loud and clear," he said.

When Sawyer's fingers suddenly curled, grasping a handful of his shirt to jerk herself toward him, it was enough for Holling. He sealed his lips swiftly to hers. He didn't want to give her a chance to change her mind. From the way she responded, Holling didn't think that it was a possibility. She wasn't going to back away from him now.

Not that he was all that convinced of his skill as a kisser. Holling was realistic, knowing that he what he lacked in skill, he more than made up for in persistence and enthusiasm. If he had any doubts, especially after her oh-so-cruel cut-down, Sawyer's new response to him bolstered his confidence. He heard her give the faintest of moans, signaling the end of her reluctance.

Sawyer kissed the way she spoke—distinctly, with an edge that challenged him to try to soften. He hadn't intended to prolong the kiss. He only wanted to give her a taste of how she was affecting him. By the way he was responding to her, he guessed that she had affected him on a level deeper than even he had considered. The longer he held the kiss, the more reluctant he was to see it end. The more pliant her lips became, the harder he pressed her. He cradled her head to him as she clutched his shoulders. His hands slid downward, resting on the small of her back as she arched toward him.

Kissing Sawyer made him forget everything—his surroundings, the pain in his head, even the emergency rescue team approaching him.

Chapter 10

The first member of the emergency response team waved his flashlight back and forth across the area.

Distracted, breathless, Sawyer pulled away, revealing Holling's prone position.

As soon as the ERT moved in, he let out a startled shout of recognition. "Mr. Holling!"

Holling lifted his hand, giving a weak wave in response.

"Hey, Reiner. Is that you over there, boy?"

"Yes, sir!" he said excitedly, kneeling down beside Holling. He called in his location with the radio clipped to his shoulder.

"You all right, sir?"

"I gotta admit, I've had better days, Reiner," Holling confessed.

The ERT pulled a pair of rubber gloves from his kit. "Lie still, sir. Let me take a look at you."

Sawyer sat back and watched as he performed a cursory examination. When he located Holling's head wound, he took out a small penlight and shone it into Holling's eyes, checking the pupils for a response. Carefully, Reiner examined the spot on the back of Holling's head. Not quite careful enough. Holling winced.

"Sorry, sir. Looks like you're gonna need stitches."

"Can't be any worse than that time your daddy's loco mare threw me over that ropin' pen. How many stitches did that take, Reiner? Three? Four?"

"More like seven," Reiner corrected.

"Seven stitches?" Sawyer repeated. "That must have been some fall."

"I've fallen harder," Holling said quietly, pinning Sawyer with a meaningful gaze.

The throw from that horse last winter was nothing compared to how he was feeling now. Then, he'd known the horse was crazy. He'd taken his chances like all of the others who'd put their money down and bragged they could break old man Rogers's horse. He'd strapped himself in the saddle, given the nod to the man at the gate, and charged into the small, private arena fully expecting to be thrown.

But this . . . this was totally unexpected. This encounter with Sawyer wasn't anything he could have prepared for. No time to strap himself down. No time to figure out if this was the way he wanted to go. The door opened and there he was, plummeting heart-first, instead of headfirst, toward her. Trouble was, he hadn't hit bottom yet. He had no idea where he was going, how long this feeling of free-falling would last. He didn't even know if she was along for the ride with him. He only knew that he didn't want it to end.

"I'm just gonna clean this wound for you." Reiner announced his every action before performing it. "Here we go with a temporary bandage. That should keep the wound clean until you can get to the county hospital."

"How far is the hospital from here?" Sawyer asked.

"Oh, 'bout six miles or so," Reiner told her. "They're supposed to be sending out an ambulance this way, if you want to wait for it."

"How long?"

"An hour, ma'am. Maybe two. That twister cut a path through here like you wouldn't believe."

"I'd believe it," Sawyer said with a shudder.

"If it's all the same to you, Reiner, I'll drive myself," Holling said.

"You can't drive yourself to the hospital, Holling. Can he?" Sawyer asked the EMT.

"I know from experience that Mr. Holling's got a hard head, ma'am. But I have to advise against him trying to drive."

"Is there someone who can come and get you, Holling?" Sawyer asked.

"I could call my pops," he suggested. "Or someone from the ranch. But I'm guessing that the sheriff's department will be turning back any traffic that isn't rescue related."

"I guess that leaves it up to me to get us out," Sawyer said, taking a deep breath.

He shook his head. "You don't have to. If necessary, we can wait for the ambulance."

"Hard as a brick or not, you need that head looked at," Sawyer said. "I can drive. I can get us there."

Reiner then turned his attention to Sawyer. "How 'bout you, ma'am? Are you injured?"

"I'm all right," she said.

"Don't listen to her, Reiner. She's got a cut on her side that needs to be tended to."

"Ma'am?" Reiner gestured toward her side. Carefully, Sawyer peeled away her blouse. She hissed in pain as the blood that had already clotted opened the wound anew.

Reiner took off one pair of gloves and disposed of them in a plastic bag, then snapped on a fresh pair. Holding her side with one hand and shining his penlight on her with the other, he said, "I should be able to tape-stitch that closed long enough for you to get to the hospital, ma'am. But make sure you get that tended to right away. You don't want to risk an infection."

He pulled out a bottle of antiseptic, some cotton balls, tape, and gauze. Sawyer sucked in her stomach and ground her teeth as he cleaned dried blood. Involuntarily, she reached for Holling's hand.

"Almost done," Reiner soothed. "Can you hold that there, ma'am?" He placed her hand over the thick gauze padding, then secured the dressing in place with strips of white tape.

Once he was finished, Sawyer pulled her blouse down over the area. Holling reached into his pocket and pulled out his keys.

"It's a dark green Suburban. Hopefully it's still in Marjean's parking lot."

She nodded and climbed to her feet. "Be back in a bit."

"Can you go with her, Reiner?" Holling asked. "You know my truck."

"Yes, sir. It's got those strands of Mardi Gras beads hanging from the mirror, right?"

"You got it."

Reiner turned his flashlight on wide beam again, pointing out a path to the café parking lot.

"Sawyer," Holling called out to her.

"Yes?"

"You ever drive anything that big before?"

"No," she confessed. "But I suppose I'd better learn fast." She looked around her, her eyes following the play of Reiner's light against the café ruins. Her shoulders slumped. "Looks like that's the only way I'm going to ride out of here. I don't see my bike anywhere."

Nathaniel Holling couldn't find his son anywhere. He waded through the emergency room and triage areas, where several of his friends and neighbors waited for their turn to be treated. His heart went out to all of them, but there was one who was first and foremost in his thoughts now.

"Cody!" he called out to one of Holling's friends. "Have you seen Holling?"

The young man shook his head slowly, keeping the ice pack on his head to keep the swelling down. "Naw, sir. I haven't. Sorry."

Nate kept walking. His booted feet thudded on the linoleum floor as he searched for his son. He ran his hand over his beard, trying not to shout and disturb the others in need of obvious medical attention. He was trying not to panic. It wasn't easy. When Holling had called the bunkhouse, letting him know that he was on the way to the hospital, Nate had popped up, raring to go, storm or no storm. Red Bone had wanted to go with him, but Nate insisted that he stay behind.

"Get whatever medical supplies you think you'll need and go check on the Osgoods." They were his neighbors to the east. An elderly couple had recently bought the ten-acre property as their retirement home. After Holling, they were the first people Nate had thought of.

"Nikki?" he called to another of Holling's classmates, a young woman working in the hospital as a volunteer. "Have you seen my son? Have you seen Holling?"

"Not since they brought him in," she said. "You might check with Gideon over there." She nodded at a tall, thin man in green scrubs. "I think he was one of the ones who wheeled him in from the ambulance."

"Much obliged." He touched his hand to his hat and continued on.

"Are you Gideon?" Nate addressed the man as he was dumping a load of used hospital gowns into a roll-away bin.

"Yes, sir. Can I help you?"

"I'm looking for my son."

"Jon-Tyler?" He raised his eyes toward the ceiling, trying

to recall. "Umm . . . I think they put him in examining room number three . . . no, number four."

"Number four?"

"Yes, sir. Go back that way, turn left, then back through the double doors. You can't miss it."

"Thank you," Nate said gratefully. However, by the time he found the room, his son was gone—replaced by another patient. She sat on the edge of the examining table, looking like so many of the others who'd been taken unaware by the twister. Disheveled. Confused.

"Come on now, Nate," he chastised himself. "You can do this."

He was frustrated that he'd been turned around so many times that he'd lost his bearings.

When Nate first peeked in the examining room, he thought he'd stumbled onto a child's room. She sat on the table, in a floral hospital gown that seemed to swallow her. Her legs dangled off the edge, swinging her feet back and forth. Her dark head was bowed, obscuring her face behind short, dark hair in a ragged, pixie cut. Her small hands gripped the edge of the table so tightly, Nate saw her knuckles lighten under the strain. She was breathing deeply. In. Out. In. Out. He watched her shoulders rise and fall. Suddenly, Nate heard her retch, curse, then retch again. Without thinking he stepped inside and grabbed a paper coverall from a tray by the door. She jumped off the table and was trying to make it to a nearby wastepaper basket, but she wasn't going to make it.

In three strides, he was at her side, thrusting the coverall in her hands. She pressed it to her mouth, heaving into it until the spasm passed.

"Th-thanks," she said, looking at up him with two of the prettiest eyes he'd ever seen. They reminded him of the sea—deep green and constantly changing. There was gratitude in her eyes, followed by mild embarrassment, and a hint of annoyance.

"Don't mention it, little missy. Are you all right?"

"I will be," she said stoutly.

"I didn't mean to barge in on you. I was looking for my son. The orderly said I would find him here."

"That wouldn't be Jon Holling, would it?" she asked, looking curiously at him.

"Yes, ma'am. It sure would be. You know him? Course you do," he said, answering his own question. "Everybody knows Holling."

It wasn't too far a stretch of the truth. Everybody who was anybody knew his son. And Nate knew everybody who knew his son. The fact that this woman knew his name intrigued him. He'd never seen her before, of that he was certain. How did his son know her? And why didn't he know that he knew her?

"He'll be back in a minute. The technician took him down to be X-rayed."

"X-rayed!" A fresh surge of anxiety hit him. "For what? Is he all right?"

She tapped her forehead with a slender finger. "I think the doctor ordered an MRI. Holling took a pretty nasty knock on the head."

"Oh, hell then. He'll be all right. Pardon my French," Nate snorted. "He's taken some pretty hard knocks. Nothing can hurt that boy's coconut."

"So I've been told."

Her mouth twisted, letting Nate know that she had a sense of humor as dry, as offbeat as his own.

He held his hand to her. "I'm Nathaniel Holling. My friends call me Nate."

"I'm Sawyer," she offered.

"Sawyer? Is that your first name?"

"Yes, sir, it is."

"Funny name for a girl, ain't it?"

"She's a funny kinda girl," Holling said from the doorway. The medical assistant that had taken him for his testing wheeled him back into the room and was profusely apologizing. "If you'll wait here for a minute, sir, I'll check on your room. Sorry for the wait, but we're full to capacity."

Nate turned around to face his son. For a minute, his face clearly showed his relief at finding Jon-Tyler alive and well. Then he folded his arms across his narrow chest.

"What happened to you, boy?"

"This is what happens when you send me after pecan pie you know good and well that you don't need."

"Hmmph," Nate rumbled in his throat. "You'd think that if I thought you were smart enough to pick up my order, you'd be smart enough to get out of the way of a twister." He grabbed a stool, dragging it across the floor to sit beside his son. He examined the bandaging, tugging on a piece of tape.

Holling slapped his hand away. "Cut that out."

"So what did the doctor say?"

Holling tapped his index finger against his bandaged head. "Mild concussion. The doc says to stay off my feet for a few days."

Nate burst into laughter. "Mighty convenient. You probably slipped that doctor a Jackson to write you an excuse to keep you from having to work, you good-for-nuthin' gold-brick."

"The bricks falling down on us weren't golden," Sawyer said, vouching for him.

"Us?" Nate said, raising his eyebrows meaningfully.

"All of us at Marjean's Café," Sawyer clarified. "That's where we all were when the tornado hit. We're lucky to come out of it alive."

"Any damage to the Way, Pops?" Holling asked.

He shook his head. "Nothing that can't be put back with a little elbow grease," he replied. "So don't go waving any doctor's excuse in my face. I'm takin' you out of here, taking you home, just as fast as I can sign the release papers."

He reached out and grabbed his son's hand and squeezed. He didn't have to say it out loud. Sawyer understood the gesture as easily as if Nate had spoken the words. He'd been afraid for his son. The hour-long drive into White Wolf, the pleading with the sheriff's deputy to let him pass, the frantic calls to the hospital to locate him—it was too much emotion to contain.

Sawyer tried to make herself inconspicuous. She didn't want to intrude on their reunion. She moved to the far side of the room, pretending to study the collection of cotton balls, gauze, and monitoring equipment.

"Speaking of homes," Holling said, clearing his throat loudly to draw her attention. "Sawyer, were you able to reach your folks?"

Sawyer hesitated before answering. "My father's traveling. I left a message with his administrative assistant and told her that I was . . . uh . . . having engine trouble. I didn't tell her that the whole damn bike was probably scattered across the state. Pardon my French." She winked at Nate.

"Bike?" Nate echoed. "You mean like a motorbike?"

"Yes, sir. That's my ride."

"You were right, boy. She is a funny kinda girl," Nate whispered loudly to his son, pointing his thumb in Sawyer's direction.

"Pops, I invited Sawyer to stay with us a couple of days," Holling announced.

"Why are you telling me?" Nate said gruffly. It was apparent to him that his son wasn't asking his permission to let the girl stay.

"I'm tellin' you so that you won't go walkin' around the house in the nude and near 'bout scare that girl to death."

"Don't listen to him, little missy. He's the one who walks around in the nude."

"TMI," Sawyer said, raising her hands and waving them to cut off of this conversation. "Way too much information."

"You're welcome to stay with us as long as you like," Nate offered.

"They're gonna keep me here tonight, Pops," Holling said. "Why don't you go on back and take Sawyer home with you?"

"I can't leave. Not yet, anyway," she said. "Not until I take care of a few administrative things. And that might take a while since I've lost my wallet, my identification . . . all my credit cards." Sawyer didn't try to hide the frustration in her tone.

"If you're worried about the hospital bill, don't. That's already take care of," Holling told her.

"What do you mean taken care of?" Sawyer asked.

"Yeah, what do you mean?" Nate echoed. He folded his arms across his chest and regarded his son with a mixture of curiosity and disapproval.

"We'll talk about it later, Pops." Holling tried to brush the matter aside.

"No," Sawyer interjected, moving closer to him. "We'll talk about it now. What have you done?"

"Ooh. Watch out, Holling. I think Sawyer's got a temper," Nate said.

"I just made some calls," Holling said simply, shrugging his shoulders.

"Then you'll just have to unmake them," Sawyer said defiantly.

"What for?"

"Because I don't need your help. I can take care of my own bills, thank you very much."

"Oh Lordy! Here it comes," Nate predicted as he threw up his hands. "I'll bet you're gonna give us one of those 'I can take care of myself' speeches, aren't ya, little missy?"

"How do you know what I'm going to say?" Sawyer challenged.

"That's the problem with all of you independent ladies.

You can do it all yourself. Don't need us menfolk to do a damn thing for ya anymore. The one thing we did have a monopoly on, the one thing we're good at it, you ladies either turn to each other for it or run to a clinic to have it artificially done."

"Pops!" Holling said sharply.

"What?" He turned, giving his son a look of total innocence.

"Pops," he said in a calmer tone. "Leave Sawyer alone."

"Aw hell. I'm not bothering her. I'm not saying anything she didn't already know. Did I offend you, little missy?"

"No, but if you don't stop calling me that, you will. My name is Sawyer. And as much as I appreciate you looking after me, Holling, I don't want you paying my hospital bill. It's too much money. I'm grateful to you for saving me from that storm, but enough is enough!"

"Sawyer, all I did was make sure that the hospital administrative staff didn't give you any hassle about tracking down your insurance information for you. You did fill out the paperwork when they admitted you, right? I know you don't have any ID on you. If Pops wants to get you out of here tonight, and you leave without making sure your bill is taken care of . . . You want that down on your credit report, skipping out without paying?"

"No," she agreed reluctantly. "I guess not."

"Then it's settled. Relax."

Sawyer opened her mouth to speak, but Holling cut her off. "If it's all right with you, Sawyer, Pops will take you shopping in the morning to a store over in Cut Bank, if it's open, to let you pick up a few things."

"I don't want to be a burden to anyone," Sawyer said quickly. "I can pay you back."

"Better let him pay, Sawyer. Pops isn't used to opening up his wallet. It's not as if it comes naturally to him." Holling's words echoed Sawyer's sentiments about nursing.

"We'll just make sure that we hit all the stores where Holling has accounts, won't we, Sawyer?" Nate winked at her.

"Do this sort of thing often, Holling? Shopping for women, that is?" she said, her tone intentionally jealous.

"Maybe I oughta try to get out of here tonight," Holling said, shifting uncomfortably in his chair. "You're gonna get me into trouble, Pops."

"You opened the door, boy. I just walked through."

Holling didn't get a chance to defend himself. The technician returned, ready to take him to his private room.

Chapter 11

"Here you go, Sawyer. You can have this room." Nate held the door open for her and made a grand, sweeping gesture for her to enter.

Sawyer brushed past him. "Thank you so much, Mr. Holling."

"I thought I told you about that 'mister' business. You call me Nate. You are gonna be stayin' with us for a while, aren't ya?"

"Until I can either find my bike and get it repaired or convince the insurance company to cough up a new one," she said. "I'm not sure how long either will take. Or if either option is even feasible."

"Well, you won't catch us countin' the days, Sawyer, girl. Like I said before, you're a guest for as long as you want to be."

He set her bag down on the floor next to the bed. The bag contained a few items they'd picked up from a twenty-four hour-superstore—two pairs of jeans, three or four shirts, personal hygiene articles, and a few unmentionables that he'd modestly turned his eyes from when Sawyer had tossed them into the basket. She was long past caring about appearances at that moment. She was near exhaustion and was only thinking about getting through the line and into bed before she'd collapsed.

If Nate hadn't forced her to eat as soon as they arrived at his home, Sawyer was sure that he would have gone straight to bed. She'd waited at the breakfast nook table while he whipped her up a large fluffy omelet.

"I thought I told you that I didn't want you making a fuss over me," she'd said. But her mouth had watered at the sound of sizzling in Nate's skillet. Chopped scallions, red and golden bell peppers, three kinds of cheeses, diced ham, and garnished with a spoon of picante sauce dribbled over the top—she'd polished off the late-night breakfast before he'd finished scrubbing the pan.

Now, with a full stomach, she was looking forward to collapsing into bed and digesting the meal for the next twelve hours.

"I'll let you get settled in. There's soap and towels in the linen closet behind the bathroom door. You've got your own private bathroom in this room, so you won't have to worry about one of us walkin' in on you." He chuckled. "I guess that would be just me since Holling's takin' a siesta at the hospital and our housekeeper, Chale, is out of town visiting family for a while."

He headed for the bedroom door, then turned and winked at her. "Just in case, Sawyer, girl, you'd better use that latch. It's been a while since we've had such a pretty little thing like you around here."

Sawyer narrowed her eyes at him and pursed her lips. "As tired as I am right now, Nate, you wouldn't get much enjoyment even if you did peek in. Wouldn't be much of a show for you at all."

"At my age, little missy, about all I *can* do is watch."

Sawyer was laughing as Nate closed the door behind him.

She didn't have the least bit of fear that he'd actually meant any of his lascivious talk. They'd been together for almost three hours, shopping, joking around, eating, and he'd been nothing but a gentleman toward her. She saw where Holling got it from. The two were cut from the same mold. Except for the dirty jokes, Nate reminded her of her grandpa George. Being a minister, Grandpa George had toned down his innuendos and double entendres. Yet, being a man of the church hadn't curbed his natural tendency for jokes. If anything, it gave him more ammunition. His congregation was a willing, captive audience that hung on his every word, waiting for him to throw in a zinger or two.

Maybe that's why I feel so comfortable around Nate, Sawyer mused. She was perfectly at ease with him. A part of her wondered if she should be more troubled. Sawyer pushed those thoughts out of her head. She'd been in tighter jams with people more menacing than Nate could ever be. She'd be all right.

"You must be crazy, Sawyer," she said aloud to herself. A nagging voice in the back of her mind made her wonder whether or not she'd lost her mind. Some folks called it intuition. Her grandma Lela called it the Angel of Reason. Whatever it was, she was tuning out that voice. Maybe she wasn't thinking clearly. Lack of sleep. The harrowing experience she'd just been through. Any other time her suspicious instincts would have told her not to trust so quickly—trust either Jon-Tyler Holling or his father.

Yet, she was trusting.

"Not like I have much of a choice."

She'd been stripped of the meager belongings she'd brought on the road with her, her bike, her wallet, her phone. Anything she could have used to get herself out of a jam was taken away from her. She had nothing but her wits about her. Now she had to rely either on herself to get her out of trouble or on the kindness of strangers. So far, she hadn't proven to be very good at taking care of herself, despite all of her brave talk in the hospital.

"Not a very good track record, Sawyer, girl," she said, sitting on the edge of the bed. She pulled off one of the tennis shoes she'd purchased. The first one hit the deep pile area rug with a muted thud.

"First you screw up and get yourself pregnant. No offense to you, baby," she said, patting her stomach affectionately.

Sawyer then pulled off the other tennis shoe and let it land next to the first one. "Then you get yourself caught in a tornado."

She shrugged out of the light sweater and tossed it on top of the bag containing the rest of her new things. In all, the bill from their shopping spree came out to almost two hundred dollars that Nate Holling had shelled out for her. Two hundred dollars! Her eyes had nearly bugged out of her head when the cashier rang up the bill. If she'd been shopping on her own, two hundred dollars would mean nothing. But this was someone else's money. A total stranger's.

Immediately, she'd insisted that he put some of the things back. She reached for the lime-green capri pants and the melon-colored cropped-top blouse that Nate had picked out for her. She could easily bear to part with those. They weren't exactly her favorite colors. Nate just laughed at her as if the money had been nothing.

"And to top it all off, Sawyer," she continued, "you get yourself stranded in a place that doesn't even rate a dot on the map, camping out in the home of people who are determined to kill you with kindness."

Sawyer imagined that if she allowed herself to lie down, her head would hit the pillow with an equal force. She was tired. So tired. She should get up and take a bath. That was the least she could do for her generous hosts, not to stink up their bed. The sponge bath she'd taken in the ladies' restroom with the baby wipes had her smelling like clean diapers. The spritzing of floral body spray she used to cover up the baby diaper smell wasn't a scent she would normally have chosen. But it would have to do.

The idea of a bath sounded so tempting. She ran her fingers lightly over the fluffed-up pillows lining the headboard of the cherry-wood, four-poster bed. The crocheted, antique-white lace pillow covers looked like overstuffed clouds. They were calling her name even louder than the thought of a long, soaking bubble bath.

"In a minute," Sawyer said through a yawn, answering the imaginary call of the bathtub. She would be up in just a minute. One more minute. She would only doze for a minute, Sawyer promised herself. And then she would get up, take a quick shower, and get back into bed. She didn't hear the light tap on the door. Nor did she see the sunlight streaming into the room four hours later when Nate peeked in to check up on her.

Sawyer lay on the edge of the bed, curled up in the fetal position. Her right hand supported her cheek. The other hand rested against her stomach. She was still fully dressed.

Nate eased the door open, grabbed the corner of the blanket near the foot of the bed, and gently pulled it up over Sawyer. With the back of his hand, he lightly brushed away her hair that had fallen across her cheek and mouth. She didn't move a muscle. In fact, if it weren't for her deep, rhythmic breathing, he would have performed the old trick of holding a mirror up to her mouth and nose to see if she was even alive.

"Lord only knows what you must've been through, Sawyer, girl," he murmured.

While they were shopping, she'd given him an abbreviated account of how she had wound up in White Wolf. Though she was animated, making light of her predicament, Nate knew that she wasn't telling the complete story. When he'd asked her what she was doing out here, traveling alone, she'd given him some cockamamie story about a cross-country charity motorcycle trip to raise awareness of breast cancer.

He didn't really buy it. Breast cancer awareness month was in October. And the *only* reason he knew that was because the wife of one of his hands was a breast cancer activist. When it came to donations, she'd been at his doorstep every October since President Clinton made the National Mammography Day observance official back in 1992 . . . No, it was 1993. Nothing makes you forget it's donation time like a four-year breast cancer survivor hounding you until you either ponied up the money or some volunteer time. He'd done both.

Nate shook his head, trying to reconcile what she'd told him about herself with what he suspected. As charming as she'd behaved, something didn't feel right about Sawyer's story. She had the look of someone on the run. He'd seen that look before often enough. Their property was worked by a handful of year-round workers. The rest were day laborers or transients. Nate could usually peg the ones who were running away from something. He'd gotten very good at judging the ones who were running away from legal trouble. They didn't stay around long, which suited him just fine. If he could, he helped them run right into the arms of the authorities. He wasn't jeopardizing the safety of his workers or his home by harboring fugitives.

But those running from personal demons were treated differently. Nothing like a day of good, honest, hard work to exorcise those personal demons. Folks like that, as long as they didn't cause trouble, were welcome to stay as long as they wanted. That's the category he placed Sawyer in. He wanted to help her, if he could. He would have done it even if he hadn't known that Holling was developing feelings for her. There was something about that Sawyer Garth. Something familiar, enough so that he was willing to take her into his home without many questions asked. He just knew that for now, this was where she should be. If she was running, she could rest here for a while. She obviously needed it.

Nate had knocked on her door at least twice that morning. Once at five o'clock to tell her that he was going out for a while to start his morning chores. He'd knocked again at six-thirty once he'd returned to tell her that he'd made breakfast for her. Now that it was nine o'clock, he thought he'd better do more than knock. He'd better check on her.

He barely made a sound as he crept into the room. He set the small tray bearing a glass of orange juice and toast down on the nightstand beside her and turned to leave. Nate stopped when he heard the bed creak, followed by a soft sigh.

"Nate?" Sawyer raised herself on her elbow and called out to him.

"Well, now, missy. You finally decided to join the land of the living?"

"Barely," she said, yawning behind her hand. She ran her fingers through her hair as she looked around the room, and squinted her eyes at the drawn curtains. "What time is it?"

"Nineish."

"Oh man," she groaned and fell back on the pillow. "I didn't know it was so late. I didn't mean to sleep so long."

"You must've needed it. Hard sleep is your body's way of tellin' you to slow down. How're you feelin'?"

"Okay." She smiled up at him. "Actually, I'm feeling much better. Amazing what a little sleep will do for you."

"A little sleep? Girl, I was about to start checking you for a pulse."

Sawyer laughed. "Usually I'm a light sleeper," she said. "Especially if I'm sleeping in a strange room."

She stretched her arms high over her head and arched her back in a catlike stretch. "This bed is so comfortable, Nate, it knocked me right out."

"You could have been sleepin' on a bed of bricks and

never known the difference. You know you snore louder than Holling does?"

"Remember when we were talking about TMI cases, Nate?" Sawyer sat up, drew her knees up, and hugged her legs close to her chest.

"Yeah?"

"Well, that was one of them," she insisted.

"Seems to me you'd want to know everything there is to know about my boy, Sawyer."

"Anything he wants me to know, I'm sure he'll tell me."

Nate pulled up a chair next to her bed. "You're the first woman I ever met that didn't try to get me to talk about him. You know, all the gals around here all want to get to close to him," he said, not bothering to hide the boastful pride in his tone.

"Is that so?" Sawyer replied blandly.

This didn't deter Nate. "Ain't you the least bit curious about him?"

She gave a noncommittal shrug. "No . . . I ain't," she said, mimicking him.

"Sure you are." Nate answered his own question to his liking.

Sawyer laughed. He sounded just like Jon-Tyler when he'd asked her whether she wanted to know what he'd have inscribed on his headstone. Her aunt Rosie used to have a saying about apples not falling far from trees. In this instance, the apple was still hanging on to the branch. These men just didn't take no for an answer.

"You wouldn't be worth your salt if you weren't even the teensiest bit curious. You gotta admit, he cuts a fine figure of a man. You do like him, don't you?" Nate insisted.

"To tell you the truth, Nate, I barely know him. There isn't much time for conversation when you're trying your best not to be smashed by a tornado." She tried to be flippant, but Sawyer barely believed her own words. In that short span of time, she felt she knew, and trusted, Holling more than she did Ryan—a man she thought she'd known for two years.

"That's not what I asked you, little missy." Nate wagged his finger at her.

"What do you want me to say, Nate?"

It was Nate's turn to shrug. "I don't know. Humor an old man, why don't you?"

"Your son's a likeable man," Sawyer said carefully.

"Go on."

"You know more about what makes him likeable than I do."

"I think you more than like him," Nate announced.

"And your basis for that opinion would be?"

Nate leaned back in his chair, his index finger absently stroking his salt-and-pepper beard.

"Well, now . . . let's just say that in the hospital I saw the way you looked at him . . . and the way he looked at you. There's something there that don't have a thing to do with how long you've known each other."

Sawyer reached for the toast and juice Nate set out for her. She nibbled the edges for a while, savoring the delectable taste of homemade bread, fresh butter, and preserves. She hadn't had cooking like this since the last time she'd eaten at her grandmother's. After she'd polished off the toast and drained the glass of her juice, she began hesitantly.

"Holling and I went through a pretty traumatic experience together. I guess you can say that we got about as close to death as anyone would like to come. You can't go through something like that and not share a bond. He saved my life. For that I'll be forever grateful."

"Pretty words from a pretty lady. It wasn't gratitude that passed between you two. I'm old but I'm not senile yet, Sawyer."

She shrugged again. "Well, whatever it is you thought you saw, it really doesn't matter. In a few days, I'll be on the road again."

"You in a hurry to leave us, Sawyer?" Nate's instincts were telling him again to have this girl checked out. He knew that Jon-Tyler had a few contacts in the sheriff's department. If there were warrants out on her, he would find out before the end of the day. What he'd do with the information, he didn't know. Would he pass it on to Jon-Tyler? Would it matter if he did? Instinct told Nate no. Jon-Tyler had already made up his mind about that girl. Don't go confusing him with the facts.

"I've got some things I need to take care of . . . some obligations I need to meet," Sawyer continued.

"And after that?"

"Who knows after that, Nate? I certainly don't."

"But your path could bring you back here again, huh? Nothing . . . or no one . . . stopping you from coming back if you really wanted to?" Like his son, he'd also examined her hands for a wedding ring.

"I go where I want to go. Do what I want to do," she said, a slight edge to her voice. "Where I go and how I go is really nobody's business but my own."

Nate backed off from his interrogation. "Well, if you've got a mind to go . . . at least go downstairs. I've got a stack of homemade buckwheat pancakes a mile high that I couldn't polish off. There's bacon and sausage and eggs and grits. I'd sure appreciate it if you made it your business to eat some of them so they won't go to waste."

That seemed to ease some of her tension. "Why so much food, Nate? You must be used to feeding an army."

"An army of one. Holling can really put it away. And when each of the rooms is occupied by guests, I want to make sure they leave here with full stomachs. No complaints. That's the best way to get repeat business."

"I'll try to do your breakfast justice. Sounds delicious," she said. "Let me jump in the shower and then I'll be down."

"Take your time, Sawyer. I'm plannin' to head out around noon to pick up Holling from the hospital."

She gave him Nate a curious look. "Why do you call him that?"

"What?"

"Your son. Why do you call him by his last name?"

Nate shrugged. "What else would I call him? It's what he calls himself. Always has, ever since he learned how to say his own name. He was about fourteen months old. Independent cuss."

"You say that like it's a bad thing."

Nate scratched his beard, considering her comment. "Too much independence can be a bad thing. Some folks might look at it like bullheadedness."

"You know, he's the spitting image of you."

"Do you think so?" Nate asked, his eyes crinkling at the corners.

Just like Holling's eyes, Sawyer thought. They had the same kindness reflected in them. The same mischievous gleam.

"He acts just like you," she said, pointing her finger at him.

"Actually, he's more like his mama," Nate corrected.

"Is Holling your only son?"

"No," Nate said. "He has an older brother, Shane Austin, and a younger sister, Aidan Elizabeth."

"Do they live here, too, with you? Holling hasn't mentioned them."

"Shane lives in Billings, to be closer to this job. And Aida Beth, that's what we call her, lives with her mama."

"What do Shane and Aida Beth do?" she asked curiously. As close as Holling and his father seemed to be, as proud as they were of their lifestyle, it seemed strange to Sawyer that other family members weren't also involved in the family business.

"Shane's into politics. He's an aide for the lieutenant governor."

"Really?" Sawyer raised her eyebrows, indicating that she was impressed. That seemed to win a few points with Nate. He puffed out his chest farther.

"Aida Beth's still in school. She's a grad student studying to be a . . . well, seein' that she's been in grad school goin' on . . . well . . . goin' on what seems to my bank account like forever, I guess she's studyin' to become a lifelong student."

"You must be very proud of them," Sawyer said.

"I am. I'm proud of all my kids. I just wish . . ." Nate cut himself off, shaking his head. He clapped his hands together and said with forced cheerfulness, "How 'bout you, Sawyer? Any brothers or sisters?"

"No. I'm an only child."

"Ahhh . . . no wonder," Nate said as if a mystery had suddenly been revealed to him.

"What does that mean?" Sawyer raised one eyebrow at him.

"You have a way about you."

"And what kind of way is that?" she said, amused.

"The kind of way of a person used to getting her way," Nate said bluntly. "In a word—spoiled rotten."

"I am not spoiled rotten," Sawyer huffed. She smiled self-consciously at him and said, "Not completely rotten. There's still a part of me at the core that hasn't been spoiled through and through."

"Then there's hope for you yet."

"Not if you and Holling keep treating me like royalty," Sawyer said, gesturing at the breakfast tray.

"Enjoy it while you can. You stick around here long enough, we'll put you to work. You being an only child, your family must be worried about ya," Nate said. "You give them another call today, all right? Let them know where you are. Call them on my dime."

"I'll pay you back, Nate, for all the kindness that you've shown me."

"Do you hear me asking for anything in return?" Nate sounded offended.

"No, you haven't," she agreed.

"I don't know what folks are like where you come from," he said sternly. "But around here, the only payback we expect for a kindness given is a kindness returned. Do you think you can handle that, little missy?"

"I can certainly try," Sawyer said earnestly.

Nate's face softened as he smiled. "Good." He then winked at her. "As long as you're our guest, I think we'll get along just fine."

Chapter 12

Holling couldn't wait to get out of there. If he could have made his escape any sooner he would have. But his street clothes were stuffed away in a plastic bag somewhere, practically unwearable. And he didn't think that he could manage a dignified escape trying to hold closed the rear opening of his hospital gown. When his pops called him that morning and told him that he'd be by around noon to get him, it couldn't be soon enough for Holling. He hated to admit it, but he was homesick. He missed his home, his own bed. His missed his father, and, he couldn't deny, Sawyer. He wondered how they'd gotten along last night. Sawyer wasn't the warmest person to get to know. And Pops wasn't the type to let a mystery stay mysterious for him for very long. If he didn't pester her with a hundred questions, he'd keep chattering at her until he got her to open up to him.

Holling lay on his back, his arms folded under his head, staring at the panels of the ceiling. When he got tired of counting panels, he pointed the remote control at the wall-mounted television and aimlessly flipped through the stations.

Flip. Flip. Flip. Static. Rerun of a sitcom. Cable movie that didn't interest him. News. He paused on that station. White Wolf didn't have a local news station. All of its television programming was broadcast through Billings. A reporter from the news station was standing on what Holling recognized as the main corridor through White Wolf. Behind him, what remained of Marjean's Café acted as the background. He turned up the volume.

"I'm standing here in front of what used to be the heart of White Wolf. As you can see by the mass of twisted metal, brick, and wood behind me, the destructive force of what some tornado chasers are calling a force-five tornado toppled buildings and destroyed landmarks that have withstood the test of time and the elements since the town's inception in 1865. Damage is estimated to be in the hundreds of thousands. At this hour, four persons are confirmed dead with nearly thirty still unaccounted for. Authorities are withholding the names of the deceased until all relatives have been notified."

Holling closed his eyes and sent up a small prayer. Whether the newscast revealed the names or no, chances were that he knew them and he felt the loss for those families.

"Local officials have already begun the labor-intensive task of sifting through the wreckage searching for the missing. And law enforcement have set barricades at both ends of the main strip, stopping all unnecessary traffic to try to prevent looting of local homes and businesses. Only vehicles with official business and those with valid proof of residency will be allowed through the roadblock.

"I have received word that the lieutenant governor is expected to fly in from the state capital tomorrow to tour several counties affected by the killer tornado. Whether or not the state will declare the towns affected a disaster area remains to be seen. I'll be bringing you live, up-to-the minute updates as soon they become available. This is Annette

Merlison, reporting live from White Wolf. Back to you, Peter."

He switched the channel, back to the predictable antics of a sitcom. A light tap on the door diverted his already shortened attention span.

"Good morning, Mr. Holling. How are you feeling today?"

"I was fine until I caught the news," he said.

"Oh, I know what you mean. Isn't it a crying shame? I don't ever remember a storm this bad."

The nurse pressed the control on the bed, raising him to a sitting position.

"You didn't eat your breakfast." She rattled the nearly full tray left beside the bed.

"I guess I wasn't hungry."

"Or are you expecting your father to sneak you in something to eat?" she asked accusingly. "Something with enough bad ingredients to keep you in this hospital bed for a month?"

"Busted," he said, lifting his hands in submission.

"You know, Mr. Holling, between you and me, I don't blame you." She fussed around him for a moment, checking his vital signs and noting the progress on his chart.

Holling submitted to her ministrations, listening to her friendly chatter with half an ear. He hadn't meant to tune her out. He was preoccupied. More than preoccupied. He was practically obsessed. Seeing the devastation on the television only reinforced his thinking.

Why was he still alive? Given the severity of the storm, there was no way that he and Sawyer should have survived it. As exposed as they were, as close as the tornado had come to them, they should have been at the top of the list of that reporter's statistics.

Yet, here he was alive and well enough to complain about the hospital food. It certainly gave a man something to think about. It isn't every day you're brought face-to-face so abruptly with your own mortality. If you're lucky like most folks, your own demise kinda sneaks up on you . . . steals your vitality bit by bit. A touch of gray here, an aching joint there. Eyes that don't see so clearly. Ears that don't hear so well. And before you know it, you're stretched out in a padded satin coffin, displayed for all of your loved ones to gawk at and reminisce about and squabble over your belongings.

He'd thought plenty about what he wanted on his headstone, enough to be able to recite it verbatim to Sawyer. But he hadn't thought much about the events that would cause someone to have to purchase one for him. He'd always figured that he had all the time in the world.

In that moment when he and Sawyer dove for the floor, hand in hand, side by side, he didn't necessarily see his life flash before his eyes. Not like he'd heard in books and movies. This was different. So completely different. Instead of reliving the events of his life, he took stock of how he'd lived it.

What kind of man had he become? What kind of person was he? As he lay down, waiting for the sky to come crashing down on him, he'd put his entire life in perspective. So much time wasted with inconsequential matters. So much emotion wasted. The times he was angry and impatient for events beyond his control could have been better spent. The hurts he'd been given and, in turn, had doled out to others, what was the sense in that? At the same time, his triumphs didn't seem all that grand, either. What was he doing chasing after material things—things that would fade or turn to dust?

Not that he felt he'd wasted his life. He led a good life, a life he'd been born into, and could at any time have walked away from. But he hadn't, because it suited him. Not like Shane and Aida Beth. He didn't exactly blame them for walking away from the Way, but he couldn't say that he understood it either. How could anyone walk away from something Holling considered about as close to paradise as one could get? White Wolf wasn't the biggest town on the map, but it had everything he needed. He couldn't ask for a better life than the one he had. He did as he wanted to do, came and went as he desired. He had good friends, made a good living. You don't walk away from a good thing. You just don't. Surviving that tornado only reinforced that belief. There were no guarantees in life. One minute you're waiting for a pecan pie. The next minute you're down on your knees, praying for your life. If that didn't put his life in perspective, he didn't know what did.

At least, up until yesterday, he thought that he'd had everything. That was before Sawyer Garth, the woman who'd blown him over with the ferocity of a tornado.

"I'm gonna get you for this, Pops," Holling said in a mixture of awe and amusement. Pops had put that whammy on him. Fixed it for him good. With the curse of his old man's prediction, what else could he do but fall in love with that little woman?

"You're where?"

The voice coming over the telephone line was staticky, breaking up every other word.

"I said I'm in Montana, Aunt Rosie. A little town called White Wolf. I'm . . . Hello? Hello? Can you hear me, Aunt Rosie? This is a really bad connection." Sawyer directed the last words to Nate, sitting across from her at the breakfast table.

"Honey, give me . . . your number. I'll . . . try . . . you back."

Sawyer placed her hand over the receiver. "She wants to try to call me back. Is it all right if I give her your number, Nate?"

"Sure, sure, no problem at all." He relayed the number to her. Sawyer spoke as clearly and as distinctly as she could, repeating the number several times before her aunt could give the number back without mistakes.

"Okay, Aunt Rosie. I'll wait by the phone until I hear from you."

She hung up the phone, shaking her head. "I could barely understand a word she said. I felt just like that geeky guy on those wireless television commercials. 'Can you hear me now? Can you hear me now?' I think she was somewhere on the road when I called. I could hear lots of traffic noise in the background."

"Is she the one you were on your way to meet, Sawyer?"

"Um-hmm . . . the ride was supposed to start in Seattle and go cross-country to Florida."

Seconds later, the cordless phone jangled in her hand. She passed the phone to Nate. "In case it's not her," she said.

"Hello?" Nate held the phone up to his ear. He paused as he listened for a minute. Covering the mouthpiece with his hand, he said, "You're right. It's not your aunt . . . but the phone is for you."

"For me?"

He passed it back to her as she looked up in surprise. "It's Holling."

"Hello?" she said into the phone.

"Sawyer, are you anywhere near a TV? Are you watching the news?"

"No, your father and I just sat down to breakfast."

"There's a portable over in the breakfast nook. Turn it on to channel five."

"He says to turn the television on to channel five," she relayed to Nate. He slid back from his seat, the wooden, mission-style chairs scraping across the linoleum floor.

Sitting on the shelf beside the coffeemaker and a toaster oven was a portable television. Nate turned it on, adjusted the antenna to clear up the reception, and then switched to the station Holling mentioned.

"It's on now, Holling," she said, swinging her chair around

so that she could see. Recognition was immediate. "Hey, that's—"

"Yep. Marjean's Café," he confirmed for her.

Sawyer watched as emergency rescue teams assisted the patrons who'd taken shelter in Marjean's storage room. The camera panned around the area, showing the bewildered, frightened, and confused faces as they were escorted out.

"I'm glad there weren't any camera crews around when we got out of there," Sawyer said with exaggerated relief.

"There's no telling where this footage is going to wind up. Just think, this may even make national news. Can you imagine seeing yourself on TV, after being all shut in, not having bathed for a couple of days?"

"I'm not nearly as worried about that as the fact that they say the camera puts twenty pounds on you," Sawyer said with misgivings.

"Like you should be worried. You could stand to put on a few pounds," Nate observed, noting that she hadn't really touched her second breakfast.

"Sawyer!" Holling said excitedly, his voice so loud that she pulled the phone away from her ear.

"I see it." She spoke almost over him. She stood up, moved closer to the television.

"What is it?" Nate wanted to know. "What's the matter?"

"See that?" she asked, touching the bottom right corner of the television with her fingertip.

Nate squinted at the screen. "Metal pipes. So what?"

"Not just any metal. Chrome," she said triumphantly. "Chrome exhaust pipes. Unless I miss my guess, that's my ride underneath all of that. I just hope she's all there."

"You're riding halfway across the country all alone on a motorcycle. You're the one who's not all there, little missy," Nate grumbled.

"How in the world are we going to get her out of there?" Sawyer said, more to herself than to Nate or Holling.

"I know some people in the sheriff's office," Holling told her. "I'll see if I can give them a call and get a wrecker truck out there. If not, as soon as I get of out here, I've got a flatbed truck that we use to haul hay. We'll dig it out ourselves, if we have to."

"I wonder if they'll let me down there to stand vigil over it." Sawyer had heard the on-the-scene reporter talking about the possibility of looting.

"The reporter said earlier that they're stopping everyone but official vehicles and residents. You can't go down there by yourself. You're gonna need one of us to go with you," Holling told her.

"Don't worry, Sawyer. That bike's not goin' anywhere," Nate assured her. "Holling will make sure of it. As soon as Holling is out of the hospital and he's feeling up to it, we'll head back into White Wolf and seeing about getting it towed to a repair shop."

"Ask Pops when he's coming to get me," Holling requested of Sawyer.

Sawyer passed the message on to Nate. "Holling wants to know when we're coming to pick him up."

"Oh, didn't I tell him?" Nate teased. He raised his voice, making sure Holling could hear him. "We're not coming to get him. I'm gonna get me a new son to take his place. One that has enough sense not to get caught up in a tornado."

"I am *not* telling him that," Sawyer said, clamping her hand over the phone and giving Nate a stern look.

"Why? Are you afraid he's not gonna help ya get your bike back?"

"Never mind," Holling said loudly. "I heard what he said. You tell that crotchety old man to come get me out of here or I'll make sure he never eats another pecan pie for as long as we both shall live."

"Holling says . . ." She started to relay the message verbatim, then improvised. "Holling says please come and get him. He's ready to come home."

Nate snorted in laughter. "You're sweet, but you're not gonna fool me with that whopper. I know my son. If anything, he's probably cursin' me and threatening me."

He held his hand out, asking for the phone. Sawyer passed it over to him.

"Ready to get off your lazy butt and get back to work, Holling?"

"More than ready. I wouldn't have stayed overnight if the doctor hadn't threatened to strap me down."

"You just sit tight, boy. We're on our way just as soon as Sawyer finishes her breakfast."

"I'm done," Sawyer insisted, pushing her plate toward the center of the table.

"No, you're not," Nate argued, shoving the plate back in front of her. "We don't let food go to waste around here. You sit down and don't you get up again until you finish off those eggs."

"Don't make her eat those, Pops. I know you and your cookin'."

"What do you mean?" Nate sounded offended.

"Eggs ain't supposed to crunch, Pops. The last time you scrambled some eggs for me, ya left half the shell in them."

"I was careful this time," Nate insisted. "Sawyer's our guest."

"Funny way for you to treat a guest," she said, resuming her seat at the table. "Ordering me around like you were some kind of drill sergeant."

"She's arguing with me, Holling. Is this the way she acted when you two met up at Marjean's?"

"Worse than that," Holling confirmed.

"Oh, I find that hard to believe."

"Don't let that little body fool you, Pops. She's got a temper."

"Yeah, we got a taste of that attitude in the hospital."

"What? What did he say about me?" Sawyer asked, straining to hear Holling's responses.

"Never you mind that. You get to eatin', little missy." Nate shooed her away.

She made a small sound of annoyance, but a moment later, Nate heard the sound of her fork scraping across her plate.

Nate moved away from her, deliberately turned his back, and whispered into the phone, "That's some kinda something you've gotten mixed up with, Holling."

"How's she doin', Pops?" Holling asked in concern.

"She looked a little puny last night. But after some good, hard sleep and a hot meal, she's lookin' less and less like some stray you dragged in off the street."

"Dragged is right. She didn't want to go down into Marjean's shelter. It was all I could to keep her inside the restaurant. If she could have, she would have hopped back on that bike of hers and taken off."

"She's runnin' from somethin', all right," Nate murmured. "Holling, are you sure she's not in some kinda trouble?"

"I'm not sure," Holling admitted. "I thought she was acting strange. But at Marjean's there was a state trooper. She didn't look nervous when he passed us. Maybe she's not wanted."

"Not in Montana, maybe," Nate observed. He glanced back at Sawyer. "I'm trustin' your judgment. I don't think she's dangerous, so I'm lettin' her stay. I put her up in Aida Beth's room."

"How long do you figure she's gonna stay?"

Nate then looked over his shoulder at her. "Hard to say. She's here for now. And with her bike being down, she won't be goin' anywhere anytime soon."

"Whatever it is she's runnin' from, I want to help her, if I can."

"Somehow I figured you'd say that. You wouldn't be a son of mine if you didn't want to help her."

"Oh, so now I'm a son again?"

Nate laughed. He'd forgotten that he'd threatened to replace Holling. "Hold that thought, boy. Somebody's tryin' to get me on the other line."

"See you in a while, Pops."

"Sure thing. We'll be there around noon to get you."

Nate pressed the button on the phone to switch over to the second line.

"Hello? . . . Yes, she is. Hold on a minute, please." He passed the phone back to Sawyer. "I think this is your aunt Rosie."

Sawyer gulped down the last of her orange juice and wiped her mouth with her napkin. "Aunt Rosie?" she said into the phone. "Oh yes, I can hear you. Tons better." She nodded at Nate, thanking him for the meal and the telephone privileges.

Nate gave her the thumbs-up sign, then motioned that he would leave her alone to hold her conversation in private.

"Sawyer, are you all right?" Rosie's voice was filled with concern.

"Yes, ma'am. I'm fine. I'm just . . . hanging here in Montana for a while, that's all."

"Montana? Who do you know in Montana?"

"A very nice family. The Hollings. They're putting me up for a few days while I get my bike worked on."

"Worked on? What's wrong with your bike, Sawyer?"

"How do I know? I'm not a mechanic," she snapped, instantly regretting her flippant tone. She knew as well as her aunt Rosie that Sawyer knew her bike well enough to be able to diagnose any problems, if not solve them, herself.

"How much work does it need, Sawyer?" Aunt Rosie said crisply.

Sawyer bit her lip, wondering how much to tell her aunt. She didn't want her to worry. "I'm not sure," she said truthfully. "I've got a mechanic lined up, but since it's the weekend, the shop could be backed up. Don't worry, Aunt Rosie. I should be able to meet up with you by the time you guys cross into Idaho."

"Are you sure, honey?"

"I'm sure, Aunt Rosie."

"How are you for cash? Do you have enough to cover the repairs and the storage fees, if you need to let it sit at the shop for a while?"

"I'm fine, Aunt Rosie. Don't worry."

"That's the second time you've told me not to worry. The first time, I'll let you get away with. You tell me not worry again and I'll be up for the next few nights with you on my mind."

"You don't have to worry about me, Aunt Rosie. I'm being well taken care of."

"If there's one thing I do know about you, Sawyer, it's that you'll always find someone to watch out for you."

"Listen, Aunt Rosie, I've got to go. If you need to, you can reach me at this number."

"What about your cell phone?"

"I dropped it in the water," Sawyer said truthfully. "It's on the blink. But I've got the phone insured so I'll replace it in a day or so."

"You're having all kinds of issues on this road trip, aren't you?"

Sawyer wanted to laugh. Her aunt didn't know how close to the truth she came.

"If you need me, you be sure to call me, Sawyer."

"I will, Aunt Rosie. I promise."

"Then I'll see you in a couple of days?"

"Two or three at the most."

"We only plan to be in Idaho a day or two. If it looks like

you're running behind, let me know. If I have to make a side run through Montana to get you, you know I will."

"Thanks for the offer, but I don't think it'll come to that."

"Give the Hollings my best, will you?"

"I certainly will, Aunt Rosie. You take care now."

"Talk to you in a couple of days."

"Bye."

Sawyer pressed the key to hang up the phone, then blew out a long, relieved breath. She hated not being completely honest with her aunt. Aunt Rosie had always been so good to her. But if she found out just how close to death Sawyer had come, she'd be here in White Wolf so fast, folks around here would think they'd been hit by another twister. If she didn't get on the road fast and allay her fears, Aunt Rosie might even have a talk with Shiri. Under a full-force interrogation, Shiri would have to crack. She'd have to tell all. Sawyer couldn't fault her. She was having a hard time keeping her mouth shut, and her aunt Rosie wasn't even providing much pressure. No, the best thing to do would be to get on the road, meet up with her aunt, and tell what she had to tell in her own time, and in her own way. But first, she had to get that bike back.

Chapter 13

Rosie Kincaid snapped her cell phone closed and slid it back into its black leather protective case. She stared at the phone for several seconds, noting the length of time she'd talked with Sawyer. Only six minutes. Not very much time at all, counting all the worrying that she'd done. Maybe she was being paranoid. After all, Sawyer wasn't supposed to meet her until the end of May for the official start of the ride. But when Shiri had called her, told her that Sawyer had taken off four days ago, Rosie sensed something was wrong.

"Is everything all right, Rosie?" Meghan Ogden, her sidecar-riding partner, asked as Rosie sat down at the table to eat.

"Hmm?" Rosie said distractedly.

"I said, is everything all right?" she repeated, slightly raising her voice.

"Yes, I think so. Why do you ask?"

"I don't know. You have a funny look on your face. Like something is bothering you."

"I finally got in touch with my niece Sawyer."

"So, is she going to be joining us or what?" Tory Ogden, Meghan's sister, asked.

"I think so. But in a few days. She ran into some trouble and needed some work done on her bike."

"What a shame," Willa Decker murmured. She dug her fork into her pile of chili cheese fries. "I was looking forward to meeting her."

"You will. Just not yet," Rosie assured her.

"What kind of bike trouble?" Tory wanted to know.

"I don't know that either. She was having a mechanic look at it."

"I thought you said your niece was a heart-and-soul biker bitch," Meghan said.

Her sister Tory elbowed her in the ribs. "Watch your mouth, Meg."

"I didn't mean any disrespect, Rosie. I just meant—"

"I know what you meant, Meghan," Rosie said, smiling to show that she wasn't offended by Meghan's choice of words. "I'm a bit surprised myself that Sawyer didn't know what was wrong with it. I made her take classes when she bought that bike, riding classes and a mechanic's course. She shouldn't have been that clueless. That's not like her."

"Where is she now?"

"Somewhere in Montana."

"Montana? That wasn't a stop on our road trip," Willa said. Washington, Idaho, Colorado, Utah, finally ending up in Texas.

"I know. She took off on her own, following her own map."

"Why are you so worried? I thought you said your niece was a free spirit," Tory said. "Seems to me from what you've told us about her, she's expected to do this kind of thing."

"She's a free spirit, but she's not stupid. If she's going to be traveling alone, she usually lets someone know where she's going. Not days after she's gotten there. I hate to admit it, but Sawyer's got some growing up to do. When she takes off, she usually wants someone to come after her. Not this time. This didn't feel like a usual Sawyer-style stunt."

"If you ask me," Willa said, "when a woman takes off and doesn't tell anyone else where she's going, it's because she doesn't want anyone else to know what she's doing. Myself, when I go incognito, it's because I'm running off to spend too much money or I'm going to meet my man."

"I don't think that's it. Sawyer doesn't need to hide how she spends. As for the other, she has a man. Ryan." Rosie's riding mates didn't have to guess what Rosie's opinion of him was. They could tell by the way she scrunched up her face when she spoke.

"He can't be that much of a man if he lets her go off to do who knows what whenever she wants to," Meghan commented.

"Do you think they had a fight?" Tory asked.

"A fight bad enough to make her wind up in Montana? If things were that bad, she would have put him out," Rosie said confidently.

"Like I said, maybe she's gotten something better that she's running to, rather than running away from what she has back there," Willa insisted. She gave a sly look all around the table. "I hear they grow 'em big and strong in Montana."

"And they do it with their boots on," Meghan chimed in.

The round of snickers from the table helped to ease the worry lines from Rosie's face. But not by much.

"Don't worry, Rosie," Willa said soothingly, patting her friend on the shoulder. "If Sawyer's anything like you at all, she knows how to take care of herself."

Chapter 14

"What are you doing, Holling? I thought the doctor told you to take it easy," Sawyer chastised him.

Holling strolled around the corner of the house, whistling a popular tune he'd heard on the radio that morning. A coil of rope was slung over his shoulder. He didn't see Sawyer as she sat on the shady side of the front porch, sipping a glass of iced tea and fanning herself with the sports section of the newspaper.

Startled, he looked up, placing his hand against his forehead to shield himself from the midafternoon sun's glare.

"Sawyer." He sounded surprised to see her.

"That's right. It's me. Who were you expecting?" She stood up and leaned over the porch rail to peer down at him.

"What are you doing here? I thought you'd gone shopping with Pops."

"Nope. I decided to stay here."

"Why?"

"I wasn't going to let him spend any more money on me."

"I thought we talked about that."

"We did," she confessed. "And you two came to a decision that you would spoil me. I just reversed that decision. I'm glad I didn't go. I knew you'd pull a stunt like this, Holling." She pointed to the rope. "Where do you think you're going with that? You're supposed to be in bed."

"You two talked about that," he said, mimicking her. "So I reversed that decision."

"Are you trying to wind up back in the hospital?"

"I feel fine, Sawyer," he insisted. "I've been sitting on my butt for three days now. If I don't get up and do something, I'll go stir-crazy."

"You haven't been just sitting," she reminded him. "Face it, Holling. You don't know the meaning of taking it easy. You're up at five o'clock in the morning, meeting with the ranch foreman or the other hands, directing the repair tasks, updating your Web site, going over payroll receipts. If your father or I weren't by your side every minute of the day, you'd be pushing it even more that."

"I can't help it, darlin'. I'm a man on a mission."

"Well, I'm here as mission control and I'm telling you to get back to bed." She pointed back toward the house.

"You sure you want to send me back?"

"Now, what kind of question is that?"

"Well, I was thinkin', as soon as I finish this one last chore, we could go into White Wolf to see about your bike."

"Really!" Sawyer said excitedly. "You mean it, Holling?"

"I told you I feel better."

"So, what's this chore? What can I do to help?" she asked eagerly.

Holling hesitated. Up until now, he'd welcomed Sawyer's company. With her hovering over him, tending to him, she'd kept him distracted, entertained. Going through stacks and stacks of paper wasn't his most favorite part of running the ranch. Still, it had to be done.

"Matías told me that one of the mares is in heat. We're

gonna try to breed her to his stud. I promised him her first colt could be his. I'm gonna give him a hand."

"What do you mean give him a hand? I thought you just put the two together and let nature take its course," she said, clasping her hands together as if it were that simple.

Holling laughed at her. "Well, it goes something like that. But his stud is a little . . . um . . . inexperienced. Sometimes nature needs a helping hand . . . additional coaxing."

"Cool . . . this should be interesting," Sawyer said, skipping down the stairs to join him at the side of the house. While recuperating, she'd been sketching out some ideas for her next novel. Witnessing an actual breeding process would lend an air of authenticity to her story that she didn't think she could get through the library or browsing online.

Holling held up his hand, the smile suddenly gone from his face. "Where do you think you're going?"

"With you," she said simply. "To help."

"No . . ." he said hesitantly. "I don't think so. I think me and Matías can handle this one without you, Sawyer."

"Why not?"

"I don't think this is something you need to see."

"You've got to be kidding." Sawyer laughed at him, but there was very little mirth in her tone.

"No, I'm not kidding."

"Why not!" This time all the laughter was gone from her face. Holling could tell by her expression that she wasn't used to anyone telling her no. She didn't like it. She didn't like it at all. "Is this some macho, cowboy, not wanting to offend my delicate senses crap?"

"It doesn't have anything to do with that, Sawyer," Holling denied.

"I don't believe you." She narrowed her eyes at him, stabbed at his chest with her finger.

"Believe what you want. I told you, Matías's horse is young

and wild. It'll take the two of us to keep him from getting out of hand. I don't want you in the way and getting hurt."

"I won't be in the way," she protested. "I'll just sit up in the loft and—"

"No!" Holling said flatly. "Once we're done, I'll sit down and tell you what you need to know."

"I don't need anyone censoring me . . . or filtering for me, Holling. I want to know for myself. I'm a writer."

"Then use your writer's imagination," he retorted, stalking away from her.

Sawyer started after him. Holling whirled around. "I mean it. Wait for me back up at the house."

"What's the matter with you, Holling? I don't see what's the big deal. It's just a couple of horses f—"

He put his hand over her mouth, giving her a look that would have cowed any of the hands working for him.

"If I had time, I'd wash your mouth out with soap," he threatened.

"You just try it," she shot back. Muffled though it was through his gloved fingers, her response didn't lose any of its venom.

"You wait for me back at the house," he repeated. "I'll be back in an hour or so. We can head out after that, if you mind yourself, that is."

When Holling pulled his hand away, Sawyer backed away from him, her eyes reflecting her anger and her disappointment. He leaned toward her, to kiss her, but she froze, her body posture sending him a clear signal.

Holling turned back toward the barn. Ahead of him, Matías was standing near the entrance. He'd witnessed their exchange, but knew by Holling's expression not to make mention of it.

The stables had a double-sided entrance. As Holling approached him, Matías swung one of the doors facing the house closed. Holling stepped inside, then indicated that Matías swing the other door closed.

The mare was already in her stall.

"Go on and get her ready," Matías said. "I've got Blaze tied off in the roping pen."

Passing the rope to Matías, Holling indicated with a simple nod to bring in his horse. Matías turned to leave, then looked back. Holling could feel him staring at him.

"Something you wanted to say, Matías?" he prompted.

"Just that . . . not that it's any of my business, but if you care to know what I think . . . I think you did the right thing, boss."

Holling didn't say anything in response. Matías took his silence as permission to go on. He never had to guess where he stood with Mr. Holling. If he didn't like something, he was quick to let you know.

"Miss Sawyer, she's a lady. I mean, anybody can see that. We all can." He gave a dry chuckle, but when Holling swung his gaze to him, he straightened his face. "Meaning no disrespect, Mr. Holling. But a lady needs to be treated like a lady. And some things a lady has got no business seeing. I wouldn't let my lady watch. No, sir. Not me."

Holling thought about the last few days. He hadn't been able to do much around the ranch. Physical activity was kept to a minimum. The time he wasn't doing paperwork, he'd spent sitting by the window and watching Pops escort Sawyer around. From what Pops had told him, she'd shown a genuine interest in everything about his business, his home—asking plenty of questions, taking notes, interviewing the hands. Not once had they complained that she was interfering or getting in the way of their business. Like Matías said, they were all too busy watching her.

The one time Pops thought she might be squeamish, she had barely batted an eyelash. He and Red Bone had taken her to a section of open range, looking for one of the cows that he'd been told was due to drop a calf at any time. The timing couldn't have been more perfect if Pops had orchestrated everything himself. They'd gone as far as they could in Pops's truck, gotten out, and walked through a section of the underbrush. There, in front of God, open sky, and Sawyer's wide green eyes, she witnessed a live birth.

"For a minute, I thought the girl was gonna puke her guts out," Red Bone admitted to Holling when he came to give him a report. "But she turned out to be a real trooper. She sucked it up . . . and after it was all over, had a million questions."

Holling wondered whether he'd done Sawyer a disservice by turning her away. He knew that she wasn't delicate. So, why had he forbidden her to watch?

"Just go get the horse, Matías," Holling said gruffly, more irritated at himself for second-guessing his decision than he was at Sawyer for being the cause of his wavering. He knew why he didn't want her to be there. He wasn't always at his best during this part of the job. A facet of his personality that he wasn't ready to reveal to her sometimes came out when he was working with the horses. The language grew a little coarser. The running commentary between him and the workers as they did what they had to do to coax or manipulate the brood mare and stud wasn't necessarily their Sunday best. Sometimes the conversation could be borderline vulgar. And he didn't want Sawyer to see him like that. Not yet.

Never mind that she'd already seen many facets of his personality so far. Flirtatious when he first met her. Frozen in fear and humbled in prayer. Injured and unconscious. Steadfast when all he wanted to do was run. Calm when he wanted to fly apart. Generous without expectations of reciprocity. Whether he realized it or not, whether it was deliberate or not, he was building a case for himself with her. He was trying to put his best face forward. Not that he didn't think he could turn away. Holling didn't know. He didn't know what type of man she was used to dealing with. He didn't know what kind of man she had back home. Whatever kind of man he was, he wanted to be sure that the one standing right here, right now, before her, was the one she wanted to keep. He could ruin all of that with a single word, a thoughtless gesture if he wasn't too careful. And *that's* why he didn't want her in that stable with him.

He opened the stall to the mare, soothing her as she moved back and forth in the stall with marked impatience. She would barely hold still as he slid a halter over her nose and behind her ears. It was as if she knew what was about to happen. He could barely attach a lead rope to her as she started for the stall gate. She could sense the presence of the stud. As Matías brought him through the opposite end of the stable, the stud trumpeted out, announcing his presence to the mare.

She neighed back—shrill and impatient.

"Easy . . . easy there now, girl," Holling said, turning her around. He backed her out of the stall, making it easier to control her speed and direction. If he'd brought her out head-first, he knew that she would have taken off without him to answer the stud's call. Her hooves slid through the hay, kicking up dust as she tried to increase her pace.

"Guess these two don't need an introduction," Matías commented. He kept a short rope on his own horse, keeping his head level, and curbing the stud's natural instinct to rear up. Instinct was driving him. But he had to learn to take instruction. If they let him try to mount the mare before she was ready, it could result in wasted time and effort. An inexperienced stud with plenty of will and stamina was no good to them if he was off the mark.

"At least give him a chance to ask her name," Holling teased.

"What then, boss? Dinner and a movie? I think he's wanting to dispense with the formalities."

Matías guided his horse around the mare, walking him in a circle around her, waiting for her to respond. She did so by turning her rear end to the stud.

"Guess that says it all," Matías confirmed. He sniffed, noting the pungent air. He knew that smell. Raw. Natural. There was no guessing. It was time.

Holling backed the mare to the center of the stable, making sure that she had plenty of room to maneuver. Unlike the inexperienced stud, she knew the routine and what was expected of her.

"Give him some more slack, Matías," Holling directed, as the stud nearly bowled him over trying to reach the mare. He pushed his chest in Matías's back, nudging him forward.

"I don't know, boss." Matías shook his head in mock dismay. "As hot to trot as he is, he could probably reach her from here. You ought to know how that goes, eh, boss?"

Holling estimated the distance still between them at two, maybe two and a half feet.

"You call that a compliment?" Holling retorted.

"Sorry, boss. Didn't mean to offend you."

"That stud of yours ain't got nothin' on me."

"No, sir. I don't expect it does," Matías said agreeably. "Looks to me like she's ready for him."

Holling guided his mare back until they'd reached the middle of the stable. Once Matías had given the stud enough rope to maneuver, the rest, as Sawyer had been so astute to mention, was up to nature. The stud reared up on powerful hind legs, pawing the air, before resting his front hooves on the mare's back and closing with her. There wasn't much for Holling and Matías to do at that point but wait until the stud had completed his task.

"Should we hit her again?" Matías asked as he backed his horse away. "Just for good measure."

"You sure Blaze can handle it?" Holling teased him,

knowing that Matías closely identified with his horse. A slur against one went against the other.

"He can go all night long if he has to," Matías bragged.

"Every stud's fantasy," Holling returned. They performed their routine again. Circling the horses. Letting them get acquainted. Watching and waiting. A third time for good measure, then Holling led the mare back into her stall.

He wiped a thin bead of sweat from his forehead with the back of his sleeve. With only one door open, there hadn't been much of a breeze through the stable. As he stepped back outside, felt the air stirring his clothing, he knew that he probably smelled as drenched as he looked. He unbuttoned his shirt, fanning the two halves to cool his skin.

"I appreciate it, boss," Matías said.

"Don't thank me yet. Not until we see if it took. We'll try a couple more times this week, as long as she's showin' that she's in heat."

"Yes, sir."

"I'm headin' back to the house. Make sure you give Blaze an extra helping of feed. He's gotta keep his strength up."

"He's a horse of mine. That means he's keepin' up more than this strength, boss," Matías retorted.

Chapter 15

Shaking his head, Holling started back for the house. A quick shower. A bite to eat. And then he'd keep his promise to Sawyer. As he approached the stairs leading to the front porch, he looked over to his right, only half expecting to see her still there. She wasn't. Her pitcher of iced tea and the newspaper were gone.

Holling pushed open the screen door, calling out to her.

"Sawyer?"

No answer.

Probably still sulking, Holling thought in irritation. Maybe he shouldn't have put his hand over her mouth. That was a bit much. But he hadn't expected her to swear at him, either. Not that he hadn't heard the word before. Or even used it himself on occasion. But as Matías had said, Sawyer was a lady. And the way he'd been raised, language like that just wasn't used in polite company. Old-fashioned maybe. But Holling figured there'd be fewer confrontations in the world if more people remembered their manners.

"Come on, Sawyer. Don't be mad," he cajoled, calling through the house. Holling peeked into the kitchen to see if she was there. Not there, either. Not in the study. Not in the common room.

Climbing the stairs, he prepared himself to form an apology. He wasn't going to apologize for not allowing her into the stable. He had no regrets about that. But he would admit to being sorry for threatening to wash her mouth out with soap. That wasn't any kind of way to win points with her.

Turning the corner, he headed for his younger sister's old room.

"Sawyer?" He tapped on the door lightly with his knuckles. "You still mad at me? Are you gonna hold a grudge against me all the way into White Wolf? You still want to go, don't you?"

When he didn't get an answer, he blew out a small sigh of frustration. "All right, then. So you're not talking to me. I'm gonna grab a shower and somethin' to eat. Maybe by then you'll feel more like talkin'. All right?"

As he started to turn away, he thought he heard her stirring around behind the door. He was going to leave, but then he heard the fall of footsteps. Soft. Hesitant at first, almost as if she was debating whether or not she wanted to open the door.

A moment later the door creaked open and Sawyer stood looking out at him. Her expression was unreadable. She leaned against the doorjamb, only her head poking out.

"Hey," he said, for lack of anything better to say.

"So, are you all done playing matchmaker?" she asked, her tone mocking.

"Yeah. We're all done."

"Just so you know, Holling, I wouldn't have been in the way. I just wanted to see what it was all about. I can't help it. I'm curious."

"I know," he admitted. "And next time . . . well, we'll see about next time," he conceded without making any definite promises.

She stepped back, pushed the door closed, then jerked it open again. "I'm sorry I cursed at you," she said. She made a face, almost as if it was painful for her to make that admission. "Some of the folks I used to hang with . . . well, with them, it wasn't anything but a word. It didn't mean anything."

"Just a word," he agreed. "And . . . I'm sorry I was gonna wash your mouth out with soap."

"You wouldn't have tried," she said, lifting her chin defiantly at him.

Holling stepped back to the door, leaning his arm against it, opening it an inch farther. Sawyer didn't back away, even though this was much closer than she would have let him get when she'd just met him. They'd been through so much together, and she was still having trouble letting him inside her personal space.

For someone so little, Holling mused, *she certainly requires a lot of room.*

"Were you tryin' to push my buttons?" he asked, wondering why she was trying to goad him. Why was she trying to push him away?

"Did it work?" she asked.

"I don't think I'm gonna tell you, Sawyer. You might make that a bad habit of tryin' to push me."

"And you don't like to be pushed around," she concluded.

"No, ma'am. I sure don't."

"And you think I do? I've got just as much pride as you, Jon-Tyler Holling. Probably more pride in my finger than you've got in your whole body," she said, stabbing at him in the chest with her index finger.

Holling reached up and caught her hand. Stroking it gently, he asked, "You don't think I know that? I figured that out from the moment you walked through Marjean's door. What do you think it was that drew me over to you?"

"My leather chaps?"

"Well," he drawled, "that, too."

"Aha! So you were checking me out."

"I'm not denying it." He shook his head. "I told you from the start that I wanted to get to know you better. Remember?"

Sawyer nodded. "I remember. Funny, but it was only a few days ago."

"But it feels like a lifetime, doesn't it, Sawyer?"

"Yes," she admitted reluctantly. "Why do you think that is, Holling?"

"Simple," he said, leaning toward her, testing her to see if she would back away. When she didn't, Holling moved even closer, making her back up to restore the distance between them.

"So, what's the answer, if it's so simple?" she said, realizing that he was deliberately herding her back into the room. There wasn't much space in the room to start with. Most of that was taken up by the huge four-poster bed.

"You already know," he said, giving her that half smile that she was finding harder and harder to resist. Sawyer wasn't mad at him anymore. She couldn't be. Not when he looked at her like that . . . with that little-boy mischievousness. For a moment, she wondered about Holling as a child. She wondered about the kinds of trouble he'd gotten himself into and how something as simple as a smile could have gotten him out.

The look he was giving her now wasn't childish. However, it was trouble. Trouble for her. It was making her forget. The burning anger she'd felt for his rough handling of her earlier now simmered to a low boil. The white-hot flare of anger that had seared her brain and fired her imagination with all kinds of awful names she could call him, or evil, vengeful things she could do to him, now settled into her stomach, radiated outward, so that she felt that she was melting.

The way he looked at her now, Sawyer knew that there

might be some more rough handling to be done. But that could be on both their parts. The way he looked at her, she wanted his hands on her. And hers on him.

"Maybe I don't know. Humor me," she said, borrowing one of Nate's phrases, talking fast to stop herself from thinking. With her active imagination, she could envision all kinds of things he could be doing to her in this tiny room, on that huge bed.

"Nothin' funny about what I'm feelin' for you, Sawyer," he said.

Sawyer kept backpedaling, until she felt herself collide with the corner post of the bed.

"Holling," she said, putting up one hand to ward him off.

"What?" He put his hands on her waist, drawing himself to her.

Sawyer felt the warmth of his broad chest against hers. "Didn't you say that you were going to take a shower?"

"Do I smell that bad?" He was laughing at her as he said it.

"You smell like . . . like . . ." She fumbled for the right word. It frustrated her that as a writer she was at a loss to find the perfect word to express herself.

"Hot, steamy, animal sex?" he said suggestively, lowering his head to kiss her neck. He didn't stop at her neck, but continued down her shoulder, over her collarbone, then on toward the swell of her breast.

Sawyer gasped aloud, "Yes!" That was it. The right word. And just the right spot.

"I'm pleased to know you're so agreeable," he said, hooking his long leg around her and falling over so that they both landed on the bed.

"Holling!" Sawyer exclaimed in protest, but she was laughing, even as they bounced several times on top of the plush, springy mattress. Holling stretched her arms above her head, pinning her wrists to the bed as he covered her body with his own.

"I thought the doctor said no physical exertion!" she said.

"This isn't exertion," he contradicted. "This is recreation in its purest form."

"I'm serious, Holling," she said, trying to squirm away from him without much success. He pinned her to the bed. The more she wiggled, the more she realized that she was only making matters worse. He mimicked the gentle undulating sway of her hips, coaxing her until her movements seemed less like protest, more like permission.

"So am I, Sawyer," he retorted. He brought one of her hands down, slid it between them, cupping it over the bulge in his jeans.

"But the doctor said—" she began.

"Forget what the doctor said! You're the cure for what's ailin' a man, Sawyer," he said, kissing her and effectively stopping her protest.

He hadn't been feeling exactly right since he'd kissed her that day at Marjean's. At first he thought it was his injuries causing his discomfort. After leaving the hospital, he blamed his feeling ill at ease on the medication. When he'd talked to his doctor and described his symptoms, the doctor had assured him that an increased sex drive was not one of the side effects of the antibiotic. If anything, it should have had just the opposite effect on him. It wasn't a medical ailment he had . . . but a physical one. Or, his pops had said, laughing at him, a hormonal one.

Sawyer moaned despite herself. Her breath came in ragged pants as Holling lifted her T-shirt. His laid his palms across her breasts, kneading, massaging, tweaking her nipples until they swelled and tingled with sweet torturous burning. Ryan had never made her feel this way about herself. Sometimes, when he came to her, she had the feeling that she could have been anybody. Any warm body would have sufficed.

She hadn't realized what was missing in her relationship with Ryan until now, though the passion must have been there at one time. She couldn't imagine opening up her heart, and her home, to Ryan without feeling that she wanted him to be there. Yet, somewhere along the way, something changed. She didn't know how, or when, or even why. She just knew that it wasn't the same.

When Ryan reached for her in the middle of the night, she'd always submitted. Mechanical. Predictable. She simply allowed him to do what he wanted for the sake of preventing an argument and his hurt feelings the next day. While he sweated and strained over her, she allowed her mind to wander, to travel back to the time when she thought she had enjoyed his midnight attention.

When he rolled over off her, she rolled over, too. Turned her back to him, closed her eyes tight, and pretended that that's the way things were supposed to be between a man and a woman. What did she expect? Fireworks each and every time? Impossible. It was the stuff of fairy tales. It was the kind of stuff she wrote about. She didn't actually believe she could expect to feel that way forever.

It shouldn't have come as a surprise to her that the condom had failed. Everything else about their relationship had failed. The fire. The commitment. The passion. It had slipped away from them so quietly she didn't even notice its passing. She'd even convinced herself that all of her passion was poured into her writing. As long as her characters sizzled on the page, there was no reason to expect that she could experience that in real life.

Until now. Holling showed her how it could be . . . how it should have been all along. As Holling kissed her, smoothed his hands over her, he was getting to know her. He was exploring, taking the time to discover what she liked, what she needed. Sawyer didn't leave him guessing. When he was right, dead-on, her throaty cries were confirmation.

She wrapped her arms around his head, cradling him to her. When she felt his lips brush against her breast, she lifted it to him, offering him more.

Holling reached for the waistband of her shorts and slid his hand palm downward. "Let me in, Sawyer," he said, huskily.

Not just into her body. Into her life. And into her heart.

Sawyer didn't know how she knew his desire was three-fold. She knew. She sensed it.

"No!" Sawyer suddenly cried out. Panic gripped her. She pushed against Holling with all her strength, rolling away from him. She sat up and clung to the bedpost with both arms wrapped around it.

"Sawyer?" He was completely bewildered by her sudden reversal. He'd had women turn him down before. Even some who'd waited until the point of no return before slamming the brakes on him. But not like this. He'd never given anyone reason to be afraid of him. He reached out, laid his hand gently on her shoulder.

"Darlin', are you all right?"

She shook her head, speechless. Even she wasn't sure what had come over her.

"I'm sorry, Sawyer," he said, anguished. "If you didn't want me touch you—"

"It's n-not you, Holling," she stammered. "I . . . just . . . just . . ."

"Maybe it's just too soon," he said soothingly. He touched her shoulder. A simple squeeze. Just to let her know that he could touch her without expecting more from her. "I shouldn't have pressed, Sawyer. I'm sorry. I guess I'm feeling a little . . . I don't know. There's no excuse for it." He shrugged.

"That must be it," she agreed. "It's too soon."

But Sawyer knew it was more than that. It had less to do

with Holling's behavior than her own. She was behaving foolishly, recklessly. As much as she wanted him, she couldn't be thinking about herself now. The decisions she made now affected her life and the life growing inside her.

He stood up, pulled his clothing back in order. "If you're still ready, I'll take you into White Wolf in a bit."

"I'll be ready," she said and smiled up at him gratefully, not only for keeping his promise, but for keeping his distance.

Chapter 16

The sheriff's deputy assigned to the White Wolf north entrance roadblock waved his hand, flagging Holling down as he drew closer to him.

"Better pull over," Nate advised, tapping his son on the shoulder. He sat in the backseat of his club-cab Ford truck and offered advice. "I don't think they're playing around with this roadblock business."

"It's just Parmon Mace," Holling said. "We've known each other since the third grade. I don't think Mace will give us any trouble letting us pass."

"Parmon Mace. You mean that kid who had the awful allergies? Always had the runny nose?" Nate asked.

"Yep. That's him."

"Then you'd better be sure to stop. If only just to hand the boy a box of Kleenex."

"Or I could speed up, run him over, and put him out of his misery," Holling teased.

"You sound like you don't like him," Sawyer observed.

"Holling's still mad because once in the third grade the boy left his snotty rag on Holling's desk," Nate said.

"The third grade?" Sawyer said incredulously. She'd wondered what kind of trouble he'd gotten into as a kid. "You've been mad at him since you were about nine years old? That must be some kind of record for holding a grudge."

"Holling specializes in grudges," Nate said as Holling rolled to a stop, put his truck in park, then let down the window. "In fact, once his brother—"

"Let it go, Pops," Holling said. As he pulled up alongside the sheriff's deputy standing next to his cruiser, he warned his father, "No snot jokes."

"Who, me?" Nate said, raising his eyebrows innocently. He then gave a sniff of disdain—loud and exaggerated. Holling shifted, reached into his back pocket, and pulled out a bandana. He tossed it at his father. "I could use this to stuff your mouth, you know."

"What's the world comin' to, Sawyer, when a son threatens his father's life because of a few sniffles?"

Holling rolled down his window and called out in greeting, "How's it goin', Officer Mace?"

"Hey, Holling. Is that you?"

The officer dipped his head, peered over his sunglasses at him.

"Sure is. What are you doin' out here, Parmon? They got you out here in this hot sun, huh?" Holling said cordially.

Sawyer raised her eyebrows, but said nothing. Holling didn't sound like a man who was holding a grudge. He sounded very friendly. If he was holding a grudge, he wasn't showing it. She filed that information away in the back of her mind. A man who knew how to set aside his differences to get what he wanted. She hadn't seen that behavior modeled in a while. When Ryan was upset, she knew it. Everybody knew it. He wasn't above throwing a tantrum or two to get his way. He'd called it being intense. Sawyer called it being a big, whiny titty-baby.

"Yeah, you know how it is. Same ole same ole," Mace responded, leaning against the door. He peered inside the truck, nodded at Nate. "How are you doing, Mr. Nate?"

"Oh, I can't complain. Though all of this wind kickin' up has got the pollen messing with my allergies."

Holling shot his father a look, then glanced meaningfully at the bandana.

"I can certainly understand that." Mace reached into his pocket and pulled out a handkerchief. "Excuse me," he said through the cloth after clearing his sinuses. He then glanced apologetically at Sawyer.

"Ma'am," he said, touching his hand to the brim of his department-issued straw hat.

Sawyer smiled back. "Hello."

"What's goin' on with you, Holling?" Mace asked him.

"Trying to pick up the pieces like everybody else."

"Your place wasn't hit too hard, was it?"

"Not too bad, though I wasn't there when the twister blew through. I was at Marjean's."

"Mother Nature sure did a number on that place."

"Yep. She sure did."

"I hear the lieutenant governor is supposed to be coming in for a personal tour. What do you know about that?"

"Yeah, I'd heard that, too."

"Looks like it's the season for visitors," Mace continued, looking pointedly at Sawyer. Though Holling couldn't see Mace's eyes behind the dark, wraparound sunglasses, he could tell by Mace's posture what was on his mind. The way he leaned into the truck, the slight movement of his head—he was checking Sawyer out from head to foot. He must have liked what he saw, because he kept looking at her, even while he was making small talk with Holling and his father.

Holling couldn't fault the man for looking. Sawyer was something to look at. She wore a pale green, button-up, spaghetti-strap top with a matching lightweight sweater. Her button-fly blue denims rode low on her slim hips. Her hair was pulled back away from her face into a ponytail, wispy bangs covering her forehead and hanging in tendrils around her ears. She wasn't wearing much makeup that he could tell. Maybe a little gloss that added just a touch of sheen to her full mouth. It didn't fit the image of the tough-talking biker woman who'd walked into Marjean's with plenty of attitude.

Holling resisted the urge to knock Mace's arms off the truck. He didn't blame the man for looking, but that didn't mean that he had to like it.

"How long do you think a roadblock is gonna be necessary, Officer Mace?" Nate asked.

"Oh, I don't know. As long as it takes to get the town back on its feet, I guess."

"A long time for you to be up on *your* feet, huh?"

"I don't mind. You get to meet some interesting folks this way, Mr. Nate," he said. "Mighty interesting." He paused, swinging his head to look at Sawyer again.

Being subtle wasn't getting him anywhere with Holling. Mace tried a different tactic. "So, Holling, you gonna introduce me to your lady friend? So I can add her to the watch list," Mace said quickly. "We've already had some reports of looters. Vultures sweepin' in and taking advantage of folks' misery and gettin' away clean. Folks gettin' so bold these days. Like they don't even care. You know that camera crew out of Billings caught some sticky-fingered lowlifes bustin' into Circuit City? They just backed their truck right up through the front window, smashed it in, and loaded up as much as they could carry."

"You gotta be kiddin' me." Holling whistled.

"You think that if a body was driving around in a tricked-out, suped-up Dodge that could be spotted for miles around, you wouldn't want to use it to do a smash and grab. But folks are stupid. Or don't care. And you know what the killer thing about all this is? The camera crew didn't do a damned thing about it. Didn't lift a finger to try to stop them. Just kept on filming and afterward promised to turn a copy of the tape over to us so we could try to hunt 'em down. They had to keep the original so it would wind up on the six o'clock news. I swear, I just don't know where people's heads are at these days. I don't know what's worse, those ambulance-chasin' reporters or those lowlifes makin' the news to bring 'em out here," Mace said, turning his attention back to Sawyer.

"Do I look like one of your lowlifes carrying contraband, Officer Mace?" Sawyer said, folding her arms across her chest.

"Is that an offer to search you, ma'am?" Mace countered, smiling. Holling figured with a smile that wide, he could count each and every tooth that he planned to knock out of Mace's head if he kept looking at Sawyer that way.

Enough was enough. Mace had pushed the bounds of professionalism. Maybe it was Mace's job to note comings and goings in town. But if you asked Holling, he was noticing Sawyer just a smidgen too much. She didn't help matters much, looking way too damned sexy, now that he thought about it. And why'd she have to smile like that at Mace? What was she trying to prove?

"This is a friend of mine from out of town," Holling said simply, deliberately not offering a name.

"Sawyer Garth," Sawyer supplied quickly.

"It's a pleasure to meet you, Ms. Garth. Welcome to White Wolf," Mace said, making it a point to add her name to his clipboard.

"Thank you, Officer."

"Sorry that it had to be under these circumstances." Mace then turned his attention back to Holling, suddenly all business again. "You heading in?"

"Yeah, for a while. Zack is supposed to meet me by Marjean's with a wrecker."

"He came through about fifteen minutes ago." Mace checked his clipboard where he was noting vehicle license plate numbers. "How long do you plan to be in town?"

"Not long. A couple of hours maybe," Nate said. "We've got a vehicle we need to tow."

"All right, then. You take it slow goin' through. We've had two accidents already today. One woman ran into a cow trying to avoid hitting a stray dog in the road. Another wrecker lost his load and sent a compact car wheeling into what was left of Lee's Cut'n'Curl."

"Will do, Officer Mace," Nate promised.

"Ms. Garth, maybe when we get things all put back together you'll visit White Wolf again," Mace said to Sawyer. "We could all hook up, you, Holling, me, and a few other folks and kinda hang out, take in the sights. Dinner and a movie, maybe?"

"Sounds like fun," Sawyer agreed amiably.

Holling then drowned out Mace's next words when he turned the key in the ignition. He put the truck into gear and drove around the sawhorses with the flashing safety lights.

Sawyer couldn't help noticing that Holling managed to spin up a small cloud of dust as he drove on.

"Snot-nosed sumbitch," Holling muttered under his breath.

"I thought he was very friendly," Sawyer said, looking back at Nate and giving him a wink.

Nate chuckled. "I think you just gave Holling fresh reason to hold a grudge against that Parmon Mace, Sawyer, girl."

Holling knew that they were messing with him. That didn't make it any easier to take. He wasn't normally a jealous man. The way he saw it, he'd been given too many blessings in his life to be concerned about what anybody else had. This thing with Sawyer was different. He didn't *have* her. He couldn't lay claim to her in any form or fashion.

So, when it became pretty obvious to him that Mace was hitting on her, there wasn't much that he could do about it. What was he going to say, stop looking at his woman? She wasn't *his* woman.

She made it clear from the first moment they met, she was her own woman. Maybe that's why she wasn't wearing a ring. She would do what she wanted to do, whenever she wanted to do it, and it didn't matter if he liked it or not. If anything, Holling could say that she had him. Had him right where she wanted him. For the moment, that was at arm's length. And that's where he'd stay until she let him know that she was ready.

"There's Zack's wrecker truck," Nate pointed out. Not that anyone could miss the high-gloss black truck blazoned on the side with a black skull and orange flames shooting out of its eyes.

"I see it, Pops," Holling said, maneuvering as close as he could.

Sawyer gave a low whistle. "Wow . . . that's a very big truck. You don't think that's overkill for my bike, do you?"

"Bigger is always better," Nate said, winking at Sawyer. "Any man will tell you that."

Sawyer shook her head, covered her eyes with her hand. "I only meant that a simple flatbed wrecker with a lift should have been enough, Nate."

"I know what you meant, Sawyer, girl. I'm just agreeing with you."

"I don't know, Nate. It's kind of hard to tell that's what you're doing."

"I guess you've figured out that everything that comes out Pops's mouth sounds suggestive," Holling said as an excuse for his father.

"Well, you know, they say you are what you eat," Nate drawled.

"Pops!" Holling said sharply. "Pay no attention to that old man, Sawyer. He gets that way when he's off his meds."

"Your pops and I have an understanding, Holling," Sawyer assured him. "We both know that he's all talk and no action."

"One of these days I'm gonna surprise you both," Nate predicted.

"You keep talking like that, Pops, and I'm sending you to bed without your supper," Holling warned.

"If you're cookin', you'd be doing me a favor," Nate shot back.

With a long-suffering sigh, Holling shut off the engine again and climbed out of the truck. He waved and called out to his friend Zack.

A young man in grungy, oil-stained gray coveralls and a John Deere cap twisted backward on his head was talking to one of the cleanup volunteers. He pulled off his cap, ran his hand through his thinning blond hair that was pulled back into a ponytail. When he heard Holling, he patted the volunteer on the arm, stuck his hands deep into his pockets, and strolled across the asphalt parking lot.

Holling held out his hand, shaking it briskly as he said, "Thanks for gettin' here so quickly, Zack. I appreciate it."

"Not a problem, Holling. Tell me now what we're hauling."

"There's a 2003 Suzuki Savage buried somewhere under all of this mess. I need to get it and haul it over to your shop to see if we can get it repaired."

"A Savage, huh? I always thought you were a Harley man."

"I am till the day I die. This ride's not mine. The bike belongs to a friend."

Holling gestured over at the truck as Sawyer opened the door, stepped out, and slid on a pair of sunglasses.

Zack gave a low whistle, pulled off his cap again, and smoothed over his hair. "Since when did you start hanging with friends with that much class, Holling?"

"Recently," Holling confessed. "Very recently. A step up from all you lowlifes."

"You say it's her bike?"

"Uh-huh. She rode in the day that twister hit."

"Talk about a good thing fallin' right out of the sky."

Sawyer approached them, with her hands tucked into her back pockets. "So, what do you think, gentlemen? Do you think there's any chance of my salvaging my bike?"

"If she's in there, we'll get her out, ma'am," Zack promised.

"Zack, this is Sawyer Garth. Sawyer, this is a good friend of mine, Zack Spenser. Zack owns Spenser Cycles. They're about the best in the business when it comes to bike repair and custom designs."

"How do you do, Zack?" Sawyer said, extending her hand to him.

"Pleasure to meet you, ma'am," he said, shaking hands with her. "I'm sorry to hear about your ride. But I suppose it's a blessing that you could walk away from it all."

"I couldn't agree with you more. I'd given up hope that I would ever find the bike."

"How did you find it?"

"I saw it on the news. They were covering the storm damage right there in front of Marjean's. And there it was, pieces of the chrome sticking up right over . . ." She turned around, searching the area for familiar landmarks. "About over there." She pointed it out to him.

Zack squinted in the direction. "Yeah . . . yeah, I think you're right, Sawyer. Come on, let's go see how much elbow grease and back-bending it'll take to get her cleared out."

Zack led the way, followed by Sawyer, and Holling bringing up the rear.

"Careful there, Sawyer," Holling said, grasping her elbow when she stepped onto a loose brick and wobbled.

"Maybe you'd better wait over there, ma'am," Zack suggested, pointing to a clear patch of ground. He pulled a pair of work gloves from his coverall pocket and tugged them on.

Sawyer stood back and supervised as Holling and his friend cleared debris.

"You be careful, Holling," she cautioned, as Holling and

Zack lifted an unwieldy section of Marjean's Café's wall away from the bike. "Don't forget to bend from the knees when you lift. Watch that piece over there. It's got sharp edges. Set that piece over there. That's it. Almost got it."

"Anytime you want to jump in and help," Holling said over his shoulder, tossing the wall section away with a soft grunt.

"No, it looks like you two have it well covered," she replied, putting her hands on her hips and smiling with smarmy charm at them.

"Yeah, that's what I thought," he retorted, wiping a bead of sweat from his forehead with the back of his hand.

After fifteen minutes of sifting through debris, Zack let out a loud "Whew, boy! I think we've got it clear enough for me to back my wrecker up to it now."

"Can you stand her up?" Sawyer asked, shaking her head at the bike still lying on its side. She hated seeing her pride and joy like that—all covered in dust and mud. She hardly recognized what used to be her black and silver beauty.

"You sure don't let a fella catch his breath," Zack complained.

Holling tapped him in the middle of his chest. "We're gonna have to get her up to get her onto the wrecker anyway, Zack. Might as well keep going while our muscles are warmed up."

"Warm? I'm gettin' close to a nuclear meltdown. You didn't tell me I'd have to do actual work once I got out here, Holling."

Zack motioned for Holling to take up a position near the front tire. He moved around to the rear of the bike, pushing aside inch-thick mud with his boot.

"On three," Holling said, wrapping his arms around the handlebars and gas tank.

When Zack took a firm hold of the chrome brace that

Sawyer had custom-added behind the rear passenger seat, he nodded to Holling to indicate that he was ready.

"One. Two. Three. Lift!" Holling sang out.

"Easy, easy!" Sawyer called out in concern, taking a step forward when Zack almost lost his grip on the bike.

"You know, Holling, something tells me that she's more worried about her bike than my back," Zack complained.

"I'm sure a big, strong fella like you can handle it, Zack," she said sweetly.

"Flattery will only get you a ten percent discount on my bill," he warned her.

While they held the bike into position, Sawyer moved in and pushed on the kickstand with her foot. Once it had lowered, they let the bike rest on its own.

"Looks like the saddlebags are still intact," Holling observed, noting the dark leather cases strapped to either side of her bike.

"Lot of good they'll do me. There's not much in them," Sawyer said ruefully.

When Holling threw her an odd look, she shrugged and said, "I travel light. If I can find my jacket, my wallet . . ." Her voice trailed off.

"You lost all of that in the twister?" Zack asked, clucking his tongue in sympathy.

"Don't worry, Zack, I'll be able to pay you for any repair work," she said quickly. "I'm not expecting charity."

"That's not what I meant, ma'am. But I have to admit that it does give me a small degree of comfort knowing I'll be taken care of."

"You will be," she said resolutely.

"Yes, ma'am. If you'll excuse me, I'll go back the truck up so we can get her loaded."

He made a small, barely imperceptible movement with his head. Sawyer was too preoccupied with the bike to notice, but Holling did.

"Be right back," he told her, falling into step beside Zack.

When they were a few feet away, Holling asked his friend, "What's up?"

"I was gonna ask you the same thing."

"What do you mean?"

"Strange lady shows up in town. No money. No place to stay. No means of transportation. Yet, you're treating her like she's royalty. What's up with you?"

Holling shrugged. "Just tryin' to help a lady in distress."

"Hey, I've got more chivalry in my big toe than you've got in your whole body, Holling. But there are limits. Are you sure you trust her?"

"If you're worried about your fees, Zack, don't. She said she'd pay you."

"And just where is she gonna get the money? You heard her. No wallet. No credit cards. No ID. Even if she has a rich daddy somewhere who can wire her gazillions, how is she gonna get access to it? You think a bank or a money transfer company is gonna open the cash drawer and let her take what she wants?"

Holling shrugged. He didn't know how things were going to work out. He just knew that they would.

"Yeah, that's what I thought. You don't know a thing about her. We may be talking a couple of thousand dollars' worth of damage to her bike. That's just the damage I could see. There's no tellin' how much there's going to be once we strip her down."

"You've got nothin' to worry about, Zack. If she can't pay you—"

Zack stopped in his tracks, putting his hand against Holling's chest. "Don't tell me that you're about to say that you're gonna pick up the bill."

"Why?" Holling looked with genuine surprise at him. "Is that so strange?"

Zack shook his head. "Now I know something's wrong. You? Offering to pick up the tab? That has to be a first."

"Are you callin' me cheap?"

"Let's just say that you've taken penny-pinching to a whole new level, son."

"Don't worry about gettin' paid, Zack. I told you, I've got it covered."

"Maybe that ain't all you've got covered," he suggested, his expression sly.

"It's not like that," Holling said quickly.

"I know you, Holling. You don't give up anything without expecting something in return."

"Oh, so now you're sayin' that I'm selfish? Tell me again why I've got you as a friend."

"Because I tell it to you straight. I don't kiss your ass like half the folks around here. You look me in the face and tell me that you're not wanting something from that girl."

Holling turned, faced Zack squarely. "I don't want a thing," he said evenly. His gaze never wavered as he spoke. He could say that to his friend with total conviction. He didn't want a thing from Sawyer Garth. He wanted *everything*.

Chapter 17

Everything's going to be all right, Sawyer thought in relief after she'd finally hung up the phone. Zack had given her the use of his office. When she'd first entered, her first reaction was to decline his offer and take her chances scouring the ruined Marjean's Café to find her own cell phone. Maybe Holling's friend was a genius when it came to chopping up a bike, but he was just a run-of-the-mill slob when it came to keeping his office.

Sawyer paced in the confined space of Zack's office. She was careful not to disturb the desk covered with multiple in-baskets containing requisitions for parts, custom requests from bike enthusiasts all over the state, and invoices and trade magazines. Sundry motorcycle parts acted as paperweights to hold down the sheer volume. Empty fast-food containers that looked weeks old, and some not so empty but just as old. A trail of ants moving around the watercooler, a few other unrecognizable bugs nesting in the corner, file cabinets filled to overflowing. It was organized chaos. If Zack had a system, she couldn't decipher it.

She'd reached for the phone with two fingers, her eyes darting around for a can of spray disinfectant. What a difference it was from the clean, orderly, sanitized home that Nate had opened up to her.

"If you're worried about catching something in here," Nate teased her, "don't. The plague is too scared of catching something from Zack to hang around for long."

"I'm not prissy," Sawyer said. "But I'm not willing take my life into my own hands either . . . literally." She raised the phone and pointed to the grease stains around the handle.

Nate pulled out a handkerchief from his back pocket and wiped away the most visible stains. "Here you go, little missy. I suggest you get to dialing."

"Thanks, Nate." Sawyer nodded and dialed information to get the toll-free number of her credit card company.

She spent an hour on the phone with her credit card company, explaining her situation. Normally, it wouldn't have been such a hassle, canceling one card and requesting another. She'd been through this before when her purse was stolen during one of her book signings. The fact that she'd requested the card shipped overnight to a different address did cause a problem.

Even though she'd given every piece of information they'd asked for, including name, current address, driver's license number, Social Security number, even the special secret identification number that was supposed to help prevent credit card fraud, she was still having trouble. She was glad that her company was making it difficult for anyone else to call up and request a card. But not her! It was supposed to be easy for her. She'd been trying for several days to get a new card issued to her. As soon as she was released from the hospital, she'd called the company. A service operator had promised that one was on the way to her, but several days later she still hadn't received her card. Sawyer began a fresh round of calls.

"No, it's not a PO box," she'd argued. "You can deliver the card to the address I gave you. It's Route 4, Box 11," she said, repeating the address that Nate had given her. He'd scribbled it down on a piece of paper and left her to watch Holling and Zack begin the careful process of disassembling her bike. Sawyer thought he'd left her alone because he couldn't stand the look of strained patience on her face and the blatant irritation in her tone.

Before he left her, he offered, "Do you want me to talk to them? I know a few choice cuss words that might light a fire under them."

"I know a few of my own," Sawyer retorted. "And I'm *this* close to using them!" She held up her thumb and forefinger pinched closed.

The second time she'd been transferred and her voice rose in exasperation, Nate had pointed at the office door, indicating that he was leaving her.

Sawyer nodded and then covered the mouthpiece with her hand.

"I'd stand a chance of finding my old card quicker than getting through to these guys," she complained.

"Hang in there, Sawyer," he encouraged. "They can only transfer you so many times before you wind up back at the first rep."

"You're a real comfort, you know that, Nate?" she said dryly.

He winked at her. "I guess I'm doing my job, then."

Sawyer turned back to her phone conversation. "It's Garth," Sawyer repeated. "G as in girl, A, R, T as in Tom, H."

Then, throwing herself against the cracked, overstuffed cushions of Zack's swivel chair, she rocked back and forth several times. The chair creaked as she rocked, making her wish for a can of WD-40. Sawyer looked up, counting the tiles in the ceiling to keep her irritation in check.

The ultrapolite voice on the other end of the line interrupted her count at around thirty-nine. "Ms. Garth, are you there?"

"Of course I'm still here," Sawyer retorted. "Where else would I be? I can't go anywhere else without access to my funds, can I now?"

"Yes, ma'am. Let me just verify this information and we'll get you all taken care of."

She listened as the customer service representative confirmed that a new card would be shipped to her and repeated the shipping address.

"That's right," she said, in relief. "White Wolf, Montana."

"Is there anything else we can help you with today?"

"No, I think you've done enough," Sawyer said testily. Then, remembering the recorded message that said that some parts of that conversation might be recorded for quality assurance, she added in a gentler tone, "Thank you for your assistance." She could see it all now . . . she finally winds up on *Oprah* or *Good Morning America* to promote her book and they drag out one of those customer service reps who would be more than willing to dish the dirt on her.

She placed the phone back into the cradle, planted her elbows on the desk, and rested her cheeks in the palms of her hands. That was how Holling found her as he poked his head in the door.

"Hey," he called out to her.

"Hey yourself," she greeted him.

Holling pushed the door open more and sat on the corner of Zack's desk. "So, did you get everything taken care of?"

"Uh-huh." She nodded. "It took some convincing, but they said I should have a new card by tomorrow. In case there's a problem, they gave me the tracking number of the shipping company."

"Let me guess, now that you've gone through all of that, they're going to start shipping your credit card bills to my home, too, aren't they?"

"All part of my evil master plan," Sawyer said, rubbing her hands together and imitating a mad scientist's laugh. "Seriously now, I hope that card does show up tomorrow."

"You can't be ready to go shopping," he teased. "Not with your mission-control duties."

"You and your daddy ought to take that comedy act of yours on the road. No, I'm not dying to go shopping. I just don't feel right about you and your father paying for everything. I've been staying at your home at your expense for a week. You treat all of your tourists that way? How do you and your father make any money on your bed-and-breakfast?"

"Now that I know you've got a card on the way, you're paying for your own bike repairs," he said, pointing at her.

"Did you honestly think I would expect you to pay Zack for me?" She sounded offended.

"I was prepared for that possibility."

"Holling, no! I couldn't let you do that."

He shrugged. "Consider it a loan."

"And how do you know I'd pay it back? Or that I could pay it back? What if I skipped out on you?" she challenged.

"I'd track you down and bring you back," he said simply. "Make you settle up."

Sawyer paused and said, "No matter how I say this, Holling, it's going to come out wrong. So I'm not going to try to pretty it up or sugarcoat it. You know I'm very grateful for everything you and your father have done for me. I don't know what I would have done without you keeping me safe from the twister and your father taking me in after it was all over. But it will all be over soon. As soon as they deliver my replacement card. I'm leaving as soon as my bike is ready, Holling," Sawyer said bluntly.

"So you've said," he returned.

"I just wanted to be clear on that."

"Clear as crystal."

"I just wanted to say it now. Call it an early good-bye. I don't like making long, complicated ones."

"So, if I wake up in the middle of the night and you're gone, you're telling me don't be surprised."

She nodded.

"You want to know what does surprise me, Trek?" he said, his tone lamenting. "The fact that you're still here surprises the hell out of me."

Pops was right. She was a runner. Holling wished he knew what was driving her, what was making her push on. There was so much he wanted to know about her. So many things he wanted to ask her. Things he wanted to say. But the timing was all wrong. She was in a hurry and he hadn't known her long enough to get her to trust him enough to slow down for him. There was panic on her face when he'd touched her.

"Say, Holling, got a minute?"

It was Zack, standing at the doorway.

"Yeah," Holling said tightly.

Zack motioned for him to meet him out in the hallway.

Holling pulled the door closed behind him and followed Zack to the end of the hall.

"I wasn't interrupting anything in there, was I?" Zack grinned at him.

"You know damned well you were, Zack," Holling said in irritation.

"Good. My office is no place to romance a woman anyway. Too much crap in the way."

"I'm not going to even try to remind you how many you've had up there, door shut, blinds closed, with the Do Not Disturb sign hanging from the chain on the doorknob."

"All right, all right, I get your point."

"What did you need?"

"The good news is, I can fix her bike."

"You called me out here for that? You could have told me that in there."

"The bad news is it's gonna take some time."

"How much time?"

Zack gave his friend a sly smile. "It's why I called you out here, son. How much time do you need?" Zack said pointedly.

"Excuse me?"

"Clean the wax out of your ears, Holling. I said, how much time you gonna need to get with that girl? You want to get into her panties, right? One day? Three days? A week? You tell me what you want and I'll make it happen. The bike's gonna need some new parts. The engine, for one, is hosed. That could take me at least a week to track down."

Holling grinned, then wiped his hand over his mouth, effectively erasing his smile.

"No, that would be wrong. I can't do that to her."

"What? Are you crazy? The girl's hot for you, Holling. You gotta strike while the iron's hot. Here am I practically handing her to you on a platter and you're going all noble on me. What's the matter with you?"

"You just order the parts she needs, get them here as fast as you can, Zack."

"You sure?" Zack sounded dubious.

"Yeah, I'm sure. Just fix the damned bike, Zack. I'll take care of the rest."

"Man, you must really have it bad. All right, then. Have it your way. Let's go in and give the girl the news."

"Sawyer," Holling said firmly. "Her name is Sawyer. Sawyer Garth."

Zack nodded. He understood. He understood maybe even more than Holling did. He'd said her name was Sawyer Garth. But he wasn't thinking Garth. Nuh-uh. No way. He was thinking Holling. Sawyer *Holling*.

Chapter 18

"Seven days!" Sawyer said in dismay. "You've got to be kidding me!"

"That's just to get the parts in," Zack said evenly. He glanced over at Holling. "And that's when the real work begins. You could be lookin' at up to ten days."

"I can't be hanging around here for a week," Sawyer retorted. "I've somewhere I need to be."

"Hey, lady. We've all got somewhere we need to be," Zack responded. "You asked me how long it'll take and I'm telling you."

Sawyer turned to Holling. "I know he's your friend and you want to give him the business . . . but something tells me that I'm getting the business here."

"Sawyer," Holling said, his tone slightly disapproving.

"I'm sorry, but I find it hard to believe that a man of his supposed reputation can't do any better than that."

"Have you looked at that bike lately?" Zack jerked his thumb back over his shoulder. "Let's go down to the workroom floor and I'll show you what we're dealing with here."

She followed him out of the office, down the stairs, and

onto the main workroom floor. Several bikes in various stages of repair were scattered on a garage floor that was half the size of a football field. Sawyer tried not to be impressed by the variety of bikes she saw—from cruisers, to choppers, to crotch rockets. Bikes of every make and model, foreign and domestic, brand-spanking-new and those that had seen their share of a few stretches of road. You didn't attract this kind of clientele without being good at what you did. Whether she liked his attitude or not, Zack knew what he was doing. She had to trust him.

He took her over to a bay where her bike was, even as they spoke, being disassembled. He patted the shoulder of the young man carefully laying out parts, sorting them between those that could be reused or revamped and those that were meant for the scrap pile.

Sawyer made a pained sound of dismay, seeing her pride and joy, her baby, gutted like that. But it also heartened her to see the young mechanic treating her bike with as much care as she would have.

He looked up when he saw her, gave her an acknowledging nod.

"Give us a minute, Leo, would ya?" Zack tapped the young man on the shoulder. "Take a break."

"Sure, boss." He set aside the socket wrench that he was using, placing it into its designated spot in his tool chest.

"Do I need to point out what type of work we're talking here?" Zack asked, pointing to the parts that Leo had removed.

She gave a heavy sigh of resignation. There was more damage than she thought.

"No, you don't," she said reluctantly. "Listen, I don't mean to be difficult. But I'm supposed to meet my aunt and thirty other women on a cross-country charity ride. They're waiting for me. I won't put their schedule at risk if I can help it."

"Well, you can't help it," Zack said. "I'm sorry."

"So, how much in storage fees is this going to cost me while we're waiting for parts to come in?" Sawyer said.

Holling came to his friend's defense. "Zack isn't out to gouge anybody."

"Because you're a friend of Holling's, I'll give you three days free. Four if you're really nice to us." He waggled his eyebrows at her.

"You sure there isn't another bike shop in town?" Sawyer asked Holling. "I can work my own deals and won't have to be *nice* to anybody doing it."

"There's Cycle World in Billings," Zack offered. "But if I have to tow your bike out there, I will charge you. For the estimate work that we've already done, I'll have to charge you. For the insult to think that I'd cheat a friend of Holling's, I'll have to charge you."

"Nobody's towing anybody anywhere else." Holling stepped between them when Sawyer took an angry step toward Zack. "And nobody's gonna have to be nice to anybody to get the job done . . . and done right." He gave the last warning to Zack.

"I'll get the job done right," Zack promised. "Even if I have to pull extra hours to do it. But I'm giving you fair warning, if any of my other customers come in with bike work, I'm going to be giving them the same treatment."

"If anybody else comes in, they're just going to have to take a number," Sawyer countered. "I was here first."

"As much as I appreciate your business, I'm not gonna disappoint my longtime customers . . . the folks who helped me to build this business, ma'am. I didn't get where I was screwin' my customers."

"I'm sure that's not what Sawyer's suggesting, Zack," Holling interceded smoothly. Sawyer shot him an angry look. He read her meaning loud and clear. Her look said to him, "You don't know me well enough to be speaking for me."

"Zack, can you give us a minute? Take a break," he said, repeating the words that he'd just told Leo.

"Sure, boss." Zack grinned at him.

Holling canted his head, indicating that he wanted a private conference with Sawyer.

As soon as they were out of hearing distance from Zack and his employees, Sawyer whispered harshly, "I know what you're going to say, Holling."

"That's a neat trick, Sawyer. Because even I'm not sure what I want to say to you right now. I don't know if I should praise you for being strong enough to stand up to Zack's mess or cuss you out for accusing my friend of cheating you."

"I don't have time for games, Holling. I've got to get that bike roadworthy."

"And he's the man to do it. You won't get anywhere with the man by ticking him off. You can't come up in here, accuse him of cheating you, and then tell him he can't do business with the customers who helped him get where he is."

"I didn't mean to come off sounding that way."

"Well, you did."

"Do you think if I apologized it would smooth things over with him?"

"Do you think you could apologize without making it sound like an accusation?"

"Oh, I don't know," Sawyer said. "Might be kind of difficult."

"Then you'd better let me handle it. Wait here. I'll go and talk to him." Holling moved across the workroom floor. He waited until he was inches away from Zack, then placed his hand on his shoulder and turned him away so that their backs were partially turned to Sawyer.

"Okay, Zack, you want to tell me what the hell that was all about?"

"What do you mean?" Zack asked, composing his face so that it was the very model of innocence.

"Don't play with me, son. Why were you so hard on Sawyer?"

"Jeez, Holling. You girlfriend can be a real bitch when she wants to be."

"She's not my girlfriend," Holling said stiffly. "And she's not a bitch. She's just had a rough time of it the last few days. Give her a break, Zack. She's been hit by a tornado and now you want to hit her with a bunch of bogus fees."

"They're not bogus. Every one of them is legit."

"Cut her some slack, Zack."

"She hates me, doesn't she?"

"Nah . . . she doesn't hate you. She thinks you're gonna gouge her and she may think you're a slob, but that doesn't mean that she hates you."

"Then I ain't doing my job. I *want* her to hate me."

"I don't think you want to get on that lady's bad side, Zack."

"So, did you talk to her?"

"Yeah. I suggested that she might want to apologize," Holling said. He was surprised by her reaction. He'd expected her to curse him out right on the spot and storm out of there.

"How'd she take it?" Zack asked.

"How do you think she took it?"

"Like a trooper. A storm trooper, that is. My guess is that she came about an inch away from ripping us both a new one."

"On the for-real, Zack. How many days to get the job done?"

"One or two days to get the parts in. Another two or three to get them installed. We're talking five days max."

"Uh-huh. So why did you tell her seven days? I thought we agreed we wouldn't pull that sneaky crap on her."

"That's right, we did. But I did you a favor. Consider that one a freebie."

"How do you figure that you've helped me out?"

"You go back and tell that impatient little . . ." He stopped himself, took a deep breath, and then continued. "Go back and tell your friend that you've got the days knocked down from ten to five. That'll get you panty points for sure."

"It's not about the panties, Zack." Holling knew that for a certainty. If it was just about getting Sawyer into bed, he wouldn't have backed off this afternoon. Not that he would have forced himself on her. But he certainly would have kept after her until she changed her mind.

"The hell it ain't. It's always about the panties. Your tongue's hanging so far out your mouth after her that you can lick your own boots clean, son."

"I told you, it's not like that. Yeah, I admit I'd like to get to know her better. But that ain't likely to happen. She's not giving me much room to get close to her."

"You know what your problem is, Holling?"

"That I've got you for a friend?"

"That ain't a problem, that's a liability," Zack shot back. "Your problem is, you're not acting like a man who hasn't had any booty in a while."

"And just what is that supposed to mean?"

"I mean, you're too concerned about following the rules. Trying to be all chivalrous. You don't have time for that."

"She's all by herself, stranded, Zack. Me and Pops are the only friends that she's got out here. How would I look if I tried to climb her every chance I got?" Holling's conscience had pricked him as the events of that afternoon came back to him.

"It would look like you meant business."

"She's not interested, Zack."

"And you're buying that act? Come on, Holling. Use your brain. This is a perfect opportunity for you both. In a couple of days, she'll be long gone out of here. Maybe you'll never see her again. Can you think of a better reason not to take advantage of that kind of opportunity?"

Holling shook his head no, whether in denial or in answer to Zack's question, he wasn't sure.

"I'll bet deep down inside, she's just waiting for you to make the first move. See how she's letting you take the lead? Offering all the suggestions? She's totally depending on you to help her through this crisis. Be a man. Take the initiative."

"And just what am I supposed to do? Club her over the head and drag her into some dark alley by her hair? I'm not gonna take advantage of her like that."

"If she's into that kinky kinda sex, why not?"

"You know, Zack, sometimes I worry about you."

"You don't have to worry about me. I know what I'm talking about. If you don't believe me, go over there and tell her what I said."

"Are you trying to get my face slapped?"

"I meant tell her how you came over here and negotiated the price and the delivery date for her. See if that don't warm her up to you."

"All of this altruism. What's in it for you?"

"Promise me that when the time comes, you'll do the same for me."

"You mean, you want me to irritate your friends and threaten to overcharge them?" Holling teased.

"I meant I want you to be lookin' out for my best interests when I meet the woman who's my perfect match, Holling."

"My what?" Holling laughed uncomfortably.

"You heard me. She's your match. I've been checkin' her out, you see."

"Yeah, so I noticed. You need to quit that, son, before somebody, someday slaps you with a horrendous sexual harassment suit."

"Not just in the way you're thinking, Holling. Though I

gotta admit, she's somethin' to look at. I meant, I've been watching how she acts around you, and you know what I noticed? I noticed that she acts just like *you*." Zack stabbed Holling in the chest with his index finger. "She's tight on money, not willing to give an inch, expects everybody to jump when she snaps her fingers. If that ain't you in a dress, I don't know what is."

Holling shook his head. "You're crazy."

"Maybe. But I'm right. You wait and see. You say you want to get to know her. Fine. Start by knowing yourself. Now get over there and impress her with your deal-making ability."

Holling hesitated. It was a dangerous game that he was playing, treating Sawyer's emotions like a toy. What possessed Zack to think he could manipulate her in his behalf?

"Go on," Zack said, making shooing motions with his hand.

"All right," he said finally, but he didn't seem to be overly anxious to get over there.

"Go on!" Zack insisted.

Sawyer looked up from the magazine she'd been flipping through as Holling approached her. Her expression was guarded, as closed as the magazine she snapped shut and tossed back onto the workbench.

"Well?" she said.

Holling shrugged. "I talked to him."

"I kinda figured that out," she retorted.

"He's gonna fix your bike, Sawyer."

"And?"

"And he's gonna do his best to get it to you sooner than he originally estimated."

"How much sooner?"

"He might be able to chop off three days, maybe four, if he pushes it."

"Did you tell him to push it?"

"I didn't *tell* him anything," Holling said, a slight edge in his voice.

Sawyer backed off. "I stand corrected."

"So, if all goes well, you should be out of here by Tuesday. Wednesday at the latest."

Sawyer smiled, and Holling couldn't help but notice how her entire face seemed to light up. He was glad to be the one to bring her the good news. But he wasn't so sure how he felt about her being so happy to leave him.

"Thank you, Holling!" she said, wrapping her arms around him and giving him a brief squeeze before letting go.

"No problem. Glad I could help," Holling said as he looked over his shoulder at Zack. He grinned when Zack gave him the thumbs-up sign with one hand and the okay sign with his other hand. Just as quickly, the smile faded when Zack brought his hands together and stuck the thumb of his right hand repeatedly through the oval made by the okay sign with his left hand.

It didn't take a genius to figure out what hint he was trying to give Holling by that crude gesture. He knew it wouldn't take Sawyer long to figure it out either, if she'd caught him at it.

"C'mon," Holling said, grasping her by the elbow and turning her away so that their backs were to Zack. "I'm starving. Let's see if we can round up Pops and go get something to eat."

"Eat? Around here?" Sawyer said hesitantly.

"I know what you're thinking," Holling said. "The last time we talked about getting something to eat in White Wolf, we wound up in a tornado."

"What do you do for an encore, Holling, call up an earthquake?"

"You lookin' for somebody to make the earth move for you, Sawyer?" he taunted her.

Sawyer didn't miss a step, just kept walking as she said

over her shoulder, "I wouldn't be surprised if more than one body fell off in this town, never to be heard from again."

"Ouch." Holling winced at her comeback.

"You sure Zack will be able to get the work done in a few days?"

"He said he'd try. I can't ask much more from the man than that."

"I don't mean to keep bugging you about it . . . it's just that my aunt Rosie and the rest of the riders are probably on the road by now. I can't ask them to delay the ride for me and I don't want them to go on without me."

"She'll wait for you, Sawyer," Holling said with certainty.

"You don't know my aunt Rosie," she said with feeling.

"You're right. I don't."

"Then what makes you so sure that she'll wait for me?"

Because anyone with any lick of sense would wait for you, Holling thought. He was waiting for her now, waiting for her decide to let down her guard. Waiting for her to realize that if she gave him just half a chance, it would be worth the wait. He knew that she was only protecting herself, keeping him at a distance emotionally while she waited to put physical distance between them. She was anxious to put some miles between them—and that was making him anxious. Maybe he should have gone along with Zack's plan. Maybe he should have agreed to let Zack pad a few hours for the chance of more time with her. But if Zack had been right about her personality, if she was more like him than he could see on the surface, then he knew that wasn't the way to go. As guarded as she was, a few more days weren't going to make a difference. No difference at all.

Chapter 19

It was the same thing all over again, just like at Marjean's Café. Sawyer sat down to eat, took only a few bites, then excused herself to go to the restroom. Only, this time, there was no Luce there to help her through the worst of the nausea. This time, her helper was less delicate in his aid.

"Hey, little missy, are you all right in there?" Nate rapped loudly on the door with his fist. "You ain't dyin' in there on me, are you?"

Instead of stopping in White Wolf to eat, they'd gone back to Holling's home. Nate had promised to cook up a meal that would rival Marjean's best.

"I'm all right," Sawyer insisted.

"You don't sound like you're all right. Open up the door."

"No . . . no, I don't think I will," Sawyer said. "I don't mean to be rude, but it's not a pretty sight in here."

"You know that's an insult to the cook, don't you, to send it back before you had a chance to really enjoy it?"

Sawyer couldn't help but laugh at his gross-out humor. "Sorry, Nate. I guess I'm just not feeling well," she apologized.

"You need me to bring you anything? Some Pepto-Bismol or Alka-Seltzer?"

"No, thanks."

"How about a power hose to wash down my commode?"

"I said no, thank you!"

"Well, you want to open the door and let me in?"

"No!" she said, with even more urgency in her voice. "I'll be out in a minute, Nate." She covered her eyes with her hand. What part of no didn't he understand?

"All right, then. Holler if you need anything."

"I will," she promised.

Sawyer listened for a minute for the sound of his footsteps in retreat. It took a while for those footsteps to start up. She could tell that Nate was still by the door listening.

"I know you're still out there, Nate," she called out.

"Okay, then. I'm leaving now for real this time."

This time, he did walk away. But Sawyer took her time trying to stand. The last thing she needed was to fall down, crack her head on the porcelain sink, and have Nate burst in through the door scolding, "I told you so!"

She rose unsteadily to her feet and gave herself a good talking-to in the vanity mirror in front of her.

"Okay, I've had just about enough of this," she said. "I'm on to your game now." She was starting to figure out the pattern of her spells of nausea. Whenever she went for long stretches without eating, the nausea was at its worst.

"I'll fix you, my little pretty," she said, imitating the high-pitched cackle of the Wicked Witch of the West. "And your little dog, too."

She laid her hand gently over her stomach. "To fix this, all I have to do is just snack for twenty-four hours and I won't have to worry about being sick again. Small, regular meals, every hour on the hour, should do it."

Sawyer took her examination further. Lifting her blouse, she placed her hands against her bared stomach and gingerly massaged. Her fingertips made lazy, concentric circles around her stomach. Four weeks along. Still much too early to notice any change in her waistline.

"But if you start eating like a pig, there's going to be a change. I could conceivably explode from the sheer volume of food I'll have to consume," she said ruefully.

Turning on the faucets, Sawyer splashed water against her face and rinsed out her mouth with mouthwash. Maybe she was taking longer in the bathroom than she should. Part of her was obsessed with rinsing the taste of bile from her mouth. The other part of her delayed because she didn't want to go out there and face Nate and Holling again. She'd been so embarrassed when her gorge began to rise. She'd practically bowled Holling over. As he brought more food to the table, she made a dash for the bathroom. The large salad he'd carried went clattering to the floor.

Fresh baby spinach leaves, strips of red and yellow bell peppers, cherry tomatoes, crumbled blue cheese spread across the wooden plank floor of the screened-in back porch. The last Sawyer saw of the salad was Holling's basset hound, Vashti, rising from her basket in the corner of the porch and leaping to lap up the crumbled bacon bits that had tumbled into the cracks of the floor planks.

Poor Holling. All that work and his salad masterpiece was ruined. He'd put up with a lot of teasing from his father.

"You trying to turn us all into cows, Holling?" Nate had teased. "Getting us to graze on them greens?"

"Consider it a healthier balance to the slab of meat you've got sizzling on the grill, Pops," he'd retorted.

The salad was the closest Nate had let Holling come to "cooking" for them.

"Trust me, little missy," Nate had warned. "You don't want that boy anywhere near a cooking stove. Did he tell you what happened the last time he tried to cook?"

"Don't listen to that old man, Sawyer. I told you that he

frequently forgets to take his medication." Holling made swirling motions around his temple with his index finger.

"Sounds like a good story," Sawyer said. She was all ready to dig into the salad that Holling had put together. But then Nate brought her that steak . . . that steaming, three-inch-thick, barely-trimmed-of-fat, flame-kissed steak. He pulled it off the grill, laying it on Sawyer's plate with blood juices dribbling off the edge.

It was her undoing. Before she could properly excuse herself, she clamped her hand over her mouth and sprinted for the downstairs guest bathroom. Maybe it would have been wiser just to step off the porch. But she wasn't going to ruin anyone else's appetite with her peculiar reaction to Nate's culinary skills.

Now she stood in front of the mirror, trying to regain her composure.

She gave herself a pep talk. "Okay, Sawyer, you can do this. Take deep breaths. In. Out. In. Out. That's it."

The deep-breathing exercise helped to settle her stomach. Now maybe she could go back to the table.

"But only if Nate takes that bloody hunk of flesh off my dinner plate. Ugh!" She made a face and shuddered in disgust.

As Sawyer turned to leave, out of the corner of her eye she caught her reflection.

"Speaking of hunks of flesh." Now her silhouette was still trim. But the time was coming. She stopped, turned her head, and regarded her reflection with a certain amount of misgiving.

"Take a good long look, Sawyer, girl," she said to herself. "Good-bye tight, sexy jeans and cropped tops. Hello stretch pants and muumuus!"

No wonder Ryan was so disgusted when she'd told him that she was pregnant. Who was going to want her now, all stretch-marked and smelling of spit-up? She'd heard it from all of her friends with children. Variations of the same story. A baby in the house might be a small blessing, but it was also a huge adjustment. A lot of married couples couldn't handle it. Mothers too tired to feel sexy, too focused on the baby to do the things that helped her get the baby in the first place. Sex was cut out of marriage quicker than you could say, "Honey, it's your turn to feed the baby."

And the fathers . . . the poor fathers . . . some were so jealous of the newcomers that they drove even deeper wedges between them and their wives. When they did manage to coax some attention from their wives, it was so brief and unsatisfying that it really wasn't worth the effort to begin with.

Sawyer figured if she had a dollar for every time one of her friends with children wound up sleeping in separate bedrooms, she'd have enough money to put her child through college.

She hadn't even had the baby yet and she was separated from Ryan. "He doesn't want me," she murmured. Saying it out loud still didn't make it ring true for her. How could he not want her? Hadn't he always said that she was everything he wanted in a woman? Intelligent. Fun. Sexy. Especially the sexy. Ryan couldn't keep his hands off of her. In public, or in private, his hands were constantly roaming over her. Her back, her rear, her breasts. There wasn't an inch on her skin that he hadn't touched. And now, just because there was going to be more skin to touch, he wanted to dump her? It wasn't right. It just wasn't right!

"He doesn't want us!" Sawyer corrected, feeling her throat constrict. "And you know why? Because nobody wants to read a spicy romance novel written by a woman who is somebody's mother. It's like . . . like . . . reading smutty thoughts penned by your own mother. Nobody wants to go there. Let's face it, you're going to blow up . . . and I don't mean that in a good way. You're going to get as big as a house. Get used to it, girl."

She couldn't visualize her body distended. It just didn't seem feasible. Holding her hands out in front of her, she guesstimated how far her stomach would precede her.

"It's going to arrive a good ten minutes ahead of me," she lamented.

Sawyer reached for one of the bath towels hanging from a decorative rod against the wall and stuffed the towel underneath her blouse. She turned left, then right, taking note of the effect.

"Oh no . . . no . . . no!" It was going to be awful. Just awful. Big, fat, swollen belly with probably a butt to match. "You might as well just give me a wide-load sign to hang on my backside and a warning siren that goes off whenever I back up, just like the sanitation trucks. *Beep-beep-beep!*"

Swollen cheeks, droopy breasts, swollen ankles, fingers puffed up like Cheetos. And through it all, what did she have to look forward to? Puking her guts out every day for the next nine months. And what was her reward for all of that torture? With her luck, she'd be in labor for a week. Give birth to twins, or even triplets, and spend the rest of her youth up to her eyeballs in diapers.

"I can't do it. I just can't do it!"

It wasn't only vanity sending Sawyer into an emotional tailspin. She was afraid. Very afraid. But not only for herself.

How was she going to bring another life into this world? She could barely take care of herself without getting into trouble. Having a child was so much responsibility—a type of responsibility she never had to face before. She'd lived in her own fantasy world of her creation, never really having to worry about much. Because she'd lost her mother at such an early age, her father had seen that she'd been given anything she could ever hope for, wish for. But from a distance. Always from a distance. Almost as if he was afraid.

Her mother had left her financially secure. And the success of her books was the icing on the cake. She had a small circle of friends she could also count on for amusement. Close ties to her family members she could always count on for emotional support. She had a man who she'd thought cared for her, and a budding career. What cares did she ever have other than whether or not her book would make it to the best-seller list?

Sawyer wasn't selfish. She just never really had to care for anyone other than herself. And Ryan of course. Now that he'd taken himself out of her life, she was back to square one. Back to only having to worry about herself. And now, of course, there was the baby—this nameless, formless thing that consumed her every waking thought. How was she going to give herself over, body and soul, to this thing she couldn't even bring herself to give a name?

Sawyer sank to the floor as a wave of overwhelming sadness washed over her. She heard herself sobbing, but couldn't quite bring herself to accept that it was she making that noise. Not Sawyer Garth. Not tough-talking, independent, self-made Sawyer Garth. But it was Sawyer. Loud, blubbering, and uncontrollable. She couldn't stop crying, even when she heard Holling's voice calling out to her in concern.

Chapter 20

"Sawyer? Open up! Are you all right?"

Holling stood on the other side of the door, shaking his head. Something about this picture seemed eerily familiar. Seemed to him the first time he'd met Sawyer, he was waiting for her outside the bathroom door.

"Y-y-yes," she stammered, then hiccupped. Holling didn't think she'd gotten tipsy off of the Listermint mouthwash kept for guests in the restroom. Something else was wrong.

"Darlin', open up the door," he insisted. "We're all worried about ya out here now."

"I'm fine," she insisted.

"I believed that whopper the first time you told it to me, Sawyer," he said. "I'm not fallin' for it again. Now, you open up that door, or so help me I'm gonna take the hinges off."

Silence for a moment, then she answered with thinly disguised reluctance. "All right. I'm coming."

Holling heard the soft release of the lock as she turned it. Gradually, the door creaked open.

"Uh . . . Sawyer, are you all right?"

She shook her head from side to side. "I swear, if I hear

that question one more time, I'm going to get homicidal!"
She gritted her teeth.

Her tone led Holling to believe that she meant what she
said. But it was hard to take her seriously. She hadn't cleared
her nose completely from all of her crying. He couldn't feel
threatened by a woman who was in serious need of a handkerchief.

"Well, okay . . . if that's the way you feel about it. Is there
anything I can get for you? Some fresh Kleenex? A semiau-
tomatic weapon to help you realize your murderous aspira-
tions?"

"Are you making fun of me, Holling?" she demanded.

"No, ma'am. I wouldn't dream of it."

"You'd better not." She glared at him.

Holling was having a difficult time keeping a straight
face. It was obvious that Sawyer was in distress. At that moment, what she needed more than his dry humor was a strong
(and dry) shoulder to cry on.

Sawyer snuffled, then turned around to reach for a tissue.
As she bent down for the box she remembered the towel that
she'd stuffed under her shirt.

That set off a fresh round of tears, this time loud and re-
strained. Without the benefit of the thick, oak door separating
them, Holling stepped across the threshold into the bathroom
and gathered Sawyer into his arms. He held her close, towel
and all, placing his huge palm behind her head to guide it
against his chest. For a moment, he didn't say a word, letting
his comfort be nonverbal. He let the strength in his arms
communicate his compassion. He swayed gently from side
to her, soothing her, calming her.

Sawyer wrapped her arms around Holling's waist and
clung to him as the drowning cling to an unexpected life pre-
server. She didn't question where her salvation had come
from. She didn't stop to wonder whether or not it was sturdy

enough to support her. She held on in gratitude and waited for the tide of emotion to carry her back to safety.

Holling smoothed his hand over the top of her head and then planted a light kiss. After her hiccups had subsided, he asked, "Feelin' better?"

She looked up at him with red-rimmed eyes.

"Don't give me that look. At least I didn't ask if you were all right," he protested.

"I'm feeling better," she confessed. "Just . . . just don't let go of me yet."

"I won't," he promised. "I'm here for you as long as you need me to be."

"I appreciate that."

"Do you feel like talking about it, Sawyer? It helps sometimes, you know."

She shook her head no. "I can't talk my way out of this mess, Holling."

"I'm not sayin' I have any answers for you, Sawyer. I'm just sayin' sometimes it helps to have another set of ears to help you figure it out."

"You're a good friend," she began haltingly. "I appreciate the offer."

"Uh-huh," he said, to encourage her to keep talking.

"But I don't want to get you involved."

"You're standing in my bathroom with one of my towels stuffed under your shirt. I can't get much more involved than that."

Sawyer laughed, looking down in embarrassment. "Oh, that . . . I only did that because . . . well, because . . . I think there's something I should tell you, Holling. Normally, I wouldn't go blabbing a thing like this, because it really isn't anybody's business but mine. But you and your father have been so good to me that I feel like I owe you . . . owe you my life and . . ."

Sawyer went on speaking, rapid-fire, without taking a breath and without really revealing what was troubling her. She would have kept babbling if Holling hadn't bent down and quickly sealed his lips to hers.

He didn't give her a chance to protest. Didn't give her a chance to reject him or push him away as she had done that morning. He hardly gave her a chance to draw in a breath as he stopped her nervous chatter.

If Sawyer resented the intrusion of her physical space, she didn't give him any indication. Whatever it was that had frightened her that morning didn't seem to be an issue. She didn't run from him. She ran to him. Lifting herself on her tiptoes, she flung her arms around his neck and deepened the kiss. She didn't know how long she stood there, swaying toward him, letting the emotional tide turn.

There was a kind of escalating urgency in Holling's touch, as if he, too, was in the process of discovery. When he'd entered the bathroom, he hadn't intended to kiss Sawyer. After the afternoon's fiasco, he was leery of approaching her with anything more than an offer of friendship and support. He was genuinely concerned about her well-being. She was in distress and he would do whatever it took to help put her at ease.

But, just like that day of the tornado outside Marjean's Café, something spoke to him, urged him on past his original, noble intentions. It wasn't Zack's voice that he heard in his head when he reached for Sawyer. It was his own, telling him to kiss her. He didn't debate whether it was the appropriate thing to do. He didn't consider whether it was the sensitive thing to do, or whether it would win him "panty points," as Zack called it. He did it because it was the right thing to do.

Oh, so right, Holling thought as he held on to her. Sawyer felt so good and right in his arms. How could this not be where she was supposed to be? How could this not be what he was supposed to be doing? *Don't let go,* she'd told him. Was she kidding? Was she crazy? Granted, she was standing there with a towel stuffed up her shirt, crying hysterically over who knew what, but that didn't make her crazy, did it? Or was he the loony one? Maybe he should have taken Zack up on his offer to stall and strand Sawyer there for a few more days.

He moaned aloud, not as much for the way kissing her was making him feel but for his conscience, which was taking on a life of its own. It was pricking him, hounding him, warning him that he shouldn't be taking advantage of her. Not like this. Not when she was in such a state.

With a concerted effort, Holling pulled away from her, held her at arm's length. He took a moment to collect himself, being careful not to look her directly in the face as he did so. He didn't want to see those wide, green eyes, glittering up at him with an odd, luminous glow. He didn't want to notice her passion-pounded lips, swollen with the eagerness of his attention. He could hear her breathing, ragged and harsh, as she struggled to regain control. No . . . no, that was him.

He dropped his arms to his sides, severing all contact with her.

"Holling?" Her voice was an unspoken question. Why had he stopped?

"Didn't mean to slam on the brakes so fast, Sawyer," he apologized. "It's just . . . things were getting out of hand, if you understand what I'm sayin'."

"I understand," she said, clearing her throat. She turned away, faced herself in the mirror, and *tsked* at her disheveled appearance. She made a show of running her fingers through her hair and smoothing her hands over her flushed cheeks.

"Besides that, the bathroom isn't my first choice of romantic places. Something about all that cold tile and how far voices carry." He moved behind her and rested his hands on her shoulders. "Not that I wouldn't enjoy kissing you any-

time, anywhere, darlin'. I just want you to know that if I didn't
stop then, I wouldn't have been able to stop. And then where
would we be?"

She met his gaze in the mirror and said softly, "Pregnant."

"Exactly," he said, nuzzling her neck.

Sawyer stiffened. She closed her eyes and gripped the
sink. "Too late."

Holling's head snapped up. "What did you say?"

"I said, it's too late. I'm pregnant, Holling."

It took a few seconds for the thought to register. He knew
things had gotten heated between them, but he hadn't completely lost control of himself. Despite his spiraling desire,
the pants had stayed snapped shut. A few seconds more and
he started to put the pieces together. Her frequent mood
swings. Her frequent illness. The emotional wall of tough-
ness that kept him at distance. Sawyer was pregnant.

"How—" he began.

"You mean Nate never sat you down and shared with you
the birds and the bees?" she asked.

"I was going to say how far along?"

"About four weeks," she confessed.

He reached out and clasped her left hand in his. No wedding ring. Not even the shadow of a band.

"No, I'm not married," she said, her tone hard.

"What about the father?" he asked.

"What about him?" she said belligerently.

"Does he know?"

"The question you should be asking is, does he care?"

"I guess you just answered that question for me," he said
calmly, in direct opposition to her increasingly hostile tone.

"I just thought you should know." When he didn't respond to her anger as Ryan would have done, she felt some
of the fight deflate from her. "He was all too willing to do
what it took to get me pregnant, but when it came to owning

up to it . . ." She clamped her mouth shut so tightly, Holling heard her teeth click together.

"Is that what all of that boo-hoo-hooin' and cryin' was all about, Sawyer?"

When she nodded reluctantly, Holling shook his head briskly from side to side. "Nuh-uh. Don't you even waste the water on him, Sawyer. His choice, his loss."

"I know that . . . I mean, if he's decided to move on, then I should, too. And I will."

He pulled the towel aside, tossed it on the floor, and then placed his palm against her stomach.

"Four weeks along, huh?"

"Four weeks," she echoed.

"You're not showin' at all."

"It's too early for that. You wait a while longer. Soon I'll be waddling around here like an elephant."

Holling looked at Sawyer, his face breaking into that irresistible crooked grin. "I hope so."

"And just what is that supposed to mean?"

"Exactly what I said. I want to be there to see it. I want you to be here."

She shook her head no. "You and your father have already done more for me than I have a right to expect. I can't stay here, Holling. I have to go."

"You mean on that biker rally ride? In your condition?"

"Condition? Being pregnant doesn't make me incompetent."

"Until I saw you with that towel, I wouldn't have argued. Now I have my doubts."

"One little lapse in sanity and you're going to hold it against me," she grumbled.

"The only thing I want to hold against you, darlin', is me. Tell me that you're going to stay for a while."

"For as long as it takes for Zack to fix my bike," she said firmly.

Holling took a deep breath. "As long as we're confessing things—"

"What?" Sawyer said, narrowing her eyes at him with suspicion. "What about my bike?"

"Nothing about your bike. Zack's fixing it."

"Are you sure? I don't know if I can trust him."

"You can trust me," he assured her. He could say that with a clear conscience. If he'd decided to take Zack up on his offer to stall her, he wouldn't have been able to ask her to trust him.

"Can I trust you to keep my secret? I don't want anyone else to know about the baby. Not even Nate."

"If you don't want me to say anything, Sawyer, I won't. But do you mind if I ask why not? He cares about you, you know."

"I know he does," she said, her expression pained. "I don't want him to worry about me more than he has to, Holling."

"You can't stop a man from feelin' the way he feels."

"Exactly. If he never starts to worry about me in the first place, I won't have to ask him to stop. Just let him go on caring the way that he does. In a few days, I'll be gone."

"Why are you in such a hurry to go? Don't you like it here?"

"You already know the answer to that. I've got some obligations, some commitments I need to follow through on. I plan to do just that. You can't tell Nate that I'm pregnant. If he knew about that baby, he'd never let me go off."

"I can't say that I blame him," Holling said stubbornly.

"Promise me, Holling. I know that if you do, you'll keep your word."

"I'll keep my word. I won't tell Pops."

"Thank you." She breathed a heavy sigh of relief, then laughed when her empty stomach rumbled, demanding that she make an effort to fill it again. Holling heard it too, and teased her about it.

"Pops is probably wondering if we've fallen in," he said. "We'd better go out and apologize for insulting the cook."

She grasped her stomach and gave an apologetic shrug when it continued to gurgle.

"You know, Holling, I do feel better. I think I could eat something now."

He wrapped his arm around her shoulder, ushering her out of the bathroom.

"Now that I know it's not the company you keep that's turning your stomach, I'll be more inclined to overlook your mad dashes for the bathroom."

"That does seem to be a distressing habit of mine. I've been doing some research. They say it's only the first trimester that's supposed to be the worst."

"Three months. You ought to build up some awesome leg muscles and lung capacity with that much sprinting," he said, leaning back to admire her backside.

Sawyer stopped short, gave him a look that chastised him for his obvious enjoyment of the view. "Or I could just save us all the trouble and set up a sleeping pallet right there in the bathtub," she retorted.

"You mean like the kind of pallet Vashti has out on the back porch?" he suggested.

"I'm a girl of simple tastes. I wouldn't need anything as fancy as that," she said, elbowing him in the side. "That's some kind of setup you have for that dog. Sheltered from the weather, extra padding. And she doesn't have to move far for food and water. I think you've got her spoiled, Holling."

Holling winked at her. "Kinda makes you wonder about my potential, doesn't it?"

Chapter 21

Sawyer sat hugging her knees on the steps of Holling's back porch, watching the last rays of sunlight fade into the evening sky. It had been a while since she'd slowed down long enough to enjoy something as simple as a sunset. She watched intently, following each change in the night sky with as much concentration as she would if she were watching a classic movie. One by one, she counted the evening stars as they winked on. Groups of ones, twos, stars by the dozens until the sky was thick with them—dotting the sky as brilliant as a jeweler's gemstones set out for display against a black velvet cloth.

She sighed, as much from the fullness of her stomach as she was from a fullness of spirit. This must be her day for discoveries, Sawyer thought with mild amusement. She didn't know the sky could hold so many stars. If she'd been back home in Birmingham, she wouldn't have taken the time to notice the night sky. Glance at it, maybe, while she thought of how to best describe the view in her next book to amaze her readers with her ability to craft a scene.

Her nightfall observances would have been merely an exercise. Seated at her writer's desk, head bent over her, fingers flying over the keyboard until the evening faded back to morning, she couldn't appreciate the beauty of the moment until now, spending it with Holling and his father.

Behind her, and to her left, Nate leaned in his chair against the wall. The evening newspaper he held between his arthritic hands rustled gently in the evening breeze. He heard her sigh and he set down his paper.

"Something wrong, little missy? Dinner disagreeing with you again?"

Sawyer looked back over her shoulder and gave him a smile.

"No. Everything's just fine, Nate."

Satisfied with her answer, he raised the paper again.

Behind her and to her right, Holling sat on the porch swing, tuning the strings of an acoustic guitar. With his head lowered, his fingers leisurely moving up and down the strings, he strummed. No tune in particular. Nothing that she would recognize. He was experimenting, trying out different chords until he found a progression that pleased him.

Sometimes meandering and melodic, sometimes a little bluesy, mingled with a hint of classical guitar, even a splash of Spanish flamenco style tossed in. It took a few tries for him to find a style that suited his mood. The longer he played, the more polished his impromptu performance became. Sawyer picked up on his musical progression, and before long found herself humming softly along . . . almost as if she could hear the words of his song in her head.

Holling noticed her humming, looked up in surprise, but didn't stop playing. He didn't interrupt her, simply kept his eyes trained on Sawyer's profile as she gazed up at the stars. Her wistful expression was the birth of his inspiration. The melody was molded by his skill and familiarity with his instrument. Its final form was a reflection of the natural sounds happening all around them. Holling plucked the guitar strings, imitating the night call of the whip-poor-will, moved his fingers up and down the guitar slide to answer the call of the stud horse to the mares penned separately from him. The tune ended on a soft sigh, dying down like the whisper of trees rustled by the night wind. He didn't think he'd be able to repeat the song if he tried. It was spontaneous, springing from the creative well in him that he hadn't tapped into for a long time. How Sawyer managed to follow along with him was as much a surprise as the song she was able to draw from him.

When the last note faded, swirled into the air, Sawyer turned around and clapped her hands.

"Bravo! Bravo!" she said. "Encore! Encore!"

Holling stood up, taking a grand bow.

"Don't encourage the boy, Sawyer," Nate muttered, his teeth clamped around a toothpick. "You might swell his head."

"Hey, no comments from the peanut gallery." Holling pointed at his dad.

"How long have you been playin' the guitar, Holling?" Sawyer asked.

"Oh, about twenty minutes," he returned, winking at his father.

Sawyer threw Nate a puzzled look.

"That's Holling's excuse for a joke," Nate translated for Sawyer.

"Oh . . . I see."

"You want to know excuse for a joke? That so-called dinner you call yourself putting together. Now, that's a joke."

"You don't like my cookin', next time you cook yourself." Nate then made a comic show of slapping his hand to his forehead. "Oh! That's right, I forgot. You can't cook."

"I guess that makes two of us, then," Holling returned.

Sawyer stood up, folded her arms, and stared at them. "Do you two ever give it a rest?" Back and forth, tit for tat, each one trying to get the last word on each other.

"Not if we can help it." Nate laughed at her.

She shook her head, then stepped off the stairs.

"Goin' for a stroll?" Holling asked.

"Care to join me?" She held out her hand to Holling.

"Sure," he said, shrugging his shoulders as casually as if he could just as easily have turned her down. Carefully, he laid the guitar down on the padded seat of the porch swing.

Nate looked over at his son over the rim of his halved-lens reading glasses, moved his toothpick to the other side of his mouth, and shook out his paper. "Don't act like you're not happy," he uttered under his breath as Holling passed. "Trying to pretend that you're all cool and nonchalant and everything. Don't keep the lady waiting."

Holling increased his pace, almost skipping down the short flight of stairs, to join Sawyer. Without a word, he slid his hand into hers, his long fingers intertwining through hers. Sawyer glanced down, noting how easily and naturally her hand fit inside Holling's. She didn't want to think too much about it. If she did, she knew that it would sour her mood.

She didn't want to count the number of times Ryan had offered to hold her hand. Most of the contact he initiated with her was much more physical. A hand around her waist, tugging her close to him, or around her shoulders, seizing the opportunity to touch her breasts whenever he could. Sometimes on the sly. Sometimes not. His public displays of affection were more about control, or showing ownership, than a simple desire just to be near her.

She walked along in relative silence. Nothing but night sounds, and the crunch of soft gravel under their feet to mark their passing.

Holling initiated conversation. "So, have you thought of a name for the baby yet?"

Sawyer shook her head no. "I'm still trying to get used to the idea that there is a baby," she admitted.

"What do you want? A boy or a girl?"

"Honestly, Holling, I hadn't thought about it."

"Why not?"

"I guess you could say I'm still shell-shocked."

"Seems to me that you've had some time to adjust now. What better time to start thinking about it? It's your future, you know. Something you need to plan for."

"You mean like I *didn't* plan for this?" she said, bristling.

Holling recognized the warning signals—the flash of anger in her eyes, the hardness in her tone. She was shutting down again, shutting him out.

"C'mon," he said, squeezing her hand and tugging her in a different direction.

"Where are we going?"

"Someplace I always go when I want to think without anybody hounding me."

"Where is that?" Sawyer asked dubiously.

"Not far. About a mile up the road."

"A mile?" she complained.

"I promise, it won't seem like a mile."

"I'm not exactly wearing my walking shoes." She looked down at her feet to her low-heeled sandals.

"I'll carry you if you get tired."

"What?" Sawyer exclaimed, but she was laughing even as she backed away from him.

"I'm serious. Hop on my back, I'll give you a piggyback ride."

"I'm not climbing on your back," she said.

"I was going to suggest that I put you up on my shoulders," he said, teasing her. "I didn't think you'd go for that idea."

"You were right!" she said, backing away. "Never mind. I'll walk."

Holling sat down in the middle of the drive and pulled off his boots.

"Now what are you doing?" she said.

"If we cut across the field that way"—he pointed with his chin—"it'll cut the trip down to about half a mile."

"And you're taking off your boots because . . ." she prompted.

"It's the softest grass you'll find for miles and miles around. Feels good when you walk across it."

"Nuh-uh. No way. There could be bugs out there. Or snakes."

"Come on, Sawyer." He reached up and tugged on her hand until she had to sit next to him. With the other hand, he grasped her foot and managed to slide off her sandal.

At the touch of his hand on her bare foot, Sawyer let out a squeal and started to giggle.

"What, are you ticklish?" he asked, running the ball of his thumb along her instep.

Sawyer squealed again and tried to scoot away from him.

"Cut it out, Holling! Nate!" she pleaded.

"Holling, you leave that gal alone!" he warned, but he didn't move from his perch.

"I'm not doin' anything to her, Pops!" Holling called out. Sawyer's giggling squeal of a response said otherwise. "Promise me you'll walk barefoot with me."

"I can't do that. What if there are—"

"What if there is nothing out there but God's green earth?" he countered. "Say you'll do it." His tone threatened to reach for her foot again.

"Okay, okay! I'll walk with you. But if I step in something squishy or disgusting, so help me, Holling, you'll be washing my feet for a week."

"We don't run livestock on the path we're taking, Sawyer," he told her. "Not yet. We've fenced off that section, trying to let it build up again. Last summer, the property was over-grazed, so we're trying to correct it."

"It doesn't have to be cow poop, or horse poop. It could

be rabbit poop. Or snake poop. Any poop at all is going to make me—"

Holling reached for her other shoe, but Sawyer jerked her foot out of his grasp. "All right, all right! Let me do this, please," she said.

He handed her back the other shoe, gathered up his boots and socks in his left hand, and then held his right hand out to her again.

"So, what is this thinking place of yours?" she asked.

"About six years ago, Pops had a man-made lake put in. The intent was to put some catfish in it . . . or trout, so we'd have fishing all year round."

"And do you fish all year round?"

"Not as much as we thought we would. But I still go out there sometimes, stick my pole in the water. I wind up doing little more than feeding the fish. I swear, those sneaky suckers are getting smarter every year."

He turned off the road, heading for the fence that divided the yard from the beginning of the pasture. Sawyer hesitated for a moment, then reached up and grabbed onto the white-painted plank when he urged her on. The fence wasn't very high, and the space between the boards was just wide enough for Sawyer to treat them as she would a ladder. Holling was already on the other side, grasping her around the waist and helping her down. They had only taken a few steps when Sawyer stopped in her tracks and looked down at her feet. For a moment, she had visions of beer cans skulking in the ankle-high grass, waiting to send her to the hospital for another set of stitches.

"Well?" he asked, for her verdict.

"It feels . . . springy," she said, wiggling her toes. "Springy in a good way."

"That's my girl," he said, giving her an encouraging smile. "C'mon."

Holling led the way, picking the easiest pass through the

pasture. The first part of the walk led up a gently sloping hill. Sawyer didn't notice how high they had actually walked or how far they had gone. Holling kept a steady stream of conversation, telling her about the history of the property, and revealing some of his family's plans for the future.

"Almost there," he promised. But the lake wasn't immediately visible. Gently rolling pasture gave way to a circular cove of pine trees, low scrubs, and pale lavender-colored wildflowers whose petals were folded and closed, drooping down almost to the ground as if asleep. She glanced back over her shoulder to check their progress. Holling's house looked small to her, partially shielded by the trees.

"Almost there," he said again, his tone dramatic and expectant.

Suddenly, he reached up and placed his hand over her eyes.

"Holling?" she questioned.

"Trust me," he murmured. "Keep walking. I'll guide you."

"You won't let me trip and fall, will you?"

"If you trip, it's only about thirty feet away from the water's edge. You'll roll right down into the lake to break your fall."

"Anybody ever tell you that you've got a sick sense of humor?" she asked.

"I get that all the time," he confessed. Actually, he was pleased that she even recognized his sense of humor. Some folks would be willing to bet that he'd lost it somewhere along the way.

"A couple more steps. Step. Step. Step," he directed, then stopped. "Ready?" he whispered, almost directly in her ear.

Sawyer nodded her head. "Yes."

"Okay, open your eyes, Sawyer," he said grandly, taking his hand away.

Sawyer blinked, then gave a gasp that echoed on the night air.

"Ooooooh! How lovely!" she exclaimed, clasping her hands together.

Holling had timed their arrival almost perfectly. The moon was high overhead now, moving in and out of the clouds and reflecting on the rippling surface of the lake below.

"Is that sand?" Sawyer asked in awe, noticing the glitter of the lake's shore.

"All around the lake," he confirmed. "We took a trip to Cozumel once. A family vacation. Pops had fallen in love with the sparkling sands of the beaches there. Most normal folks want to take home souvenirs to remember the trip. But no, that wasn't good enough for Pops. He arranged to have enough sand shipped to him to give him the illusion of the vacation paradise. All that he couldn't get from Cozumel, he mixed with some sand from local landfills."

"So, if I go walking around the beach down there, I'm not going to have my foot cut on a beer can, am I? My cousins aren't here to help me to the hospital." Her tone was a mixture of amusement and distrust.

"Maybe your cousins aren't here, but I am," he said. "And I won't let anything happen to you. This is my private place. A place I come to when the whole world seems full of beer cans waiting to get you. None of that here. C'mon, Sawyer. Let's take that walk on the beach that I promised you."

"Beaches in Montana," she murmured, shaking her head. "Will wonders never cease?"

Not as long as I can help it, Holling thought. He took her hand, leading her closer to the water's edge.

Sawyer stopped close when she thought she heard a splash echoing louder than the usual waves.

"What was that?" She stepped closer to Holling.

"If you listen real close," he said in a hushed whisper, "you can hear the fish jumping in and out of the water to catch the bugs skating on the surface."

"Ew!" She made a face.

When she got to the edge of the lake, she bent down and swirled her hand inside.

"This water's ice cold!" she exclaimed. "And so pure. What have you done? Hung a giant commode deodorizer over the edge so when you flush the lake it makes the bowl sparkling fresh?"

"Anybody tell you that you have an overactive imagination?" he asked.

"I'm a writer." Her tone wasn't apologetic as she shrugged. "It's what I do."

"Tomorrow there's another place I want to show you. That ought to really get the creative juices flowing."

"Where is it?"

"I'm not going to tell you . . . you'll see," he promised. He bent down and cupped his hands in the water and let it pour out again. "The lake's being fed from an underground spring. Before Pops had the lake dug, we had a couple of survey teams come out. A geologist and several folks from the environmental protection agency. The first spot we considered was about ten miles back that way closer to the mountains." He pointed. "In the spring, we'd get the runoff to help replenish her."

"What made you change your mind? Why put the lake here and not near the base of the mountains? That would have made such a lovely setting."

"If we get a particularly harsh winter, we couldn't control how much water actually flowed into the lake without building a few levees or tearing up the land even more than we had to in order to redirect the flow. It could have gotten nasty with flash floods or mud slides. Once you start digging holes in the ground you gotta be real careful, Sawyer, about how that affects the rest of the land around it."

"I guess I never gave it much thought. In Birmingham,

everything's already built up. So modern and urban. It's still got its Southern charm, but you have to drive to the rural areas to see nature."

"Out here, Sawyer, we think about the land all the time. A good third of the land we're sitting on is protected, reserved either for grazing or natural state parks."

"It's beautiful out here, Holling." She looked up into the night sky. "It absolutely takes my breath away."

"I know the feeling," he responded, his voice husky with emotion.

The change in the timbre of his voice brought Sawyer's attention back down to earth. She glanced over at him. He wasn't looking up at the sky. He was looking directly at her. There was an intensity in his lean face that caught Sawyer off guard. The shadows played tricks on her eyes, so that all she seemed to see were his dark eyes, pinning her to the spot. Up until now, everything had been easy. The walk. The conversation. Teasing. Flippant. Even buoyant.

"Holling," she began hesitantly, backing away from him.

"What?" he said, smiling at her with the crooked smile that somehow always seemed to get to her. His expression was usually so stern, so no-nonsense. His smiles were rare. And when he turned them on her, she felt the full force of their effect.

"Don't." She uttered a single word, but it covered a multitude of commands.

"Don't what?" he murmured, approaching her. Sawyer held out her hands, pushed against his chest.

Don't come any closer, Holling. Don't smile at me. Don't look at me that way. The way that makes my stomach turn flips and my heart switch from wildly beating one moment to frozen solid in time the next. Don't fall in love with me, Holling. I'm not ready! And you, Sawyer, don't you dare fall in love with him either. Don't. Don't!

She wanted to scream at him. Instead, she kept her tone low, cool. "Don't get too attached."

"What are you talking about, Sawyer?" His tone of innocence didn't fool her. Not one bit.

"You know what I'm talking about," she insisted. "Don't get too attached to me."

"And why not?" He covered one hand that lay against his chest, and gently massaged her fingers. Sawyer recognized her mistake by touching him. She felt how his heart beat beneath the fabric of his shirt. It was as wildly erratic as her own.

"Because I won't be around long enough to figure out whether or not we could make it work."

"You could change that, Sawyer," he suggested. "You could stay."

"What if I don't want to?"

He spread his hands out. "I'm such a great guy. No reason for you not to want to take advantage of my hospitality."

"I have my reasons."

"Name one."

"I already did."

"No, you didn't," he contradicted. She gave him a look that made him amend his statement. "Oh. . . . Well, if it's the baby you're talking about as one of your so-called named reasons, I'm not counting that one. You haven't given the baby a name, remember?"

"That's not funny!" she snapped.

He kept his tone even to keep from making her even angrier. "You don't see me laughin', do you?"

"I don't want to talk about the baby with you, Holling."

"Why not? It's why I brought you out here. I told you that I come out here when I have difficult things to think about. You've got a very difficult topic to tackle. It's why I brought you out to my thinking place."

"So I could think about you?"

"Partially. I can't think of a better subject to think on."

"Your shortsightedness and one-track mind are not my problem."

"My thinking place. My rules. Looks like it is your problem, Sawyer Garth."

"So, if I come out here on my own, does that mean I get to choose the subject I want to think about? I didn't know that if you brought me out here, there would be conditions on my thoughts."

"Being pregnant makes you grumpy, too, doesn't it?" he goaded her.

Sawyer took the bait. "I swear, Holling, if you mention this baby one more time, I'm going to—"

"To what?" he interrupted, challenging her. He placed his hands on her hips, pulling her closer to him. *Maybe I could have been gentler,* Holling thought in hindsight. He hadn't meant to manhandle her. But his aggression was twofold.

Part of him was tired of the way she was always running away from him. Did she think it was easy for him, practically begging her to stay? He wasn't used to working so hard to get a woman's attention. The other part of him was genuinely concerned for her safety. If she'd kept backing away from him, she would have found herself falling, floundering in the lake.

"I don't know," she faltered. "I'll think of something."

"Let me give you a suggestion," he offered, bending his head down to kiss her.

Sawyer started to lean away, then swiftly decided that she didn't want to. She lifted her face to him. "This isn't a good idea, Holling," she murmured as he kissed her. "There's so much that we should talk about first."

"All I'm askin' for is time," he said, smoothing his palm over her cheek. He brushed aside her hair. "Just a little more time."

"Five days," she conceded. "If I'm not totally, completely, irrevocably head over heels in love with you in five days, you'll let me go? Swear to me that you will."

"You'd take my word for it?"

"You're a man of honor, aren't you?" she countered. "Code of the West and all that jazz?"

"Yes, Sawyer, I am."

"Then I'll have to accept that, won't I?"

"Five days," he repeated. "You don't give a man much time to pull off a miracle, do you, Sawyer?"

"Five days. Take it or leave it."

"Five days. Take me or leave me," he corrected.

"Then we're in agreement," she whispered, as his lips closed over hers, sealing the covenant between them.

Chapter 22

"Promise me," Nate entreated his son for the third time. "Promise me that you'll be agreeable and that you and Shane won't fight. Promise that this time you'll try to get along."

"I can keep that promise, Pops," Holling said, yanking on the straps to tighten his saddle. He yanked too hard, causing his horse to huff and stomp in protest. "Not a problem. I won't say a single unkind word to him. And you know why?"

Nate didn't respond. Instead, he patted his hand along the horse's rump to soothe him. "Easy there, big fella," Nate said. But he was looking at Holling when he said it.

Holling gave a shrill whistle, calling over to one of their stable hands. "Cale, bring out that sorrel for Ms. Garth, would ya?" he directed to a young pie-faced man.

"Yes, sir, Mr. Holling," he said briskly, trotting off.

"I'll tell you why." Holling followed in the pattern of his father, answering his own questions. " 'Cause I don't plan to be here *if* and when he finally decides to show up."

"He said he'd be here."

"Sure he did. He always says he'll be here. And then you get your hopes all up. Regular as clockwork, he'll call and make some excuse why he can't be here. You know what that does to you, Pops? Tears you to pieces. And then you spend the next couple of weeks with your lip all poked out."

"Shane's a very busy man, Holling. You think his job is easy? Helping the lieutenant governor run the state is not an easy job."

"If Shane spent as much time running this state as he does running his mouth or running up personal debts, I bet we'd all be better off," Holling snapped. He turned around, cupped his hand to his mouth. "Hey, Sawyer! Shake a leg, darlin'. We're burnin' daylight."

"You sure you don't want to hang around, Holling? Introduce Shane to your new gal?"

Holling said an unkind word, and then on reflex apologized to his father for the slip. "If I can help it, I don't want Shane within ten miles of Sawyer, Pops."

Nate shook his head at his son. "What's the matter, Holling? Afraid Shane will snatch that little missy right out from under your nose? You two always were competitive."

Holling shot his father a concerned look. Shane was a slick one with the ladies. He had it all. Looks. Brains. Position. *And* the Holling name.

Nate quickly eased his son's fear. "Don't worry, boy. Not a chance of that happening."

When Holling looked at his father, his expression was unsure. Nate clasped his hand on Holling's shoulder. "That gal's only got eyes for you, Holling. As far as she's concerned, there is nobody else."

"I don't know, Pops," Holling said doubtfully.

"Well, I do. Let me tell you something, Holling. I've been watchin' her . . . and watchin' some of these peacocks hanging around, struttin' and trying to get her attention. She might as well have blinders on. You've got nothin' to worry about."

"I keep telling myself that, but every time I think I'm

gonna get close to her, she pushes me back. She's a hard woman to get to know."

"Give her some time, boy."

"She gave me five days," he said ruefully.

"Five days to sweep her off her feet, huh? You're good. But you're not that good," Nate said. "If I were you, boy, I'd kick it into gear."

"Don't worry, Pops, I've got a plan," Holling said, tapping his temple with his index finger. He turned again, shouting for Sawyer to hurry.

"I'm coming, I'm coming!" Sawyer called out, racing down the stairs as she shrugged into a light jacket. As she drew closer, she took one look at the strained looks on their faces and apologized. "Sorry I took so long."

"It's all right, Sawyer," Holling said gruffly, turning his back on her to check his saddle.

She threw a puzzled look in Nate's direction. Nate shook his head, cleared his throat, and said, "So you and Holling going for a ride?"

"Uh-huh."

"Where you headin' off to?"

"I'm not sure," Sawyer said, giving a self-conscious laugh. "Holling said it's a surprise."

"What time you gonna be back?"

Holling's voice rumbled a low warning. "Pops."

"I'm just askin' so I'll know what time to put supper on for you."

Again, Sawyer shrugged. "We're going exploring, Nate. I'm not sure what time we'll be back."

"Don't worry, Pops. I won't have her out too late," Holling said.

"So, you're saying that you'll be back for . . . for supper."

Holling relented. "Yeah, Pops. I'll be back in time for supper if it's that important to you."

"It is," Nate said, his dark face lit by his smile.

"You'll be riding Taffy," Holling told her, pointing out the horse being led toward them by one of the stable hands.

Sawyer smiled at the tan pony with the white blaze on her face and the white markings on her hind legs.

"Here you go, Mr. Holling." Cale handed the reins to Holling.

"Thanks, Cale." He double-checked the saddle, all of its cinches, before addressing Sawyer again.

"A couple of questions before we head out, Sawyer. You're not afraid of horses, are you?"

"Now's a fine time to be asking me that, Holling." Sawyer's tone was mildly chastising.

"Well, are you?" he insisted.

"I don't think so. I mean, standing here with the possibility of a very long ride ahead of us isn't striking fear in my heart."

"I guess I don't have to ask you whether or not you can ride, huh?"

"Now we're talking a different kind of horsepower. I'm out of my element here. If you give me something with two wheels and a hand clutch, I can handle it. This one has got four legs and no visible throttle. But the last time I was on a horse, I was about six years old. My father took me to a state fair. This guy had six Shetland ponies attached to a wheel. All we did was go round and round and round."

"How was it?"

"I thought I had the time of my life. My father said I looked like a stone statue sitting up there. I wasn't laughing or smiling like the other kids."

"You don't have to be afraid of Taffy here."

"I wasn't afraid then," Sawyer quickly denied. "I remember riding that pony and thinking that I should write a story about it. I wasn't afraid, I was just in my own imaginary world."

"What about now?" he teased.

"I'm not afraid now either," Sawyer said stoutly.

"Even if you were, something tells me that you wouldn't want to show it."

"I'm a big girl now and can move in and out of my fantasy world without the fear showing on my face."

"I picked Taffy for you because she's a good trail horse," Holling explained. "She'll follow the lead horse, with you barely having to control her. Just hang on to the reins."

"Is that all?"

"Mostly all you need to know. Just like the pony ride when you were a little girl."

"Two more things I need to know." Sawyer held up two fingers. "Minor details."

"What's that?"

"How to climb on and how to get off."

Holling burst into laughter, startling his own big buckskin horse.

"Whoa . . . easy."

He patted the stud's warm side, making soothing noises. Then he waved the stable hand over.

"Cale, you're about Ms. Garth's size. Show her the best way to mount a horse."

"Yes, sir. Ma'am, you take the reins like so. Grab the saddle horn with this hand. Step up into the stirrup, swing your leg over, and plant your foot in the other stirrup."

Taffy barely twitched a tail as Cale settled himself on her back. She lifted her head slightly, ears perked up as if listening for the command to go.

"When you dismount, it's just the reverse." He demonstrated the technique again. "Simple."

"Come on over here, Sawyer, and get to know her."

"I guess introducing myself is the least I can do before asking her to haul me across the countryside," Sawyer said, eyeing the horse with a certain degree of mistrust.

Holling held on to Taffy's bridle as Sawyer moved closer.

She stroked the length of Taffy's velvet face, smiling when she felt the warm rush of air as Taffy whooshed in her direction, and stamped her foot.

"I think she's ready to be off, Holling," Sawyer said.

"Are you ready?"

"As ready as I'll ever be, I suppose."

"All righty then. Let's go."

"Any hints as to where we're going?"

"You want a hint?"

"Just a teeny one," she said.

"Here's your hint. You'll see when we get there."

"That's not a hint. That's a secret."

Holling chuckled softly, his mood lightening. "Let's just say that I'll be giving you inspiration for your next book."

"You do know I write romances, don't you?" she reminded him.

"Uh-huh. I looked you up."

"Excuse me?"

"On the Web. On one of those online book-ordering sites. You've gotten some pretty good reviews."

"You sound surprised."

"More like impressed. I ordered a couple of copies. Are you gonna autograph them for me?"

"Sure."

"You promise?"

"I said I would."

"And you're a woman of your word," he pressed.

Sawyer looked askance at him. It was the same question that she'd asked him last night. "What's your game, Holling? What are you up to?"

"Why do you think I've got to be up to something?"

"You think I fell off the turnip truck yesterday?"

Holling's eyes crinkled up at the corners. "No game, Sawyer. I just asked if you're gonna sign my books for me . . . when they come in."

It took Sawyer a moment to realize that somewhere in that simple admission was a big fat "Gotcha!" waiting to jump out at her.

"And when are they supposed to be in?" she pressed. "You didn't have them shipped overnight, did you?"

"I saved a few pennies on the ordering. The books should be here any time between next week and the week after."

"You've got to be kidding!" she scolded. "Holling, I thought we agreed that you only had five days. About as long as it would take for Zack to fix my motorcycle."

"It's not my fault that you just extended the deadline," Holling protested with mock innocence.

"You are absolutely incorrigible!"

"Incorrigible?" he repeated. "There you go with those big writer's words again, Sawyer."

"If I had a thesaurus, I'd thump you in the head with it."

"If being incorrigible is anything like being devious and underhanded and totally committed to making you stay, then thump away."

She shook her head. "I don't understand you, Holling. I don't understand why you're going through so much trouble with me. Is this more of your 'hopeless causes' charity cases? Do you think you're gonna get extra stars in your crown in heaven for making me feel wanted?"

Holling paused before answering. He wondered what kind of relationship she'd been in with that ex of hers. What had he done to her self-image? Why couldn't she see that, in his eyes, she was worth fighting for?

"I've got at least five days to make you see," he said softly. "Clock's tickin', darlin'."

He held the bridle, then nodded for her to climb into the saddle.

"All right, Taffy," Sawyer murmured near the horse's ear. "Just you and me, girl. You and me. You treat me right and I'll treat you right."

"She will," Holling promised.

"Do you mind?" Sawyer said, raising her eyebrow at him. "This is a private conversation between me and the horse."

"Far be it from me to eavesdrop," Holling said, as if injured.

Sawyer grasped the reins and the saddle as Cale had demonstrated. She placed her left foot in the stirrup, then swung her leg over the saddle.

Holling held on, keeping Taffy steady for her. But that didn't stop him from appreciating Sawyer's form as she settled herself into the saddle. He told himself that he was checking to be sure that she was comfortably seated, yet he couldn't help appreciating the beauty of her seat.

He made a low sound of appreciation under his breath. The girl sure did know how to sit a horse well, even without formal training. Some things he figured were just natural— God-given assets that no amount of formal training could imitate. He had to admit, it wasn't just the way she sat that pleased him. He liked the curve of her thighs, how it gently swept upward to form the sweep of her firm bottom. Sawyer sat straight-backed, proud, and fearless even though he knew she must be quaking inside. From the ground, Taffy didn't look so big. But once she was sitting on top of her, the ground must have looked very far away for Sawyer.

Holling didn't notice how long he was staring at her until, after she'd finished adjusting herself in the saddle, she stared down at him.

"What are you waiting for?" she prompted.

"Nothin'." He shook his head.

"Then come on, let's go. Like you said, Holling, we're burning daylight."

"Yes, ma'am!" Holling touched his hand to his hat and then swung easily onto own his horse. His powerful thighs rested against the horse's flanks. He adjusted the reins and gave the slightest nudge to his horse. Sawyer imitated him as best she could.

As Cale scurried ahead of them to open the gate and let them out of the pen, it was Sawyer's turn to admire Holling's physique. As he headed out to open pasture, Sawyer tried to keep her focus and attention on what she was doing, and not the ripple of Holling's muscles across his back and shoulders.

Holling whistled softly, getting Taffy's attention. Sawyer didn't even have to dig her heels into Taffy's side, urging her forward, when the well-trained sorrel lifted her head, then fell into step behind Cochise.

Sawyer waved to Nate watching them from the porch. "Look at me, Nate!" she called out. "I'm riding a horse."

"Hold on tight, little missy!" he shouted back. "Don't you fall off, now."

"I won't," she promised, holding tightly to the reins. They plodded along a quarter of a mile, Sawyer getting used to the gentle sway of Taffy's gait.

Holling twisted around to check on her. "You doin' all right back there?"

"Just fine," she said. "Do you want to tell me where we're going now?"

"You don't want to wait to be surprised?"

"I hate surprises," she said. "They make me nervous."

"Is that why you don't want to talk about the baby? 'Cause it makes you nervous?"

"I thought we weren't going to talk about that anymore."

"*I* want to talk about it, Sawyer."

"Why!" she demanded. "I don't see what business it is of yours. It's my baby. My business. End of story, so just let it go."

Wrong, Holling thought stubbornly. It wasn't the end of the story. Not yet. Not while he had at least four more days to make it his business. He looked back at her, noticed the stubborn set of her face. Sawyer's expression was matched by the equally determined look in his. She thought that he was meddling in her business. Well, maybe he was. No maybe about it. He definitely was. And for the life of him, he wished that he had a rational reason why he was so concerned about her. It didn't make any sense. He barely knew her. What did he know? That she had family in Birmingham. She rode a motorcycle. And that she was carrying another man's child . . . a man who didn't want anything to do with her. It was enough for him. Enough to know that he had tender feelings for her, feelings that ran too deep for him to yet determine their true depth. It must be right. It must be real. Women he'd known all his life hadn't evoked emotions of the intensity that he had about Sawyer.

Was he in love with her? Maybe. Certainly felt like it to him. He'd been in love before and recognized the feeling for what it was. Wild and unpredictable. Being in love meant being unsettled, unsure, plagued with doubts and insecurities that made a man constantly debate. That's the way he felt about Sawyer. Always questioning, always wondering what little thing he could do or say to set her off.

Holling felt what he should really be asking was, did he love her? Was he ready to commit himself to her and only her? A tiny voice inside him told him that he was. It was a voice that grew louder every waking moment. It told him that he wanted her. He wanted to be with her. He could accept her unconditionally for who she was and what she was. It didn't matter about her past. He would embrace her, and all that she was, if only she'd let him.

The first time she'd rejected him and his offer, he thought maybe she didn't share the same feelings. She'd had a man. Maybe she still had feelings for him and held out the hope that he would change his mind and accept the child. If that were true, Holling didn't think he could compete with that. All he could ever hope from Sawyer was her friendship.

But then, he'd kissed her last night. He'd kissed her and she'd kissed him back with the kind of passion that Holling sensed couldn't have been meant for her ex. It couldn't have been. That kiss was meant for him and only him. He didn't know how he knew. He just did. Maybe it had something to do with the way she clung to him. Fiercely. Possessively. She couldn't let go. Wouldn't let go. She wanted him, too.

It sounded crazy to his own ears, as if he were some kind of obsessive nutcase who couldn't take no for an answer. If he'd seen his behavior in anyone else, he'd figure that person to be some kind of lowlife loser who couldn't take no for an answer. If a woman didn't want you, then let go. Move on. But Sawyer did want him. She did.

Maybe it had something do with the way she murmured his name. Was it the way she molded her body into his, moving sensually against him, making him moan, that let him know that she needed him? She knew just the right places to touch him to fire his senses. She'd found out through tentative exploration and grown bolder, less reserved as each touch tore from him an unfettered response. Like the strings of his guitar, she stroked him, strummed him.

It was instinct that told him that she was for him. It was instinct pushing him to keep at her, to help her realize that she belonged *with* him, if not *to* him.

His pops had told him to come up with a plan. He did have one. Nothing as devious and underhanded as Zack's plan to delay her. It was simple. He would stay by her side, every waking moment. Maybe if she saw how he was with her, how perfectly they seemed to fit together, she wouldn't be so quick to break them apart.

Chapter 23

Side by side, Holling and Sawyer rode along the path leading to Holling's "surprise." With each mile they rode, Sawyer grew in confidence of her ability to handle Taffy, enough so that she wasn't content to ride behind Holling anymore. Three miles into the ride, she kicked Taffy in the sides as she'd seen Holling do to Cochise. Taffy only needed a mild nudge. Sawyer knew that without spurs she couldn't hurt her gentle sorrel. In fact, when Taffy quickened her step, Sawyer wondered whether or not Taffy herself was getting bored with the dawdling pace they'd set.

When Taffy came up alongside Holling, Sawyer pulled back firmly on the reins, slowing Taffy down so that they were even. Otherwise, she would have overrun Holling. Might even have kept running clear on to the next county if Sawyer hadn't stopped her.

"So, you're tired of eatin' my trail dust?" he teased her.

"I got tired of talking to your backside," she explained. "And I'm sure you were getting a cramp in your neck turning around to talk to me."

"So, are you enjoying the ride so far?" Holling asked.

"I certainly am. The more I see of your home state, Holling, the more I think how fortunate you are to be surrounded by all of this. I'm a writer and I can't find the words to explain how it makes me feel."

"What's Birmingham like? I have this picture in my head of old, Southern-style plantations and ladies in big dresses sipping mint juleps."

Sawyer laughed. "You've been watching *Gone With the Wind* too many times. True, Birmingham has its own Southern charm. But it's also very modern. It's a metropolis. Not as notorious as New York or Chicago or L.A., but certainly enough people and buildings to make you feel closed in. Out here, I look around and all I see is land and sky. A girl could lose herself in all of this."

My plans exactly, Holling thought. "You won't get lost," he said. "Not with me here to guide you."

"I'm not used to anybody guiding me," she retorted. "I'm used to finding and making my own way."

"You can't do it all by yourself, Sawyer. Sometimes you've got to have help. Even your writing . . . as solitary a profession as that is . . . you've got to have help. A whole slew of people to bring that book from the thoughts in your head to the books on the shelf. So tell me, Sawyer, how long have you been writing?"

"It's hard to say. I've been writing stories ever since I was old enough to pick up a pencil." She laughed softly. "I used to write these squiggles on pieces of paper and then 'read' them out loud to my cousins. It was funny how I could read the same squiggles and come up with a different story every time. A natural-born storyteller. That's what my aunt Rosie used to call me."

"You had a very active imagination, huh?"

"More like hyperactive. If my imagination had been an actual child, I think the doctors would have prescribed Ritalin for me to calm me down. I was such a strange kid. I lived in my own fantasy world. Everything I thought I needed out of life, I created in worlds of my own making."

"And now you're making that imagination work for you."

"It's not work," she said, winking at him. "That's what some of my family members think. They think that I'm playing for a living." She shrugged off the sentiments. "Is there a crime in enjoying what you do?"

Holling nodded. "I know what you mean. Guess what I used to play when I was a kid? Go on, guess. I'll bet you'll never guess."

"When you were a kid, you wanted to be a cowboy," she said promptly.

"Nope."

"What do you mean no?"

"Guess again."

"An Indian?"

"Nuh-uh."

"I give up."

"You're not even trying," he accused her.

She paused for a moment, as if thinking. "A race-car driver?"

"We'll be at this all day. When I was a kid, I wanted to be an astronaut."

"An astronaut!"

"Up until the time I was about nine, I just knew I was going to be in outer space."

"What changed your mind?"

"Pops caught me trying to launch myself into orbit with a homemade rocket. I'd taken an old barrel that we'd sawed in half and used to feed the horses, tacked on some wings made from plywood, soaked some rags in charcoal lighter fluid for my fuse . . . I almost had it lit, too, but Shane ran in complaining that I wouldn't let him be the captain. Snitched on me to my pops. That ruined my trip real fast."

Sawyer had to pull Taffy to a full stop, she was laughing so hard. She was certain that she'd tumble out of the saddle if she didn't stop to catch her breath.

"But that was before I decided I wanted to be a pro wrestler. I think I was about eleven when Pops derailed that career move, too."

"What killed that dream?"

"The whuppin' Pops gave me when I broke my brother's arm trying to imitate a wrestling move."

"When did you finally settle on being a rancher?"

"I didn't settle on it. It settled on me," he admitted. "It kinda snuck up on me. One morning, I was out helping Pops with the chores. The next thing I know, living and working the property wasn't so much what I was supposed to be doin' but who I was. An extension of me. I just woke up one morning and knew that's where I was supposed to be."

"How old were you when you came to that conclusion?"

"Twelve," he answered promptly.

"Twelve? Wasn't that too young to be deciding what you wanted to do with the rest of your life?"

"How old were you when you read your stories to your cousins?"

"About five," she admitted.

"Sometimes you just know what you know. And nothin' can convince you otherwise."

Sawyer gave an unwilling smile. She'd sensed that about Holling. He had an unmistakable confidence about him. This was a man used to making decisions, whether snap ones or after long, careful consideration. In either case, his manner was the same. Steadfast. Self-assured. Convinced of his own rightness.

"Haven't you ever felt that way, Sawyer?" Holling continued. "Ever felt deep inside so strongly when something's right . . . so convinced that nothing in the world could change your mind?"

She looked down at her still-flat stomach, placed her hand over where she imagined the fetus to be nestled, safe and protected, inside her. It was exactly the way she'd felt when she left the doctor's office. She couldn't go through with the abortion. Despite her doubts and misgivings, despite her fear and her anger at Ryan's rejection, deciding to keep the baby was the right choice for her. She felt it in the very core of her being. Let others come to other conclusions. This one was right for her.

"Yes," she said simply. "I've felt that way."

Holling reined in his horse and then reached out to close his gloved hand over Sawyer's. "Then you know how I feel for you now, Sawyer. You know why I can't explain it. I just know. From the moment I saw you, I knew. I know you don't believe me yet. But you will."

"I suppose you're going to tell me that you just know that, too," she said, trying to make her tone mocking. It didn't come out sounding right. It didn't sound harsh at all. To Holling's ears, she sounded hopeful, as if she wanted to be convinced.

"Since you won't believe me, I'm gonna hang around until you tell me that you know it," he said smugly. He clucked to his horse, starting him up the path again.

"How much further?" Sawyer asked.

"Not much. Should be just beyond that line of trees up there ahead." He pointed to a section of land that slanted upward. "When I read an excerpt from one of your books online, I thought about this place and thought about you . . . how you'd enjoy it."

"Quite a buildup you're giving it, Holling, whatever this place is." Sawyer tried raising herself up in the saddle, craning her neck to see beyond the trees obscuring the rest of the road. The road wasn't very well traveled. Portions of it were overgrown with weeds and obscured by low-hanging branches from trees that looked as old as the land itself. As they approached the base of the hill, underbrush gave way to a path barely wide enough for the horses to climb.

"You won't be disappointed. I promise."

Sawyer didn't immediately take him at his word. She continued to ask questions, trying to get him to give her a hint as to where they were going and what she could expect to see. But like the mood he had set for her first sight of the lake, Holling was teasing and mysterious, playful and dramatic.

"Here's were we get off," he said, swinging down. He tied Cochise's reins to a nearby tree, then reached out to help Sawyer down.

"Oomph!" she exclaimed as her feet touched ground. She hadn't thought the ride was a rough one until she felt the muscles in her rear tighten. Sawyer stretched her arms above her head, then leaned forward to loosen her thigh and calf muscles as Holling tied off Taffy next to Cochise. Close to the leafy twigs, the horses munched contently.

"Ready?" he asked, indicating the rocky footpath leading up the hill.

She nodded. Holling grasped her elbow, then started the climb up.

"Easy," he said. "The last rains may have made the dirt path unstable."

It was the last thing he said to her before guiding her to the top of the hill. Once at the top, Holling held out his hand and said, "Ta-dah!"

Sawyer burst into laughter—not in ridicule for his grandiose gesture, but for his correct assessment of her delight in his latest sightseeing adventure.

"What is this?" she gasped.

"A ghost town, of course," he explained. "Some say the original site of White Wolf. But I don't think so."

"Why not?"

"If it was, somebody would have claimed this as a historical landmark by now. Maybe set it up as a tourist attraction, charging gullible tourists twenty bucks a head to tour."

"What do you think it is?"

"I think it's an old movie set."

"A movie set? In Montana?"

"The early Western filmmakers didn't always film on the back lots, Sawyer. Some of the early film moguls went for authenticity. Just look at the view . . . the mountains in the background, the prairie we came through to get here. Relatively secluded. They could shoot without being bothered by the locals."

"Then why wouldn't they tear it down when the movie wrapped?"

"Who knows? Maybe it was cheaper to leave the structures standing and let Mother Nature do the tearing down for them? The point is, it's still here. And if you can close your eyes, for a moment, just a moment, you can pretend you really are in the old West."

Sawyer looked down on the collection of rustic buildings, circa the early 1800s. A livery stable, a mercantile, a saloon, and a church—only two or three of the original structures still stood. But they were enough to fire Sawyer's imagination. She squeezed Holling's hand. "Come on, cowboy. Let's see what this one-horse town has to offer."

She started down the opposite side of the hill, tugging Holling after her into the first building she came to that looked as if wouldn't come down on their heads—the saloon.

Holling pushed open the swinging doors, letting Sawyer in before him.

She ambled around the building, running her fingers over what appeared to be hand-hewn furniture. "If it was a movie set, someone sure did their homework," she murmured, impressed. "It all looks so real." She spun around, pointing out imaginary landmarks. "Over there is where the piano player sits," she said.

As she skipped across the room, Sawyer grew more animated. "And here . . . here is where they play roulette . . . no, poker!" When she crossed the room again, kicking up dust and leaving footprints to mark her crossing, she stood behind the long bar dominating the room.

Sawyer pretended to grab a mug from behind the dilapidated bar. She pulled down on the handle of a tap, coughing a bit as the nozzle hissed air and a small puff of dust wafted into the air. She waved aside the dust with one hand and passed Holling the imaginary draft with the other.

"Sit down, Marshal Dillon, and have a beer."

"Why, thank ya, Miss Kitty, I believe I will." Holling fell easily into the role-play from the Western television drama. He held up the imaginary glass to the sunlight streaming through the cracks in the warped planks of the wall.

"Must be light beer," he mused.

"The good stuff's in the back," Sawyer returned.

Holling leaned his elbows on the bar. When one of his arms went through the thinning wood, Sawyer laughed and helped him to pull some of the splinters from his shirtsleeve.

"Just a flesh wound, Marshal Dillon," she said. "You'll live."

He pantomimed raising the mug to his lips, then wiping off the foam with the back of his hand.

"That sure did hit the spot, Miss Kitty." He poked out his stomach, deliberately making it look as if he were carrying a spare tire around his waist, and then patted his paunch. "Well, I guess I'd better mosey on back down to the jailhouse."

"Oh, Matt, must you go?" Sawyer raised her folded hands to her cheek, leaned her head on her hands, and fluttered her eyelashes at him. "It's so dangerous out there. I hear that every bit-part actor who ever starred in every *Gunsmoke* episode is out there gunnin' for ya."

"It's a dirty job, Miss Kitty, but a man's gotta do what a man's gotta do." Holling hooked his thumbs in his belt, pretending to hitch up his pants. "Dodge City is my town and no two-bit, tenderfoot with a notch on his gun belt is gonna run me out of it."

"One last kiss before you go, Matt. It's the least you can do for me after all of those episodes when all I got from you was a consoling arm around the shoulder after I was either kidnapped, beaten, or shot just for the privilege of being the marshal's woman."

Carefully, Sawyer leaned over the bar, puckered up, and made loud, obnoxious smacking noises in his direction.

"What? I think I hear Festus calling me." Holling cupped his hand to his ear and leaned toward the door.

"Not so fast, cowboy! You'd better get back here and make an honest woman out of me!" She reached out, grabbed two handfuls of his shirt, and pulled him to within inches of her face.

"Why, Miss Kitty! I didn't know you could be so forward," he murmured. "You know, lewd acts like this can get you arrested."

"Hold on to your spurs, cowboy. You ain't seen acting yet!" Sawyer said. She gave a final yank, pulling him so that his chest leaned against the bar. His fingers gripped the edge for support.

When Sawyer pressed her lips to his, she could barely continue with the charade for her laughter. The stubbly beginnings of the beard that Holling was starting to grow tickled her face.

Sawyer heard the bar creak under his weight and threaten to collapse. Still, she couldn't stop laughing. She tugged harder, pulling him over the bar.

"Whoa!" Holling cried out, wrapping his arms around

her waist as they tumbled to the floor in a cloud of dust, splintered wood, and the dried leaves that had blown inside the room over time.

"Oh! Ouch!" Sawyer exclaimed as she fell on her side to the hardwood floor. Holling fell on top of her in a tangle of arms and legs and wood.

"Sawyer!" Holling quickly rose up on his elbows to take the bulk of his weight from her. He waved his hand in the air, brushing away the debris that had fallen near her head.

Sawyer sneezed, giggled, and then sneezed again.

"Are you all right, darlin'?" he asked, smoothing his hands over her face, brushing away cobwebs that clung to her hair.

Sawyer lay nestled next to him, her forearm resting against his chest.

"I'm all right," she said softly. "Nothing hurt but my pride."

"This is the last time I let you serve up drinks, Miss Kitty," he teased. "Your concoctions sure do pack a punch."

"I'm not the only one who packs," she retorted. Smiling up at him, Sawyer murmured in her best Southern belle imitation, "Why, I do declare, Marshal Dillon. Is that a six-gun in your pocket or are you just happy to see me?"

Holling sat up quickly, rolled away from her, mentally cursing his inability to mask his feelings from her.

"You think that's funny?" he retorted.

She put her hand over her mouth, trying to cover her grin. "Oh, lighten up, Holling. I didn't mean anything by it."

"That's the killin' part, Sawyer. I *did*," he said tightly. He'd been so focused today on trying to connect with her, trying to get to know her, that he hadn't thought about how being close to her affected him physically.

Holling had done the best he could to push his desire for this woman to the back of his mind. It was only clouding his thinking. Getting in the way of what he really wanted her to know. Sure, he wanted to make love to her. He knew it. And she knew it. But he also wanted her to know that he wanted more from her than that. Body and soul. That's what he wanted. He would have nothing less from her. Until she was ready to offer that to him, he'd have to be patient.

"We'd better go," he said hoarsely. He rumbled, cleared his throat as if the settling dust was irritating it.

Sawyer dropped her eyes. "Do we have to?" she asked softly. "I mean . . . so soon? Can't we, uh, stay a while and . . . explore?"

"Explore?" he echoed. He didn't want to read too much into her request. On the surface, it sounded like a plausible enough excuse. After all, he'd brought her out here knowing that the ghost town would intrigue her.

"Uh-huh," she whispered. She reached out, laid her hand against the back of his neck, and applied subtle pressure, drawing him closer.

Holling leaned forward, hovering just inches away from her mouth.

"You want to explore. I think I can arrange that, darlin'," he said.

"I always thought you were a man of considerable . . . *ummm* . . . resources," Sawyer said. The rest of her comeback was lost, cut off by Holling suddenly covering her again. This time, there was no unexpected free fall. No clumsy tangling of limbs. As he eased her back, his movements were controlled, deliberate. He never took his eyes from her face. He watched for every change in her expression, any shift in her emotion. He saw himself reflected in her deep green eyes. Where he was used to seeing suspicion, or at the very least secrets upon secrets, he saw himself in an open, honest expression of love.

There. He'd said it. At least to himself. He didn't dare say it out loud for fear of sounding like a lunatic. He was in love with her, just as sure as he was breathing. From the first time he'd met her, spoken with her, and protected her, his every waking moment was consumed with figuring out if she could ever love him back.

Holling was afraid of the answer. It had all happened so fast—as swiftly and as strongly as the storm that blew over them. He could hardly trust himself to think that he could have found a woman who could make him feel this way. Not after years of searching, wanting. It didn't make sense. He didn't know enough about her to be able to explain rationally why he felt she was a perfect match for him. Then again, there was nothing rational about love. It was like faith. Either you had it or you didn't. Either you believed or you didn't. He had it. He believed it with all his heart. And if he had to give all his heart to Sawyer to make her see it, he would do it.

"Sawyer," he said hesitantly. "You don't have to—"

"I know that, Holling. I want to," she insisted, and to prove her sincerity, she reached for him. She laid her hand on his thigh, stroked upward to rest against his groin.

Holling's eyes fluttered closed. A small moan escaped his lips. "I didn't bring you out here to . . . you know . . . seduce you or anything. I didn't even think about it. I mean . . . of course I thought about it. Every time you're around me, I'm thinkin' about you, Sawyer. Darlin', you've got me in such a state that I'm always thinkin' about you. But that's not all I think about. I mean, I don't want to disrespect you—"

"Sh!" She placed her fingertips against his lips. "I thought you cowboys were supposed to be the strong, silent type."

"I'm just giving myself some breathing room. And giving you some time for you to change your mind."

"I don't want to change my mind," she said resolutely.

"I didn't bring any condoms," he blurted out. When she laughed softly at him, Holling said defensively, "I told you that I wasn't prepared."

"Well, it's not as if you're going to get me pregnant, Holling," she retorted.

"I just wanted you to know that I was thinking about you. I won't ever do anything to hurt you, Sawyer." He placed his hand on her stomach. "Not like the man who did this to you."

"I don't want to talk about him," she said harshly, turning her face away.

Holling clasped her face between his large hands. "I just want to say that he wasn't any kind of a man. If he can't step up and be a man, then there are plenty of us out there who are more than willing to move up in line to take his place."

"What . . . what are you saying, Holling?"

"You know what I'm sayin', Sawyer. If you need a father to your child, if you want one, I'm volunteering."

"You have completely lost your mind," she whispered. "Maybe they should have kept you in that hospital. You don't know what you're saying."

"Maybe I am crazy. I'm willing to accept that. A person gets one chance on this earth, Sawyer. One chance to live life right. Sometimes we muddle through and do and say and be all the wrong things. Sometimes we correct our mistakes. Sometimes we don't."

"This was my mistake," she said, holding her stomach. "Not yours. I don't expect you to have to fix anything for me. I'm sick and tired of having others step in and fix what I've screwed up."

"It doesn't have to be a mistake," he insisted. "Maybe this was the way it was supposed to happen. You. Me. At that place at that time. Haven't you wondered why things turned out the way they did? I don't believe in luck. I don't believe in fate. I do believe in life and making the most of what's put into yours. You came into my life, Sawyer. And I believe I'd be makin' one hell of a mistake if I let you out of it."

"You don't know me. You don't know anything about me."

"I don't have to. All I know is that I want you, Sawyer. All of you. Every part of you. That means the both of you."

"What kind of man are you?" she said, shaking her head in disbelief. "What kind of man would be willing to take on another man's child? Just like that. No questions asked. No hesitation. No doubts."

Sawyer couldn't imagine that a man like that could exist. Not really. She could easily imagine a man like Holling. She had. She'd written men like him onto the page. But for one to actually exist? Yet, of course he could. He was the kind of man who'd risk his life to save a perfect stranger.

"No doubts," Holling said firmly. Sawyer opened her mouth to protest and found herself flinging her arms around Holling instead, kissing him, clinging to him with a ferocity that belied her slender frame.

Chapter 24

Sawyer let go. She let it all go. Her anger. Her suspicions. Her doubts. All of the emotional baggage she'd brought with her on this road trip, she tossed it up into the air and scattered it beyond the big Montana sky.

As she lay back, her gaze locked with Holling's. In that instant she knew that she wasn't going anywhere. She couldn't. She couldn't leave this man—this man who'd given her so much. As important as she thought her publicity charity ride was, part of her knew why she was really going. She was running away.

Maybe her initial reason for joining her aunt Rosie on the ride started out as altruistic. You couldn't get any more unselfish than wanting to raise awareness for breast cancer. But that was before . . . before her visit to the doctor. Before Ryan's brutal rejection. Before that damned blue stick. After that, all her feelings changed. When she took off on her motorcycle, she wasn't thinking about saving the lives of other women. Those other women couldn't help her now. She'd taken off on her bike wondering what the hell she was going to do with her own life. Plain and simple—she was running away. Away from Ryan. Away from his rejection.

She could only imagine what her grandmother was going to say when she found out about the baby. Her grandmother, so proper, so uncompromising in her values. And Grandpa George, a leader in the church. Just because she didn't attend their church didn't mean her life wasn't touched by its members. Since her book had come out, she couldn't attend a publicity function without running into someone from Grandpa George's congregation.

It was bad enough when she let Ryan move into her home. She had to deal with her grandmother calling her at least once a week demanding to know when he was going to put a ring on her finger.

"Why buy the cow when you can get the milk for free?" Or her personal favorite. "There are only two kinds of ladies, Sawyer, those you marry and those you don't. So far, you're exhibiting far too many qualities of the latter."

She didn't want to hear any more of that. Not until she could feel stronger about herself. Not until she could defend her life and her life's decisions, no matter what the decision had been. It took a chance meeting with Jon-Tyler Holling to realize that she didn't have to defend herself. She didn't have to justify her behavior to anybody—not to her family, not to him.

He'd opened up his arms to her, saved her from nature's fury. He'd opened up his home to her for as long as she wanted to stay. She knew she could never outstay her welcome. He'd opened up his wallet, sharing his wealth, seeing to her every need, her every want. And now, as he carefully settled over her, Sawyer knew that he was opening his heart to her.

For a brief moment, the thought occurred to Sawyer that she was only responding to him out of gratitude. Holling and his father had done so much for her and had asked nothing of her in return. No one but her own family had ever treated her with such unconditional kindness. She hoped that she wasn't confusing desire with duty. Was it her obligation to submit to his touch? Was she allowing him to make love to her, as she'd done for Ryan, because she didn't know any other way to repay to him? Ryan had often reminded her how much she owed the success of her first book to him. Even though he was getting a whopping 30 percent of the profits, he'd held it over her head that it was his connections that got her published in the first place. She would have been knocking on proverbial doors, trying to get noticed if it wasn't for him. She owed him. And he could collect any time he wanted.

Not so with Holling. The moment he touched her, Sawyer realized that he wasn't taking from her but giving. Oh, so giving! If she had any doubts about the way he made her feel, they dissipated, completely evaporated like icicles under the summer sun. Warmth suffused throughout her body, growing steadily, reaching a slow, steady burn.

"Don't let me go, Holling," she pleaded. "Don't let go!"

Sawyer clutched his shoulders, her fingernails digging into the cotton cloth of his T-shirt. She tugged, trying to free him from it. Frantic, she needed to touch him, feel his skin against hers. He reached for the hem of her shirt, pulling it over her head and shoving the material under her head for a makeshift pillow. He bent his head, touching his tongue to the swell of her breast. When she gasped, then reached behind his head to pull him even closer, Holling pulled the lace-trimmed cup aside and caught the swollen dark nipple between his teeth. With a skillful combination of swirling his tongue and pursing his lips, he tweaked the nipple until the sweet torturous ache brought a cry from her lips. As if by an invisible connecting cord of pleasure, the attention to her breasts awakened an ache between her thighs that would not be soothed by the mere proximity of his groin against hers.

Sawyer moved her hips—a rhythmic rotation that spoke

clearly of her desire. Words weren't necessary. Speech would only be a hindrance, taking away precious air and energy.

Holling unsnapped her jeans as Sawyer's fingers worked to unclasp his belt. She yanked on the leather strap, pulling it from the loop. The large silver filigree buckle made an odd ringing noise as it *clinked* against the floor. Her breath came in short, erratic pants as she managed to peel the pants past his hips, over the taut muscles of his rear and he did the same for her. Cupping Sawyer's bottom, as much for comfort as for leverage, Holling positioned himself between her thighs that had parted for him. Part of him wondered if perhaps he should decline the invitation. There was still time for cooler heads to prevail.

"Sawyer, wait," he began, pulling his mouth away from hers long enough to suck in air.

"No." Her refusal was calm, direct. Holling knew by her tone that she wasn't responding to him in the mindless frenzy of passion that could overtake you when you were deep in the throes of lovemaking. She knew exactly what she was doing. She knew exactly what she wanted. Sawyer was in complete control. She threw her leg over him, then rolled over until she was sitting on top of him. Her palms planted firmly on his shoulders, her knees resting on either side of his thighs, Sawyer pinned him to the wooden floor.

Before, he had been the pursuer. He'd had her moaning, squirming with need, begging him not to stop. *Funny how quickly the tide turned,* Holling thought with mild amusement as she settled on top of him. Not that he couldn't dislodge her if he really wanted to. Why should he? He'd have to be crazy to try. She felt so good. As light as a summer breeze, as warm as sunrays streaming over him. When she lifted her hips and eased the tip of his shaft into her, Holling gave an involuntary moan, raising his buttocks off the floor.

As she rocked against him, rotating, drawing him into her deeper, deeper still, Holling could feel himself swelling, lengthening, spurred on by the warmth that surrounded him, convulsing and completely accepting him. She was so small. He'd had concerns that he could hurt her. Not anymore. Sawyer could handle herself—and him. Like Taffy, she'd taken him by the reins and was riding him with a kind of bold confidence. Before, he'd been impressed by her ability to handle a bike. That was nothing compared to the way she handled him now.

For now, Holling was content to lie back and let her set the pace and the direction. Whatever she wanted from him, he would give. This was a new role for him. He wasn't used to being on the receiving end of a woman's attention. Not like this. Plenty of women had chased him. And some, he'd let catch him. But once behind closed doors, the story changed. Once they were behind closed doors, Holling made sure that they knew what they were in for. He gave them a glimpse of the *real* Holling. He was the big boss man, the one in control. Every woman in White Wolf knew that Jon-Tyler Holling had to make the rules.

And then Sawyer came into his life. New game. New set of rules. Hers. He either had to learn to play or get out of the game. With the way she was making him feel, he wasn't going anywhere. Except maybe out of his mind. The things this woman was doing to him! The look she flashed him in those luminous eyes. The pout of her lips. The upward tilt of her breasts she flaunted sometimes just out of his reach. Even the rhythmic roll of her flat stomach. She worked them all to her favor . . . to his undoing.

Holling clutched Sawyer's hips in an unspoken signal. Time to switch riders. He raised himself up, started to turn sideways. Sawyer understood completely, sensing the shift in his mood. He'd gone from willing and amused observer to demanding partner, wanting his equal share. He'd experimented, seeing what it felt like to let someone else assume control. She'd risen to power, imposing her will over him.

But it was Holling's turn now. As his nature had risen, he'd come back to reclaim the advantage. She held on to him, her hands gripping the bulging muscles in his forearms as he repositioned her. Smoothly. Seamlessly. Face-to-face. Hip-to-hip. Holling thrust into her, sealing them heart-to-heart. He withdrew almost the entire length of him, then surged forward. Time and time again, each stroke growing in intensity. The duration between each stroke shortened so that Sawyer barely had time to recover before he sent another wave of pleasure rippling through her. Their bodies slammed and slid together, slick with perspiration. Twisting, intertwined, melded together so that it was difficult to tell where his skin ended and hers began. Unrestrained. Uncomplicated. Nothing pretentious or fabricated about what they were doing. For the moment, it was about greed. Greed and need. Basic. Instinctual. Clutching. Clawing. Gripping. Gnawing.

Release came to Sawyer first. She called out Holling's name as spasms gripped her body and sent her senses spiraling out of control. It was the sound of her voice, calling out to him, pleading and grateful, raw and rejuvenated, that pushed Holling over the edge. Gripping her hands much like he'd done the day the twister hit, Holling groaned as he felt himself spilling into her.

"Sawyer!" He couldn't stop himself. Couldn't control the rush of liquid heat that shot from him even as his breath expelled from his lungs. Even if he had the presence of mind to withdraw, Sawyer wouldn't let him. She'd wrapped her legs around him, pinning him to her and accepting all that he offered.

"*Damn!*" Holling muttered, his voice muffled as he rested his forehead against her shoulder. It was both a curse and a compliment. She continued to move under him, matching the pulses as his orgasm subsided. Finally, completely spent, Holling withdrew. He lay next to her, cradled her in his arms.

"You know what we've just done, don't you?"

"I've got a general idea." She giggled, snuggling closer to him.

"I'm serious, Sawyer."

"When are you not serious, Holling?"

He reached out and touched his hand to her stomach. "Darlin', I think we just made a baby."

"News flash for you, cowboy," Sawyer said, sitting up on one elbow. "I'm already pregnant. Remember?" She tapped his forehead twice with her index finger.

"I can't help how I feel, Sawyer. When I was inside you, I felt it . . . my seed, your body, our child. Are you gonna deny that you didn't feel something, too? A spark. Somethin'?" He shrugged helplessly, at a loss in searching for the right words to express his feelings.

"I'll admit that we connected, Holling." She smiled shyly up at him, smoothing her hand over his chest. "And I don't just mean in the physical sense. But to say that we made a baby together . . . well, that's just plain impossible."

"Impossible like surviving a tornado with nothing more than a few sheets of plywood and plastic between us and it?" he challenged.

"That's different," she said stubbornly.

"I don't see how. A miracle is a miracle is a miracle."

"Holling, you're so sweet. But saying so won't make it true. This isn't your baby. As much as I wish it was . . ." She bit her lip. Perhaps she'd said too much.

"You know, my pops used to have this saying. Every time I wished out loud for something, he'd say, 'If wishes were horses, Holling, beggars would ride.'"

"And what is that supposed to mean?"

He winked at her and flashed her that crooked grin. "You certainly had me beggin' for you, darlin'."

"And so I let you ride," she completed for him.

"So, tell me again how wishes can't come true."

"Holling, I—"

"Sh!" He silenced her, leaning toward her to touch his lips to hers. "You think what you want. I'm thinkin' what I want. And what I want is you, Sawyer Garth. I want you to be mine. All of you. Every living, breathing, precious part of you. All mine. For my very own. Knowing that, tell me again that won't make that baby mine, too."

Chapter 25

It just wasn't like her, Rosie Kincaid thought. Not like Sawyer at all. Something wasn't right. And no matter how much she tried to push it to the back of her mind, Rosie couldn't pretend that it was.

Sawyer told her that she'd be here. She'd promised her that, as soon as her bike was repaired, she would meet them. A couple of days tops. Rosie had given the name of the motel and exact directions on how to get there. It was a motel on the state line between Idaho and Montana—off their travel plans, yet close enough to keep them from losing too much time. She was also very clear about when they would be pulling out again.

Since Rosie and the other ladies were running behind schedule—a summer storm caught them so that they had to pull off the road and take shelter at a truck stop—she fully expected Sawyer to be there at the motel waiting for them when she got there. But she wasn't. She hadn't even checked in. Nor had she left a message letting her aunt know what had happened to her.

Rosie didn't like it. Didn't like it at all. It wasn't like Sawyer to be so inconsiderate, so uncommunicative. Not to her. She may have cut herself off from the rest of the family—probably at that sycophant Ryan's insistence. But Sawyer had always been close to Rosie. She'd grown even closer when Rosie confessed that Sawyer was her favorite, though Rosie admitted that she said that to all of her nieces and nephews. But Sawyer really did have a special place in her heart. Sawyer was so much like her. Maybe that's why she was often so frustrated with the girl. She knew what was in store for her if she didn't find a way to curb her natural tendencies. If it weren't for her cousins, helping to settle her, Rosie was convinced that Sawyer probably would have seriously hurt herself before now. Sawyer could call Shiri or Rosie and talk to either one when she had nowhere else to turn. So, why wasn't she talking now? What was wrong with that girl? She couldn't begin to fathom. Rosie figured that there was one who would know.

After she settled into her motel room, she reached for the telephone and dialed Shiri's number. At three o'clock in the afternoon, Rosie didn't expect Shiri to pick up. So, she'd intended to leave a message and then wait for her to call her back. But Shiri answered after the sixth ring.

"H-hello?" Shiri said into the phone, sounding breathless.

"Shiri?" Rosie lifted her eyebrows.

"Aunt Rosie?"

"Yes, dear. It's me."

"I wasn't sure. You don't sound like you."

"You caught me off guard. I was expecting your answering machine to pick up."

"N . . . no, I'm home. I came home early."

"Is everything all right, Shiri?"

"Of course, Aunt Rosie, why do you ask?"

"It's just, you sounded, um . . . distracted," Rosie said for lack of a better word. Rosie smiled when she thought she heard the deep rumble of Shiri's husband in the background.

He was home, too? Both of them? Together? Three o'clock in the afternoon? It didn't take a genius to figure out why Shiri sounded so distracted.

Rosie tried not to laugh. It must be true love. Jack and Shiri had been married for two years now and they still couldn't get enough of each other.

"As enthusiastic as rabbits," Rosie's sister Lela had remarked often enough. That was her delicate way of talking about an indelicate subject. Jack and Shiri. When they walked into a room, you could feel the attraction they still shared for each other. As passionate as they were for one another, Rosie was surprised that Shiri hadn't announced that she was expecting before now. After the way Lela was claiming that she'd been dreaming about schools of fish the past few weeks, somebody had better make an announcement soon. With Brenda about to deliver any day, the race was now on between Essence and Titan and Jack and Shiri.

"I'm sorry, dear. Did I catch you at a bad time?" Rosie tried to sound sympathetic and failed miserably.

"No, of course not," Shiri said in that dry tone that let Rosie know that just the opposite was true.

"I won't keep you long, Shiri. I was just wondering whether or not you'd heard anything from Sawyer."

"Sawyer? I thought you'd been in touch with her."

"I was. But that was several days ago. We were supposed to meet at the next stop on our road trip."

"She didn't make it?"

"No, she didn't. That's why I'm calling."

"What about her cell? You can't reach her on that?"

"She said she lost it. She gave me the number of some friends that she was staying with in Montana."

"Montana!" Shiri exclaimed. "Who does Sawyer know in Montana?"

"You mean you don't know them, either? A family named the Hollings."

"She's never mentioned them to me before."

"That girl!" Rosie said in exasperation. "I'll bet anything it's someone she's hooked up with on the road."

"Sawyer's flaky, but she's not irresponsible," Shiri began, then had to cross her fingers against that stretch of the truth.

She'd wondered about Sawyer's judgment when she hooked up with that Ryan. But, as her cousin and her friend, Shiri'd held her tongue because Sawyer was convinced that she was in love. When Shiri'd fallen for Jack, after a few initial misgivings, no one could have convinced her that it wasn't right. She'd looked past his celebrity status, his party-hard lifestyle, and his obvious chick-magnet appeal and found her soul mate in him.

Sawyer had proclaimed how good Ryan could be for her career. Who was she to frown on the relationship? When he'd moved into her home, again she'd held her tongue, even though Sawyer had admitted that Ryan wasn't pulling his share of the weight. Not the upkeep. Not the bills. Why she allowed it to go on, Shiri couldn't figure out. Not until Sawyer had confessed that Ryan had been her first—and had sworn to be her last. The girl was in love. Love had a funny way of closing your eyes, even as it opened your heart.

And apparently, Shiri thought snidely, opened her legs. She'd kept the secret of Sawyer's pregnancy from everyone, including her own husband, even when he pressed her to know the details of that late-night conversation.

"I didn't say she was irresponsible. But I do think she's working through something. Some issues. I thought you might have a hint. I'm just worried about her, Shiri."

"I know, Aunt Rosie. But Sawyer's a big girl. She can take care of herself."

"That's Sawyer talking," Rosie said intuitively. "We're all big girls. But that doesn't mean that we can't use a helping hand every now and then. Remember when you and Jack were going through some troubles? Where would you be if it weren't for me, and your mother, and your grandmother helping you through, holding your hand . . . or kicking your butt when you needed it?"

"And I'm grateful to you all," Shiri said with feeling. "That is, after I got over being mad at all of you for getting into my business."

"You got our help whether you wanted it or not. Whether you needed it or not. We can't do any less for Sawyer. If you know something, Shiri, now's the time to tell me."

"I swore that I wouldn't tell. I gave Sawyer my word."

"If she's in trouble, then she wants you to tell. Especially if she told you *not* to tell. She knows good and well that we Johnson women can't keep a secret to save our lives."

Shiri burst into rueful laughter. "We do tend to run off at the mouth, don't we, Aunt Rosie?"

"Like Old Faithful."

Shiri gave a reluctant sigh. "You're right about one thing. Sawyer does have some things on her mind. But she'll get them resolved, I promise you, and it won't take her long to figure it out . . . to get it out of her system, so to speak."

Rosie paused. Shiri was trying to tell her something, trying to tell her and still stay true to her promise to her cousin.

"It'll only take about . . . oh, say, eight more months," Shiri said meaningfully.

"Eight months," Rosie echoed.

"Uh-huh. She's already had about a month to dwell on it, Aunt Rosie."

Rosie was silent on the other end of the phone.

"Shiri, are you telling me that Sawyer's pregnant?"

"I didn't say that," Shiri exclaimed quickly. "If it ever gets back to me, I never said that, Aunt Rosie. You remember that."

"The girl's pregnant! What in the hell is she doing traipsing around the countryside on that motorcycle!" Rosie exclaimed. "Is she out of her ever-loving mind!"

"Aunt Rosie!" Shiri pretended to be shocked. There wasn't much that her grand-aunt could do to shock her these days. Shiri had ceased being surprised when Aunt Rosie showed up at the airport to pick her up sporting her shoulder tattoo the day that she met Jack. She was a free spirit, coming and going as she pleased. Doing what she wanted. Saying what she wanted. The day Aunt Rosie truly shocked Shiri would probably be the day she was laid out in her grave.

"Why didn't she tell us?" Rosie murmured in concern.

"You're better able to answer that than I am," Shiri said. "I know she didn't want to disappoint you."

"She could never disappoint me."

"Except now when you're disappointed because she didn't want to disappoint you," Shiri observed.

"If she's only a few weeks along, she doesn't need to be running around the countryside, stressing herself out. Do you know if she's even seen a doctor?"

"We went before she took off to join you in Seattle, but she didn't go through with the . . . uh . . . examination."

"You mean abortion," Rosie said tightly. "She was going to terminate the pregnancy, wasn't she?"

"She thought about it," Shiri confessed.

"Is that why she went to Montana?"

"Be reasonable, Aunt Rosie. She wouldn't have to go all the way to Montana for that."

"I can't be reasonable. How could she think we'd want her to do something like that?"

"What you or I or anybody in the family wants shouldn't have been the point, Aunt Rosie," Shiri said. "The decision was Sawyer's and Sawyer's alone. Now, I can imagine her taking off, to be alone, to make that decision. She's a lot like you, Aunt Rosie. She does what she wants to do."

"I just hope that she hasn't . . . uh, done anything . . . that she'll regret later."

"If she does, Aunt Rosie, it'll be hers to regret. Not ours.

We can't make her decisions for her. And we certainly can't judge her for those decisions. All we can do is stand by her."

"I *want* to stand by her, Shiri. I want to give her all my strength to lean on, if she needs it. But I haven't heard from her. I'm not even sure where she is . . . if she's still staying with that family."

"The Hollings, right?"

"In a town called White Wolf."

"Sounds . . . rustic," Shiri said dryly.

Aunt Rose slammed her palm against her forehead. "He certainly did."

"Excuse me?"

"Mr. Holling. Nathaniel Holling, if I remember correctly. He had the cutest accent. Sexy in a rustic kind of way."

"Euwww! Too much information, Aunt Rosie!" Shiri protested.

"He gave me his phone number and said I should feel free to call him anytime."

"Don't tell me that he was trying to flirt with you, Aunt Rosie."

"And why shouldn't he? You're not the only one who can still turn heads, honey. I still got what it takes."

"Who are you telling? We girls get our special charm from the female side of the family. Are you going to give that Mr. Holling a call?"

"I will. Just as soon as I hang up with you."

"When you catch up to her, Aunt Rosie, tell her that I'm praying for her."

"I will, honey, I will."

"And, Aunt Rosie?" Shiri said quickly, before her aunt had a chance to hang up.

"Yes, dear?"

"When you talk to Grandma Lela . . . and I know you will talk to her because, as you said, we Johnson women can't keep anything to ourselves—"

"I won't give away Sawyer's secret. Not until I've had a chance to talk to her myself."

"I appreciate that. I really didn't want to be the one to snitch on her."

"I'll tell Sawyer that I beat it out of you," Rosie teased.

"Thanks for the sentiment," Shiri said. "But that's not what I want you to think about."

"And what would that be?"

"Just tell Grandma Lela to keep dreaming about those fish."

"She'll be happy to know that she was right. Everybody kept saying that it was Brenda's twins that kept her tossing and turning with those dreams. But she kept insisting otherwise. Said that there had to be someone else in the family. The dreams were just coming on too strong. Now that I know that it's Sawyer, she can stop dreaming."

"Not necessarily," Shiri said hesitantly, then began to laugh self-consciously. "Grandma Lela might have to keep dreaming a while longer."

"Shiri!" Rosie said breathlessly into the phone. "Are you trying to tell me that you're—"

The excited squeals of joy didn't need phone lines to be heard cross-country.

Chapter 26

"Do you hear that, Holling?" Sawyer sat up on her elbow, looking around.

"What? I don't hear anything," Holling said, yawning lazily and pulling her back down to snuggle in his arms.

"I'm serious, Holling. I thought I heard something out there." Sawyer paused, lured by the comfort of his arms, and then sat up again, straining to hear.

"It was just the wind. Come on, Sawyer. Stay with me for a while longer. Pops will be expectin' us back soon and who knows when we'll get a chance to be alone together like this again?"

"Wind with the rumble of a diesel engine?" she retorted.

"You can tell the kind of vehicle by the sound of the engine?" Holling said, his tone slightly disbelieving.

"Maybe I'm starting to get my mommy ears early. I'm telling you, I heard something."

She reached for her shirt. By the time she'd stepped back into her jeans, Holling realized that their intimate moment was over. Whether she'd heard something or not, the mood was lost. Groaning in resignation and dismay, he sat up, too.

Holling shook out his shirt from the floor dust and pulled it over his head.

"If it makes you feel any better," he said, "I'll go check it out."

"My hero," she said dryly. "Maybe I'm being paranoid. I just don't want anyone sneaking up on us."

He winked at her. "If it turns out to be nothin' more than the wind, darlin', you owe me another ten minutes."

"Only ten?" She raised an eyebrow at him. "What's the matter, Holling? Did I wear you out?"

Holling snorted in derision. "Wear me out? Darlin', you just don't know. I was *trying* to be good. So as not to scare you off."

"Oh, you were," Sawyer said, stretching languidly. "Very, very good. And all that trembling I was doing wasn't exactly from fear."

Holling started toward her again, with that undeniable look in his eyes.

"Oh, no, you don't!" Sawyer laughed, backing away from him. "You said you were going to check out that noise." Grasping him by the shoulders, she spun him around and shoved him toward the door. "Remember?"

"I'm going, I'm going," he said. Holling scooped up his boots, pointing his toe to pull on one and then the other as he hopped toward the door. He stood in the doorway, peering out.

"See anything, Holling?" she called from across the room.

"A cloud of dust," he said, looking back at her. "Like I said . . . nothin' but the—"

He stopped suddenly, then cast a quick glance in Sawyer's direction.

"What is it, Holling?" she said in alarm. She couldn't explain the sudden panicky feeling in the pit of her stomach when he'd looked at her. Something was wrong. Holling had that same sense about him like the day of the tornado. Tense. Alert. And like that day, totally committed to seeing her out of harm's way.

"Wait here, Sawyer," he said in that tone that Sawyer knew so well. That tone that wouldn't accept argument from her.

"What? What is it?" she said in a stricken whisper.

He shook his head. "I'm not sure. Like I said, wait here and I'll be right back."

"Wait for me, Holling. I'm coming with you," she said, hurrying into her clothes.

"You're just trying to get out of that last ten minutes," he teased.

But Sawyer wasn't fooled. In his way, he was trying to assure her that everything was going to be all right even though he wasn't so sure himself.

"If it turns out to be nothing, I'll give you twenty," she promised. But she already knew that something was happening.

As they stepped out onto the wooden plank walkway along the main street, the rumble of a truck engine grew louder. Holling had to smile. Couldn't help but love a woman who knew her engines.

"Ford 350," she suggested.

He offered his own suggestion. "Dodge Ram."

He couldn't see the truck at first. But something was coming. The cloud of dust it kicked up as it came up from the far side of the hill rose up, swirled as if caught in a dust-devil windstorm. Holling thought at first that it might be somebody four-wheeling, kicking up dust and pushing the limits of some new boy toy. That wasn't an unreasonable assumption. Even though this ghost town was off the beaten path, far from the sites summer tourists would usually take in, it was just the kind of area that would appeal to some ad-

venturesome types—Generation Xers with more money
than brains, hell-bent on imitating the SUV commercials on
television. Plenty of mud and music and motion.

Hand in hand, Holling and Sawyer walked all the way to
the end of the street, waiting to see what would appear on the
horizon. Instead of flying over the crest of the hill, as he expected the truck to do, it lumbered over the ridge and carefully made its way down the slope. As the independent
suspension kicked, all four wheels spinning over the boul-
ders and navigating deep ruts dug into the ground by the last
summer storm, Holling muttered under his breath, "What
the hell . . ."

"Are you expecting a delivery, Holling?" Sawyer asked,
turning a puzzled expression to him.

"If I was gonna have something delivered, it would be a
deep-dish pizza with extra cheese and pepperoni. Not that,"
he said, gesturing toward the truck.

As one tire rolled up and over a jagged boulder, the truck's
cargo teetered precariously to one side. The nylon tie-downs
crisscrossing the bed to hold the cargo in place were frayed.
They strained and threatened to snap under the sudden shift.

Sawyer held her breath as unopened boxes of brand-name
electronics, including televisions, computers, and DVD
players, slid sideways.

"They're about to lose that load," Sawyer said. "Do you
think we should warn them? Flag them down?"

"No!" he said sharply, backing away from the edge of the
street out of sight.

Something didn't feel right. What was that truck doing
out there, this far from the highway, without a visible resi-
dence or even a department store to deliver its load to?

What he and Sawyer were doing out here could easily be
explained. One look at her mussed hair, the passion marks
he'd left on her neck and shoulders, and the rumpled clothing and it wouldn't be too hard to figure out. That truck was

a mystery that couldn't be so easily solved. And because Holling couldn't think of a plausible explanation, it made him uneasy in his mind. He didn't want to alarm Sawyer, but he didn't want to take any chances either.

Holling moved back, pulling her back to the shadow of the building as the truck reached the bottom of the hill and made its way toward the center of the ghost town.

"What are you doing?" she asked.

"Nothin'," he said simply. Absolutely nothing at all. He didn't plan to move until the truck had passed them by.

As the truck approached their vantage point, he moved farther back, keeping Sawyer behind him. She tried to peek around his shoulder, but he kept one hand behind him, continuing to ease her back.

"This is silly," Sawyer murmured. "There's probably a perfectly logical explanation for why that truck's out here."

"How many ghosts do you know who watch Sony flat-screen TVs?" he retorted.

"The ones with more money than spirit." Sawyer tried to make light of his severity.

"Let me put it this way, those TVs are so hot, those ghosts might as well be watchin' TV in hell."

"You mean . . . you think those were stolen?" She paused as the conversation with Holling's friend came back to her. "Oh man! What was it Officer Mace said about that store break-in?"

Holling looked back over his shoulder at her. "You mean before he blew snot all over me or after he kept lookin' down the front of your blouse?"

"You were jealous!" she accused him, punching him on the back.

"Of booger nose? I don't think so."

"Do you think it could be those guys?" she asked.

"I don't know." He shook his head. "But this doesn't feel right. We ought to get out of here."

"Do you think they saw us?" Sawyer whispered, though she wasn't sure why she was whispering. The loud rumble of the truck engine probably could have drowned her out even if she shouted.

Holling cursed under his breath as the truck drew closer. In a moment, it would drive right past them.

"Around the back," he said harshly. "Whether it's them or not, I don't want to take any chances."

Sawyer nodded. By now, she'd learned to trust Holling and to rely on his judgment. Out here, in this still wild place, she was out of her element.

Holling glanced back over his shoulder, checking on the truck's progress. It cruised on past their hiding spot. But Holling wasn't feeling secure just yet. It kept going, slowing down as it approached the saloon.

"Shit," Holling spat. He'd hoped they would continue past.

"The saloon?" Sawyer confirmed.

"Yeah." His belt, hat, and cell phone. Sawyer's sweater. They'd left them behind. If he weren't so concerned that their visitors walked on the shady side of the street, he wouldn't have cared about leaving them behind. But the very fact that they were there was enough to make even the dumbest criminal wonder—wonder and look around for the owners.

The only way out of the valley was back up the path. Back over the same ground that the truck had covered.

It came to a halt. Holling could tell by the idling of the engine. Voices now. Three. Maybe four calling to each other. Laughter drifting back. Calls of congratulations on the success of this haul and a woman's voice urging them to hurry and load before they lost the daylight. If Holling had had any doubts about what they'd gotten in the middle of, he didn't now.

He pulled on Sawyer's arm, drawing her down to a crouch. The walls of the saloon were warped and cracked. The last rays of sunlight shining through would cast a shadow inside and draw as much attention to them as if someone had shown a floodlight on them.

Holling debated. What should he do? Should he stay put and wait for cover of darkness? Maybe they would be too busy unloading to notice the signs of obvious occupancy that he and Sawyer left behind. Maybe they would be too anxious to be gone to try to search for them.

Or should they try to get out of there now? They could try to claw up the hill. It was steeper, rougher going than the path. But if either one of them lost their footing and sent down a rain of loose dirt and shale, they might as well send up a flare. If they continued on past the saloon, there were only two more buildings to provide cover. Once they were gone, they would be exposed, out in the open.

Sawyer laid her hand on his arm, communicating her feelings without words. Fear and trust mingled together, letting him know that even though by now she was scared, whatever he decided to do, she would support him. He'd seen her through that damned tornado. Surely he could see her through a few petty larcenists.

Move, Holling said to himself. Move while they still could. These people hadn't yet found the items he and Sawyer had left behind in the saloon. Maybe they were buried under the bar that had collapsed. Maybe the looters would be too busy unloading to notice. Every foot away from them was a foot closer to getting Sawyer to safety.

He put his index finger to her lips, indicating silence and caution, then began to crawl on his hands and knees beyond the saloon. Sawyer followed, biting her lip to keep from crying out against the jagged rocks that dug into the soft flesh of her palms and worked their way through the knees of her jeans. With each inch that they crawled along, she felt her heart beating so loudly she thought that it could surely be heard—heard over the sound of the idling truck engine, the woman's frantic demands to "get their lazy asses in gear," and, to her sudden dismay, the sound of a dog barking. Sniffing. Scratching. Whining to be set loose.

Holling heard it, too, looked with wide eyes toward the wall where the dog's paws scratched at the wood.

"Holling!" Sawyer mouthed to him.

"Keep moving," he said, his voice a ragged whisper. She nodded tightly and picked up her pace.

Once they were past the corner of the saloon, Holling looked over to his left, made sure that they could not be seen from the alley, before darting over to the next building. He started to move forward, then froze when he thought he heard voices coming from the street. He heard them. He couldn't see them just yet. He prayed that it meant they couldn't see Sawyer and him, either.

"Go on and let 'im out, Andy," a voice, whining and irritated, called out. "Rather he take a piss now than on the carpet of the truck."

"Hell naw, I ain't gonna let 'im out. If he takes off now, we won't never get him back tied up. Stupid, mangy flea-bitten mutt. I don't see why you brought him along in the first place. He'll just go chasing after some rabbit or squirrel and we'll be half the damned night tryin' to get him back."

The dog whined, then gave two resounding yelps. Big dog, Holling could judge by the deepness of the bark and how it echoed off the boxed canyon walls. Disgusted, he lifted his eyes to the sky. Why couldn't they have brought some stupid fur ball of a yappy dog? Rats on a rope, Pops called them. One that he could brush away with the flick of his hand if it was set on him. This one sounded big, rottweiller or Doberman.

"But he's gotta go, Andy."

"Let 'im hold it. We'll be done unloadin' in a minute and then you can walk him so that he can do his business."

The voices drifted off. They were moving away from them again.

"Go! Go!" Holling urged. Time to make their move. He pushed Sawyer in front of him. Twenty feet to the path. Maybe fifteen. Maybe, if they could get there before being seen, before they set the dog loose, maybe they might still have a chance. . . . So many maybes.

Sawyer was moving in earnest now. Trying to be quiet, but opting more for speed than stealth.

Fifteen feet. Thirteen . . . a little farther now. Just a little more. Ten feet.

Suddenly, the dog stopped barking. Sawyer breathed a sigh of relief. They were going to make it. Almost there. Almost.

Suddenly, Holling grabbed her roughly and spun her around to face him. "Sawyer, listen to me . . . listen good and do exactly as I say. When I say go, you make a straight line for that path. Keep going. Don't look back, darlin'. Don't look back."

"What do you mean 'me'?" This time she *did* argue with him. "It's 'we.' *We're* making a straight line for the path, right?"

"Don't argue with me. They've set the dog loose. It's got our scent and soon it'll—"

"But how do you—"

"I know dogs. Vashti . . . when she's on the hunt, she'll come up on you real quiet like. It's coming after us . . . me. I'm gonna go back and—"

"No!" Sawyer snapped, tugging on his arm. "You're not leaving me. I'm not leaving you. Dog or no dog."

"We don't have time to argue."

"Then don't waste it," Sawyer countered.

Ten feet. Nine . . . If they could get around the bend where the rock jutted sharply, near the spot where she'd almost clipped her head as they were coming down into the canyon, they'd be completely concealed. At the end of the footpath, the horses were still tied off in the shrubs.

"Go on!" He shoved her, sending her up the incline. "I need you to get to the horses and bring 'em as far up the path as you can. Go!"

"Holling!" Sawyer reached out to him, but he'd already started back down the path. Sawyer looked beyond him, saw the dog easing from the shadows. It came out of the alley between the saloon and the trading post, its dark, wet nose plastered to the ground. It was huge. She didn't recognize the breed. It had to be something mixed.

Mixed all right, Sawyer thought grimly. Part dog. Part hellhound. All evil. Large paws dug into the ground as it loped along. Wide muzzle filled with teeth. So many teeth!

"That's not a dog," Sawyer snapped. "That's a bear!"

"Now, Sawyer! Get to the horses," he urged her. Holling kept moving until he was at the base of the hill. There he stopped, planting his feet, forming a wall between him and Sawyer. So far, it was just the dog. The others hadn't followed it, assuming that the dog was only going to do what came naturally to dogs who'd been cooped up. As long as there was just the dog, maybe there was a chance, Holling hoped. Maybe he could calm it, soothe it, or give it a command to sit, lie down. Anything to buy more time. Time for Sawyer to get away.

Cautiously, Holling raised his hand. A display of friendship. Peace. But as the dog's nose lifted, testing the air, it drew back its black lips to bare jagged yellow fangs. Holling felt the maybes fly out of his head, leaving his heart to sink.

He looked back over his shoulder once more, pleading with his eyes for her to go.

Chapter 27

Sawyer turned, clawing up the steep hill, nearly stumbling in her haste. Carefully, she edged around the bend in the path where the boulder jutted out in the middle of the path. Another few feet and the path would begin to slope down again. Easier to navigate. But only easy in the daytime. The sun was slipping beyond the horizon now, casting long shadows on the footpath that made it difficult to see. In that dimming light, even walking could be treacherous, let alone trying to take the path at a dead run.

Scared, angry, and frustrated, Sawyer ran full tilt down the hill. Running. Running. Doing what she did best. Running away. She tore through the underbrush, nearly in a panic when she reached the base of the footpath and didn't see the horses.

What if those looters had seen them and driven them off? Or what if the sound of their truck had simply scared them off? Even if she could find them, what if she couldn't get mounted again? It was easy getting on the first time because Holling was there to support her.

Holling! Seemed as though he'd done nothing but support

her, shelter her, from the moment she arrived in White Wolf. When he needed her to return the kindness, what had she done? Done what she'd always done. Turned and run.

"Coward!" Sawyer berated herself. She talked so big, so bad, so tough. Where was all of that bravado when she needed it? Why didn't she stay behind to help him? She didn't know what she could have done against that snarling mass of mange and meanness. But at least he would have known that he wasn't alone.

"Please, God," Sawyer sobbed in prayer. "Please let him be all right. Please! If there's any way on this earth that you can see fit to help me help him . . . *please!*"

Maybe she had no right to ask for divine intervention. She hadn't necessarily been a model believer these days. Sawyer didn't want to hold her life too closely under a spiritual microscope. Too afraid of the glaring flaws that she would find.

If she thought it would help matters, she could promise to do better in the future, but Grandma Lela had always warned her against trying to make bargains with God.

"Sawyer, either you live your right life or you don't. When you don't, there's no sense in trying to make a deal with the Lord. What could you offer that He doesn't already rightfully deserve?"

No bargains, then. All she had left were prayers. Simple, heartfelt prayers.

Help him! Help me, help him!

That's all she wanted. She wanted Holling back—safe and whole. He had given her so much and never asked anything in return. What had she done for him? How had she shown her gratitude? By taking off her clothes. Responding to his touch. In the grand scheme of things, what did that really mean?

She had done that much for Ryan. And she had done it without much thought, hardly any emotional involvement at all. She'd thought she was in love. It paled in comparison to what she was feeling now. Only now did she realize that it was true love she had given to Holling. She'd loved him in every sense of the word. Physically. And now emotionally.

She truly cared for him. Running off and leaving him like that didn't do justice to those newly discovered feelings. She couldn't leave him like that. Holling deserved more than that. So much more. She owed him her life. She could give nothing less than that in return.

"You get your scary butt back there, Sawyer Garth, and help that man." She didn't know how she was going to help him, she only knew that if she didn't try, the love and faith he'd shared with her would all be for nothing.

"Come on, girl, think! Think. Stop panicking!"

Sawyer took a moment to stop and take better note of her surroundings. She stood stock-still, slowing her breathing, trying to calm the pounding of her heart and the rushing in her ears.

She couldn't hear the diesel engine anymore or that dog barking. She heard the rustling in the trees as the evening wind picked up. She turned her head. Off to her left, she thought she heard a soft whinny.

"Taffy?" she called out, moving toward the noise. Whistling softly between her teeth as she'd seen Holling do, she called out to the sorrel.

Pushing aside low-hanging branches, Sawyer made her way to a small copse. She didn't recognize this as being the place where Holling had secured the horses. But that didn't surprise her. In this light, nothing was as it seemed.

What did surprise her was the sight of Luce, standing between the two horses, holding the reins out to her as she approached.

Luce? Sawyer mouthed the word, no sound coming out.

"These belong to you, honey? I found them wandering loose over that ways a bit."

She moved toward Sawyer, clucking her tongue to the horses to bring them along. Sawyer couldn't help her reaction. She took a step backward.

There was no way Luce could be here. No way. Holling said very few people knew of this place. Obviously not, if it turned out to be the hiding place for looters and great-grandmas alike.

"How . . . how did you . . ." Sawyer rasped.

"Don't worry about that now, honey." Luce closed her warm hand over Sawyer's, pressing the reins into them. "These are your horses, aren't they? You were calling out to them."

"I was, but—"

"Climb onto your horse, honey, and go after your man. He needs you now."

Sawyer placed one foot into the stirrup and tried to pull herself up. But Taffy shifted impatiently, causing her to mis-step. She hopped on one foot, trying to keep her balance, and wound up flat on her backside.

"This is impossible!" Sawyer exclaimed, slamming her fists into the dirt in frustration. Huge tears welled up in her eyes. "I don't have time for this!"

"Easy," Luce soothed, grasping Taffy's bridle and holding her steady. "Try again, Sawyer," she directed.

Biting her lip in determination, Sawyer wiped her eyes and nose on her sleeve, and then reached up for the saddle horn to haul herself back into the saddle. She wiggled her foot around until she had it firmly in the other stirrup.

"Luce, I don't know how you got here," she began.

"It doesn't matter. What matters is that I'm here for you now."

"But what are you doing out here! I don't understand how you could possibly—"

"You will understand when the time is right and proper. Trust me, Sawyer. Now's not the proper time. Right now, your time belongs to him. If you want to be there for him when he needs you, go now."

Leading Holling's horse Cochise with one hand and with a firm grasp of Taffy's reins in the other, Sawyer wheeled Taffy around and pointed her through the opening of the trees.

"Come on, Taffy! Come on, girl!" she said, pounding her heels into Taffy's flanks. Sawyer learned forward, bending her head over the saddle horn to avoid a low-hanging branch. Part of a branch still whipped at her face. Spring-green leaves and branches caught her, leaving a welt she knew she would feel for days. But the sting of the branches couldn't compare to the ache in her heart if something happened to Holling.

On instinct, she glanced back over her shoulder to see how far she'd gone. She also looked back to give a thankful nod to Luce for her aid. She didn't know how she managed to be there. Perhaps it didn't matter. Her being there was an answer to a heartfelt prayer.

"Thank you, Luce," Sawyer mouthed. *Luce?* As suddenly as she'd appeared she was gone. Nothing visible but the line of dark trees swaying back and forth in the evening breeze.

Maybe he hasn't caught our scent, Holling thought. From his vantage point at the base of the hill, he could see the dog lower his nose to the ground. Snuffling around, first toward him, and then away again. Holling had hopes that perhaps the dog was just looking for a good place to do his business. Maybe the dog's distress had nothing to do with him and Sawyer at all. Holling didn't mind being wrong about his familiarity with animals this time. He would have welcomed being wrong if it meant that they could get out of there without being detected.

"That's it, boy. Have yourself a good old time," Holling murmured as the dog stopped pacing, opened its hind legs, and squatted low to the ground.

Holling looked back over his shoulder, making sure that Sawyer really had gone. He waited for a minute, then two. It seemed like hours since he'd sent her ahead of him. He had to be sure that the dog wasn't going to follow them. Judging from the way the dog was straining, he was going to be there for a while.

Still, Holling didn't trust it. He didn't know anything about the looters and how well they'd trained the animal. If it didn't have any training at all, Holling could almost bet that it would take off after him if it saw him or caught wind of him. He didn't have any faith that it wouldn't eventually find him out. But he didn't want to make any sudden moves, nothing to draw the dog's attention. So, he started back up the hill, quietly, stealthily, never once taking his eyes from it.

His feet barely made a sound on the rocky path as he inched backward, keeping one hand along the face of the canyon to guide him. One step. Then another. And another. He didn't count his steps just as he didn't count on his luck. Anything could happen. He could knock a pebble loose, sending it clattering down the hill. The dog could suddenly decide that the call of hunger was greater than the call of nature and take off on a hunt. The looters could come looking for it.

Step. Step. Step. Farther. Farther still. A small voice in the back of mind was already starting to celebrate. He was going to make it! If he could get past the point where the road curved, there'd be no more of this sneaking around. He'd haul ass down the far side of the hill as if his life depended on it. Holling had no doubt that it probably would. Anyone fool enough to smash their truck through a store-front window right in front of the all-seeing eyes of a television camera probably wouldn't have any hesitation about cutting him down if they had the chance. He just wished that he hadn't left that cell phone behind. He could have called Parmon Mace and had someone out here to investigate.

Another step. Then another. Holling kept going.

"*Ah hell!*" Holling swore as someone came around the corner of the trading post, whistling for the dog.

"Pepper! Here, boy! Get on back here, now. Get on back to the truck, you lazy pile of kibbles and crap."

The man's command drifted up, carried up the canyon walls by the wind. The dog ignored him, not quite ready to go. So his owner stopped, turned his own face to the rear wall of the trading post, and opened the front of his pants. For a moment, dog and master mirrored each other as the man took a moment to relieve himself.

Time to go, Holling thought. It was getting way too crowded out back for Holling's tastes—crowded and unsanitary. He paused under cover of darkness, waited for both to finish and return to the truck. As long as he could hear almost every word the man said, Holling knew that the wind was working with him. As long as he stayed upwind of the dog, pressed to the shadows, he could wait them out.

The man shook himself, then started to zip his pants. "Did you hear what I said, spit for brains? I said get on back to the truck!"

He stooped, picked up a rock, and hurled it at the dog's head. Yelping more in irritation than pain, the dog scuttled away from the spot where the rock had dug into the ground and knocked up a cloud of dust. It started to lope away, heading for the alley.

"Mitch!" another voice called out, frantic, feminine. She came tearing around the wall even as the one named Mitch scrambled to adjust himself and his clothing.

"What the hell's wrong with you, woman? Don't you know better than to come up on a man in the dark like that?"

"Shut up!" she screeched at him, then hurled something at him. "Somebody's been nosin' around. We've got to get outta here now!"

Holling felt something grab his guts as the item she'd thrown at Mitch fell into the dirt. He might have been mistaken about what he saw, but he wasn't about what he'd heard—the unmistakable strains of "Für Elise" floating on the wind.

Holling made a mental note to himself. *Pops, remind me to work on your sense of timing.*

He heard them yelling at each other, their curses and accusations tumbling over each other in their haste. As if they weren't already, things were starting to get ugly. One of them wanted to take off right away, the other wanted to reload the truck since their stash had been discovered.

"You gotta be out of your freakin' mind. Do you know how much that stuff is worth?"

"You won't collect a dime if we get busted."

"Quit your panickin'! Ain't nobody around here, Iola." Mitch was trying to assure her. But Holling's cell phone was still ringing. A grim reminder that their private place wasn't as private as they thought. Holling knew how they felt. He would bet that there hadn't been a soul around that ghost town except him in the past five years.

Iola gave an ultimatum. "I'm leavin'. Stay here and wait to be picked up if you want to."

She spun around, marched off. Mitch started after her, still arguing. He took one look behind him. For a moment, Holling thought he'd been spotted. He froze as Mitch took a few steps away from the back of the saloon. He looked up, his gaze sweeping back and forth across the high canyon walls. Suddenly, he spun around.

"Pepper! Get over here!"

When the dog responded and came over to him, Mitch grabbed him by the collar, dragged him over to the ringing phone. He knelt down, first trying to push the dog's nose into the phone. Pepper shied away. The vibration accompanying the ring was not to his liking. Mitch then lifted the phone, rubbing it all over the dog's nose and muzzle.

"Get 'im, Pepper! Fetch 'im back. Go on, boy. Earn your keep for tonight."

Holling cursed it all. His bad luck. The audacity of some people who thought that an extra helping of meanness gave them free license to spread it around. He even cursed the dog's willingness to please, despite being obviously mistreated. There was nothing for him to do now but run as Pepper lifted his nose to the air and brayed.

"Iola!" Mitch shouted. "Iola, come out here! We got something. We got the sumbitch!"

Holling didn't need any more encouragement than that. No more wondering whether stealth would win out over speed. He had to go now and trust that Sawyer had brought the horses far enough up the path to stay ahead of them.

He turned, running as fast as he dared on the darkened path. He didn't waste any time checking to see if Pepper was gaining on him. Holling figured that he would find out soon enough how close he was when he felt the dog's fangs clamp down on his backside. He could hear Pepper howling. He thought he heard the dog once it reached the base of the path. No reason why he thought that. He certainly wasn't going to look back to check. He wasn't going to risk looking back and missing a step, just like in one of those cheesy horror flicks he used to love as a kid. He and his friends, sitting in the back row of the movie theater, feet up on the seats and throwing popcorn at the screen. "Run, you fool!" they'd yell, laughing all the while so loud and obnoxiously that more than once they were asked to leave the theater.

It wasn't so funny now. The fear was real. So real that Holling was starting to rethink now whether those horror flicks were completely unrealistic. He could completely empathize with that poor fool running for his life.

"Go, Pepper! Get 'im, boy. You bring 'im down and you'll get a whole damned box of those rawhide strips!" Mitch was urging. His voice echoed off the canyon walls, bounced so that it was hard for Holling to tell whether he was spurring the dog on from below or trying to keep up.

Holling ran with one hand pushing off the wall to help guide him along the path. At the rate he was going and with such recklessness, he didn't want to run smack dab into that boulder jutting out just before the bend. If he ran too fast, he could give himself another concussion. If he ran too slowly, he would give the dog a chance to catch up.

As Pepper brayed, Holling got a better sense of how close the dog was. Close. Too close. His gaze scanned ahead. No sign of Sawyer or the horses. He didn't know whether that fact relieved him or not. For her own safety, he was glad that she wasn't here. For the sake of his own safety, the sight of her would have warmed his heart. His only prayer was that she had reached the horses, and that she was okay. It hadn't occurred to him before now that he might have done her a disservice by sending her on her own. He hadn't thought of what might be waiting for her on the far side of the footpath. He'd simply reacted on instinct, sending her away from the most immediate, imminent danger.

Holling reached the bend in the footpath, over half a mile from the ghost town. Another half mile to go. Might as well be ten miles. From the sound of Pepper's frantic barks, in a minute, maybe two, the dog would be right on top of him.

As he braced himself, waiting for the inevitable, Holling risked one quick glance behind him. Pepper was still barreling toward him. His wide mouth was open, snarling and snapping with mindless frenzy. Powerful legs stretched out in a full run.

Holling turned, his heart racing as fast as his mind raced with possibility. Flight or fight. Flight wasn't going to work. So, it was time to fight. He glanced around, looking for something to defend himself with. A stick. A rock. A doggie treat. Anything to keep Pepper off of him.

As the dog approached, Holling felt an odd sense of calm settle over him. It wasn't an unfamiliar feeling for him. He remembered feeling something like this the moment he realized that the twister would not pass over him. It was going to strike and there was nothing on this earth that would stop it. Being exposed as he and Sawyer were, all they could do was to sit back and wait for it to happen. If that moment was going to be his end, then let it come quickly. He didn't know about Sawyer, but he certainly had few regrets in his life. He'd lived his life as he should, gladly accepting all that he was given, taking no more or less than his due share.

He'd felt that same sense of calm when he awakened to find Sawyer watching over him. He'd come through a miracle. The fact that she'd shared it with him, faced the danger and come through by his side, only confirmed what he'd initially thought of her. She had an inner strength that he could rely on. There was also a vulnerable quality about her that made him want to lend her whatever strength he had.

If he had just one regret, it would be that he had not met Sawyer sooner. In the brief time that they'd shared, he'd loved a lifetime's worth. He'd given more of himself to her than he ever imagined he could give a woman. Even believing that, it made him angry that something as stupid and as wasteful as someone's else greed could end all of that. He'd discovered that there was more of him yet that he wanted to share with her. And now, he might not get the opportunity. He had no illusions. That dog had the potential to *kill* him.

The dog got to within three feet of him when—

"Holling!"

He could hear her, but he couldn't see her. Sawyer! She'd made it!

"Sawyer!" As he glanced back, she appeared to him on the path, leading Cochise. There was only room on the path for one horse at a time. *Smart lady,* Holling thought in admiration. She'd brought Cochise because he was large enough to carry them both. Yet, she was savvy enough not to try to ride him. She couldn't risk stumbling in the dark.

"Sawyer!" Holling ran up to her, nearly colliding with her and the horse in his haste to stop.

"Holling, are you—" she began. Holling didn't give her a chance to finish her sentence. He pressed his lips firmly to hers, then grasped her by the waist and hauled her up into the saddle. Sawyer landed with a soft sound of dismay, grasping on to the saddle horn for dear life. Holling's horse Cochise stood several hands higher than her mare Taffy had. Being so far off the ground wasn't a feeling she'd soon get used to, especially not under these circumstances.

Holling swung up behind her and urged Cochise back in the opposite direction. When he checked on the dog again, he almost stopped in startled surprise. The dog hadn't moved an inch from where he'd stopped to signal to his master that he'd caught up to his prey. Instead of rushing them, leaping for the horse's neck as wild dogs on the prowl were prone to do, it hunkered down, wagging its stump of a tail. Suddenly, Pepper rolled over, sticking his feet up in the air and whining.

What the hell? Holling barely had time to wonder. He kicked Cochise in the flanks, spurring him on at a fast walk. As much as he didn't want to, he held the horse in check, waiting for the moment when the path widened again to let him run full speed. The more distance he'd put behind him, the better he'd feel. With his arms wrapped around Sawyer, making sure that she was firmly seated, he said in relief, "Come on, boy. Let's go home."

"Is that hellhound still following us?" Sawyer asked breathlessly, almost too winded to speak.

"I don't know. I don't think so," he said, looking back again. Sawyer leaned over, too, her curiosity getting the better of her fear.

Her eyes widened. No sound could come out of her mouth

as she watched what seconds before was a canine menace romp and scamper on the footpath, as friendly and as harmless as a puppy. It leaped and wagged its stump of a tale for the friendly attention. Seeing Pepper's transformation didn't astound her nearly as much as witnessing what caused it.

As Holling slapped the reins against Cochise's side, sending him trotting down the far side of the hill with increasing speed, Sawyer looked back and mouthed a fervent "*Thank you.*" She whispered it softly, knowing that she couldn't be heard. Or could she?

Her last vision of the footpath as Holling reached the shrubs was the sight of Luce, kneeling beside the dog, lifting her hand in farewell.

Chapter 28

Holling paused only long enough to snatch Taffy's lead rope in his hand as he pulled up alongside her. As he yanked on the reins, Cochise lifted his nose, snorting in protest of the abrupt halt.

"Do you want me to switch?" Sawyer asked.

"Nuh-uh," Holling said. "No time." He was riding hard and wasn't going to stop until they'd cleared the gates of Holling's Way. He had no way of knowing if those looters were bold enough to come after them. Sawyer was just learning to ride. He'd rather lose some time riding double than risk letting her fall behind.

Sawyer hung on, trying not to wince as she was jarred along. "Are you all right?" Holling murmured in her ear, sensing her discomfort.

"I'm fine," she said, gritting her teeth to keep them from chattering as she spoke.

"Hang on tight, darlin'," Holling said soothingly.

"I will. But don't you dare let me fall!" she warned him.

He wrapped his arms tightly around her. "Don't you worry. You're not goin' anywhere."

Closing her eyes, Sawyer concentrated on maintaining her balance and making herself as small as possible in the saddle. Though she was afraid, she felt secure. He would not let anything happen to her. Holling leaned forward, pressing his chest against her back. As they cantered over the uneven ground, she could feel his heart beating, wild and strong, against her. Holling was afraid. It showed in the tense lines of his profile as his cheek grazed hers. But not fear for himself. He was no coward. Sawyer knew that she was first and foremost in his mind. As he'd done in Marjean's Café, he'd put her safety above his own.

Sawyer leaned over the saddle horn and tried to peer behind her.

"I don't see them," she said. "I don't think they're following."

She couldn't hear the truck engine, only the sound of the horses' hooves pounding into the soil and the wind rushing in her ears.

Holling glanced back, too. Not yet, they weren't. No glare of headlights between the trees. Still, he didn't slow down. Soon they would be on open ground, crossing the pasture bordering their property. They could make better time then. Unfortunately, so could that truck. Once it cleared the canyon, it wouldn't be anything to gun the engine and run them down.

"There!" Sawyer exclaimed, needlessly pointing ahead of her. She didn't have to tell him where they were. Holling's heart soared at the sight of the warm, pale glow of lights streaming from the windows of his home. He whooped as he pulled back on the reins, just enough so that Cochise would finish the ride at a moderate trot. As they passed under the gate bordering the main road and the drive leading up to the house, the clamor brought Nate out of the house and several of the hands from the sleeping quarters just beyond.

"Where the hell have you been!" Nate shouted at him. "Do you know what time it is?"

"Not now, Pops!" Holling said brusquely, sliding down from the saddle.

"I've been tryin' to reach you for two hours."

It might as well have been a gnat buzzing in Holling's ear for all of the attention he gave his father. Right now, the only thing on his mind was Sawyer.

"Been holding dinner for you, too. Big fancy spread," Nate complained.

"It'll keep," Holling tossed over his shoulder.

"I only cooked it because that girl's aunt's on her way and—"

"I said not now, Pops!" Holling snapped. He called out to Matías and Corey, standing far enough away to give them a respectful distance but close enough to offer help if Holling requested it. "Take Cochise and Taffy up and down the road a couple of times and let 'em cool off. Then give 'em a good rubdown and plenty of feed, fellas, won't ya? These horses sure earned it tonight."

"Yes, sir, Mr. Holling."

Nate placed his hand against Taffy's side, noting the lather dripping down her legs. He moved to Cochise, even more wet having to carry the weight of both of them over several miles.

"Aunt Rosie?" Sawyer queried, her voice barely above a whisper. "She's coming here?"

"That's right, little missy. She called about an hour after you two took off," Nate said. His eyes narrowed as it dawned on him that Sawyer was seated on Cochise, not Taffy. She was clinging to the saddle as if she could not let go. Her breathing was shallow and strained. The tightness around her mouth, her pallid complexion, and Holling's urgency made him mentally shift gears.

"What *happened?* Did Taffy throw a shoe or something?"

Holling ignored him as he reached for Sawyer.

"Let's get you inside," he said, holding his arms out to her.

"Don't let me go, Holling," she whispered tightly, leaning toward him.

"I won't . . . I won't," he continued to assure her as he walked with her into the house.

Sawyer groaned as she lifted her foot to take the flight of stairs. It seemed as though every muscle in her body ached, felt as though her bones had been wrenched out of position and set back into place without much regard for whether they'd put them back into the proper location.

"Oh, Holling," Sawyer said, her voice stricken. "I don't feel so good."

"It'll be all right, darlin'," he returned. Holling swept Sawyer into his arms, taking the steps two and three at a time. Pops had left the front door ajar. He swung it open, shoving it with his shoulder, and carrying her to the first comfortable seat he saw.

"Will somebody please tell me what's goin' on?" Nate demanded, trailing behind him.

"Pops, get on the phone and call the sheriff's department. Tell them to check out that old ghost town in Weeko Canyon," Holling said, helping Sawyer to the sitting room couch. She lay back, one hand covering her eyes, the other clutching her stomach. Holling strode over to the bar, pouring Sawyer a glass of water.

"What for?" Nate asked. "What do you want me to tell 'em?"

"Here ya go, Sawyer," Holling said, holding the glass to her lips. "Drink this."

Sawyer sat up and reached for the glass. But her hands were trembling so badly that she didn't trust herself not to spill the contents. She gulped down the first few swallows.

"Easy," he soothed, brushing her hair away from her face.

"What happened out there, son?" Nate said. "Is Sawyer all right?"

"What about my aunt Rosie, Nate?" Sawyer demanded.

"She's on her way, little missy. I expect her at any time now."

"Did she say why she's coming here?"

Nate shook his head no. "She only said that she was making a detour and that she wanted to see you. Said something about your cousin being worried about you."

"Shiri," Sawyer muttered. "She must have told her."

"Lie back now," Holling directed. He reached for the decorative throw tossed on the back of the couch and draped it over her. Taking her empty glass from her, he stood and started for the bar again.

As Sawyer lay back and closed her eyes, Holling leaned his head, indicating that Pops should follow him. He returned to the bar, pouring himself a shot of something stronger than the water he'd given Sawyer. He tossed it back quickly, feeling the amber liquid burn his throat as it slid down.

Wiping the back of his hand across his mouth, Holling said in a hoarse whisper, "Pops, you remember those looters Parmon Mace was talkin' about rammin' their truck into that electronics store?"

"Yeah. What about 'em?"

"Mace couldn't find them . . . but we sure as hell did."

"Damn," Nate muttered. "You mean that's where they'd holed up? At Weeko Canyon?"

"Not holed up for long. I took Sawyer out there to have a look around at the ghost town and they showed up. We tried to get out of there, but they set a dog on us. A mean one. Biggest rott you ever saw. They might be long gone by now, but if Sheriff Tanner and Parmon hurry, they might be able to get back some of the stuff they took."

"You took Sawyer out there? Put her in the middle of all of that?" Nate admonished him as he picked up the phone and dialed the sheriff's department. It was after hours, so he had to be transferred a couple of times before reaching a live person. He put his hand over the receiver and said sharply, "Next time you want to impress a gal, Holling, why don't you take her to dinner and a movie instead?" Then he turned back to the telephone, giving the dispatcher his name and address, and briefly relaying what Holling had told him. After he hung up the phone, he and Holling stood on the other side of the room, their voices low but excited. Several times Nate gestured in Sawyer's direction. He even thumped his son on the head, and Sawyer thought she heard the word "knuckle-head."

Sawyer sat up on one elbow.

"You lie down, little missy," Nate said, shaking a scolding finger at her. "You don't look so good."

"Don't be mad at Holling, Nate," Sawyer pleaded. "He saved my life. Again." She swung her gaze to him. "That's twice now I owe you."

"I'd be more grateful if it was ten minutes that you owed me instead," he teased, reminding her of their conversation before their run from those looters.

"Don't make me laugh." Sawyer's giggle mingled with a painful groan as she clutched her aching stomach muscles. She lay back again. As she did so, her expression suddenly shifted.

"What's wrong?" Holling said, immediately moving toward her.

"I . . . I don't know," Sawyer uttered, sounding confused. She sat up and swung her feet off the couch. She stood up, clutching her stomach. Her eyes were wide and frightened.

"Something's . . . something's wrong, Holling. I . . . I . . ." She cried out suddenly, doubling over.

"Sawyer!" Holling crossed the room in three steps, catching her to him as she swayed forward. When she looked up at him, her face was mingled with perspiration and tears. The sudden wrenching of her stomach, the unexpected flow of warmth staining her jeans—the feelings were familiar, but not to this intensity.

"Help me, Holling!" she moaned. "I think I'm losing the baby."

"Baby!" Nate exclaimed. "Who . . . what . . . Do you want me to call a doctor?" he asked, reaching for the phone again.

"No, there's no time for that. Bring the truck around," Holling ordered. Wrapping the blanket around Sawyer, he lifted her again. "Call ahead to the hospital and let 'em know that we're on our way. We'll be comin' in fast."

Nate nodded. "I'll stay here and wait for Sawyer's aunt. Don't you worry, boy. Everything will be just fine."

Nate patted his son's shoulder as he headed for the garage. A thousand questions ran through his mind, but he held them all in check. He wasn't the sharpest tool in the shed, but it didn't take a genius to figure out that now wasn't the best time to be pestering the boy with fool questions. The way Holling looked, Nate didn't figure Holling to be able to answer them anyway. When it came to certain matters, Holling had the proverbial one-track mind. And right now, the only thing on his mind was that girl.

"Baby," Nate murmured again, reaching for the keys hanging on a hook by the door. He shook his head. "Well, I'll be damned. I *knew* my cookin' wasn't that bad."

Chapter 29

They'd taken good care of him when he was brought in from Marjean's with a concussion. Holling had no doubt that they'd take equally good care of Sawyer. That still didn't stop him from wearing a groove in the hospital floor as he paced in the waiting area.

His frustration level increased when he realized that he couldn't answer very many of the questions from the hospital paperwork shoved into his hands as part of normal hospital procedure. He didn't know anything. Her name. That was all. Not her address. Not her blood type. Was she allergic to any medications? How the hell should he know? He certainly didn't have a clue about her last menstrual period. He took a stab at an answer, guessing from how far along in the pregnancy she'd tearfully confessed that she was. He didn't know a damned thing of substance about her. He only knew how she made him feel. Soaring with joy one minute, irritated as all hell at her stubborn independence the next. Proud and protective. Fierce and forgiving. He loved her and it was killing him that she was in pain, in serious trouble, and there was nothing that he could do about it.

If it weren't for the hospital aide who'd been assigned to him and Sawyer when she was treated after the storm for that cut at her side, the thought that they already had paperwork on her would never have occurred to him. She directed the head nurse to Sawyer's file, then returned to the waiting room to check on Holling.

"Can I get you anything, Mr. Holling?" the young woman offered him. "Some coffee?"

He shook his head, trying to remember her name. Brenda? Brandy?

"No, thanks."

"You really ought to sit down and try to relax, sir. All of this worrying won't do her any good." She gestured toward the waiting room sofa.

Holling settled on the edge of one of the overstuffed couches lining the wall. He planted his elbows on his knees, leaning forward with clasped hands.

"How long has it been?" he asked, glancing up at the wall clock. Seemed like hours, though it really couldn't have been more than twenty minutes. The late-night local news was still on the television mounted overhead. The volume was turned low so that he couldn't hear. But they were covering the weather now. And that didn't usually happen until near the end of the half-hour forecast.

"I don't know," she confessed. "I know waiting is hard, but the doctor will be out soon."

Holling wasn't sure that he *wanted* a speedy report. Not if that meant it was pretty obvious there was nothing that could be done to save the baby. He hadn't just been trying to impress Sawyer when he'd claimed the child was now his, too. He'd meant every word of it. She might not have believed him. Not a hundred percent. Part of her still doubted. That was okay. She was welcome to her doubts. It was his intention to spend the rest of their days together proving how much he'd meant those words.

He leaned back and rubbed his hands over his tired eyes, listening to the raspy sound his callused palms made over his stubbled face.

"You're sure I can't get you anything? It wouldn't be any trouble, Mr. Holling. No trouble at all."

Holling looked up at her with tired, red-rimmed eyes. *No trouble at all,* she'd said. He almost wanted to laugh out loud. Seemed like the moment Sawyer Garth rode into his life, she was nothing but trouble. One near miss after the next. But he'd give his right arm to be able to hear that she'd keep on giving it to him. She was the link in a chain of miracles he'd been allowed to witness.

"Sure," he relented. "Thanks, uh . . ."

"Brynn," she supplied, pointing to her name tag and smiling at him. It was a pleasant smile, Holling noted. Practiced. Sympathetic. But not insincere. A perfect combination for somebody whose profession was soothing the pain of others.

"How do you take it?"

"Doctored," he confessed, smiling back. "As somebody told me once, I like just a little coffee with my cream and sugar."

"Be right back." She disappeared around the corner, to the courtesy area stocked with sodas, light snacks, and a coffee and vending machine. Holling could smell the coffee streaming from the machine after Brynn made her selection. She returned, carrying a small Styrofoam cup and a cellophane-wrapped sandwich.

"I took the liberty of bringing you somethin' to eat, too, Mr. Holling. Ham and cheese sandwich. It may not be the most appetizing thing to put in your stomach this late at night, but the cafeteria's closed."

"Thanks, Brynn," he said, eyeing the sandwich.

"I checked the expiration date. Good enough."

"Good enough," Holling repeated, startled. When he glanced at her, saw her dark eyes dancing, he realized that she was teasing him. He chuckled softly, peeling aside the paper.

"Well, I suppose if I'm gonna get food poisoning, the hospital's the best place to be."

"I know for a fact that we've got the best stomach pumps in the state," she assured him.

She stood by, watching him take a couple of bites. Satisfied that she was leaving him in a better state than she'd found him, Brynn excused herself. "I've got to go check on a few patients," she said. "But I'll be back, Mr. Holling, as soon as I can. Sooner if I hear any news."

"Thanks again, Brynn. I appreciate your kindness."

She smiled at him again before leaving the room. Holling took another bite of sandwich, another swig of coffee, then set the rest aside, his appetite gone. He leaned back, stretched his legs out in front of him, and crossed his arms across his chest. To any casual observer, he might appear to be resting. Anyone who knew him better than that would know that Holling was far from calm. He was doing his best not to fly apart from sheer frustration and fatigue.

"Garth?"

Holling's eyes flew open on hearing Sawyer's name. He sat up.

"Yes?"

"Mr. Garth?" An elderly woman in light screen scrubs and a white lab coat consulted a clipboard. Her iron-gray hair was held away from her face with a tortoiseshell barrette.

He shook his head no. "Jon Holling," he corrected. "Sawyer's my . . ." He fumbled for the right word. What exactly was she to him? Did hospital protocol make allowances for a commitment of the heart?

The doctor gave a nod of understanding and held out her hand to him. "I'm Dr. Egan. Can you come with me, Mr. Holling?"

"How's Sawyer?" Holling asked immediately.

"She's resting comfortably now. We gave her a mild seda-tive."

Dr. Egan motioned for Holling to follow her, away from the waiting room and curious eyes and ears.

"Where is she?"

"The maternity ward. In room 23."

"The maternity ward," Holling said. "Does that mean—"

Dr. Egan cut him off before he made any assumptions. "It means that things are still touch-and-go. She hasn't lost the child. Not yet. The next twenty-four to forty-eight hours will tell. She's a strong young woman. If we can get her through this, there's a good chance that they'll both be fine, mother and child."

Holling blew up a heavy sigh. "Is there anything I can do?"

"Do what you've been doing, Mr. Holling. Stay by her side. Give her your support and your prayers. That's what she needs most now, more than any modern medicine."

"Can I see her, Doc?"

"Just for a while. Remember, she needs her rest." She patted him on the arm, then directed him to Sawyer's room. "She's very lucky to have a friend in you, Mr. Holling."

"That works both ways, Dr. Egan. Both ways."

Holling walked down the hall, checking room numbers. He couldn't help but notice the brightly colored, oversized birth announcements decorating some of the doors. Storks and cherubs. Names of newborns. Ribbons and balloons. He sighed again, wishing and wondering whether in eight months he would be walking this hall again.

He found the room number and knocked softly. No answer. Holling pushed the door open and peeked inside.

"Sawyer," he called out. He passed her private restroom on his left, the closet and sink area on his right. The privacy curtain was only half drawn, partially obscuring her from the door. Holling moved farther into the room and approached the bed. He reached for the curtain, started to draw it back, and was surprised to find someone already in the room. At first glance, he thought it might be another nurse. Dressed all in white—white blouse, loose white trousers, and comfortable, rubber-soled white shoes—she sat on the opposite side of Sawyer's bed. She wasn't doing anything. Not checking her vitals. Not rearranging her bedcovers. Just sitting there with her hands folded primly in her lap. She didn't even turn her head when Holling entered, but continued to look upon Sawyer with concern.

"Excuse me," Holling said, trying to get her attention. "I don't mean to disturb you. The doctor said I could sit in for a while."

She turned her head and regarded him with wide gray eyes.

"You're not disturbing us. Sit down, Jon-Tyler," she said gently.

Holling blinked in surprise. How did she know his name? He didn't recognize her, and he knew most folks in White Wolf. He reached for another guest chair and pulled it close to Sawyer's bed. His eyes never left the woman's face.

"She's resting more comfortably, now that you're here, Jon-Tyler."

Holling reached out and laid his hand on top of Sawyer's resting on the covers. Her hand was cool to the touch. When he closed his hand over hers, slightly squeezing her fingers, she didn't respond. Didn't bat an eyelash.

"How do you know that?" he challenged.

"How is it that you don't?" she countered.

Holling felt in his heart that Sawyer would be all right. Part of him had faith. The other part of him was so assured because of Dr. Egan's prognosis. He would take her word for Sawyer's condition. She had seemed so kind and competent. Her very presence evoked in him a sense of efficiency.

He didn't get that same sense from the woman standing vigil over Sawyer. That's exactly what he considered her to be doing. Within the past few moments, the woman had made no move that led him to believe that she was there in an official, medical capacity. If she wasn't a nurse, then who was she?

"Are you . . . Sawyer's aunt Rosie?" he asked. He knew the answer even before he finished asking the question. His father was supposed to bring Sawyer's aunt with him. Since there was no sign of Pops, he couldn't reconcile this woman as a relation to Sawyer. Why was she there? What was she doing there?

"No."

"Then who are you?"

"You can call me Luce. Sawyer does."

"Luce!"

"Yes."

"Sawyer's mentioned you. You're a friend of hers, then."

"And yours." She smiled gently at him. "We're more than just friends, Jon-Tyler."

"She told me that you helped her dig me out of Marjean's. I'm grateful to you."

"You're welcome. I did it for Sawyer. She loves you, Jon-Tyler. Very much." The woman turned to him. "Do you love her?"

"Something tells me that you already know the answer to that, Luce," Holling said wryly.

"Sometimes it helps if you say it out loud."

Holling opened his mouth to speak, but Luce held up her hand to stop him. "Oh, not to me, child. I already know the answer. But Sawyer . . . our poor, sweet Sawyer." Luce clucked her tongue. "Even through all of this, she's the one who still has doubts."

"I don't know why," Holling said in frustration. He massaged her hand between his own, then brought it to his lips. "I've done just about all I know to do to make her understand how I feel."

"It's only been a couple of weeks, honey. How are you going to convince anyone of anything in that short a time?"

"If I could convince myself, I ought to be able to convince her. I'm one of the toughest skeptics around." He sighed, turned his gaze ceilingward. "Maybe you're right, Luce. Maybe I've handled this all wrong from the start. She's probably used to guys like me hittin' on her all the time . . . givin' her every line in the book for a chance with her. I got nothin' new to say. Who was I foolin', making her believe that I could love her so quickly?"

"Maybe you shouldn't focus so much on the how, Jon-Tyler."

"What do you mean?" He shook his head, his expression puzzled.

"Sometimes, honey, the *why* you feel the way you do is just as important as the *how*."

"I don't even know if I know why I feel the way I feel about her," Holling murmured, more to himself than to Luce.

As Holling considered Luce's words, he turned to glance over his shoulder when someone knocked on the door.

"Mr. Holling?"

"Brynn?" He recognized the voice of the nurse's aide.

"Yes, sir. I came to tell you that you'll have to leave now. Dr. Egan says that Ms. Garth needs her rest."

"I understand," Holling said reluctantly. "Thanks for the reminder."

He didn't want to go. There was still so much he wanted to say to Sawyer. Even though she was sleeping, he'd once read that if you talked, sometimes messages made it through to the subconscious mind. He just wanted her to know that he was there for her. He would always be there. He'd only held back from voicing those feelings aloud because he didn't want to expose his deepest thoughts in front of Luce.

He stood over Sawyer, kissing her tenderly on the forehead. "I'll be back, darlin'," he promised. "You sleep well."

Sawyer stirred a bit, murmuring softly in her sleep. Holling listened closely to see if she understood. He thought he heard her whisper his name.

"That's right, Sawyer," he whispered back, his lips hovering inches from her cheek. "I'm here. I'm not going anywhere. I'm not going to let anything happen to you. So you just take your time, get well."

Holling straightened. "We gotta go, Luce. Doctor's orders. Luce? *Luce?*"

Chapter 30

Holling stepped into the hall. He looked up and down, searching for Luce. Now that they were out of the room, he could speak freely to her. There were questions that he could ask, questions that he did not want to raise while he was in there with Sawyer. Yet, there was no sign of the woman.

Down the hall, Brynn was talking to his pops. He'd finally arrived. And beside him stood an elderly woman with gray-streaked hair worn in two plaits pinned on top of her head. Her long denim skirt was studded with silver along the hem. She wore a long-sleeved black shirt with a pink ribbon tied in a bow pinned just below her right shoulder.

Aunt Rosie.

He lifted his hand, trying to get their attention without shouting. Rosie noted them first, tapped his pops on the shoulder, and pointed to him.

Pops said a few more words to Brynn, then met Holling outside Sawyer's door.

"How is she?" Nate said by way of greeting. "What did the doctor say? Is Sawyer all right? What about the baby?"

Holling held out his hands, stemming his father's questions. "First things first, Pops."

"Oh yeah, right. Sorry. I guess I checked my manners at the door. Rosie Kincaid, this is my son Jon-Tyler. Holling, this is Sawyer's aunt Rosie."

"How do you do, Jon-Tyler?" she said, grasping his hand and shaking.

Holling smiled. She had a warm, firm grip. Kinda reminded him of Sawyer's style. Strength must run in their family.

"My friends call me Holling," he said.

"Do they?" Rosie said, lifting an eyebrow in surprise. "My friends call me Rosie."

"Sawyer's resting comfortably, Rosie," he said. "They ran me out of there, but I'll bet if you go in, nobody will try to stop you. I'll stand right here at the door and make sure that they don't."

He leaned against the wall, folded his arms across his chest, and looked to Rosie for all the world as solid and as immovable as the wall that he leaned against. She reached up and patted his cheek.

"You know, Holling, with friends like you, I don't know why I even worried about our little Sawyer." She canted her head, regarding him with snapping brown eyes. "Something tells me you're more than friends, eh?"

"Yes, ma'am. That would be so."

"I knew it. I can tell. I can always tell. You're in love with her, aren't you?"

"Right on both counts."

She leaned close and asked in a conspiratorial whisper, "I may be overstepping my bounds here . . . but I'm going to ask you a very personal question. If I'm out of line, just tell me. You won't hurt my feelings. But I have to ask. I have to know . . . is that baby yours, Holling?"

"Yes," Holling said firmly, just as assuredly as Nate gave a resounding "No!"

Rosie raised her eyebrows, looking back and forth between the both of them.

"Seems to me that you two have got some details to get sorted out," she observed.

"Nothing to sort out," Holling said stubbornly. "I know the baby's mine."

"Details my left eye. Even I know you can't know a woman for only a couple of weeks and make a baby almost two months old," Nate said testily.

"How do you know how far along she is, Pops?" Holling asked.

"I'm afraid that's my doing." Rosie raised her hand to volunteer her confession. "On the ride over, your father and I did some talking."

"Looks like I've got some *more* talking to do," Nate said, pinning his son with a hard stare.

"While you two work it out, I'm going to slip inside and check on my niece," Rosie said. She pushed the door open, closing out the heated sounds of Nate and his son. As soon as the door swung closed, she heard Nate's strident tone clearly through the door.

"Have you lost your ever-lovin' mind!"

Rosie didn't mean to eavesdrop. She'd been raised to believe that it was rude. Yet, something in that young man's response to his father kept her glued to the spot, her ear pressed to the other side of the door. Instead of giving Nate a smart-assed response, his tone was calm, persuasive.

"Yes, sir. I sure have. My mind *and* my heart."

With a sigh of sweet sentimentality, Rosie closed her eyes. She placed her hand over her heart as she moved to Sawyer's bedside.

* * *

Nate grabbed his son by the elbow, trying to draw him to a more secluded location. "Holling, are you sure you know what you're doin', boy?"

Holling pulled away from him. He'd promised Rosie that he'd stand guard by the door. He wasn't budging. "I know *exactly* what I'm doing." Even if his tone hadn't attested to that fact, his expression certainly did.

Nate made a small sound of disbelief. His son had always had his own brand of confidence, a certain assuredness that sometimes bordered on cocky. Most times, that self-assurance worked to Nate's advantage. Whenever he took Holling on a livestock auction, no one could bluff or pull one over on him. He knew what he knew, and no one was going to tell him differently.

Nate called to mind one time a horse trader tried to tell Holling that the palomino stud he was interested in was only three years old. Holling took one look at the horse and told that trader where he could stick that three years. After dickering a round or two with Holling, the trader was lucky if he knew his *own* age by the time it was all said and done. After that, he always had his story straight, his facts in place, before trying to do business with Holling.

That same stubbornness, an unwillingness to sway from his position, was working against Nate now. Holling had that look on his face, the look that told Nate his son would not be moved—emotionally or physically. Not by brute force, anyway. Chewing his lip in concern, Nate tried a different tack.

Nate tried sympathy and reason. "I know you have feelin's for the girl. It's as plain as that big, broken nose on your face. And I'm sure she's got a tender spot for you, too. Though, for the love of Pete, I don't know why. Whatever it is between you is your own business. But to take on the responsibility of a child . . . one that ain't even yours . . . that's when I have to get involved, son."

"No, sir, you don't. This is my affair."

"Not anymore, it ain't. Holling, what we have, what we've built together, I've built for us. For our family. For you and for me and for Shane and for Aida Beth. To let another man in . . . to give him access to *your* inheritance, I won't stand for it."

"Do what you want with your part, Pops," Holling retorted. "As for me, everything that I have . . . everything that I am . . . I want Sawyer to have."

"Listen to me, son. Listen to what I'm saying. I'm just saying that if that baby's daddy realizes the wealth you're handing over to the child, what do you think he'll do?"

"He doesn't want anything to do with Sawyer or the baby," Holling protested.

"Now he doesn't. But if he finds out about our net worth, do you think he'll be happy to remain on the sidelines?"

"We have ways of takin' care of claim jumpers, Pops. Nobody, I mean nobody, messes with us or our own. Six generations of Hollings living on the Way . . . You ought to know that more than anybody."

"Why even go through that hassle of a legal battle if the custody of the child ever comes into question?"

"You sayin' that I can't?" Holling challenged.

"All I'm sayin' is that maybe you shouldn't."

"Why not?" Holling said softly. "*You* did."

Blinking in surprise, Nate stammered, "That . . . that was different."

"I don't see how," Holling said stubbornly. "You make me see the difference."

"I was married to your mama."

"As soon as Sawyer's feelin' stronger, I'm gonna ask her, Pops. You know that I am."

"Be reasonable, Holling. I could propose to your mama because I'd known her since we were kids. We had ten years together before you came. Ten years of lovin' between us."

"Ten years of lovin'," he echoed. "But it still wasn't enough, was it?" Holling's jaw clenched tight. So tight he could barely speak. "Ten years couldn't keep their hold on her, could they?"

"Your mama . . . well, Janeen is a special breed. She needed more than I could give her."

"So she stepped out on you." Holling put bluntly what Nate had trouble saying, even after all these years. "Year after year. Man after man. Hoppin' from bed to bed."

"Don't you talk about your mother that way!" Nate stepped up to his son. He had to look up at him—and had been looking up since Holling hit his growth spurt.

"Why not? It's the truth, isn't it?" Holling returned.

"You didn't know your mother like I did."

"Kinda hard to get to know her when she only came home long enough to change her clothes or to take some money," Holling retorted.

"She always came back to me," Nate said, stubbornly defending his wife.

"You mean you always went after her."

"Doesn't matter. Janeen knows she always has a home with me if she wants it."

"If she showed up on that doorstep tonight, you'd let her in, wouldn't you? Just take her back as if nothing ever happened."

Holling's tone was awed. He didn't know if he admired his father's devotion to his wife or pitied it. They hadn't bothered divorcing, just gone their separate ways as if sacred vows weren't worth the paper they were printed on. As long as Janeen Holling carried his father's name, Nate Holling would continue to love and accept her shortcomings. As a boy, Jon-Tyler couldn't understand it. It didn't seem right to him that a man would *let* himself be stepped all over. The older he got, the more Holling came to understand his father. Nate knew that he'd never be able to change Janeen Holling. He could either accept her for who and what she was, or not.

If he didn't, it was Nate's problem. Not Janeen's. She was going to keep on doing what she wanted. Some folks called it selfish. Some folks called it spirited. Others weren't quite so kind.

Holling also grew to understand that his father coped the best way that he could. He was no saint. Holling never had that delusion about his father. If he strayed outside of the proverbial marriage bed, he did it quietly . . . and never let it get in the way of raising his children the best that he knew how. He was there for them. Always. Unconditionally.

If Holling loved Sawyer so completely, he only had his parents to blame for the example they set. Blame Nate for showing him uncompromising devotion and the willingness to let the loved ones in his life be who they were, no matter how much it hurt him.

Blame Janeen for the wounds she inflicted on Nate, he did. And often. Holling blamed her when he had to fight to defend her name, even when he didn't want to. He blamed her for all of the snickers behind his back, the gossipy whispers, and the looks of self-righteous pity. He blamed her for the nights Nate walked the floor, dejected and lonely, wondering what was wrong with him that he couldn't keep his woman. He blamed her for setting the wedge between him and his brother Shane. The brother whose parentage was never questioned. He blamed her for showing him the hard way that to be happy in your life, sometimes you had to make sacrifices.

"I can see why you're attracted to that girl. I look at her and I see shades of Janeen in her, too. Completely independent. Gonna do whatever the hell she wants with just the right mix of good-girl sweetness to make you want to forgive her every time she crosses you. You can't help yourself. Like a moth to a flame, scorched wings an' all."

"You can't blame me for feeling the same way about Sawyer. Just because we didn't know each other as kids doesn't mean I can't want her with me now."

"She's carrying another man's child!" Nate insisted.

"And so was Mama. Did that stop you from loving her?"

"No," Nate said, turning away from his son. "Heaven help me, I still love that woman."

"Look at me, Pops." Holling's strained tone drew Nate's focus back to him. "I know you do, Pops. No power on this earth can stop you from lovin' her . . . or from lovin' me! Did that stop you from takin' me into your home and lovin' me, Pops? Even suspecting that you weren't really my father?"

Nate shook his head, his eyes reddening and brimming with tears. "I tried not to show a difference between you and your brother Shane."

"You never did." Holling placed a hand on his father's shoulder and squeezed.

"But somehow you knew . . . even from the time you were just this high, though I couldn't figure out how." Nate held his hand out from the ground level with his knee.

"First time I ever heard somebody say, 'Mama's baby, Daddy's maybe,' I suspected. When Mama took off for good to be with . . . well, the flavor of the month . . . that kinda sealed it for me."

"I know it did, son. I guess that's why I let you call yourself Holling—as strange as everybody thought it sounded. I wanted everybody to know that no matter what, you were a Holling, through and through. *My* son."

"You raised me, Pops. Gave me everything a man could want. And I'm grateful to you for that."

"I'm not askin' for your gratitude. I'm askin' you to stop and think before you go rushin' in. You sure you're not doin' this because you want to do for Sawyer what I've done for you? Are you sure about her, son?"

"I'm sure about *me*," he corrected. "I know how I feel, and . . ." He paused, remnants of the conversation with Luce coming back to him. "And I know why I feel the way that I do. And it's got nothing to do with any kind of karmic balance—trying to give back to the world what you gave to me. I'm not that noble."

"Then why?"

"I've known from the moment I laid eyes on that girl that she was the one for me, even before I knew anything about her. I took one look at her and I just knew. Call me crazy."

"Crazy," Nate obliged.

"You don't have to be so literal, Pops."

"I guess that's that, then." Nate shrugged fatalistically.

"Yes, sir, it sure is." Holling couldn't have been more matter-of-fact. He knew what he knew. If he couldn't convince his father, it really didn't matter. He was going to do what he wanted to do. Always had. It was up to the rest of the world to follow along.

"I'm gettin' too old to be bouncin' any babies on my knee," Nate said. He reached up, stroking his full beard. "But, if comes right down to it, I suppose I could put the little crumb snatcher in a wagon and strap him to Taffy."

"Now you're thinking, Grandpops!" Holling praised, clapping his father on the shoulder. Nate winced, not so much from his son's enthusiastic patting but at the idea of being a grandfather. Holling could almost read Nate's mind.

"You'd better get used to the sound of being called Grandpops."

"Don't go off buying any diapers yet. The doctor says she's not out of danger yet. She could still lose the baby," Nate reminded him.

"She won't," Holling said confidently.

"How do you know?"

"Don't ask me how I know. I just know. Call it faith. Some things you've just gotta believe."

"You believe you can make her want to stay. You haven't convinced her yet," Nate reminded his son. "Now that her aunt's here, there's nothing stoppin' her from leaving. You can't compete with family, no matter how much you care about a woman. I know that for a fact. If she wants to go, what can you do?"

"I'll think of something," Holling said.

"If you care to take some advice from your old man, I think I might just have an idea. Just sit back and let your old father work his magic."

"You're good, Pops. But you're not that good. You'd better have a plan. A better one than the ones you've tried on Mama to get her to stay."

Nate screwed up his face, trying to look offended. "Now, that was low. That one was way below the belt."

Holling shrugged apologetically. "The last act of a desperate man."

"There's desperate," Nate said, wagging his finger in his son's face. "And then there's pathetic. And you know what, Holling?"

"What is that, Pops?"

"I know beyond a shadow of a doubt that you're my son. If anyone could be more pathetic than I was about Janeen, it would have to be you and how you are about that Sawyer Garth."

"So, what's your plan?"

"Can't tell ya. Not yet. Let me get a few things together. But I can promise you this. By the time we get finished with that Sawyer Garth, whatever she has back in Birmingham will become a distant memory."

"I'm with ya, Pops," Holling said eagerly. "Just as long as you're not planning to smack her on the head with a two-by-four to give her a sudden case of amnesia."

Chapter 31

Rosie sat at Sawyer's bedside. She didn't speak for several minutes. She simply sat beside her and regarded her with a mixture of pride and irritation. How could something so little cause so much trouble? Sawyer was a miniature dynamo, stirring up trouble and leaving a mess for others to clean up. Ever since the girl could get around on her own, someone was always performing damage control.

Pressing her lips firmly together, Rosie vowed, "Not this time, Sawyer Garth."

No more running. Too long, the family had made excuses for Sawyer. They'd put up with her wild behavior because she was the odd child out. Mother gone. For all intents and purposes, no father to speak of. She was too rich for her own damned good. No one wanted to tell her no when there was money to be tossed around to fix her messes. Too pretty. Too smart. Too much of some things and not enough of others. Like good old-fashioned common sense. It was a wonder she'd turned out as "normal" as she had. All the power in the world and none of the responsibility. She'd grown up thinking that consequences were something for other people to worry about. Well, it was time that Sawyer had a healthy dose of reality.

"I'm just the woman to get that bitter pill rammed down her throat, too," Rosie murmured. But first, she'd coat the pill with a spoonful of sugar.

"Sawyer? Sawyer, honey . . . it's me. Aunt Rosie. I know you're sleeping and you probably can't hear me. But I want you to know, honey, that I'm here. I'm right here."

Sawyer stirred, moaning. She turned her head to the sound of the voice speaking to her, and cracked her eyes open to mere slits.

"Aunt Rosie?" Her voice sounded weak and scratchy.

"Yes, honey. It's me." Rosie's smile lit up her entire face. She placed her warm brown hand against Sawyer's forehead. "How do you feel?"

Sighing deeply, Sawyer shook her head. "I don't know . . . I feel strange. A little out of it."

"That's the sedative."

"Sedative . . . it won't hurt the baby, will it?" she said in alarm, clutching her stomach.

"No . . . no, it won't. Trust the doctors. They know what they're doing."

"I should have known that from the first time I was here," she said ruefully, then gave a dry cough.

"Here, let me get you something to drink." Rosie grasped the pink pitcher bearing the hospital's logo, and the lidded plastic cup with attached sipping straw sitting on the bedside table. She pressed the button on the panel beside Sawyer's bed to adjust it. The bed whirred softly, raising Sawyer to a partial inclined position. "Are you comfortable now, honey?"

Sawyer took a few swallows, then nodded at her aunt when she'd had enough. She then lay back, with her eyes closed.

"How long have you been here, Aunt Rosie?"

"Not long."

"How long do you plan to stay?"

"Well, now, that depends on you, Sawyer," Rosie replied.

"On me? I'm not holding you up from the charity ride, am I? I know how much you were looking forward to going."

"The ride can wait. Right now, you're my priority. Seeing you strong again. You can't very well go back with me in that condition, can you?"

"No . . . I suppose not," Sawyer said.

When do you *want to leave?* Rosie wanted to ask. Instead she said, "Just as soon as you let me know that you're ready, Sawyer."

"Well . . ." Sawyer paused. "My bike won't be ready to go for a few more days," she said as an excuse. "It's in the repair shop."

"So you told me. What you didn't tell me was what happened to it. Were you in an accident?"

"No," Sawyer said truthfully. She still couldn't quite meet her aunt's gaze. "Nothing like that. I've been very careful."

"What happened to it then?"

"A tornado," Sawyer said, then flinched at Rosie's squawk of surprise and condemnation.

"Don't worry, Aunt Rosie. I wasn't hurt . . . not really."

"A tornado! Sawyer, were you out riding in storm weather? How many times have I told you to get off the road when it rains?"

"I did, Aunt Rosie!" she protested. "That's how I met Holling. He was at the café where I'd stopped to get out of the weather."

"At least you showed that much good sense," Rosie muttered under her breath.

"A friend of Holling's is doing the bodywork to get me back on the road. I can't leave until he's done so I can pay him."

"We could always have the bike shipped," Rosie said offhandedly.

"Oh no. We don't have to do that. It's too expensive. We can at least stay until the work is complete, can't we?"

"The nurse's aide tells me that, if all goes well, the doctor will probably release you in a couple of days. We can head out then if the weather holds, since I rented a car."

"Oh," Sawyer said. "That's . . . uh . . . that's good. So, as soon as I'm released you can take me back to Birmingham."

Rosie mentally shook her head. The girl was *still* running away. Rosie wanted to throttle her. A perfectly good man waiting outside, willing to give his heart to her, and she was running back home to that low-down, no-good, slick-talking what's-his-name.

"Not quite so fast. Mr. Holling offered me a place to stay for a few days, to rest up before the long trip back."

"He is nice," Sawyer said tenderly. "Too nice. I don't know how I'll ever repay him for his hospitality."

"From the way he was talking, he's not looking for any kind of repayment, Sawyer."

"Still . . . I don't like the fact that I owe him."

"And what about Holling?" Rosie asked. She scooted to the edge of her seat, regarding her niece with piercing brown eyes.

"Why do you ask about him?"

"He's standing right outside, you know."

"I know." Sawyer couldn't help but smile. "He has a thing for lurking just outside of doors."

"Excuse me?"

"Nothing, Aunt Rosie." Sawyer sighed. "It's a private joke. And a very long story."

"You've only been gone from home a couple of weeks. How long a story could it be?"

"I feel like I've been gone and lived a lifetime," Sawyer said, turning her head aside. *And loved a lifetime,* she mentally added. "If you knew only half the things I've been through, Aunt Rosie, you wouldn't be sitting there so calmly."

"You've got that right!" Rosie said sharply. "Instead of sitting here, coddling you, I should probably be trying to whip some sense into you." Rosie balled up her fist and shook it at Sawyer.

Sawyer closed her eyes to mentally prepare. *Uh-oh, here it comes.* She was wondering when it would happen. Maybe she should have remained under the influence of that sedative a while longer. Anything to get away from Aunt Rosie's razor-sharp tongue and her eyes . . . those eyes that could bore down into her soul and witness all of her imperfections.

She slid under the covers, pulling them up to her nose. "Yes, ma'am," she said meekly.

"You're pregnant, girl! What makes you think you can just hop across the countryside and not be accountable!" Rosie's voice rose as she scolded Sawyer. She took a deep breath, forcing herself to remain calm. "Lord, *please* don't let me strangle this child in her bed," Aunt Rosie prayed aloud.

"I don't mean to cause trouble. It just follows me," Sawyer complained.

"When does it ever change, Sawyer? It's one drama after the next with you. When does it ever stop? When you're dead? Or when you get someone else hurt or killed?"

Sawyer sighed. "I guess I deserve that, Aunt Rosie. I haven't been behaving very responsibly lately."

"You should count yourself blessed if you get what you *don't* deserve."

"What?"

"Do I have to spell it out for you? I'm talking about Holling. I heard him out there talking, Sawyer. That young man cares so much about you."

"I know," Sawyer said.

"No, I don't think you do!" Rosie snapped.

"He saved my life, Aunt Rosie. Twice! You don't have to convince *me* of his capacity for love."

"You got him caught up in your mess, too?"

"What Holling does, he does because he wants to. No one makes him do anything. He's stood by me because he wanted to."

"So, what are you going to do about it?"

Sawyer shrugged her shoulders. "I don't know. I want to believe that we could make it work . . . but I'm so afraid. What happens if I really care for him and he decides later that I'm not the one he wants? What if I'm not worth his love? I've made so many mistakes, Aunt Rosie. What if I'm incapable of loving Holling back the way he deserves?"

"That's ridiculous! You can love just as much as anyone, Sawyer. Do you want to know what your problem is, child? I'm going to tell you. Your problem is that you've convinced herself that you don't need anybody's love. You're so damned self-sufficient, so proud of being independent that you think you can do without. You'd rather run back home to that lowlife, who is using you like all of your other so-called friends. You'd rather go back to *that* life because you know it's safe and predictable. The one opportunity you have to take a chance and love someone who doesn't want anything from you and you're ready to toss it aside like yesterday's garbage. You're thinking about running now, aren't you?" Rosie accused her.

Sawyer ground her teeth together, trying not to interrupt her aunt. It was hard to sit there and listen to her life being analyzed and found lacking by the one woman she cared so much about.

"I can't help it. Old habits are hard to break."

"I don't know what it is about your generation. I swear, you and your cousins are all alike. When things don't go your way, or are just the least bit difficult, the first thing you want to do is turn tail and run."

"That's not fair, Aunt Rosie!" Sawyer protested.

"Fair? You want fair? Fair is a midway, a Ferris wheel, and a fat lady with tattoos," Rosie shot back.

Sawyer burst into laughter. "Now, where did that come from?"

"You think I'm joking?" Rosie demanded.

"I'm . . . I'm sorry, Aunt Rosie," Sawyer gasped. She reached behind her, pulled a pillow up to her mouth, and stuffed the corner of it inside.

"This is no laughing matter. If you leave that young man, you'll break his heart." Rosie thumped her fist against her chest.

"I know," Sawyer said, her voice muffled. She pulled the pillow down. "I don't mean to laugh. I wouldn't hurt Holling for the world, Aunt Rosie. He's been a true friend to me."

"Just a friend?"

"More than a friend," she confessed.

"Go on. Say it. I dare you," Rosie challenged. "Say it out loud. Speak the truth and shame the devil."

"I do love him!" Sawyer exclaimed, encouraged by her aunt's passion.

"Love and friendship are rare commodities in this world, Sawyer. And you're going to throw away both?"

She shook her head no.

"Then what are you going to do about it?" Rosie repeated.

Sawyer heaved another sigh. "I know what I want to do. I'm just afraid."

Rosie leaned close to Sawyer. "Seemed to me that young man out there seemed big enough, and bad enough, to chase away anything foolish enough to try to scare you, honey."

"He's been so good to me," Sawyer murmured. "It's going to tear me apart to leave him."

"But you are going to leave him?" Rosie tried not to let her disappointment show. This was Sawyer's life. Her decision. Rosie had no right to meddle. She just didn't want to see Sawyer make the kind of mistake that could cost her happiness.

"I have to go back, Aunt Rosie," Sawyer said firmly. "I have a life back in Birmingham. Not a perfect one. But it's mine. Like you said, I've been running away for too long. Time for me to grow up and face it."

Chapter 32

Sawyer turned her face toward the window, listening to the rain drizzle down the windowpane in tiny rivulets. She couldn't see how badly the weather had turned; the curtains were drawn. But she could certainly hear it. Through the tiny slit where two curtain halves joined, she could see the flashing red and blue of warning lights as an ambulance pulled into the emergency-room entrance. The wail of its siren was drowned out by a sudden clap of thunder.

It was the weather that had originally awakened her. Midnight—and she was wide-awake. In a few minutes, the nurse would come in to check on her, adjust her IV drip, and record her progress on her chart.

She glanced over at one of the machines to which she was connected, a heart and blood pressure monitor, noting the steady rhythmic recording. The last few times the nurse had been in to check the readings, she'd given Sawyer encouraging news. Everything looked fine. The medications they'd given her to stop the contractions and prevent the miscarriage seemed to be doing their job. If she continued to progress, they'd release her tomorrow. Tomorrow she would be free. Free to go about her business—the business of breaking Holling's heart, as Aunt Rosie had so passionately put it. And she didn't want to have to do it. But what choice did she have? She couldn't stay here in White Wolf, as much as she'd come to love the place. She had too many loose ends to tie up . . . ends that she knew would someday come forth to haunt her if she didn't address them now while she had the will to do it. If only he could be patient with her . . . just a little while longer.

Ryan was first and foremost in her mind. She hated to admit it, but he'd been on her mind ever since Aunt Rosie refused to mention his name during her visit. She didn't have to tell Sawyer how much she disliked the man; it was evident in her disgusted expression. She was too much of a lady to say what she really thought of him. Sawyer knew what she thought, and she had to admit, she agreed with her aunt.

Sawyer was convinced that she had no more feelings for Ryan. At least, not feelings she wanted to cling to. Maybe she had loved him at one time. She was young and impressionable when she'd met him. He had a certainly quality that drew her. He praised her budding talent, worshipped her body, and had just enough bad-boy appeal that catered to the scandal-seeking side of her. Yet, youth was not an excuse for allowing him to continue to take advantage of her naïveté. Not anymore.

Now that Holling showed her what true love meant and how good it could be, she wouldn't be satisfied with anything less. It made her angry to think that all this time she had been settling. So desperate was she for attention that she'd let Ryan do as he pleased to her. To make it worse, she'd let him chase her out of her own home.

Well, that would soon change, Sawyer thought with grim determination. As soon as the hospital staff chased Aunt Rosie out of the room, reminding them of visiting hours, Sawyer was on the phone dialing her home number.

She let the phone ring. No answer. But Sawyer would not be deterred. She hung up again and dialed again. She kept calling. Either he wasn't home or he didn't want to pick up. Either way, that wasn't going to stop her from saying what she had to say. That didn't stop her from taking that first step toward true independence.

She kept calling until now, near midnight. When the answering machine picked up, she started to talk—unsteadily at first, then with growing confidence.

"Ryan, this is Sawyer. I know you probably thought you'd never hear from me again. It wasn't my intention to call you. But I am calling, so I want you to listen and listen well. The ride is over, Ryan. This gravy train has pulled to a halt. I'll be home by the end of the week. I want you, and everything that belongs to you, out of my house. That's right. *My* house. Make sure that you only take what's yours . . . what you came with. If I find as much as a coaster out of place I will report it stolen. You got that? Five days."

She knew she only had a few more seconds on the recording, so she talked fast and crisp so that there would be no misunderstanding.

"And another thing. How dare you accuse me of sleeping around on you! You know you were my first. My only. But that too has changed. And you know what, Ryan? He's a better man than you'll ever be. In every way . . . every inch of him."

She placed the emphasis in her voice that she knew Ryan would completely understand. She couldn't believe that she'd bought into that "not my baby" crap. How could she have been so weak? Of course it was his baby. But if he didn't want it, it was his loss. But she wasn't going to let him slide without acknowledging the part he'd played in creating this life that she was fighting so hard to save. If he was going to abdicate responsibility, then he had to let go of all of it—all of her.

"In the morning, you'll be hearing from my lawyer. No, I don't want child support from you. I'm making sure that you don't try to leech any more from me than you already have. As of now, tonight, our relationship, business and pleasure, is over!"

She didn't want anything more to do with him. Whatever it took to get out of the contract she had with his publicity firm, she'd do. She didn't care if she had to spend every last dime of her trust fund.

Having said what was on her mind, Sawyer slammed the phone down. Her heart thudded in her chest. Enough so, she hoped that it wouldn't bring the nurses monitoring her readings running to see what had caused her agitation. She was agitated, yet strangely calm. Cathartic. She didn't feel the least bit cowardly for saying those harsh things to an answering machine. Once she was back in Birmingham, she would have plenty of opportunity to say them to Ryan's face. She counted herself as having a victory because she'd said them. She'd cut off the broken record that played over and over again in her mind and told her that there was something wrong with her . . . that she wasn't deserving of unconditional love. She wasn't perfect. But she didn't have to be in order to deserve a perfect love.

Sawyer turned over on her side and drew the covers up over her shoulders. As she lay in bed, she felt herself start to tremble. Pent-up anger finally released itself, as poison drains from a wound. She trembled in anger . . . and as the summer storm wore on, a new emotion took its place—pure terror. She whimpered softly and placed the pillow over her head to drown out the sound of pea-sized hail slamming against the window.

Holling! Sawyer wished for him. Wished for his strength and his comfort to help her through this night.

Curled up into a fetal position, Sawyer closed her eyes

tight and tried not to remember the first time she experienced the might of a Montana storm.

"It might not be as bad as the weatherman's sayin'." Nate opened the back door and stared out past the porch. He watched the rain dripping down from the porch overhang. It was coming down hard, forming a solid wall of water as it fell. "Why don't you go on back to bed, son?"

Holling looked back over his shoulder to address his father. "I don't know, Pops," he said, his tone clearly worried. "It's been goin' steady since we left the hospital. What time was that?"

" 'Bout ten or so," Nate confirmed.

Holling nodded. He stood with one hand resting against the support pillar, the other tucked into the front pocket of the jeans. Almost as an afterthought, he'd slipped on the pants before coming downstairs. His first impulse was to roam around, as his pops would say, "naked as the day he was born." But then he remembered that they still had a house-guest. Sawyer's aunt Rosie.

His denim shirt was unbuttoned, open, and fluttering in the strong winds whipping through the backyard. As his gaze swept over the yard, he noted the damage the storm had already caused. Over to his left, the branches of the hundred-year oak whipped furiously, causing the rope and tire swing to swing back and forth like a pendulum gone haywire. Several branches had already been stripped from the tree and were sailing across the lawn.

The picnic table and chairs would have been strewn all over the yard if one of the hands hadn't had the presence of mind to gather them all up and shove them into the storage shed. The decorative shades covering the lights that lined the path leading from the main house to the stables had also been stored away. The wrought-iron posts that held the lanterns were on their own. Holling suspected that before the night or the storm was over, more than one of the posts would wind up on the ground.

He'd told his pops not to get those things installed. They were more decorative than functional. Yet, the guests seemed to like them. Even Sawyer had commented on them, saying how they added a "rustic" flair to the property. Holling couldn't help but smile at that. Rustic? They were on a ranch, sitting in the heart of the West. How much more rustic could they be? Then again, Sawyer did have a funny way of looking at things. A writer's way.

Sawyer. He said her name, almost on a sigh. If she could see so much, why couldn't she see how important it was for her to stay? He was worried about her. Then again, when wasn't he worried about her? She was constantly on his mind. From the moment he woke up in the morning, to the time his head hit the pillow at night. Even in his dreams, he couldn't escape her. Now, past midnight, he was standing out in the rain, letting the weather cool heated thoughts of her.

"What am I gonna do, Pops?" he asked, not really expecting an answer.

Nate didn't answer right away. Even though his gaze remained fixed on the stormy horizon, something told Nate that Holling wasn't necessarily talking about the weather. Even if he was, there was nothing to be done about it except ride it out.

It was the same advice he was going to give him about Sawyer. Ride it out. Maybe the storm would pass. Maybe it wouldn't. Either way, there was nothing Holling could do but wait and endure.

Nate wished he could take Holling's pain from him. Poor Holling. Nate knew exactly what Holling was in for. He knew the tough time he was going to have when Sawyer left. It was just like him and Janeen. Holling was more his son than anyone knew. He'd found the one woman he couldn't do without. And that was the one woman who couldn't be with him.

Rosie was taking Sawyer back to Birmingham as soon as the doctor released her. He'd been right. Nothing like the pull of blood kin. Holling couldn't compete with that. Nate didn't even know if he should tell his son to try. After all he and Sawyer had been through, after all they'd shared, what more could Holling do to make her see how much he wanted her to stay?

"Go and get her," Nate said quietly.

Holling turned around, not sure if he'd heard him.

"What did you say?"

"I said go and get her. Get to her before Rosie does."

"You mean kidnap her?"

"Knock her on the head with a two-by-four if you have to," Nate said teasingly . . . or only half teasingly. In the dim light, Holling wasn't sure which.

"I can't just walk in there and take her. The doctor won't release her until tomorrow. Maybe the next day."

"Then you go and camp out in her room until she does release her. Do whatever it takes, Holling. She's your woman, ain't she?"

Holling nodded once.

"And you're claimin' that baby for your own?" Nate pressed.

"Yes, sir, I am."

"Well then, boy, what are you waiting for? Don't do like I did. Don't sit back and wait for her. Go . . . get . . . her." Nate enunciated each word.

He didn't have to say it again. Holling reached for the boots he'd left by the back porch, buttoned and tucked in his shirt, then grabbed the keys from their hook by the door. As he was shrugging into his denim jacket and pulling his hat low over his eyes, an amused voice made him turn around.

"I see I'm not the only one who can't sleep through this."

Holling turned in time to see Rosie entering the kitchen. She belted her robe tighter as she headed for the cabinet to pull down a drinking glass.

"No, ma'am. Storms make me restless," he said.

"I see. Not a very nice night for a drive, Holling." She nodded at the keys in his hand. "Mind if a nosy old lady asks where you're going?"

Holling paused, considering whether or not to tell her. He might as well. She'd figured it out as soon as she arrived at the hospital to take Sawyer away from him.

In a tone that invited no discussion, no debate, no denial, Holling informed her. "I'm goin' after my woman, Rosie. I'm going to bring Sawyer home."

A wide, pleased smile lit Rosie's face. Imitating his soft twang, she said, " 'Bout damn time somebody came to their senses."

Epilogue

Three months later

Sawyer had sensed it days before Dr. Egan confirmed her suspicions. *Something* wasn't quite right. It was hard to explain. She wasn't in discomfort. No cramps. No bleeding. Even the spells of nausea didn't seem as bad as they had been now that she was past her first trimester. Still, *something* was different. It took her a while to figure it out. Now that she had, with Dr. Egan's help, she could focus her attention on more important things. Adjusting to her life as Holling's wife was her top priority. It wasn't an easy transition. As her aunt Rosie had charged her, she'd grown addicted to a life of chaos. Moving from one drama to the next. With her commitment to Holling, she'd given up that life.

Not that living on the Way was boring. Far from it. With Holling, there was *never* a dull moment. He was an adrenaline junkie himself. His fondness for fast horses more than once made her flinch. But with Holling, his passion always had a purpose. He knew what he was doing. And he'd never risk his safety for the sake of the thrill alone.

"I've got too much to stay healthy for," he'd reminded her more than once.

Now, as they lay side by side, enjoying the sunset of an August evening, Holling was performing the one action that always got his heart to racing—spending quiet time with Sawyer.

"What about Jacob?" Holling asked, flipping through a book of baby names. "Jacob's a good name, huh?"

"No," Sawyer objected. "Then folks would want to call him Jake. I had a Jake in my book."

"Had?" Holling picked up on the word. "What happened to him?"

"He died of a snakebite."

"No . . . on second thought, maybe we don't want to call him Jake," Holling hastily agreed.

"How do you know it's a he? It could be a she," Sawyer said.

"A girl named Jake might be kinda interestin'," Holling teased. His laughter shook the hammock, nearly making them flip over. That made Sawyer want to laugh even harder.

"A girl named Jake. Hmmm . . ." she murmured, considering the idea. "Couldn't be any stranger than a girl named Sawyer."

"Nope. That's about as strange as they come," Holling agreed. "Or a boy named Sue."

"You're not helping." Sawyer kissed him on the cheek, then snuggled close to him and curled herself around him. Holling encircled her in his arms, much like he'd done the night he came to her in the hospital. Sawyer didn't know why he decided to come back to her that night. Part of her thought that maybe she'd wished him there. When the storm had blown in, she'd been so scared. Even though the weather reporter never indicated the storm could be as bad as the one that leveled Marjean's Café, that didn't stop her from being afraid. She didn't want to be alone.

As if by magic summoning, he'd appeared to her, soaking wet, standing in the doorway, calling out to her. How he got past the nurses stationed at the desk, Sawyer didn't know. It wasn't important. What was important was she'd wanted him and he was there.

Holling shifted in the hammock again, wrapping around Sawyer so that his hand rested on her stomach.

No more cute little outfits, Sawyer thought, then gave a secret smile. She supposed it didn't matter. Holling preferred her with fewer clothes on anyway. And the looser-fitting outfits gave him easier access to the skin he so loved to caress.

"I suppose we should be thinking on two names, Sawyer," he murmured.

Sawyer gave a contented sigh. Two names. He hadn't made the suggestion lightly. Two names, but not as if in case she carried a boy or a girl. Two names for two babies. Dr. Egan's ultrasound had confirmed it when Sawyer went in for a checkup. Two babies! Each developing inside her. She couldn't explain it. Couldn't deny it. But there they were.

"Twins?" she'd asked Dr. Egan. It was not an unreasonable question. Her cousin Brenda had given birth to twins.

"Not identical. This one here seems slightly more developed than the one here." She drew two circles so that Sawyer and Holling could see the two individual babies developing on the ultrasound monitor. "I would say fraternal. And judging from the growth and development of this one, I would say that he . . . or she . . . has a good three to four weeks' head start on the sibling."

Holling and Sawyer exchanged glances. She could see him doing some mental calculations. When he smirked at her and mouthed, "I told you so," Sawyer exclaimed, "Impossible! I thought everything was supposed to stop once you were pregnant. No more ovulation. No more fertilization."

"Not impossible. But certainly not very common. If you

like, I can do some research and give you some information on multiple-birth pregnancies. Because of the differences in development, when it comes time to deliver, we're going to have to consider some options. In the meantime, make sure you get plenty of rest, Sawyer. You're going to need it."

"Does that mean we can't—" Holling began.

"It's crowded enough in there as it is," Sawyer interrupted, sensing what his next question was going to be.

Dr. Egan had laughed at them. "You can continue your . . . um . . . normal activities until or unless it becomes uncomfortable."

Sawyer heaved a mock sigh. She could almost hear her grandma Lela muttering under her breath about the peculiar habits of newlyweds and rabbits. Yet, she didn't question how she came to spark two lives within her. However it had happened, it only meant that she was capable of containing the abundance of love granted to her. Holling certainly didn't question it. He only reminded her in that smugly assured way that he knew she was carrying his child. He knew. And Sawyer couldn't argue with that. She could only marvel at the miracle that was her new life and extend the same degree of love and commitment that Holling had offered to her. Wholly. Completely. *Unconditionally*.

Dear Readers:

I hope you enjoyed *Unconditional*, my follow-up to the Johnson family reunion series. So many of you have asked whatever became of Shiri and Jack, which tells me that these characters mean as much to you as they do to me.

My inspiration for writing *Unconditional* came from a couple of sources. In telling Sawyer's and Holling's story, I wanted to express that a perfect love can happen—even for imperfect people. And, I have to admit, I always wanted to write an old-fashioned western—where the hero sits tall in the saddle, saves the day, and rides off into the sunset with the girl. Only, you and I both know about those Johnson women—the hero may ride, but it's the heroine who holds the reins.

As always, I'd love to hear from you. You can drop me a note at geri_guillaume@hotmail.com. Until the next time, take care.

Geri

ABOUT THE AUTHOR

Geri Guillaume is the pseudonym of Krystal G. Williams. Ms. Williams was born in Jackson, Mississippi, in 1965. She received her undergraduate degree from Rice University in Houston, Texas, where she double majored in English and legal studies. She is currently a full-time technical writer and mother of two.

Her motto, "too many words, not enough paper," has helped her publish several contemporary romance novels, a play for her alma mater, and a planning guide for family reunions.

Ms. Williams currently makes her home in Houston, Texas.

BOOK YOUR PLACE ON OUR WEBSITE AND MAKE THE ARABESQUE ROMANCE CONNECTION!

We've created a customized website just for our very special Arabesque readers, where you can get the inside scoop on everything that's going on with Arabesque romance novels.

When you come online, you'll have the exciting opportunity to:

- View covers of upcoming books

- Learn about our future publishing schedule (listed by publication month and author)

- Find out when your favorite authors will be visiting a city near you

- Search for and order backlist books

- Check out author bios and background information

- Send e-mail to your favorite authors

- Join us in weekly chats with authors, readers and other guests

- Get writing guidelines

- AND MUCH MORE!

Visit our website at
http://www.arabesquebooks.com